Newton Thornburg was
After a Fine Arts degree at
in a variety of jobs. In 1973, he became a full-time novelist
and screenwriter, whilst owning a cattle farm in the Ozarks.
Cutter and Bone was first published in 1976, and the film
version, *Cutter's Way*, appeared in 1981.

Newton Thornburg now lives in Kirkland, Washington.

Praise for *Cutter and Bone*

"A thriller, and a whacking good thriller, too . . . but also a class, big-league act . . . Shows how much can be done within a classic form by a writer who knows his business" *New York Times*

"Tense, funny, and despairing . . . charged with a passion that makes even grotesques seem likable and, more important, credible right up to the last, startling sentence" *Time*

"A searing knockout . . . A thriller . . . It will make you wince, but it will hold you until the very last shattering line" *Business Week*

"Thornburg is a born storyteller, riveting his readers with a book so galvanically charged that it truly is nearly impossible to put down. Characterization here rings true in every case, the details . . . are frighteningly accurate, and the plotline surges ahead with the brutal force of madness" *St Louis Post-Dispatch*

Cutter

and Bone

NEWTON THORNBURG

Introduction by George P. Pelecanos

To Karin, my wife, my love, my life

First published in 1976 by Little, Brown and Company, Boston

First published in this edition in 2001 by Serpent's Tail,
4 Blackstock Mews, London N4 2BT

website: www.serpentstail.com

Printed in Great Britain by Mackays of Chatham plc

10 9 8 7 6 5 4 3 2

Introduction by
George P. Pelecanos

Why is it that certain groundbreaking novels often disappear from the radar screen while other lesser works remain in print? Along with James Crumley's *The Last Good Kiss*, Kem Nunn's *Tapping the Source*, and most anything written by Elmore Leonard in the early to mid 1970s, Newton Thornburg's *Cutter and Bone* seemed to challenge the very foundation of the traditional crime novel when it was first published in 1976. But today the book is largely remembered as the source material for *Cutter's Way*, a film which has gone on to gather a cult following of its own.

The New York Times did attempt to rescue the book from the genre ghetto in its initial review, calling *Cutter and Bone* "a classy big league act," and "the best novel of its kind for ten years." But the *L.A. Times* review was more typical, predictably describing it as a "superlative novel out of Ross Macdonald country." Well, they got the superlative part right, but the connection to Ross Macdonald's Archer series, apart from the Santa Barbara setting, could not be more wrong. Macdonald and his fictional detective never did seem to "get" the younger generation; it was, famously, a thread of bafflement that continued throughout the Lew Archer books. In *Cutter and Bone*, Thornburg not only got young people, he nailed them to the wall.

When we first meet Richard Bone, one-time ad exec turned gigolo/bum, he is shaving with a Lady Remington razor after his latest trick. Bone has been in love only a couple of times, once in adolescence and briefly to his ex-wife. He's currently in love with Mo, the alcohol-and-pill-freak live-in of his best friend, Cutter, quite possibly the most cynical lead character ever to appear in a work of mainstream American fiction. Cutter stepped on a claymore during his tour of Vietnam, and now he walks with a cane that complements a reconstructed leg of plastic and steel. What's left of him is best described by Thornburg with the typical, dead-on, economic prose style that hits the right staccato notes throughout the novel:

> What a sight the man made, what a celebration of the grotesque: the thinning Raggedy Ann hair, the wild hawk face glowing with the scar tissue of too many plastic surgeries, the black eyepatch over the missing eye and the perennial apache dancer's costume of tight black pants and black turtleneck sweater with the left sleeve knotted below the elbow, not pinned up or sewed but *knotted*, an advertisement, spit in your eye.

Late one night, walking to his temporary home at the Cutter residence, the drunken Bone witnesses a body being dumped in an alley garbage can by the silhouette of a husky older man. The victim was a young runaway hooker, found with a stoved-in skull and semen in her mouth and on her face. The next day, glancing at the newspaper photograph, Bone makes the mistake of telling Cutter that he thinks — *he thinks* — that the man he sees in the news photo, a major business tycoon, is the killer of the girl.

The remainder of the novel involves Cutter and Bone's attempts to make some sense of the murder and their own wasted lives, but don't expect a tidy resolution. The idea that a murder can be "solved" is the Great Lie of the mystery novel to begin with, and here the author turns that peculiar notion on its soft head. For once, a writer chooses not to patronize us, singing us softly back to sleep as one would a child awakened by a nightmare. Thornburg tells us, very plainly, that the nightmare is real.

So this isn't about a puzzle, and though there is a love story, beautifully rendered, the novel describes the death of love rather than its bloom. What the novel seems to be about, ultimately, is America's festering wound in the wake of Vietnam. Set and written in its time, and remarkably wise without the benefit of hindsight, *Cutter and Bone* describes a crippled country, chronically high or hungover, shell-shocked but looking forward to "the better days" which will soon arrive — careful what you wish for — in the form of Reagan and Thatcher. Thornburg doesn't dwell on Vietnam specifically, but he does give one mindblowing soliloquy to Cutter, describing to Bone the *Life* magazine photos — My Lai, the napalmed child, *those pictures*, we have all seen them — of the horror and what it really means:

I studied them all right. I went to school at those pictures. And you know what I found out? I found out you have three reactions, Rich, only three. The first one is simple — I hate America. But then you study them some more and you move up a notch. *There is no God*. But you know what you finally say, Rich, after you've studied them all you can? You say — I'm hungry.

This is flat-out brilliant writing, but Thornburg is not done. If anything, the last third of the book, where Cutter and Bone travel to middle-America Ozark country to confront their suspect, is where the author really turns on the juice, hurtling the reader towards a climax that reads like a paranoid's fever dream. Guaranteed, the last few pages of this novel will leave you reeling; the ending is both shocking and right.

There are very few novels, in fact, that have rocked my world to the degree that *Cutter and Bone* did the first time I read it. My copy, bought in a secondhand store in 1990, has been through several continents with me more than once, and it looks it. Long out of print, this is the first republication of Newton Thornburg's masterpiece in over ten years. Protect and cherish the book you now hold in your hands.

1

IT WAS NOT THE FIRST TIME RICHARD BONE HAD SHAVED WITH A
Lady Remington, nor did he expect it to be the last. Nevertheless he felt a distinct breath of revulsion as he drew the instrument back and forth above his mouth, and he was not sure
whether this was because he detected on it some slight residue
of female armpit musk or whether the problem was simply his
image in the mirror, old Golden Boy all tanned and sleek and
fit. What a liar it was, this image. An honest mirror would have
thrown back something more along the lines of Cutter, he felt,
a figure with missing limbs and a glass eye and a smile like the
rictus of a scream. Idly Bone contemplated the reaction of the
shaver's owner had she known a little more of the truth of him,
for instance that he was not so much interested in keeping the
old corpus tanned and fit as he was in merely keeping it alive,
feeding and clothing it, checking its occasional vagrant impulse
to swim out into the channel a tantalizing hundred yards too far
or to push his senile MG around a curve a few rpms faster than
it was meant to go. Wait, he kept telling himself. Have patience. Something will happen. Something will change.

Though he had finished now, he was reluctant to turn off the
razor, anticipating that the woman would pick up her lament
again. He still could not believe her lack of cool. In the past,
when he had gone straight for the money like this, most of
them simply had walked, a few had thrown him out, some

3

even had come across. But this one preferred to hang in there and suffer.

When he put the razor away finally, there was a knock at the bedroom door, followed by the swish of her Sears robe as she got up and answered. It was room service: champagne and deep-fried fantail shrimp, an enthusiasm of hers. Coming out of the bathroom, Bone slipped into his peppermint-stripe shirt, which was going into its third straight day of wear. The Chicano roomboy, leaving, gave him a conspirator's wink, probably because the woman had signed the check. Bone ignored him.

"Want some shrimp?" the woman asked.

"Sure."

"Shellfish, they're supposed to be good for virility, aren't they."

"Men in my line of work, we couldn't get along without them."

"I didn't say that."

"Didn't you?"

"I'm sorry, then. It's just that this thing is — well, it's kind of hard on a woman's vanity."

"What thing?"

She laughed wistfully. "You don't have any idea?"

"Your friends," Bone said, "you going to join them again?"

"Would you like that?"

"I thought maybe you would."

"Not particularly."

"It's up to you."

"Is it really?"

He shrugged. There was nothing to say, nothing that would make any difference. The woman was one of three Fargo, North Dakota high school teachers who had come here to Santa Barbara for the spring vacation. Their rationale apparently had been that if no men turned up they could fall back on touring the local historical sites or scavenging through curio

4

and antique shops. When he had found her sunning herself alone on the beach — her colleagues were late risers — she had not been at all bashful about abandoning them, taking this new room in the motel, and spending two days and a night with him so far, footing all the bills of course. He was having his troubles, he had told her. A tight period. It would pass. And she had accepted this with a fine contemporary aplomb, in fact had seemed to take an almost indecent relish in cashing her traveler's checks and slipping him money under the table and sometimes over.

The trouble had begun only hours before, in bed, when she had broken their after-sex silence with some vague moist words about love and commitment and settling down. He had been swift in reply, coming back with his request for "a loan." Just three or four hundred, he had suggested. Something to tide him over.

Occasionally it had worked. But not this time.

At the table, Bone lifted the lid on the chafing dish and drew out a pair of shrimp. Dipping them in sauce, he devoured them in one bite.

"What will I say to them?" she asked.

"Who?"

"My friends. What will·they think?"

"About what?"

"You. This thing we've had going. What do I tell them?"

"The truth."

"And what's that?"

Bone had poured the champagne. Now he reached over to give her a glass but she ignored it. He set it down. "That you found out I was a loser," he said. "Broke. A bum."

"You don't look it."

"I don't even have a room, for Christ sake. Got locked out a couple weeks ago. And the guy I'm staying with now, he's two months behind in *his* rent. A loser too."

"You don't look the part."

5

"Well, I feel it."

She sagged into an orange vinyl chair.

"Come on, eat," he told her. "It's getting cold."

"I'm not hungry."

"Suit yourself."

"And I wouldn't think you'd be hungry either — all the *eating* you've been doing."

That made Bone look up from the table. "I enjoy it, lady. Thought you did too."

Though he called her lady, he judged she was a few years younger than he, twenty-nine or thirty, not likely the dewy twenty-five she laid claim to. In the beginning she had been reasonably attractive, good company, good in bed. But the woman confronting him now was someone brand new, a stranger with a trembling mouth and long Dakota winters in her eyes. Meredith, she called herself. Meredith Saunders.

Bone ate more shrimp. "Didn't figure you for a romantic," he said. "You came on like a realist."

"And you came on like a human being."

"False representation, huh?"

"Something like that."

Despite his hunger, Bone was beginning to wish he had already walked out. He had hoped for a reasonably friendly parting, starting with this late evening snack together, the two of them sitting here warts and all in the crummy motel room, eating, swilling, a chance for her to adjust her vision to the reality of the situation and see it as it was and had been all along, a one- or two-night stand and nothing more. *Love.* Where could she have gotten such an idea?

"Is it always so easy for you?" she kept on. "This gigolo bit? Don't you ever have any trouble 'rising to the occasion,' so to speak?"

"It ain't much of a 'bit,' I'm afraid. Nothing regular. I come to the beach to run and sometimes I see someone who interests me. Someone attractive, like you."

"Someone to fuck. Someone to sponge off of."

6

He did not respond.

"It never reaches you? Never bothers you?"

And suddenly he was out of patience. He could feel the anger beginning in him, like the first hot breeze of a Santa Ana. Getting up, he slipped into his seedy sportcoat.

"See you around," he said.

She called his name as he left, a tearful "Richard!" that made him slam the door behind him all the harder as he headed for the elevator at the end of the corridor.

His car was parked across Cabrillo, the beach drive, which curved west in a long graceful sweep of streetlights to the distant wharf and yacht harbor, beyond which the drilling platforms in the channel winked green and red at the rim of the sea. As he crossed the street and entered the parking lot, he could almost feel the woman's eyes on his back, their cloying outrage following him every step of the way. He halfway expected her to call out his name again, but gratefully all he heard was the surf breaking lightly on the beach, that and a kind of chant rising from a group of hippies sitting on the sand in lotus position around a driftwood fire. Why couldn't they be singing? he wondered. Why couldn't it be laughter and hot dogs instead of prayer beads and theological posturing, weird amalgams of fire worship and Zen? Christ, he hated California, or at least this coastal strip of it, this crowded stage where America kept trying out the future and promptly closing it, never letting it open for long on Main Street. And yet Bone could not bring himself to leave. It was like loving the meanest, gaudiest whore in the house. You got what you deserved.

But then that was more than a little specious, he knew, because he was indisputably one of them now, just another player indistinguishable from the evangelists and fire-worshipers, the pornographers and primal screamers. And his casual abuse of the schoolteacher only proved how well he fitted in. For his reason had not been the money he had pointedly asked for and not the few days of high life either, the good food and drink and service he still had not lost his taste for, even three years after having walked away from it. No, his reason at bottom was probably nothing more than simple boredom, that and the always attractive prospect of spending a few days away from Cutter, free of him and Mo and their kid and all their problems, their booze and battles and squalor, their crisp invective and soggy leftovers.

But as he reached his car now, and took in its bald tires and rusting fenders and the springs coming through the rotted leather of the seat, he had to admit the three- or four-hundred "loan" would have come in handy. At the very least it would have meant new rubber and a valve job, so he could stop dragging behind him a long blue tail of exhaust gases wherever he drove. It was funny how indifferent he had become to the thing, a classic 1948 MG-TC with running board and wire wheels and all the rest. Yet now it was transportation, that was all, no different from the gleaming Detroit iron he used to buy new each year in Milwaukee, before he had cut out on Ruth and the girls and his problems at work. But when he had first drifted here two years ago in the company of a nice lady he had met in Acapulco — and eventually was given the car by her, to remember her by, she had said — well, for some reason these four wheels had become nothing less than the symbol, the bright red emblem, of the new life he was to lead, not this year's model of some cheap chrome and plastic dream but rather wood, leather, steel, a work of care and art, honest, real. That had been about the scope of his expectations, the measure of his innocence. The reality had turned out somewhat different. Now he would have settled in a second for some of that Detroit chrome and plastic, wheels that ran fast and quiet and did not trail a spoor of smoke.

On the way home, he stopped in for a few drinks at Murdock's, a Chicago Loop tavern misplaced in Santa Barbara, a cool dark narrow room with thick carpet underfoot and a new color television behind the bar and a gaudy Wurlitzer that played bland pop music, not the sort of place the Montecito or Hope Ranch sets were likely to turn up even in their more desperate slumming forays. Murdock's clientele was basically working-class Anglo, enough of a minority in Santa Barbara so the place was rarely crowded, and the prices reasonable, the service good.

Bone still had twelve dollars of the schoolteacher's money left, five of which he put on the bar now, so Murdock would know he was not planning to add to his already embarrassing tab. Seeing the bill, Murdock quickly fashioned Bone's customary vodka and tonic and brought it to him.

"Long time," Murdock said. He was about forty, lean for a bartender, with thin red hair and blotchy skin.

Bone shrugged. "No bread."

"Someday you got to face it, Rich. This world, you work. No other way."

"That's what I hear."

"Believe it."

"I try."

"Hell you do. I mean really try. So the old stomach acts up again — so you get wound up — so what? Who don't? No one lives forever."

"Just hurry up the process, huh?"

Murdock made a face, knowing, envious. "You got it made, man. You know that? You got it wired. If I could be a professional like you and sit around some fancy office all day thinking up ways to con suckers like me, you think I wouldn't do it?"

"I think you would."

"You bet your ass. And you will again too, for a fact. You know why?"

"No."

"Cutter," Murdock said. "You still staying with him, right?"

Bone nodded.

9

"That's it then. Anyone sane, that guy drive him crazy. Anyone don't drink, he'll put him on the sauce. And anyone don't want a job — hell, he'll have you punching a clock before the week's out."

Bone smiled wearily. "I take it he was in."

"You take it right, pal. Couple hours ago." Murdock looked down the bar, where a rheumy-eyed old man was anxiously regarding his empty glass.

"Tell you later." Murdock moved away.

Bone lit a cigarette, grateful for the interruption. He was not in any mood for conversation. Ever since he had left the woman he had felt the anger growing in him, the resentment. He had a pretty good idea how she pictured him, as some sort of footloose swinging stud blithely moving from woman to woman, victim to victim, taking what he could and skipping on, no sweat, no lost sleep. The irony of it galled him, for right this minute he felt about as swinging and free as a Carmelite monk. Like the quinine water, fear ran cold in him. And it was the sort of fear white middle-class Americans just were not supposed to know about, fear of things like hunger and cold and toothache, all quite minor unless you had twelve dollars to your name, five of which you would blow this night on liquor. Would he eat tomorrow? The coming week? Would he have a place to sleep? The ridiculous truth was he didn't know, for both right now depended on Cutter's disability check, which would probably last about as long as a Southern California snow, considering that the man's tastes ran to abalone steaks and Cabernet Sauvignon and Packard restorations.

But then Bone was his own man, was he not? Free, white, and thirty-three, sound of wind and limb? Couldn't he simply do as Murdock suggested, get a job, pay his own way? The evidence indicated otherwise. For he had tried, every now and then had bowed to necessity and taken a job, probably a dozen of them in the past thirty months, two in marketing again, relatively high-paying positions in which he was expected to do only what he did best, and yet within weeks the stomach had begun to go bad just as in the past, sleep would not come, and his exhaustion was as if he had been drugged. So he had quit. And even the other jobs, the frequent blue-collar gigs as a gardener or truck driver or laborer — the story there was no different. Always the tightening in the stomach would come, the feeling of entrapment, and finally the inevitable flare-up with some asshole boss or other. Then it would be the street again, the women again, his only real security.

Later, if he drank enough, he would pass the problem off as philosophic, reflecting that he simply could not think in the old terms anymore — man, job, life — not when the death of Richard Bone was no more than a sudden leg cramp out in the surf tomorrow morning or a drunk driver coming his way just beyond every curve ahead or an exotic virus even now prospering in his flesh. When your mortality was that real for you, how could you spend what might be your last hours in someone else's hire, making or selling or serving disposable junk?

But now, sober, Bone had no answers, no certitude, nothing but the fear, the coldness trickling through him.

Murdock returned. Wagging his head ruefully, he lit a small cigar. "Yeah, he was here all right, your landlord. About two hours ago. Came in with this hippie freak and a girl."

"Mo?"

"Who's Mo?"

"Maureen. His old lady. Mother of his kid."

"What's she look like?"

"Blond. Kind of thin. A chain-smoker."

"Christ no," Murdock laughed. "This one was a spade. But some looker, let me tell you. Real cool, you know the kind. Anyway they come in here about nine and take that table over by the jukebox. Hardly drink anything, the three of 'em, just stand there feeding quarters into the thing and breaking up over the music. Now I say, you don't like a number, well and good, you don't have to play it."

"Cutter does."

11

Murdock frowned in consternation. "He's a leaker, all right. You know, I had the feeling he was kind of playing it double, making fun of the three of them same as he was the rest of us."

Bone knew the routine. "Now you see him, now you don't."

"Another thing. The guys here like the fights on TV, so naturally I turn 'em on. So what does your boy do? He sits over there telling this hippie and the girl — just loud enough so if you wanted you couldn't help but hear him — he tells 'em how sick American men are, that the only way we can get our jollies is through secondhand violence, like the fights, watching one poor creep pound on another. Only he served it up with a lot of psychological mumbo jumbo, you know?"

Bone drained his glass. "Cutter knows the words."

"Yeah he does. But believe me, by then the cats in here wasn't digging his words very much. Fact, most of 'em didn't like it from the beginning, him bringing the hippie and the black girl in here. But what could they do, huh? Him hobbling around on a cane and with one arm missing and that goddamn black patch over his eye. He uses all that, you know? He takes advantage. Hell, he ain't the only cat got shot up over in the paddies."

Bone slid his empty glass across the bar, hoping for both a refill and an end to the tirade.

"Man's got his problems," he said.

Murdock picked up the glass, dumped out the ice, the twist of lime. "One final word on the subject," he said. "Move out. Get away from him. Sleep on the beach if you have to."

"I'll keep it in mind."

"Sure you will."

In the next few hours Bone bought four more drinks himself, accepted one from an off-duty cop who had taken the stool next to his, and finally got a freebie from Murdock himself. So he was without anxiety when he left the bar at eleven-thirty, walking through a cold spring rain to his car parked up the street. The rain meant that before he could drive anywhere he first had to get out a towel and dry off the seat and dashboard, for the MG's torn old canvas top was about as effective as rattan in keeping out the weather. And even then the drying off was not totally successful, because the worn-through seat absorbed much of the wetness and would surrender it only to the pressure of Bone's weight, which it began to do as he started for home — a sensation that always made him feel as if he had been time-warped back into wet diapers and a crib. But even this feeling did not altogether kill his pleasure in the night, the almost midwestern lushness of it, with the wind soughing in the sycamores and pepper trees and the palms whipping back and forth, raining dead fronds on the darkly gleaming streets.

He was moving along Anapamu, under its graceful canopy of stone pines, when the car's engine began to cough and rattle. Then abruptly it cut out. He knew he had been playing things close, not having bought any gasoline for almost a week, so he was not surprised at running out now. And yet he could not completely check his anger either, his disgust at the god-damn miserable little limey heap with its leaky top and useless gas gauge and general debility, and he had to resist a strong impulse to steer the thing off the road into a tree and just leave it there, abandon it for good. Instead he coasted to a stop along the curb and, taking the ignition key, set out on foot the rest of the journey home, most of which was sharply uphill. He knew he could have gone for gas at one of the all-night stations on Milpas, but they were not much closer than Cutter's place, and this way, leaving the car overnight, he would not have to walk back but could use Cutter's car in the morning, if by some outside chance it happened to be running.

To his right, the high school sprawled low and dark and very Californian in its parklike setting, an almost collegiate campus compared to the bleak diploma factory Bone had attended in his native Chicago Plains. He was not surprised that given this

13

setting and climate students tended to overachieve mostly in illiteracy and venereal disease. And it made him almost wish he was sixteen again, mindless and full of juice, embarking on that long road of teenage ass. Certainly compared to the road he walked this night it would have been more pleasant, and a lot easier on the nerves. First there was the rain, which suddenly became a cataract as he turned uphill away from the school. Then in the first block a huge Doberman dragging a broken chain came snarling out of the darkness at him like the hound of hell itself, and he found himself circling gingerly around the beast, walking backward in a cold feral sweat, jabbering pleasantries. Then no sooner was he out of danger and on his way again when a late-model car came speeding down the hill and, braking suddenly, swung into an alley next to an apartment complex. There the car came to a stop and Bone saw a man get out, a squat, large-headed figure silhouetted against some distant garage doors floodlit by the car's headlights. Moving rapidly, stumbling once, the figure scurried around to the other side of the car and opened the passenger door, apparently getting something out of the front seat, though Bone could not be sure since he was across the street and approaching from the driver's side. But as he walked on, the angle changed rapidly, and he saw the man just as he finished stuffing something — golf clubs, it looked like — into one of a half dozen trash barrels evidently left there from a pickup earlier in the day. Immediately the man slipped back into the car through the open passenger door and roared on up the short alleyway, fishtailing the car as he accelerated and then braked again, turning left as the alley turned. Seconds later Bone heard the tires shrieking once more as the man turned onto Anapamu and floored the car again. Already a few lights were coming on in the apartment buildings as outraged widows and retirees checked their alarm clocks to see what time it was, at what ungodly hour they had been wakened by

14

what drug-crazed hippie freak. Bone hurried on, not eager to have to answer any questions, especially any put by a policeman.

As he reached the next corner he found the sidewalk effectively blocked by an old man and a toy poodle, both dressed in oversize yellow slickers and connected by a leash. The dog, a male, was spritzing a dwarf palm tree.

"You the one making all the racket?" the old man demanded.

Bone deliberately did not break his stride, so the man had to haul the dog in on its leash, one leg still airborne.

"Hey!" the old fellow complained. "Who do you think you are?"

Bone told him to go fuck himself.

Between the main part of the city and the mountains was a great long foothill beginning at the Old Mission and running almost to the sea. Billed as the Riviera by the natives, it offered vistas and property values that ranged from the breathtaking along the top to the merely desirable farther down. These latter were generally older neighborhoods with smaller lots and smaller houses, most of which had been cut up into apartments that offered little for the money except a view, and sometimes not even that. Cutter's place, however, stood alone, a small gray frame structure built in the forties on the outer edge of one of the goat-path roads that veined the hillside, a perch so precarious there was no backyard at all, just a rickety wood deck whose unobstructed view probably accounted for half the three-hundred-dollar rent Cutter and Mo scrounged to raise each month, often unsuccessfully.

As Bone reached their street now and saw the house ahead, he found himself hoping that Mo would be in bed already, preferably sound asleep. And this irritated him, for he knew there was seldom a time when the sight of her failed to give him pleasure and thus he had to wonder if his desire not to see her now wasn't a kind of fear, a gut need at this late stoned hour to slip past the fast guns of her scorn. How was it he had described her to Murdock? Blond and kind of thin. Which she was. But she was also kind of beautiful, a fact he had not seen fit to mention. And this too irritated him.

As he let himself into the house, softly closing the front door behind him, he was relieved to see that all the lights were out except one over the kitchen sink, which as usual was buried under a clutter of dirty dishes. Even in the darkness Bone could feel the squalor closing in on him, for the place was truly a house without a keeper. The little house that couldn't, Swanson called it, Swanson from the good old moneyed days of Cutter's childhood. Cutter and Mo had lived in the place two years, Bone understood, yet to a large extent they still were not unpacked. Random supermarket boxes full of books and stereo albums and other junk sat on the floor next to unhung pictures and piles of clothing no one had bothered to put away or get hangers for. The tiny kitchen, however, was the true disaster area. There the groceries — the bags of Fritos and Cheetos and potato chips, the cans of Spaghetti-os and Hamburger Helper, the rafts of Hostess Twinkies and Ding Dongs and other such chemical concoctions — all sat exactly where they had been brought in from the store and dumped, amid the burned pots and empty fifths and accumulated TV dinner trays.

So Bone was grateful for the darkness as he ventured into the kitchen now and, rinsing out a dirty coffee cup, tried to cool his smoker's throat with water that tasted like pure chlorine. Just as he was setting the cup back on the sink, the bathroom door opened and a shaft of light poured across the living room. In it Mo moved dreamily, carrying a drink in one hand and a lighted cigarette in the other. She was wearing chinos and the beautifully ornate silk kimono Cutter claimed to have stolen from a Hong Kong whore during one of his R and Rs from Vietnam. Reluctantly Bone left the kitchen.

"You're up," he said.

16

"How very keen we are tonight." Her smile was heedless, stoned.

"Feeling good, huh?"

"Good enough."

Bone turned on a table lamp and dropped onto the davenport. "Don't tell me, let me guess. Quads and vodka."

She shrugged indifferently. "Could be. I didn't bother to notice."

"Considering, you're looking good."

"You too. But then of course you always do. Sort of a dry Mark Spitz, aren't you?"

"Drier. And blonder."

"And older," she said.

"Much older."

Clumsily she slipped down onto the floor. Setting her drink on the coffee table, an old boat hatch resting on cement blocks, she chain-lit another cigarette. "Well, how'd we do these last few days?" she asked. "Did we score big? Did we make them pay for the honor of balling the champ?"

"You're stoned."

"Could be."

"I don't like you stoned."

"I don't like you sober."

"How would you know?"

"I asked you, how'd we make out?"

"Not so hot."

"Just food and drink, huh?"

"And a respite."

"One of those, huh? From what, if I may ask?"

"You can't guess."

She smiled, all radiant innocence. "From *me*? Your sweet old Mo?"

Bone shook his head. "Even bullshit like this, some reason I can take it from you."

That seemed to bring her out from behind the downers and

alcohol. "But Alex's generosity, that you can't take, huh?"

"All I can get."

"But resent it in the bargain?"

"Not at all. I'm grateful to him. Why, sometimes I almost like him. Let's just say I find it hard to stay with a man and his old lady."

"And why is that, do you think?"

"Maybe it's like in the Bible. Maybe I covet my neighbor's ass."

She regarded him coolly. "Don't waste your time, Rich."

"I didn't say I was trying to get it, Mo. Only that maybe I coveted it."

The cool watchful look lasted a few more seconds, then abruptly she threw back her head, laughing. "Poor Richard. The man they never say no to. And yet here he is, playing second fiddle to a one-eyed cripple. That must really gnaw on you."

"Not too much. No, I'd say my problem is more curiosity than anything else. I keep asking myself if all this isn't just an act. I mean, consider — here's this tough ballsy liberated female, this pampered alumnus of —"

"Alumna."

"Of Beverly Hills and Radcliffe—"

"Hunter."

"I keep wondering why she'd play barefoot squaw to anyone, least of all a —" Bone faltered, wanting the right euphemism.

"A what?"

"A Cutter."

"You don't have any idea?"

"I don't mean because of how he looks either — his *injuries*."

"His character then?"

Bone shrugged.

"What then? Think, Richard. Strain."

"Don't want to hurt myself."

18

"Chance it."

"It's late, Mo."

"I'm sure it is. But keep trying. The Lord loves a trier."

"That's comforting."

"Come on, Richard — why do you resent him?"

"Cutter? I don't."

"You do. Now try. Think of something."

"Anything?"

"Anything."

Bone lit a cigarette. "Well, let's see. There's you. There's always you."

"Fine. What about me?"

"How he treats you."

"And how is that?"

"Lousy."

Mo smiled wearily. The argument was beneath her. "Wrong. Alex treats me fine."

"Sure. While he goes out every night, you sit at home minding the baby."

"It's my baby."

"Not his?"

"Men don't have babies."

"So there's no need for marriage."

"Did it do your wife any good?"

There was not much Bone could say to that. "You've got a point," he conceded.

But that did not make a winner of Mo. If anything, she looked more troubled now, less sure of herself. She sat on the floor staring down at her lap and the drink she cradled. Then slowly, carefully, she got to her feet, one hand on the overstuffed, overworn Salvation Army chair that sat on the other side of the coffee table. Sipping her drink, she wandered to the front window and stood there for a time looking out at the darkness, the wet street shining in the corner light.

"I suppose it does seem kind of screwy," she said finally.

"Like it does to my parents. They think I've flipped, you know. They think their poor dear Maureen took one acid trip too many. And I can't blame them. Or you either. But I don't have any answers. There just comes a day, that's all. You come to the point where you've got to make a commitment. And for me, Alex is it. I think he has a kind of greatness in him, Rich. I really do. At least he's suffered greatly, I know that. I look at him, at that poor torn face of his, and then I think of the rest of us, all the frightened little faces like yours and mine, all the mild, hungry little faces, and I ask myself if any of us by any stretch of the imagination could ever do anything, be anything, that mattered. And the answer is no. Always no."

"But Alex could, huh?"

"I believe he could."

"I don't."

"His family, you don't know what monsters they were. And the drugs. I was in the life myself for a few years, so I have some idea what it cost him. And then Vietnam. He caught all of it, you know? But all it could do was cripple him, disfigure him on the outside. Inside —"

"Inside he limps."

"You bastard, Rich. You poor bastard."

"Inside we all limp, Mo."

"Not Alex."

Bone shrugged. "Okay. You're right, I'm wrong. You go on playing barefoot squaw."

"I'm not *playing* anything!"

"Whatever you call it. Just so it makes you happy."

"Well, it *does!*"

Bone got to his feet and went over to her. With mock tenderness he took her by the hair and turned her head, forcing her to look at him. "Then why the downers, Mo? Why the booze? How come you can't get through a day without all that junk?"

Tears welled in her eyes. "I need it," she got out.

Bone let go of her. "Enjoy it then. I'm gonna take a shower."

Even over the roar of the water Bone was able to hear the new voices in the living room, especially Cutter's nasal rasp, that fitting instrument of the bawdy sardonic character he pushed in public, so different from the one whose soft and stumbling, almost elegiac voice Bone often had to listen to out on the deck at night as the man worked closer to his pain — a voice then in fact not unlike the other Bone heard now too, only this one bearing the softness of babyfat instead of pain. And Bone decided he had known that was what the hippie would sound like. The black girl, if she was as cool as Murdock said, would naturally prefer her meat nice and white, soft breast of chicken. He would be tall and slender, Bone judged, a pale Anglo-Saxon ectomorph with rimless glasses and pony-tailed hair and a Mexican peon's blouse and elaborately patched Levi's. He would smoke grass and drink cheap wine like all his peers of course, but in careful moderation, almost as a generational tokenism, with none of the verve he would bring to his clandestine use of mouthwash and underarm deodorant. He would be working on his master's in ecology or comparative religion at no-cal state and had temporarily dropped out in order to "get his head on straight." Idly Bone wondered why he felt so much contempt for the type — because he himself in his mid-twenties had been pulling down twenty-five thousand a year, with a wife and child to support, a house and cars and debts and responsibility? Was it their purblind luck he resented, the fact that simply by being born a decade later than he, they almost automatically had inherited a life-style and values that had taken him long years of blood-sweat to reach? Or was it his suspicion that they were the reverse of him, secret establishmentarians in counterculture drag. Not that Bone wanted to play their hippie game, with its bare feet and stink, its hashpipes and costumery and funky

21

minibuses. He was content to leave all that to them, wanting for himself only the substance of the life, the sweet and simple state of freedom.

He had just turned off the shower and was beginning to dry himself when Cutter came gimping through the bathroom's unlockable door. Giving Bone a salacious wink, he carefully positioned himself over the toilet bowl, thrust the index finger of his right hand — his only hand — down his throat, and promptly threw up. Bone still found it incredible that this was part of the man's daily existence, like eating and urinating. His stomach, an even less dependable organ than Bone's, simply would not tolerate food on top of alcohol. This was his solution.

"When in Rome," he said finally, shuddering.

"You couldn't wait till I came out."

"Apparently not."

"Bullshit."

"Bad booze," Cutter reflected. "Or escargots, I'm not sure which."

"Who gives a fuck?"

In answer, Cutter raised his hand, a prelate blessing his flock. "Be still, my child. One cookie yet to toss." And again the finger wriggled down his throat. Again he gagged, vomited.

Bone, dry now, felt like killing him. What a sight the man made, what a celebration of the grotesque: the thinning Raggedy Ann hair, the wild hawk face glowing with the scar tissue of too many plastic surgeries, the black eyepatch over the missing eye and the perennial apache dancer's costume of tight black pants and black turtleneck sweater with the left sleeve knotted below the elbow, not pinned up or sewed but *knotted,* an advertisement, spit in your eye.

After flushing the toilet, Cutter tore off some toilet paper, wiped his mouth and blew his nose. Bone was hurriedly slipping into his Jockey shorts, but not fast enough. Cutter wagged his head in mock appreciation.

"What a bonny lad ye are, Rich. Not a mark on ye. Not one li'l old scratch."

Bone slipped into a pair of jeans. "Could be I'm not accident prone."

Cutter grinned happily. "You got me there, kid. That about says it."

"We have guests?"

"You could call them that."

"How late they staying?"

Cutter shrugged. "Don't sweat it. The one's a boogie chick, real cute. Maybe you could score there. The boyfriend was in Nam same time as me. Served under a buddy of mine, cat I knew at Stanford before I got the boot. The kid's a bomb-thrower and figures I still am too, which I didn't disabuse him of, 'cause he was buying. Gonna blow up the energy establishment, he is — how's that for ambition, huh? While all you want to do is pull down some poor cunt's panties, he wants to pull down Exxon. I don't know about you, Rich. You lack ambition."

"How late?" Bone persisted. And got a Cutter response:

"Time will tell."

After Cutter left, Bone found himself staring down at the toilet bowl and the shreds of vomit that flecked its rim, vomit that would still be there a week from now, dried by then, but still there, still vomit. And suddenly he knew that Murdock was right — he had to get out from under Cutter's roof as soon as he could, in any way he could, even if it meant finding a job.

Still toweling his hair, Bone returned to the living room to find everyone but Mo settled in around the coffee table. The Negro girl, sunk in the beanbag chair, turned out to be every bit the "looker" Murdock had said, a high-fashion type, all skeleton and sinew and great black eyes that swung insouciantly on Bone as he came in, questioning his right to be there or for that matter anywhere. Without any real satisfaction, Bone saw that her hippie friend fell safely within the parameters of his preconception of him, departing chiefly in his woolly mop of blond hair, almost an albino Afro. Across from him, Cutter sat draped on the davenport, his steel and plastic right leg propped on the boat hatch amid a clutter of paperbacks and bottles and ashtrays and bowls with leftover popcorn from the week before.

"Behold, the squeaky clean Richard Bone," he said. "Rich, this is Steve Erickson and Ronnie. Say hello."

Bone nodded, but said nothing.

"Steve was in Nam too," Cutter went on. "He and Ronnie are just passing through, trying to line up talent, you might say. They were kind of wondering, Rich — think you'd be any good at blowing up drilling platforms?"

Erickson suddenly looked ill. "Jesus, Alex," he protested. "Knock it off, huh?"

"Oh, you can trust Rich," Cutter assured him. "He's totally apolitical, aren't you, kid. Sort of an ideological blob. At best, a tits-and-ass independent, you might call him. Votes the straight party ticket."

Bone yawned. "You missed the bowl in there, Alex. You got some on the floor."

"See, you can trust him," Cutter said, grinning.

Bone went over to his pile of suitcases in the corner and rummaged out an old maroon silk robe, one of the few artifacts remaining from his upwardly mobile days in the Midwest. Putting the robe on, he remarked how late the hour was, almost twelve-thirty. He did not add that he wanted to go to bed, or that bed was the davenport.

"You in Nam too?" Erickson asked.

Cutter answered for him. "Unfortunately Rich couldn't make it. Couldn't be spared. He was doing vital work in marketing at the time." He looked over at Bone. "What was it you were pushing up there in Milwaukee, Rich?"

24

"Toilet paper was our big item. We gave away flags once."

Cutter nodded gravely. "I knew it was something like that. Something big."

Erickson smiled thinly, embarrassed. The black girl, however, seemed totally with it, and totally bored. She looked up wearily as Mo came in from the kitchen with a bowl of corn chips, the same bowl Bone had seen twenty minutes earlier, filled then with rotted grapes. He did not have to wonder if she had washed it in the interim. As was her habit, after she had unceremoniously popped the bowl onto the coffee table, she sat down on the floor near Cutter's feet and lit a cigarette, listened.

He'd only been putting Erickson on, Cutter confessed. Actually Bone was one of the few cats around a man could trust. It was true Bone had worked in marketing paper products for a number of years, but that was the measure of the man, that he was here in Santa Barbara broke and free instead of pimping for the establishment in Chicago and Milwaukee, and making a bundle doing it, by God. A v.p. by thirty, Cutter said, a real corporate tiger, with the big house and cars and wife and kiddies and the whole schmeer. Yet he'd walked away from it all.

"And why?" Cutter concluded. "Because he's one of us. Because he couldn't stand all the lies. All the newspeak. *Exxon wants you to know,* sure they do. But what, huh? Just what do they want you to know?"

Once again Erickson was caught, a believer. And it was a forgivable mistake. You had to know Cutter, almost live with him, to understand the savagery of his despair, that it precluded his responding to any idea or situation with anything except laughter, sometimes wild but more often oblique and cunning, as now. His mind was a house of mirrors, distortion reflecting distortion.

Erickson looked from Bone to Cutter. "You mean, I should — ?"

"Sure, let him in on it. Tell him what's up."

Bone almost told the kid to forget it, but then decided not to spoil Cutter's fun. "Yeah," he said. "I'm interested."

Erickson cleared his throat. "We call ourselves ViVA."

"Like the paper towel," Cutter put in, ever helpful.

"Yeah. But with a small *i*. Means life, of course. But it's also an acronym. Stands for —" Erickson paused pregnantly, looking from Bone to Cutter and then back again. His voice grew husky. "It stands for Violate . . . the Violators . . . of America."

"The big polluters," Cutter assisted.

Erickson nodded. "The big energy companies. Power companies. Conglomerates. The government even. We don't care who — if they pollute — if they violate us —"

"You violate 'em back," Bone said.

"Right. Fight fire with fire. Make 'em hurt. Make 'em realize the energy crisis hasn't changed a thing — we're still gonna fight 'em all the way."

Cutter finished lighting a small cigar. "Your group," he said, "you're a spin-off from the Sierra Club, right?"

And this seemed to upset the young hippie. "I said *kind of*, Alex. Nothing official. Certainly they don't know what we're planning, and wouldn't approve if they did know."

"But most of you once belonged."

"Not anymore. We've got our own thing now. And believe me, they're gonna be hearing from us, the polluters — they're gonna find out there's still some of us left, a few who haven't been coopted or scared off."

"Right on," Cutter said.

"Why, you know, they're having some kind of big energy symposium at the university here right now, today. All the captains of pollution and their purchased Ph.D. eggheads, all sitting around *talking*. Well, let me tell you, pretty soon we're gonna be doing the talking."

"Right on," Cutter said again, this time grinning cryptically at the girl. Then he looked over at Bone. "Steve and Ronnie

26

are trying to get chapters started all up and down the coast. Now the local one, Rich — well, you can see what a fertile field this would be. How many drilling platforms they got out there in the channel now, ten or twelve? Think of the mess you could make. Why it'd be pure crude all the way down the coast. The whales in the spring could just slide on down to Baja without so much as moving a fin."

And finally it began to dawn on Erickson that someone was driving a truck back and forth over his body. He put down his can of Coors. "What is this, Alex, huh? You putting us on?"

Cutter made a face. The idea obviously had never occurred to him. "Not you and Ronnie. Jesus no, my son. Just your approach, that's all."

"But I thought you were —"

"A militant?"

"Well yeah. Dunhill said —"

"Vietnam Veterans Against the War — right. But that was years ago, kid. And I got this hangup. I think. *Cogito ergo sum.* And what am I, it turns out? Peaceable. A peaceable fatalist. Like Solomon, I looked about me and decided all was horseshit."

"*Horseshit!* What we're doing is horseshit?"

Cutter shrugged amiably. He wished it were not so, but so it was. "You know what you are, Steve? You're a do-badder. And you're going to be just as ineffectual as all the do-gooders. I'm afraid life just doesn't respond properly. You give it a bone and it bites your leg. You bite its leg and it'll bite your balls."

Ronnie evidently had heard enough, for she got up and wandered out onto the deck, letting in a blast of cold damp air. Bone too felt no great compulsion to stick around and went back to the kitchen to make coffee, either that or another drink, though he doubted that he would find both vodka and tonic on hand, since Cutter and Mo both liked their liquor neat. He knew from having heard it before the lecture Erickson was in for, or actually not so much a lecture as Cutter simply giving in to the bent of his mind, a bent that inclined steeply toward hopelessness. Essentially his position was that even if the unlikely occurred, even if a cabal of enlightened socialists and egalitarians somehow came to power, and the longed-for millennium of benevolent despotism finally arrived, and even if the political technicians managed to repeal all the laws of supply and demand and somehow miraculously wrought a society of both plenitude and liberty, man would still be in a funk. He would quickly begin throwing bombs at his benefactors, and for no more complicated reason than that in the dark, secret oozings of his entrails he was as mad as a hatter, a jolly assassin, a lover of crisis and war and pestilence, anything but the dreaded menace of peace and boredom. And then Cutter would illustrate: vignettes of casual barbarism culled from his years in Vietnam and veterans' hospitals, My Lais apparently without end.

Bone had heard it all. And if he did not dispute it, neither did he much like it. So he took his time heating water and making himself a cup of Maxim. As he went back into the living room, Ronnie was striking a supercool pose in the deck doorway.

"There's some kind of hassle down there," she announced.

Erickson and Cutter ignored her, but Mo and Bone followed her out onto the deck. Bone had heard the sirens too, more than once, but that was not unusual, especially at night in a Southern California city. Below them the town stretched out like a small Los Angeles, a tinsely grid of light, beautiful now in the darkness but all of it mere foreground by day, bracketed by the chameleon peaks of the Santa Ynez mountains on one side and the sea and channel islands on the other. Within the grid, no more than a quarter mile down the hill, a pair of red domelights swiveled. In the distance another emergency flasher, this one yellow, sped in the direction of the other two.

"Looks like it's near the high school," Mo said.

"Wonder what happened?" Ronnie put in.

And so did Bone — for suddenly he realized exactly *where* the red lights were flashing.

Next door one of Cutter's neighbors, a young sculptor named Fishman, had just pulled in and parked his Jeep in front of the garage apartment he rented. As he got out, Mo asked him if he had driven up Anapamu.

"Yeah — you mean all the racket down there? They found a girl's body. A teenager. And in a trashcan yet. Can you believe that? In a trashcan."

The man's words hit Bone like a bucket of ice water, as in his mind the remembered golf clubs began to take on shape, flesh.

"Was she white?" he heard Mo ask. Gliding with her quads and vodka, she seemed to have forgotten Ronnie at her side.

"Yeah, she was white," Fishman said. "A white teenager." He went on into his apartment.

"Some big old buck nigger prolly do it," Ronnie said.

Mo caught herself then. "Oh I didn't mean that," she protested.

"What then? Just what did you mean, missy?"

But Bone was not interested in their problem. He still had his own. *He had been there, had actually seen the body discarded.*

"I saw it happen," he said now. And both girls looked at him.

"You *what?*" Mo asked.

"I saw it. I was there when it happened, across the street. Only I didn't see what it was he put in the barrel. I thought it was a set of golf clubs, with the heads sticking out, you know? But it must've been her feet."

Ronnie said nothing, just stood there looking at him.

Mo smiled in amusement. "You're putting us on."

Bone shook his head. "I ran out of gas down there, near the school. So I was on foot. And this character pulled into that

29

apartment complex, the driveway. Then he dumps this thing and drives off. I didn't think anything about it. As I said, I thought it was golf clubs or something like that. I just kept on going."

"You're *not* putting us on." Mo went over to the door and called for Cutter to come out. "We have a little excitement out here," she said. "Rich has been seeing things."

Erickson came out first, bumping into the doorjamb on the way and pretending nothing had happened, like a drunk in a comic routine. Behind him, Cutter moved carefully on his walnut cane. Mo dryly recounted what she had just learned from Bone and their neighbor. And Cutter grinned.

"In a *barrel?*" Apparently the idea amused him.

"It didn't look planned," Bone said. "More like an impulse. When the man saw the trash barrels he just pulled in and dumped the girl."

Erickson had turned to go back in. "I'll call the police," he said.

But Cutter blocked him with his cane. "You serious, boy?"

"Well Jesus yes, Alex. He's got to tell them what he saw."

"He does?"

"Of course he does."

"Why? Maybe the girl had it coming."

Erickson stared at Cutter in panic. Then he turned to Bone. "Is he serious?"

"I didn't see the man's face," Bone said. "Or the car license. I couldn't be any help."

"Well, the car. Didn't you see the car?"

"Late model is all. I couldn't tell the make. But that's beside the point."

"What point?"

"That no one here's going to report anything. No chance. So drop it."

"*Drop it!*" Erickson's eyes widened with disbelief and indignation. "Look, my whole bag is fighting crime, man. Corporate

30

crime, I admit. But that doesn't mean I approve the other. And this guy of yours, this cat you saw down there, Rich — goddamn it, he's a criminal! He's committed a crime. And it's our duty —"

"I told you what I saw," Bone cut in. "Nothing. I've got nothing to tell the police."

"Well, I'd say we'd better let them be the judge of that." And very primly, very businesslike, he started for the phone again, brushing Cutter's cane aside.

Bone caught him in the doorway, lightly taking hold of his arm for a moment, still hoping to talk some sense into him. But the kid pulled away with all his strength and went toppling back over one of Cutter's cheap aluminum folding chairs. Bone did not like violence, usually avoided it like any other rational man, but right now he had an even stronger aversion to sitting in the police station all day tomorrow trying to convince a squad of law officers that he had nothing to tell them.

So he reached down and pulled Erickson to his feet, holding him by his deerskin vest. Then he slammed him back against the clapboard wall.

"No phone calls," he said. "No police. Understand?"

When Erickson did not respond Bone took a handful of his woolly hair and jerked his head up and back, so the youth had to look at him. "*Understand?*"

This time Erikson nodded. Bone let go of him and the kid stumbled back into the house. They heard him go into the bathroom and slam the door and then struggle unsuccessfully to lock it. As Bone turned back to the others, Cutter shook his head sadly.

"You big bully," he said. "You mean person."

"Kid doesn't listen."

"He's a crime fighter."

"So I heard."

"Carries a silver bullet, I bet. Up his ass."

Bone did not want to look at Ronnie but could not help

31

himself finally, and he was not surprised to see that her cool sullenness had taken on a glint of self-satisfaction and even triumph. Feeling unreasonably angry, he returned his attention to the scene below, which was now a spreading web of light as more and more cars converged on the scene. Here and there flashbulbs went off like bursts of daylight, and finally the vehicle with the yellow domelight swung around and retraced its route, this time traveling more slowly and without any sound at all. On the deck, they all just stood there watching the scene and saying very little, especially after Erickson made a sheepish return. Then, as the cars began to leave and scatter, Cutter and Mo went back inside, followed by Erickson. But Ronnie stayed.

"I'm not with him and this jive-bomb gig of his."

"You're just his girlfriend, huh?"

"No chance."

"His companion, then."

"Look, the cat pick me up two days ago down in Hollywood, at some creep fag party, it turned out to be. I was broke just like now, no place to go. So when he offered, I took him up."

"Naturally."

"And he nothing to me, man. No more than you could be."

"It doesn't make any difference."

"You say that a lot."

"Yeah."

"Well, how about it?"

"What?"

"Don't what me. You know what I'm talking."

Bone considered the offer. It was late and he was tired, and the two days with the Dakota schoolteacher had left him feeling about as erotic as a steer. Then he thought of Mo, the fact that she would have to lie in her room with Cutter and listen to *him*, Bone, for a change, rather than the other way around. And for some reason the prospect gave him pleasure. But at bottom he knew his real reason would be the same as ever, the faithful old juices already beginning to rise in him.

"What about your friend?" he asked.

She shrugged. "Well, he do kinda like this li'l old black ass."

"But not enough."

The girl laughed. "You know, I think you right."

He took hold of her shoulders then and kissed her, lightly at first, almost exploratory, as if in token homage to their racial difference, and then more deeply finally, open-mouthed, discovering a faint trace of grass on her breath.

When they went back inside, Erickson verified that he indeed did not like his black ass anywhere near enough. Bone told him that the only way he could stay the night was alone out on the deck in his sleeping bag, and the youth fussed and fumed for the five or ten minutes it took him to gather up his things and get his backpack in order. But not once during that time did he direct a critical word at Bone. No, Ronnie was the only one at fault, Ronnie the cheap opportunistic little slut if ever he found one, in fact a no-good nigger bitch that was what she was, yeah, nigger, they'd heard him right, and if he hadn't ever used the word before it was only because he'd never run into one before.

When he left, there was not much said. Cutter, shaking his head in mock sorrow, told Bone and Ronnie to miscegenate if they must, but to please be quiet in the process because he needed his sleep, he planned to meditate all the next day. He and Mo went into their bedroom then, where the baby was still sleeping, and closed the door.

While Ronnie was in the bathroom, Bone got the cushions off the davenport and arranged them on the floor in front of the fireplace and then he pulled one of the Salvation Army chairs over to the foot of the makeshift bed, knowing Cutter would be up a few times during the night to go to the bathroom or limp out onto the deck to smoke and brood.

Finally Ronnie came out of the bathroom, naked and very handsome, her lean brown body lifted from some Egyptian frieze, a royal harlot.

Their lovemaking was about as he had expected it to be, loveless and humorless and yet better than he had had it for a long time, actually more like combat than any act of love, a silent and brutal plundering of each other there in front of the dead ash–filled fireplace. Even before they were finished, Bone began to wonder if she despised him as absolutely as he did her. For her sake, he hoped she did, had at least that much pride.

Afterward Bone fell asleep almost immediately, but not so deeply he could not hear sounds from time to time, the baby crying and doors opening and pans banging in the kitchen and finally a harsh bell ringing somewhere, a sound that cut through him like rough steel and pinned him wriggling to the past, all the hated risings day after day to shave and shower and dress and *hurry*, hurry nowhere, hurry to the one place in all the world where he wanted least to go.

Then suddenly he was aware of pressure on his elbow. Waking, he saw Mo standing over him, wearing the kimono again. Her bare foot was nudging his arm.

"Wake up, Rich," she said. "It's the police."

Beyond her he saw them, two men in business suits looking down at him and the black girl as if they had been scraped onto a microscope slide.

"You Richard Bone?" one of them asked.

Bone did not answer.

"Get dressed," the other said. "We're going downtown."

34

2

AT TEN-THIRTY THE NEXT MORNING BONE FOUND HIMSELF SIT-
ting — once again — outside the office of Lieutenant Milton
Ross, a small, neatly attired man in his early forties, initially
very polite and soft-spoken when he came on the job at eight
o'clock and thought he would quickly get from Bone what
lesser officers had not been able to manage in long hours of
predawn questioning — the "truth" of what he had witnessed.
But as Bone refused to change his story or add to it, the lieutenant's composure had begun to crack and peel. And Bone's
popularity plunged. Suddenly he was a liar, a lousy goddamn
anti-authoritarian deadbeat. He was a small-time con artist
bucking for the big time, like say a hitch in prison for obstruc-
tion of justice. But Bone was not to worry; his story would
change. Ross would see to that.

So Bone felt no great pleasure as the office door opened
again now and the lieutenant motioned him inside.

"Sit there," Ross commanded, indicating a straight-backed
wooden chair placed almost in the center of the office and
facing a row of glaring sunlit windows under which Sergeant
Verdugo and another, older man stood waiting. Ignoring the
chair, Bone walked over to a conference table that sat across
the small room from Ross's desk. Leaning back, he lit a cigarette, casually, determined not to let the little storm trooper
intimidate him. Under the windows he thought he saw a trace

of smile on Verdugo, one of the two detectives who had picked him up at Cutter's house almost seven hours before. The older man was new to Bone, big and white-haired, with the scarlet nose of a heavy drinker. He was leaning back against a radiator, arms folded, softly wheezing authority.

Ross addressed him now:

"Captain, first let me give you a short make on our witness here. Name is Bone. Richard Kendall Bone." Ross picked up a sheet of paper and began to read. "Age thirty-three. Born Chicago Plains, Illinois. Graduate University of Wisconsin nineteen sixty-four. No service record. Worked in sales and marketing, was marketing manager for a pretty large paper products company in Milwaukee at age twenty-eight. Wife and two kids, daughters. Suburban house, country club membership, etcetera. No record at all until three years ago. Then suddenly two busts for driving under the influence. License suspended. Then arrest on a charge of rape — which the woman then dropped. Lost his job and came here to the coast, alone. No steady job since. We got a Wisconsin warrant for desertion and nonsupport, then the wife dropped the charge. A year ago we brought him in on a grand theft charge, a fifteen-hundred-dollar tape recorder a local woman claimed he made off with. But she backed off too."

The captain, who had taken out a fat cigar and lovingly unwrapped it, now puffed it into life. "Fascinating," he wheezed.

Ross was undaunted. "And though there haven't been any signed complaints on this yet, some of the men say he's got a rep around the beach motels as a cocksman. Preys on women who —"

The captain laughed. "*Preys?*"

"That's what I hear."

"Still fascinating."

"Well, it does bear on his statement, I think. It bespeaks a certain life orientation, I'd say."

36

The captain waved his cigar in surrender. "All right, Milton. Jesus Christ, let's get on with it."

Nodding primly, the lieutenant returned to his paper. "Let's take it from the top then. We've checked with the bartender, Murdock, and these people he's staying with, the Cutters, and they all pretty much back up the time frame he's given us. He left the bar at approximately eleven-forty. Ran out of gas on Anapamu and abandoned his car, which puts him on the scene at approximately eleven-fifty. And that coincides with the testimony of the tenants there — that's when the body was dumped, when they heard all the racket. Bone then proceeded on foot to the Cutter place. The body was discovered — and we got our first call — at twelve-twenty. At one-forty-five we received the anonymous call regarding Bone."

"Anonymous to *you*," Bone put in.

Ross looked up from his sheet of paper. "The Cutters bear you out on that. Maybe it was this Erickson. But we haven't been able to locate him yet."

"Why bother?"

"What's this?" the captain asked.

"A young friend of Cutter's passing through town," Ross explained. "He was at the Cutters' house last night. Left after an altercation with Bone."

The captain nodded vague comprehension. "Go on."

"That's about it. And you've got his statement."

"So I have." Sighing, the captain worked a sheet of paper out of his rumpled suit-coat pocket and unfolded it, scanned it. "Yeah, and it ain't much, is it? A man in silhouette . . . heavy . . . large head . . . period."

"That's what I saw," Bone said.

The captain looked up at him. "Oh, we understand that, Mr. Bone. And we've got no quarrel there, believe me. Last thing we need is inventive witnesses. No, that's not the problem. It's the other — your refusal to go through our mug file or view a lineup. You know, we keep pretty close tabs on sex offenders

37

around here, and a case like this, well it's no trouble to run 'em in front of a witness, no trouble at all. You never know, one of 'em just might ring a bell."

"I didn't see a face," Bone said. "I can't identify a face."

"Just a silhouette, huh?"

"That's right. A shape. A dark shape."

The captain smiled coldly. "Maybe the Prince of Darkness."

"I wouldn't know," Bone said.

"Don't know the gent, huh?"

"Can't say I do."

"Well, you are indeed fortunate." The captain, apparently a realist, slowly stood erect. Putting away Bone's statement, he added, "So be it, then. Just thought I'd put in my two cents. Because this thing's really got folks all shook up. You wouldn't believe the calls I got this morning already. People want this guy awful bad. And I think I know why. It's the trashcan, I figure that's what bugs them. Why not dump the body in a ditch somewhere or on the beach, huh? Or up in the foothills? No, not this guy. He chooses *a trashcan*. And I think it says something about him, something not very nice. Something people can't accept."

Bone said nothing.

At the door, the captain looked back at Ross. "You tell him about the autopsy?"

"Not yet."

"Crushed trachea and fractured skull," the captain told Bone. "Semen in the throat and on her face. Blood type O." He shook his head slowly, in wonderment. "Seventeen years old too. A cheerleader. I don't know. I just don't know."

Still Bone said nothing.

The old man lifted one hand slightly and let it drop as he went out, a gesture of futility or parting, Bone was not sure which. And he did not care. He had been patient up to now, very patient, considering that he had spent half the long night and morning trying to convince platoons of detectives that he was a witness to a body-dumping, that was all, not the murderer they at first thought him to be, hoped him to be, and then once they had accepted this, to have to battle through the rest of the morning to defend the integrity of what he had seen, or more accurately, not seen. So he figured he had been patient enough, had played that poor man's game as long as he could.

Crushing out his cigarette, he moved toward the door. "I'm leaving now," he said. "Either that or I call a lawyer."

Ross lifted his phone, stabbed a button. "One minute, Bone. Just one minute more, I promise." Into the phone, he said, "Send her in."

Through the office door window, Bone saw one of the secretaries in the bullpen area nod to a young woman sitting next to her desk. The young woman got up and headed for Ross's office. She was small and very trim, with eyes that looked incapable of surprise, expected anything from anybody.

"Who's she?" Bone asked.

"The victim's sister, Valerie. Supported the girl, I understand. The mother too, an invalid."

"What's this got to do with me?"

"Just tell her what you saw, that's all."

"Why not you?"

"I don't think she'd believe it from me. She'd think we were snowing her, not doing our job, you know."

"So you want me to do it for you."

Ross shrugged. Finally he was enjoying himself. "It's your story, not ours."

After the girl came in, Ross curtly introduced her to Bone and then explained that Bone had been on the scene last night and had witnessed the "disposal" of the body, a word choice that did not seem to embarrass the lieutenant at all. Then he gave the floor to Bone, who told her exactly what he had told the police, not embellishing his story or apologizing for its inadequacy.

She turned back to Ross. "So you don't really have anything yet. You don't know who."

"Not yet. No."

She smiled slightly, brutally. "But you will, of course."

Ross did not return her smile. "You can count on it," he said.

"Sure."

Bone liked the girl. He regretted not having more to give her. But he said nothing. His minute was up, his long night of patience. As he opened the door, Ross tried to get in a few last words:

"Don't leave town. If you have to, get in touch with me or Verdugo. And try to remember. Try —"

But Bone had already closed the door behind him.

When he emerged from the police station he found Cutter waiting for him, stretched out like a lizard in the sun on one of the stone parapets bordering the front stairs. He knocked on Cutter's false leg, and the one eye opened.

"I'm out," Bone announced.

Cutter sat up, yawned. "So you are. Jesus, this sun feels great." He struggled erect and started to cane his way down the stairs. "You know, if I'd had a tin cup here I could've made a fortune."

"You'd only blow it."

"Car's down the street," Cutter told him. "Mo and the kid too. Nobody's slept worth a shit. You really screwed us up, you know that? I had to baby-sit out here while they grilled Mo and then vice versa."

"What about Ronnie? They have her in too?"

"Wanted to, I guess. But she took off. Your little black piece is long gone."

"Good."

"Not all that great, huh?"

"Not worth this."

40

"Amen to that."

"What about my car?"

Cutter ignored the question. "The gendarmes had me in there almost two hours, can you believe that?"

"Why?"

"Who knows? Maybe because I got bored — I asked one of them if this was all they wanted me for, to find out about you."

"Smart," Bone said.

"Yeah, wasn't it though?" Cutter grinned like a demented wolf. "First thing I knew there were three of them working on me, all with the same question: *What else is there?* So I broke down and confessed. Sodomy . . . double parking . . ."

His laughter rattled down the street.

Bone shook his head. "They're gonna lock you up one of these days. They're gonna eat the key."

"But when, huh? You never tell me the important things."

Bone tried to go back. "My car, Alex. You still haven't told me."

"Guess."

"Twenty-five?"

"More."

"How much?"

"Ten for parking on a thoroughfare. Thirty for towing. And four-fifty storage a day."

Bone's stomach knotted. "Oh, Christ no. That much?"

"Don't worry about it."

When they reached the car, they found Mo lying back on the front seat smoking a cigarette while the baby stood next to her crying and pulling on her hair, trying to make himself heard over the radio, which was booming a Carly Simon number. Cutter, who ignored the infant almost entirely, simply opened the car door and stood waiting until Mo finally crawled into the back with the baby and started to change him.

"I was waiting until you got here," she explained, as the men

41

slid into the front. "One diaper left, and if we're going out to lunch —"

"Damn!" Cutter was trying unsuccessfully to start the car. "I told you not to play the goddamn radio with the motor off!" he yelled.

Bone lit a cigarette and settled back, trying to loosen the knot in his stomach. His MG was bad enough, but at least it was a gift. He had not paid a dime for it. This, on the other hand, this grossly ugly 1948 Packard Clipper convertible, was Cutter's by choice, something he had intentionally acquired and expensively restored for no better reason than that it was the same make and model his late father had once owned and made his rounds in, tooling back and forth between the country club and the yacht harbor and the family digs near the Mission, a huge old house now converted into a warren of apartments.

"They getting anywhere yet?" Mo asked Bone.

He shook his head. "Same as before. One blind eyewitness."

"What did they say, you don't *look* blind?"

"Something like that."

"I imagine they're — well, disappointed."

"I guess."

"And you really can't blame them," she said. "I mean, here's this grown man, this nice clean-cut sort of establishment type, and he sees the culprit right across a little old side street dumping a body, practically eyeball-to-eyeball with the guy — and what can he tell them about it? Nothing. I'd be, uh, disappointed too."

Cutter was still grinding his foot against the starter. "Get off his goddamn back, will you, Mo!"

"What do you mean, off his back?" she protested. "I'm not on your back, am I, Rich? My God, I come down here to testify for him. I clean up the floor after him and his little Afro friend. Why I even wash his come towels."

Cutter was not listening. "Come on! Come on!" he yelled, as the engine turned over faster.

Bone, however, *had* heard her. Glancing back at her, he tried to read her look, weigh the pain or contempt hiding behind the slight smile of mockery. But she turned to the baby and began to nuzzle him. And just then the engine caught.

"Old Faithful!" Cutter gloated. "Well, let's go get a sandwich. We got big bidness to discuss."

They drove the few blocks to Ziggie's, a new self-serve sidewalk café located close to that point on State Street where the smart shops and neat tree-lined brick walks of downtown Santa Barbara began to go sour, in fact became the local skid row or at least what had to pass for one in the absence of any truly rundown area. In most American towns, the strip probably would have been the high-rent district, which pointed up one of Cutter's favorite themes, that the city was the victim of creeping affluence, or, as he expanded on the subject, Blockbusting Whitey Style. Every few days the bulldozers would press a little farther into the barrio, razing a few more Mexican shanties, which would then be replaced by some exquisitely designed orthodontists' office building resembling the Ponderosa hacienda and costing about a million dollars a square foot. In time there would be no hovels left, Cutter would complain, no place at all for the Mexicans to live. Who then would cut the Anglo's grass and clean his toilets? Who would raise his children? Obviously the time to act was now, before the burro was out of the barn.

They took a table in the sunshine and for a time the three of them barely spoke, all hungrily downing Ziggie's doughy hamburgers and fries. The baby, however, standing in Mo's lap, had much to say about his mother's nose and eyes and lips, which he kept touching and squeezing and kissing. And Bone for some reason found himself unable to look away from the two of them, this blond handsome young woman sitting across the small table in the pale lemon light, with her fat year-old son jabbering happily in her lap. He tried to think of his own family, Ruth and the girls, but there was nothing there,

43

nothing comparable. He had courted the girl and married her, had lived with her and slept with her for over seven years, and together they had made children, together had raised them, or at least begun the process. Yet when he tried to *feel* now what those years had been about, he could not come up with much of anything except possibly habit, that tedious old whore habit. Yes, he was afraid that pretty well covered their relationship. Ruth finally had been a habit, that was all, and probably the girls too, Janey and little Beth, somehow so like their mother, so cool and correct, so contained.

Whatever the reason, he could not remember feeling then what he felt now as he sat watching Mo and the baby.

For Cutter, however, they might as well not have been there. He had other problems.

"Money," he said to Bone. "That's what we got to talk about, kid. Bread. The staff of life."

"What about it?"

Cutter took a bite of his hamburger. "Ain't none," he chewed.

"You're short, huh?"

"You might say that, yeah. No food stamps. Disability check two weeks away. Mo and I got about four bucks between us. And the cupboard is bare."

"That's short, all right."

"I'm already into so many cats around town, people dive through windows when I hit a place. And Sister Venereal here won't call home to her mama and beg, so where does that leave us?"

"You tell me."

Cutter drained the last of his Coke. "With you, buddy."

Bone laughed. "You sure you got the right man?"

"Yeah. But let me say first, Rich, this hasn't got anything to do with your staying at the house, the few bucks of groceries you may cost us. Nobody's keeping tabs, nobody cares. We're happy to have you."

44

"I thank you, sir. But I'll be out in a day or two anyway."

"No reason to. We like having you."

Bone looked at Mo, and she smiled cryptically.

"I appreciate that," he said to Cutter. "But you got a lousy davenport. I think I can do better."

"Dreams of glory," Cutter said. "But even if you could, it's beside the point — which is we need a short-term loan. Enough so Mo can go do her thing at Alpha Beta."

"Right. I understand. But where do I fit in?"

With his one hand Cutter had taken out a cigarette. Now he lit it deftly, in a swift flow of movement. "You is duh loan*er*," he said. "We is duh loan*ees*."

"You're out of your tree."

"Yeah, I know — you're flat too. But your old buddy's been busy. Let me ask you — how you gonna get your car back?"

"I don't know yet."

"You'll try to hit somebody, right? Well, let me tell you, sweetheart — you won't connect. Everybody's really up against it lately, I don't care how goddamn much money they're making. It's like asking for blood."

Bone plucked the last french fry out of its paper tray, ate it. "What're you getting at?"

"As I said, I've been busy."

"And — ?"

"I've got a buyer for your car."

"A buyer?"

"That's right. He buys, you sell. Push-pull click-click, we've got some bread again. He'll give you two hundred."

Again Bone looked over at Mo, hoping to see her reaction to this bit of footwork. But she was inscrutable, as usual firmly in Cutter's corner.

"Who says I want to sell my car?" he asked Cutter.

"What good is it in the city garage? And anyway it's a mess, right? You can't fix it. Well, this guy can. He's got his own shop. Did most of the body work on the Packard."

45

Bone shook his head in appreciation. "Beautiful, Alex. Just beautiful. I sell my wheels and give you the money."

"*Loan* it."

"Loan it then. Either way, how do I get around?"

"My car."

"When it works."

Cutter shrugged. "Well, it's up to you, man. Think about it. Meanwhile you better eat slow. All we've got at home is Cocoa Krispies and booze."

Bone said nothing for a time. He lit a cigarette and watched the thin parade of winos, hippies, and straights moving along the sidewalk. At the near corner a truck pulled up and its driver, a young black man, got out and loaded a stack of newspapers into a vending machine. Mo handed the baby to Cutter.

"I'll get it," she said, reaching for her purse. "I want to read it first."

As she left the table Cutter pushed the baby out to the end of his knee.

"Jesus, I hope this ain't my kid. What an anal character. He's done it again. Old brown pants himself."

Bone did not trust his voice for a few moments. "What a prick you are, Alex," he said finally. "What a real first-class prick."

Cutter forced a laugh. "What's all this about, huh? What's with you now?"

"You know goddamn well."

"About selling your car?"

"About Mo, you prick. That's your kid and you know it."

For a time Cutter sat there pretending to be surprised and puzzled. Then the old look of amusement lit up his wounds again. He knew something you did not. Slowly he shook his head. "I don't know any such thing, kiddo. I don't know nothing about nobody. What do you think the girl is, some kind of tin saint? Man, she was in the life from her teens. Then that

46

Jesus Freak commune bit and a rebound after. You think you go through all that and come out a vestal virgin?"

"I'm talking about *now*, the last two years. The kid's a year old, isn't he? So he's yours."

"Don't ask me, ask her."

Mo had just returned to the table. "Ask me what?"

"If I made the front page," Bone said.

She handed him the paper. "Not by name. At least, I didn't see it. The story mentions a witness, that's all."

It was not the headline story — the worsening economy still reigned there — but it did get second billing. And there were two photographs, one showing the trashcans and the driveway leading through the apartment complex, the other a school portrait of the girl, Pamela Durant. Next to the pictures was a deck headline:

LOCAL GIRL SLAIN
BODY FOUND IN TRASHCAN

The accompanying story had nothing in it Bone did not already know. A man walking on Alvarez Street was alleged to have seen the car turn in and stop, but it was reported that he saw the suspect only in silhouette. His statement and tire markings on the driveway indicated that the vehicle at the scene was a late-model, full-size car. Residents in the apartment houses reported hearing the vehicle brake sharply, and then moments later depart with tires screeching. The victim, pretty seventeen-year-old Pamela Durant, had been a cheerleader and homecoming queen candidate at Santa Barbara High School. She was described as very popular, an active student with a keen interest in ecology and contemporary music. She was survived by her mother Angela Durant and sister Valerie, twenty-three, an employee of Coastline Insurance.

Bone handed the paper to Cutter, who had already given the baby back to Mo. Now he scanned the front page rapidly

47

and then turned inside, where something caught his interest. He seemed surprised for a moment. Then he recovered his customary look of amiable scorn.

"Hey, maybe our friend Erickson was even busier than we thought last night." He handed the paper back to Bone to let him see the item.

Glancing at the third page, at a large newsphoto there, Bone suddenly felt the sidewalk opening under him. The photograph came at him from inside as much as out, negative and positive. And he heard himself mutter, "My God."

Cutter looked at him in puzzlement. "Hey, I'm not serious, man. That cat couldn't blow up a balloon."

Bone barely heard him.

"Hey, what's with you?" Cutter pressed.

"It's *him*."

Mo too was looking at Bone now as if he had taken leave of his senses. "Who?" she asked.

But Bone had caught himself by now, realized the absurdity of what he had said. "*Like* him," he amended. "That's all. It's *like* the man."

Cutter leaned across the table to get another look at the photograph. His voice soared. "You putting us on, man? *J. J. Wolfe?* The conglomerate? The man on *Time?*"

Mo, who still had no idea what they were talking about, unceremoniously snatched the paper from them and looked at the picture Bone still could not believe: a heavy large-headed man in his forties standing next to a burned-out car and smiling happily, as if he were displaying a prize bull. Above, a banner headline explained:

CAR OF J. J. WOLFE BLOWN UP
FBI CALLED IN ON FIREBOMBING
OF VISITING TYCOON'S CAR

"He's *like* the man," Bone repeated. "Same size and build. Similar. That's all I meant."

Cutter was staring fixedly at him, almost squinting, as if there were small print all over Bone's face. "Ain't what you said at first," he said.

"I'm saying it now."

Cutter affected a look of deep confoundment, and turned to Mo. "Now isn't that weird. One second he eyeballs the picture and tells us *It's him,* just like that. And the next second he takes it all back. That is passing weird, wouldn't you say?"

But Mo was busy reading the story of the firebombing. "Happened at one-fifteen in the morning," she reported. "He'd been driving around late, alone, in a rented Ford LTD. Got back to his motel about midnight, ran out of cigarettes, and went back to his car to get more. On the way — bang. He saw it go up. But that was all. Didn't see anyone running or anything else. And he's got no idea why anyone would want to do such a thing to him." Mo smiled maliciously now. "I quote: *All my companies work for America. They create jobs and opportunity and prosperity for thousands of people. We don't take, we give.* Unquote." Mo bowed humbly, playing folksy tycoon herself for the moment. Then she returned to the paper. "So he knows this thing wasn't intended for him. It was either a prank that got out of hand or someone simply got the wrong car. Nevertheless he appreciates the fine job the local police and the FBI are doing."

"What a sweet guy," Cutter said. "It say what he was doing out so late?"

Mo reported from the paper. "He admires our fair city so much he just drives around it any chance he can get, day or night."

"He's here for the energy conference, I take it?"

"That's what it says."

Cutter looked at Bone. "What do you say now, man? Driving at midnight, all by himself. In an LTD, which I believe qualifies as a full-size car."

"Along with a few million others."

Cutter shrugged. "All right, Rich. Okay. I agree. The odds

49

against this cat being your trashcan freak are — well, astronomical. Because he's here in town, and heavy-set, with a large head, and driving the right kind of car at the right time — I agree, it doesn't mean anything. Must've been scores of other gentlemen around town — maybe hundreds — that would fit the same bill of particulars." Cutter had begun to light another cigarette but forgot it now, let it dangle unlit. His eye narrowed conspiratorially. "But you know, I must admit two things about this do just bug hell out of me. First, why you said *It's him*. Not it *looks* like him, not it's *similar* to him or a *double* for him, but *him period*. And second, the firebombing of his car — not even ninety minutes after the girl was dumped. Now isn't that strange? Doesn't it intrigue you a little, Rich?"

Bone looked at his watch. It was past twelve o'clock and people on their lunch hour were beginning to crowd the sidewalk café. Many were standing in line, waiting for tables.

"We're through eating," he said. "Let's go."

"And my two problems?" Cutter asked. "No answers?"

"Your only problem, Alex, is your imagination."

Driving back uptown, Bone found it hard to believe the amount of traffic they had to fight through. Even in his small MG the going was rarely swift, but it was decidedly slower with the one-armed Cutter maneuvering the 1948 Packard, which reminded Bone of a beached whale, a great bloated tin fish. With the traffic already this bad, he hated to think of summer and especially Fiesta week, when tourists would glut the city like starlings in a favored tree.

As they moved along, stopping, starting again, smoking and rattling past the handsome old fake-adobe structures along streets lined with palm trees and hibiscus and jacaranda, Bone could almost feel with Cutter the sick outrage of the native Santa Barbaran. For the town quite simply was perishing of its own spectacular beauty and climate, was on its back almost full time now, putting out for all kinds of pimps and promoters and developers, anyone with the price of a lay. Santa Condominia, Cutter called it, relishing how it too had betrayed him.

But Bone could not work up much of a sweat over the problem. In fact he could not even keep his mind on it. The photograph in the newspaper kept intruding. He had played the thing casually back at Ziggie's, but the truth was he had no answer to Cutter's question. He had no idea why he had blurted *It's him!* And that uncertainty, he was sure, worried him even more than it did Cutter, for only he knew how immediate and thoughtless the connection had been. It was not the face, of course, for he had not seen the man's face. Nor was it simply that both men had the same bearlike body and large head. No, it was something beyond that, an animus, an almost inhuman arrogance that flowed as equally from the dark shape dumping the body in the trashcan as from the face in the photo, the celebrated new conglomerateur grinning amiably next to the burned-out shell of his rented car. And for that matter, Cutter had a point there too, the car going up in flames within an hour of the dumping of the body — how many coincidences added up to noncoincidence?

But again Bone caught himself. Had he flipped or was it just exhaustion? As if to prove to himself the absurdity of his thoughts he picked up the paper now, which had been lying between him and Cutter in the front seat, and absently, almost carelessly, he opened it to the third page, expecting to find nothing there but a grinning stranger. Instead he found the same sick feeling as before. And Cutter did not miss it.

By the time they reached the house, Bone had begun to feel the need for both solitude and exercise, and he asked Cutter if he could take the car onto the beach. But Cutter crossed him.

"Great idea. I'll join you. We can race."

After Mo got out, taking the baby with her, Cutter drove off.

51

On the way they went past the apartment building that once had been Cutter's home, a huge three-story white stone structure sitting back amid the surviving palms and sycamores, its sprawling lawn all asphalt and parking places now, its porte cochere glassed in and modernized, a lobby. Behind the house rising young stockbrokers and communications specialists lived the chic life in converted stables and servants' quarters and drank mai-tais around the same pool where Cutter's mother, drunk, had fallen in and drowned a few years after his father, Alexander the Third no less, had met a similar fate, going down with his heavily mortgaged hundred-thousand-dollar yacht in a storm off Point Conception. By the time of the mother's death the executors of the estate could scrape together only enough for Cutter to have a year at Stanford, and then it was all over, done, three generations of money and privilege canceled like a subscription. And Cutter moved on without a backward look, slipping easily into the mid-sixties, that golden age of cant, of bare feet and acid and Aquarius, followed by either disillusionment or boredom, Cutter was never sure which, except that it led to turnabout, metamorphosis into a marine of all things, a hard-gutted grunt who reached Nam just in time for Tet of 1968, just in time to step on a claymore.

Most of this had come from Mo. What little Cutter ever revealed about himself was usually in the form of black humor, as when he referred to his parents as the aquatic branch of the family. Even now, driving past the old house, he did not glance its way. Nevertheless Bone could not forget the make and model of the car they were in, and he could only wonder what significance it held beyond the obvious, precisely how and where its psychic tendrils linked Cutter to the flesh and spirit of his past.

At Arroyo Burro they parked the car and made their way down over the huge winter boulders to the beach itself, where a ragtag school of scuba bums was preparing to go into the water, all looking to Bone infinitely weirder than anything they were likely to spear in the deep. Limping past them, Cutter asked one to keep a sharp eye out for his dog Checkers, a Labrador that liked to float out in the kelp beds for days at a time, especially at this time of year. Though the man looked dubious, he nodded.

"But be careful," Cutter called back. "He bites."

Bone walked on a short distance under the cliffs, to a boulder where he knew Cutter would wait for him. There he took off his shoes and jacket and started out, jogging at first, then slowly gathering speed as he ran toward the lowering sun, which was setting red fire to Isla Vista's lonely Stonehenge of high-rise buildings. Out at sea, storm clouds moving in from the southwest had snagged on the channel islands like old newspapers blown against a fence row. For over a mile he ran, between the cliffs and the sea, past low-tide-uncovered rocks bristling with mussels and sea anemones. And then he started back, keeping up the same steady pace, until in time he could feel the cleanness coming into him as his body burned first its fuels and then its poisons too, all the tensions and angers and other gunk of this long day disappearing down the swollen river of his blood. And still he kept on, even after the cleanness had become only pain, an ax stuck in his side and sinking deeper with every step until finally it reached the point where he felt almost severed by it, and only then did he let up, slowing down for a time and then walking and jogging the last half mile to the boulder where Cutter sat staring out at the sea.

"Used to run here myself," Cutter said. "But I guess I already told you that."

Bone, still out of breath, did not respond.

"I'd have beaten you then, Rich. Because you coast, man. You glide. You don't press. Me, I pressed."

"I believe it." Bone lit a cigarette and dragged, wondering

53

whether it would undo whatever good the run had done for him.

"But back in your old v.p. days at twenty-eight, I don't figure you did much coasting then, huh? No sir, I'll bet you ate old men for lunch back then."

"I don't particularly care for the metaphor."

Cutter laughed. "You got a point."

Neither of them said anything for a time. A pretty teen-age girl walked past, leading an English bulldog on a leash, and Cutter gave her his customary greeting — "Want some candy, little girl?" — but it lacked all edge. Smiling, shaking her head, she walked on. And both men watched her, the long legs and small fine buttocks moving eloquently as she went on around the headland up the beach. When Cutter looked back, his eye had a strange bleakness in it. Nevertheless he grinned. He grinned crookedly and said, "Lately I been thinking of killing myself, Rich. You got any advice?"

Bone dragged on the cigarette, buying time. Out beyond the surf a pelican plunged into the sea. Bone shook his head. "No," he said. "I don't think so."

"I figured not. Guy talks about it, naturally he's not gonna do it, right? He's just fishing. Dramatizing himself."

"I didn't say that."

"I would, in your place."

"Then why tell anyone?"

"No good reason. Except it's true."

And Bone began to feel a breath of alarm now, like a breeze off the kelp, fetid, a touch ominous. "Why, Alex?" he said.

Cutter shrugged. "I don't know. It's not the goddamn eye, or the arm and the leg — some list, huh? They don't help, Christ knows. But they're not it, not the real problem. No, that's in here," he said, tapping his head. "And I can't fix it. Can't change it."

"What is it?"

Cutter flipped him a look, spare, flat. "Well, it goes kinda

54

like this — you make me ill, Rich. I mean physically ill, a feeling like having to puke all the time, like having the goddamn flu or a hangover. You get the picture. And it isn't just what you say or what you do. It's what you *are*, what I know you are, inside." He must have seen some of the resentment Bone was beginning to feel, for he raised his hand, signaling that there was more to come. "And the problem, kid, the big problem is you're the best. Yeah, I guess I probably like you best — or despise you the least, I guess I should say. Less than all the others, less even than me. Probably just a matter of style, the low key, nothing important. It doesn't change the fact that I get out of bed every day like it was Armageddon. I can't stand the thought of looking at faces and listening to voices. I can't stand communicating. I'd rather kiss Mo's clit than her mouth. I'd rather bounce a ball than the goddamn kid. I don't want to read anymore, I don't want to see movies, I don't want to sit here and look at the goddamn sea. Because it all makes me want to puke, Rich. It gives me the shakes. I guess the word is despair. And it's become like my heart. I mean it pumps day and night, steady. I'm never without it. I'm sick all the time. So I think about death. I think I would as soon be dead."

Cutter broke off there, not even looking at Bone for a reaction. Absently he scarred swastikas in the sand.

"I can't say I understand," Bone tried. "I feel depression myself, Alex. And fear too. But nothing like this. Mo, doesn't she — ?"

"She doesn't figure in. She doesn't matter. With her or without her, it's all the same."

"What about the VA?"

"You mean the shrinks again?" Cutter laughed at that. "No chance. A bunch of cripples in bathrobes sitting in a circle telling each other how they've copped out or how uptight and hostile everybody else is. And the shrink getting off on it all, sitting there with one hand stuck in his fly." Cutter shook his head in disdain. "No thanks. Anyway I don't figure I'm sick. I figure I'm well, one of the few. I figure I see life whole and honest, exactly as it is. And the only normal healthy response is what I have, this despair."

Bone knew that with Cutter the possibility of a put-on was always present. But he went along anyway. "You're serious, then?"

"About killing myself? In my head, yeah. I see no reason not to. But doing it, actually doing it, well I couldn't say till afterward, could I. After I'd brought it off. And then of course I couldn't say anything. So I guess all I can say is yeah, I'm serious."

Bone dropped his cigarette onto the sand, buried it with his foot. "At the beginning you asked for advice. Okay, I advise you to wait. You can't lose. Things might change."

"I'm already into that," Cutter said. "I've been waiting for some time now."

"Good. Keep waiting."

Cutter shook his head matter-of-factly. "Not this way. Not with this setup. Mo and the kid and the food stamps. And this fucking boom town. It's like living in the middle of a Jaycee parade."

"What else then? Where?"

"Nothing very grand, Rich, believe me. First, money, of course. I'd need that. Enough for some decent surgery on the old physiognomy, tone down the scarface routine. The VA, they *added* scar tissue. I believe the surgeon was an orderly out of Watts, used an old switchblade. And no new 'prosthetic devices' either. The foot's enough. I refuse to jack off with a steel claw. Unesthetic." Cutter grinned disparagingly. "As for *where*, I'm afraid I'm gonna have to disillusion you, old buddy. Because what I want is truly square, really and truly square. Would you believe an exotic island somewhere, with ceiling fans and dusky natives? Peter Lorre and Sidney Greenstreet and me, all sweating through our palm beaches. Say someplace like Ibiza, Clifford Irving and his freaky, decadent friends. Which after all is what I am, right? Freaky and decadent. I think maybe in a place like that, with people like that, I might lose this — nausea."

Bone too had begun to smile now, for he was sure if the other had not been a put-on, this certainly was.

"Ibiza, huh?" he said.

"*An* Ibiza."

"Good luck."

"Take more than luck. It'll take money."

"Right. Well, let's head back." Bone was already on his feet, waiting for Cutter to join him, which he did now, slowly pushing off on his cane.

As they started up the beach, Cutter changed the subject, or at least for a brief time Bone thought he had.

"Back in the car I saw you look at the paper again. The picture. You still ain't sure, are you?"

"About what?"

"J. J. Wolfe."

"I keep repeating, Alex. I didn't see a face. So how can I identify a face?"

"You tell me."

"You talk in circles."

But now the circles tightened. Picking up a stone, Cutter skipped it at the surf. "A rich man, J. J. Wolfe," he mused.

And Bone laughed out loud. Next to him Cutter limped along, smiling crookedly, culpably.

"So what's funny? A rich man, that's all I said. Which he is, right?"

"Which he is."

"So what's the big deal?"

"Come off it, Alex. Or rather, come out with it. Say it."

"Say what?"

"First, all this shit about despair and your crying need for

57

bread. Big bread. And now suddenly we segue neatly to J. J. Wolfe."

Cutter was still grinning. "Blackmail, you mean? You think I'm suggesting blackmail?"

"The thought does cross the mind."

"Bone, you been in too many police stations lately. Your brain's going soft. What the hell do you think I am anyway, some half-assed mick toilet-paper salesman, some aging ever-ready beachboy who'd go down on a crocodile if the money was right?"

Bone smiled at the description. It was not all that wide of the mark. "If not blackmail, what then? Why this consuming interest in the man?"

"Why not, for Christ sake? What if it was him? Society's got a right to know, hasn't it? Got a right to protect itself."

"You and Erickson — our junior crime fighters."

"Rich, you are too cool, you know that? Ain't you curious? Don't you wonder if it really was Wolfe?"

They were walking past a fisherman, a heavy-set man in boots and a slicker standing in the surf, dejectedly watching his line moving slowly in upon him. In two years of running the beach Bone had yet to see a surf fisherman catch anything but minnows and kelp.

"Why not this character?" Bone asked Cutter. "He's about the same shape. And maybe he drives a full-size car and was by himself last night, no alibi. Could be he's the one. Why don't we investigate him?"

"Oh bullshit."

"Why bullshit? It makes as much sense."

"Look, man, I know you. I was there, remember? The second you saw that picture, it was all over your mug — that first split second before you had time to think, to sickly the thing o'er with the pale cast of apathy."

They were at the car now. "You talk funny, mister," Bone said.

"Then laugh."

"Ha ha."

Cutter backed the car around and headed out of the lot, moving slowly, as if they were in a funeral cortege. "Are we gonna do anything about it?"

"Not me. What would a man like that be doing with a cheerleader?"

"What else?"

"Bullshit."

Cutter nodded. "Of course it's bullshit. It has to be bullshit. Except for one thing — you, friend. Mister Cool. Daddy Clear-Eyes. I don't know who I'd trust as a witness if not you. And what do you give us right out of the box? *It's him.* You can't explain that away, man. No way."

Bone said nothing for a time. He was as much exhausted as indifferent. But finally he responded. "So what do you propose?"

Cutter shrugged. "We find out what we can. Check out his car. Check out where the girl was. Play it by ear."

"You got too much time on your hands, Alex. You're going bananas."

"Maybe."

"And anyway, what's the connection? If not for blackmail, how does all this relate to your — despair?"

"I just want to know, that's all. If it was him."

"Why him?"

" 'Cause I don't like him, that's why."

59

3

THAT EVENING CUTTER'S OLD PAL GEORGE SWANSON CAME
through for him as usual, dropping in at the house with a
magnum of Mumm's champagne and a family-size bucket of
Kentucky Fried Chicken. Bone joined him and Cutter and Mo
at the kitchen table but ate hurriedly, adding almost nothing
to Alex's long sardonic account of the events of the last twenty-
four hours, an account that unexpectedly avoided any mention
of J. J. Wolfe and Bone's reaction to the picture in the newspaper. At the time, Bone did not give the matter thought,
probably because he was too tired to think about much of anything. When he finished eating he took his sleeping bag out
onto the deck and zippered himself into it, and the sleep that
came to him almost immediately was dreamless and timeless, a
deep black hole he did not begin to work his way out of until
ten the next morning.

By that time Cutter was up and gone and Mo was already
coasting on her first downer of the day, lying on the living
room floor playing with the baby while a broken Seals and
Crofts record kept repeating the same cloying phrase over and
over. In the kitchen Bone found milk and Pepsis and a large
cellophane bag of powdered doughnuts that tasted like uncut
sodium propionate. They meant that Cutter, the Great Nutri-

tionist, had already been shopping, undoubtedly with money from Swanson.

Bone would have taken some of the milk — unlike Cutter he was not an aficionado of cola for breakfast — but he knew the baby needed the stuff more than he did, so he settled for another doughnut and some reheated coffee. Then, after shaving and getting dressed, he called the man Cutter had told him about, the mechanic who wanted to buy his car. Yes, the man was still interested, but he would not go higher than two hundred dollars, less the cost of getting the car back from the city. Bone said okay, it was a deal — if he could use the car that afternoon, after they got it back. The man was not enthusiastic, but he finally came around. He even agreed to come by and pick Bone up.

As he put the phone down, Mo finally made it to her feet. In her customary chinos and sweatshirt she meandered over to him.

"My, aren't we all business today," she said. "An atavism, is it? Back to the halcyon days of paper pushing?"

"I'm busy, yes."

"Why?"

"Necessity."

"What necessity?"

"Food and shelter."

She smiled indifferently. "Oh yes, those."

Bone looked at the baby on the floor, dirty and happy, shaking a rattle. "How's he doing?"

"Baby's doing fine. But Daddy's not so hot."

"What's his problem?"

She shrugged. "Who knows? He was up half the night. With you most of the time, I think — out on the deck."

"I was asleep."

"So I gathered."

"Was it pain? His leg?"

"Pain maybe. But more in the head, I'd say. He was very

excited. Agitated. He kept saying something about 'a way out.' You know what he meant by that? A way out? Do they still have those?"

"If I find one, I'll let you know," Bone said.

By two o'clock he had his car back — temporarily — plus one hundred and sixty dollars in his wallet. And he was driving up into the Montecito foothills along serpentine blacktops past low-slung California homes hugging their little patches of hillside amid scraggly live oak and chaparral, all of it tinder eight months of the year, a torch waiting to be lit. The view explained: an often breathtaking vista of the sprawling red-roofed city below, the harbor and channel islands, the dazzling sea. It was a view that did not come cheap. Lots sold for thirty and forty thousand dollars an acre, and the houses were not built on them so much as into them, expensively tethered, like craft meant for flight.

So the socioeconomic range in the foothills was a small one, running from rich to richer. It was the sort of place where people ran the sort of ad Bone was answering now:

> WANTED — Young man for live-in, part-time yard
> and pool work. Nice room, meals, plus $50/mo.
> Call 969-2626.

Bone had called after seeing the ad in the noon edition of the paper. The lady who ran the ad, a Mrs. Little, evidently had liked his voice or what he said on the phone, for she made a pretty big thing out of granting the interview — he was the first one she had gone that far with, she explained, which of course brought Bone close to tears. He almost told the lady to go play with herself, but the position sounded too good not to look into, offering not only freedom from Cutter but a bed, food, and a few extra dollars in the bargain. Right now he would have put up with a good deal for all that.

When he reached the address he was not surprised at the

opulence of the house, all glass, redwood, and rock set behind a cut-stone fence that would have stopped a tank. At the door he had to wait quite a while before a stout little Mexican maid finally answered his ring. He started to tell her who he was and why he was there, but she turned and walked off, apparently knowing a handyman when she saw one. A few minutes later the lady of the house came in, smiling warmly, introduced herself, and asked him to join her in the sunroom. She was tall and black-haired, probably about fifty, though carefully reconstructed to resemble a thirty-year-old. The resemblance was poor.

With a careless little-girl insouciance she dropped into a chair, threw out her legs, lit a cigarette. "I've been out in my studio welding," she said, explaining her denim pants and jacket, her workboots. "I'm a sculptor."

"I thought maybe you'd been riding."

"Horses?" She laughed at that. "Not on your life. Montecito horsey set — now there's a group for you. Weird. Really weird."

Bone said nothing for a moment and the woman just sat there looking up at him, appraising him, as if he were standing on a slave block. And he almost groaned out loud as it crossed his mind just what sort of handyman she might be looking for. He began to wonder if there was some kind of mark on him, a big red F advertising his wares, condemning him to their traffic.

"Well sit down," she said. "Take a load off."

He did as he was told.

"You sure you're interested in this job?" she asked.

"Yes."

"Mostly I've had students before. College boys. It kind of fit in with their needs. You know."

"Sure."

"You're older."

"I'm thirty-three."

63

She smiled slightly, almost coyly. "And may I say you don't look like the handyman type."

"I've been other things."

"Such as?"

"Business. Marketing and so forth."

"A dropout?"

"You could call it that."

"And what'd you leave behind? Wife and kids?"

"Yes."

"Just like that?"

"Nothing's just like that."

"Where was it you dropped from?"

"Chicago." He wondered why he did not tell her Milwaukee; it wouldn't have mattered.

"And has it worked out for you — the dropping out?"

"Not exactly."

"Well, at least you're honest."

"At times."

The smile had gone over the edge now, was openly ironic, knowing. "The work here's simple enough. The yard and the pool, like I said in the ad. And then I have this truck I use for junk, stuff I pick up at junkyards, usually down the coast, Oxnard and around there. Stuff I use in my sculpture. You'd help me there too. Some of it's pretty heavy."

"No problem."

"My husband's got a computer service company. Software Systems Inc., he calls it. You know what software is?"

"Yes."

"He has to travel a lot. He's almost never here."

"I see."

She put out her cigarette now, carefully, and moved forward on her chair. For a moment he wondered if she was going to reach over and put her hand on his knee or just go straight for his fly. Close, she was all makeup, heavy eyeliner and false lashes and face color. Looking at the taut line of her jaw, the drum-tight skin, he could almost see the incisions above her hairline, the cunning face-lift scars running through the gray roots. And he felt his gut tighten. Could he bring it off? Would he be able to close his eyes and do his thing? Stoned, maybe. He would need grass, bales of it.

"One important thing," she said. "And I hope you'll be straight with me. I don't want someone who just needs a place to crash, someone who'd be here a few days and then —" She threw her hand in the air. "Gone. Split."

Bone assured her that was not his intention. "I think this is just what I'm looking for," he added. "What I want."

"Good." Smiling, she stood up. "Come on then. Let me show you your room."

When they reached it, a small efficiency apartment at one end of the three-car garage, she put her hand on his arm, just a friendly little gesture, nothing much, but sufficient to tell him what he had to know. He had not read her wrong.

"All right?" she asked.

Bone looked about him, at the tasteful expensive furniture, including a twin-size bed, a color TV, an air conditioner. "It's fine," he said.

"When can you start?"

He could have been back with his things in a few hours, but that was too soon for him. He was not ready for the job yet, not ready for her.

"Tomorrow," he said.

She looked disappointed. But she smiled. "Tomorrow it is, then."

When he got back to Cutter's house Bone found it empty except for the baby, who was sobbing disconsolately in his crib. Bone picked him up and quieted him and then changed his diaper, an operation he had not performed in many years. Then he warmed a bottle of milk he found in the refrigerator and fed him most of it, all the while feeling not only ridiculous but angry too, disgusted at Mo for having left the kid alone. It was something Ruth would never have done. No, her problem was the reverse, that she had almost never let the girls out of her sight. Of the two, Bone was not sure which was worse. The kids undoubtedly knew. But they weren't talking.

In time he decided that a little sunshine would not do the two of them any harm either, and after writing a note to Mo — "Baby's with me. Think I've found a buyer for him. B." — he put a cap and jacket on the kid and drove him the few blocks to the park across from the Mission.

Little Alex Five, as Swanson called him, was thirteen months old and just now beginning to toddle. So Bone carried him to a bench near the sprawling rose garden, which was not yet in bloom, and the baby immediately began to work his way around the bench, holding on most of the time but occasionally letting go and taking a few tentative steps out into the grass, where he would stop and do a little balancing act and then abruptly turn around and lunge back to the safety and support of the stone seat. Bone moved about ten feet away and sat down on the ground, trying to play this new role of superannuated baby-sitter as coolly as possible. If he were seen at it by someone he knew, so be it. But he did not particularly want to appear to *like* it; that would have been a touch precious, he thought, possibly even sick. A grown man alone with someone else's baby — in modern America it was definitely a combustible situation. So he sat his distance and glanced over at the infant every now and then. And in time he realized that little Alex did not like the new gulf between them, in fact was about to challenge it. Twice he started out and then stopped, sat down and crawled back to the bench, where he immediately pulled himself up and resumed his enterprise, scowling over at Bone like a quarterback trying to read a new defense. Finally Bone offered him a little encouragement and the baby set out again, carefully stepping the first half of his journey and then falling the rest of the way, plunging into Bone's hands. Bone told him he was pretty big stuff and the kid gurgled happily. But he wanted more. He crawled back to the bench, pulled himself up, and made another beeline for Bone. Then he kept doing it, over and over.

Still Bone had time to sit and smoke and observe the park scene. As usual there was the Frisbee set, young hippie types who had piled out of their minibuses to spend a fruitful afternoon sailing Frisbees back and forth, to each other as well as to their dogs, the inevitable pack of mangy Dobermans and German shepherds and other kindred gentle breeds they seldom went anywhere without. When Bone thought of his own young stud days, the college years and after, he could not conceive of having to drag a dog through all that. To his way of thinking, young men needed dogs about as badly as they needed clap. Yet these characters clung devotedly to their canines. And about the only reason he could see was the species' unselective capacity for instant adoration. To feed a dog was to become a god of sorts. Maybe not to Mom or Dad or to the creeps back in school, or to the pigs and straights of the world, but to your dog, oh yes, you were a winner, you were bright and beautiful, you were *loved*.

But then Bone had to admit the syndrome was hardly confined to raunchy kids in minibuses, especially not in Santa Barbara. Downtown or on the beach or here in the parks, or for that matter along any residential sidewalk, the story was pretty much the same — dogshit. Or as Cutter put it, "*Pedigreed* dogshit. You can always tell by the slight royal purple cast it leaves on your sneakers."

It was not the sort of day, however, to sit and ponder dogs and their waste. The afternoon sun, warm and brilliant, lay like a coat of fresh paint on the adobe façade of the Mission. On the stone steps in front, a number of tourists sat in shirtsleeves while others wandered the colonnade or snapped the mandatory snapshots around the old Moorish fountain. And closer, beyond the rose garden, the Frisbee throwers and a few strollers and huddled groups of teenagers were scattered across the wide greensward, which rose gently to the queen palms and great shaggy eucalyptus at the far edge of the park. So for the moment the world did not seem such a bad place after all. Alex Five certainly was enjoying it. He had just teetered across the chasm again and into Bone's hands. And as Bone got up now, carrying the baby back to the bench, he picked up a strong new odor that reminded him of Cutter's monicker for the kid, old Brown Pants. Yet Bone felt no revulsion toward him. He was such a happy uncomplicated little bugger. At the same time Bone was unable to take any real pleasure in the child. The plump pink skin, the almost hairless head, the sweet breath and clear, clear eyes — for some reason they reminded him all too vividly of Mrs. Little's painted and butchered flesh, the dead black hair and glop-rimmed eyes, the desperation that oozed from her, like yet another cosmetic. For the baby was on his way too now, just a few steps behind. It was only a matter of time before blood would appear in the old brown pants or the sweet lips would begin to exhale the sour deaths of lungs and stomach, and the pink skin would run to white ash as the heart began to tire. Mrs. Little or the kid, it was not much of a choice really, just a matter of time.

"How touching," a voice purred. "How too, too sweet."

Turning, Bone found himself looking up at Mo, half hidden behind a pair of dark sunglasses. "Well, the mother of the year," he said.

"If only I had a Polaroid," she came back. "*Ladies' Home Journal*, certainly they'd buy a print. And then I could give one to Alex, show him what fatherhood is all about."

Bone smiled wearily, watching as she sat down on the other side of the baby, took him onto her lap.

"He didn't give me much choice," he explained. "He was yelling his guts out."

"Oh, I can imagine. Mother takes a five-minute walk around the block and —"

"An hour's more like it," Bone cut in. "I changed him at the house. I gave him a bottle. And we've been here —"

But Mo was already laughing. "*Changed* him! *Fed* him! Oh that's just too much, Rich. Now if he was a little girl I think I'd understand. I mean, knowing your proclivities."

"You get more like Alex every day."

"Honest, you mean."

"Sick, I mean."

Lighting a cigarette, she shrugged indifferently. "Okay, I plead guilty. I guess it was longer than I thought. But it was so nice out, you know? And he was sleeping. I thought I'd just get a little air, and then once I started walking —" She gestured helplessly at the park, the glorious day.

"That's why the rent's so high."

"I guess. How'd your job interview go?"

"I'll be out of your place tomorrow."

She smiled again. "My two Alexes will miss you."

And as usual Bone played her game. "I'll come around still. Don't worry."

"Oh good." Taking off her glasses, she looked straight at Bone for a change. "Now, why do I do that, huh? I mean always coming on so bitchy with you. I don't mean anything by it, Rich, I really don't. For some reason you just bring it out in me."

"My natural vulnerability. It invites attack."

"Oh sure. Maybe it's just your looks, you think? I mean, loving Alex, maybe I just naturally resent a handsome bastard like you. And yet I don't really, I mean resent you. I —"

"Drop it, okay?"

"Gladly."

The baby had taken hold of her ear and she shook herself free, nuzzled him in the neck and he giggled. And as she looked up Bone saw that her eyes had filled with tears. Because she did not try to hide them he asked her if anything was wrong.

"I don't know."

"You and Alex?"

She did not bother to nod. "Has he said anything to you?"

"About what?"

"Anything. Everything. Me, the baby, the whole setup."

"No. Nothing special."

"I don't believe you. I can't. But if he was splitting, you'd tell me, wouldn't you?"

"Wouldn't *he?*"

"Please, Rich. Help me. Tell me if he's said anything."

"I have. He's said nothing."

She sat there looking at him. "God, I despise the lot of you. You're like birds of prey, you know that? Above it all except when it's time to eat or screw."

Bone shrugged. "I'm sorry, kid. You asked."

"And a fat lot of good it did."

"What makes you think something's wrong at home?"

"You were married. You live with someone, you can tell. It's just different lately. He looks right through me."

"Money problems. It's usually money, Mo. You ought to know that. Once he gets his next government check —"

"Oh sure. Everything will be roses."

Suddenly she got to her feet and picked up the baby. "You take us home?"

"Of course."

As they walked to the car she told him that Cutter had phoned home earlier. "He said he's bringing a guest for dinner," she added. "How about that, huh? Dinner at the Cutters'. Or Alex and Mo's, I guess I should say. Anyway, he asked me to ask you to be there?"

"Who's he bringing?"

"The victim's sister."

Bone did not miss a step, but the news hit him like a small stone thrown hard. "The girl last night?"

"The cheerleader, yes. Her sister."

"Goddamn him."

"Alex? Why? What's he up to?"

Bone put her off. "I'd rather not know."

Cutter did not make it home until almost nine o'clock that evening, hours after Mo's small roast had turned black in the oven and she had calmly abandoned it in favor of martinis in front of the fire with Bone, who was responsible for both, having that afternoon cleaned out the fireplace and bought some ersatz logs and real booze at the supermarket. While he liked the fire too, and the drinks, he did not share Mo's indifference to food, and had first raided the kitchen, cutting off an end of the burnt roast and downing it along with a rocklike baked potato and some scattered greens, the makings of a salad that never did get tossed.

So he was feeling fairly comfortable in front of the fire now, his stomach full, a drink in one hand and a cigarette in the other and a good-looking girl to share it all with. The only problem was the girl — for her, he might as well not have been there. One moment she would be goddamning Cutter, shaking her head in futility and bitterness, and the next she would give in with a wistful smile and say something inane, like it was good she and Cutter weren't married, because this sort of thing would really piss her off then. She might think she owned him then, you see. But of course no one owned anybody else, and anyone worth his salt would not let himself be owned. So of course all she had a right to do was wonder where he was and what he was doing, and for that matter admire him too, precisely for this, for pissing her off, because it meant he was his own man, he was free, he was worthy of her. Bone, listening to her run on, occasionally lifted his glass in a toast. White woman speak with dumb tongue, he said. White woman full of shit.

But she was not listening.

And finally they heard Cutter arriving home, the Packard's

old engine laboring up the hill. Bone absently went over to the window, in time to see Alex bring the car to a stop out in front, unable to pull in because of a Toyota that blocked half the driveway. But he was not stymied. Abruptly he threw the Packard into gear and roared ahead, slamming into the Toyota and driving it backward a few feet. At the crash, Mo got up and came running over to the window, just as Cutter finished backing up a short distance and now took another crack at the tiny foreign car, this time smashing the front end over the curb onto the grass, totally clearing the driveway, which he calmly entered now and parked. If there was a scratch on the Packard, Bone could not see it. The Toyota, however, looked as if it had been in a head-on collision.

In the driveway, Cutter got out of his car, alone, grinning.

"He's drunk," Mo said, opening the front door.

Bone laughed. "What makes you say that?"

Across the street and next door people were beginning to come out of their houses and apartments. Among them was a thirtyish elementary school teacher, the owner of the Toyota. She ran to her car and examined it as if it were bleeding to death and there might be a chance of saving it. Then she turned on Cutter.

"You maniac!" she cried. "You drunken maniac!"

"It was in the driveway," he said. "I didn't even see the goddamn thing."

"You lying bastard. You dirty rotten cripple."

Cutter shook his head at that, like an adult reproving a youngster. "Peace, my child. Listen, why don't you come in the house with me and we can talk it over, okay? I tell you what, you come in and I'll let you see my thing and maybe even play with it, and we'll call everything square. That sound all right to you?"

"Oh God, he's flying tonight," Mo said.

The woman was crying now and her apartment neighbors were telling her to go back inside and call the police and her

72

insurance company, because he wasn't going anywhere, she didn't have to worry about that, and they would back up her story.

One man, a Negro across the street, gave Cutter the black power salute. "Right on, brother," he yelled. "They block my driveway too."

Cutter returned the salute with his left arm, the stump. "Power to duh people," he said, and the black man grinned.

Cutter came on in.

"That was beautiful," Mo told him. "Absolutely beautiful. You know our insurance has lapsed?"

"That's her tough luck."

"And if you lose your driver's license?"

He had gone into the bathroom to urinate, leaving the door open behind him. "It's already expired," he said over the splashing. "And anyway, where's it written you got to have a license to drive a car? Mine runs just fine without one."

Mo made herself another drink and resumed her vigil in front of the fire. As Cutter came back out, Bone asked him where his guest was.

"What guest?"

Bone looked over at Mo.

"The Durant girl's sister, remember?" Mo said. "That 'real dinner' you told me to make for her. 'Not our usual slop' — I believe that's how you put it."

"You two are hallucinating, you know that? Acid heads, that's what you are."

"You didn't call me, is that what you're saying? You didn't say you were bringing this girl home, and that you wanted Rich here too?"

Frowning, Cutter looked from Mo to Bone. "You part of this put-on?" he asked.

"Yeah."

"Someone else must've called," Cutter said. "Some sinister force." He had just finished combing his hair in front of the

73

hall mirror, and now he went into the bathroom and came out with Mo's bottle of Lavoris, which he proceeded to chugalug, gargling it and spitting it into a dead potted cactus Swanson had given them, "something harmonious with Alex's character," as he had put it.

"Pigs probably be here in a minute," Cutter explained. "Gonna do a number on them. A neat little number."

Mo asked him where he had been all day. "If I may ask," she added.

"Of course you may, love. Went driving, I did. Picked up this group on one-o-one, a nigger fag and two spic girls with a pet monkey. We went up to El Capitan and had an orgy. The guy was all right but that monkey, Jesus, did it ever bite."

Mo sipped at her drink. "What's the use?" she said to Bone. "What's the goddamn use?"

Bone said nothing. Outside, the police had arrived. The flash of their red domelight washed over Cutter as he stood gargling in the middle of the room. Putting the bottle down finally, he passed his hand over his face, magically creating sobriety. Then he moved toward the door.

"Come on with, old buddy," he said to Bone. "I may need your support."

But he did not. Playing the role of humble wounded war veteran, he limped eloquently down the stairs and went over to the police car, where the officers were already listening to the schoolteacher's complaint. Cutter waited patiently, and then politely answered all their questions. Gosh, he was awfully sorry about the whole darn thing. And a little confused too. He hadn't even seen the car the first time he hit it, when he turned in — a passing car with its brights on had temporarily blinded him. And then when he tried to back up, after the first impact, the gearshift apparently slipped into first instead, and that was why there was a second crash. Of course he took full responsibility for the accident, and of course his insurance company would pay, the lady had nothing to worry about there. But he had no idea what all this other was about, his supposedly insulting her and using obscene language. He recalled asking her to come into his house, yes, but only to discuss the incident away from the crowd and to give her a chance to calm down, while he called the police and his insurance company. Was he aware that his license had expired? No, but he understood the officers had no choice except to issue him a citation for the oversight; they were just doing their duty, and duty was something he knew a little about. As he said this last, Bone halfway expected him to hike up his pants and show everyone his false leg, but all he did was modestly look down at the ground, affecting embarrassment and pain.

And the officers reluctantly did their duty, giving him a citation for driving without a license. And that was all. The schoolteacher began yelling and spitting at them, calling them storm troopers and stinking fascist pigs, but they were used to that, in fact were smiling as they drove away. Cutter waved goodbye and then put a friendly hand on the teacher's shoulder.

"Forget about it," he told her. "Toyota's a shitty car anyway."

From that point on the night limped steadily downhill. Cutter vomited shrimp and half-shell oysters and other condiments he had gobbled at El Paseo's free "cocktail hour" snack table. Then he settled his stomach with a Pepsi and followed that with vodka on the rocks. Nothing strong, he said. He did not want to puke again. Along the way he admitted that he had called Mo earlier and that he had indeed spent some time during the day with Valerie Durant, the sister of the murder victim. But she had not been able to come with him.

"The goddamn funeral," he explained. "Or what do they call it the day before — visitation?"

Bone watched him with a tight, growing anger. "What'd you see her about?" he asked.

"I needed some questions answered."

"About what?"

Cutter grinned. "You sound uptight, Richard."

"What'd you see her about?"

"Oh, nothing important. Just this little project of mine. This bump of curiosity, you might call it."

"Curiosity about J. J. Wolfe?"

"You could say that, I guess."

"And how does Miss Durant fit in?"

"Call her Val. A real nice girl, Val."

"Val, then."

For a time Cutter did not answer. He had finished making himself another drink, and now he limped back around the coffee table and sank onto the davenport, grunting like an old character actor, grimacing as he lifted his false leg above the boat hatch tabletop, held it there for a moment, and then dropped it like a bomb. Near the fire still, Mo was pretending a vast indifference to everything but her drink and the flames. But there was gray flint in her eyes, a look that had begun to form and harden at Cutter's mention of "Val."

"Well, it goes something like this," Cutter was saying. "I wake up this morning you might say still *intrigued* by your reaction to Wolfe's picture — you know, the *It's him* number you did for us. Somehow I just couldn't expunge it from the old brain, you know? Kept going round and round, like a haunting refrain. So I decided, what's to lose? Check the cat out and see where he was that night, and at what time, and so forth. But the more I thought about it, the more I realized none of it would do much good unless I also knew where Val's sister was at the same time. You know, see if there were any star-crossed coincidences, any unexpected intersecting of Wolfe's path and the girl's. But to find out where she was — well, I couldn't go to the police, could I, not without involving my old buddy Bone. Which of course I absolutely refused to do. So what choice did I have, except to go to Val?"

"And tell her about the picture?"

76

"Your reaction to it, you mean? Well, hell yes, man. That's the whole bit, isn't it? But don't worry — I told her you backed off right away. I said you weren't about to identify anyone to anybody, ever."

Bone was furious. "You bastard, Alex. You cocksucking bastard. She's probably already called the cops."

"No chance."

"And of course you're sure of that."

"Would I say I was if I wasn't? Weren't?"

Bone, barely able to control himself, looked over at Mo, who seemed to have gone down into herself now, drifting with her vodka and quads. "Aren't you interested in any of this, lady?" he asked. "This 'bump' your old man's got, you're not interested?"

She shook her head.

"Don't you remember what he told you last night, that crap about a way out? Well this is it, kid. This is your escape hatch he's talking about."

"I'm afraid you lost me," Mo said.

Bone turned to Cutter. "Tell her."

Alex grinned. "How can I? I don't know what the hell you're running on about anymore than she does."

"This great interest of yours in J. J. Wolfe, that's what I'm running on about. Now tell us — tell *her* — what's behind it."

"As I said, curiosity."

"Of course. And a keen sense of social consciousness."

"That too, yes."

Shaking his head, Bone got out a cigarette and lit it. "I give up," he said. "You win, Alex. Go do your thing, whatever gives you pleasure. And if I wind up sweating out another day in the slam, so what, huh? It ain't you."

"Aw, come on, man. I just told you. The girl understands. She's not going to call the police. She knows you didn't make a positive ID, and that this is just something of mine, that's all, a wild hair, you know."

"Wonder why I can't believe you?"

Cutter shrugged. "Forget all that, huh? We got more important things. Don't you want to know what I found out?"

"From *Val*?" Mo said.

"Among others. Let me tell you, I been busy."

And Cutter went on then, telling them what he had learned about the victim. All that in the newspapers about her being the typical high school teenager, the wholesome pretty cheerleader and so forth, was just a lot of bullshit. According to her sister she was virtually uncontrollable, especially by their mother, an alcoholic semi-invalid with high blood pressure and bad nerves. The girl came and went pretty much as she pleased, a seventeen-year-old free spirit dedicated to rock music and especially its performers, for whom she was a kind of local groupie, a welcoming committee of one, which meant of course that she was already into sex and drugs. A month before her death, her sister had given her three hundred dollars for an abortion that was performed in Los Angeles. Since then the girl had not returned to school. And she was almost never at home. Lastly, she was an inveterate, habitual hitchhiker — a fact Cutter's voice underscored.

"Anyway," he went on, "night before last she was at the Stone Sponge, that new rock bar out in Goleta, real big with the kids. She went with a couple girlfriends, older girls. The police of course have hauled in these two plus everybody else they could, anybody who might've seen who she was with or left with. But from what I hear all they got so far is zilch."

Yawning, Mo poked at the dying fire. "You're not going to tell us J. J. Wolfe was there," she said.

"That's right, I'm not."

"Big surprise."

But Cutter was looking as if he had just dined on missionary. "He was across the street," he said.

"Across the street?"

"At the Calif, that big motel they just put up, that sprawling mess of orange offal out on Fairlane."

"Wolfe stayed *there*?" Mo said.

Cutter gave her a pitying look. "The woman with total re-call. If you'll remember, Earthmother, the newspaper yester-day, the one *you* read to us. He was staying at the Biltmore then, right? Where his car went boom boom. Ring a bell?"

Mo pretended to accept this abuse as her due, giving Cutter a mock humble bow of her head.

"No, Wolfe was at a party there, at the Calif, a cocktail bash for the energy conference delegates. He left around ten or eleven."

Bone asked Cutter how he knew this.

"The conference's PR man, a cat out at the university. I told him I was doing a story for *Sunset* magazine. So naturally he broke his ass for me, told me all he could. Guy like Wolfe at your conference or your party, you want people to know."

"But he left early?" Bone said.

"That's what this fellow said, yeah. But Wolfe was there all right — right across the street from the Stone Sponge."

Getting up to mix himself another drink, Bone dropped a pair of ice cubes into his glass, an erstwhile jelly jar. In the silence, the crack of the ice sounded like a comment. Now he added to it.

"That all you've got?"

"*All?*"

"Well, think about it. It doesn't change what was in the paper, does it? The man is still alone. You don't put him with the girl. You don't know where he was around midnight any more now than you did before. And I still haven't heard any-thing about a motive."

Cutter spit at the fire, and it hissed. "Christ, you don't want much," he said. "I spend half the day getting in touch with the girl's sister and trying to get my story across to her, and still I got time to find out where Wolfe was last night. And what do you hand me? *Is that all I've got?*"

"Big deal," Bone said. "Listen, pal, before I sack in, and before Mo passes all the way through the looking glass, why don't you tell us, just the two of us. Just come right out and tell us, in plain and simple English —" And now Bone almost shouted. *"What the hell are you up to?"*

Mo looked up from the floor in bewilderment. But Cutter was unimpressed. Slowly he finished off the bottle of vodka. Then standing, swaying, he did a fair impression of John Wayne.

"A man does what he's got to do," he said.

He limped toward the bathroom, burlesquing Wayne's rolling gait. Through the open door Bone heard him retching.

All through the night the carnival went on. Bone was half asleep on the davenport when Cutter began yelling at Mo. He evidently wanted to make love or at least have her make him come, but she was already gone, stoned. So he did what he had to do. He jumped up and down on the bed and woke the baby and kicked a hole in the closet door. And he yelled all the while, spewing out a soliloquy of sexual frustration. Mo was not just frigid, he declaimed, she was dead, a cadaver with a welded womb and a cunt like a rathole, full of dust and bits of straw and feathers from old nests left undisturbed for generations. Her tits were going soft just like her brain, because she was dying, didn't she know that? She was in the death grip of frigidity, in fact had a terminal case. But this was it for him, the last time he would ever try with her. Never again would he risk his balls this way, exposing them to such death and decay. No, from now on it would be whores for him, whores and little boys and sheep if he could find any, anything alive, anything but a cold rathole for him.

In time Bone slept. But he was awakened later by the sound of the deck door opening, and when he finally rolled over to look he saw Cutter out on the deck, on the deck railing actually, teetering there as he urinated down the hill into the darkness, all the while singing "Jesus Loves Me" and whipping his penis back and forth like a small boy.

And later still — how much later, Bone was not sure — he

was shaken awake and looked up to find Cutter sitting next to him, on the boat hatch. Even in the darkness Bone could see the desperation in his eye.

"I want to explain, Rich," he said, in an urgent whisper. "I want to explain about this cat Wolfe, okay? When I was in Nam, I guess I've told you, we did pretty much what all the outfits there did. Not exactly My Lais, not that big anyway, but we did our part, everybody did his little part over there. To women and kids too, because we never knew, there was no way of knowing, all slants were VC far as we were concerned, and you just didn't give a damn anyway. Not there, on the spot, not while you were doing it, it was nothing, you were a machine, nothing touched you, nothing mattered. But later — later, back here, when the My Lai thing broke — you remember those pictures in *Life*? The peasants? That one young woman with her old mother and her kid, and they're all hugging each other and crying, waiting to be offed. And the next picture, there they all are in the ditch. Well back here, with time, you know, you had time to study them, those pictures. And that's what I did. I studied them all right. I went to school at those pictures. And you know what I found out? I found out you have three reactions, Rich, only three. The first one is simple — *I hate America*. But then you study them some more, and you move up a notch. *There is no God.* But you know what you say finally, Rich, after you've studied them all you can? You say — *I'm hungry.*"

He tried to smile as he said this, he tried to laugh, but his mouth twisted more in pain than anything else.

"Sleep," he said. "You sleep now, Rich. I just wanted you to know."

4

IN THE MORNING ALEX FIVE REMINDED THE GROWN-UPS THAT though they might step to measured, faraway music, his own drummer was a noisy sort who came on duty promptly at six o'clock. Mo let him cry for a while and then finally gave in, laboriously struggling out of bed and picking him up, changing him and feeding him and trying to keep him quiet, all the while moving like a somnambulist.

From where he lay on the couch, hung over and still exhausted himself, Bone could feel some of her misery. But he did not move or get up until after the baby was fed and dry, toddling around the living room and jabbering and occasionally sticking his finger in Bone's eyes or exploring one of his ears. By then Mo had finished trying to regenerate herself in the bathroom, and now Bone followed her example, relying as always on a cold shower to bring him back to a semblance of life.

When he came out, Mo had already prepared his breakfast, scrambling some of the eggs he had bought the previous afternoon, and serving them with stale doughnuts and the usual instant coffee. He would have given his last dollar for a tall glass of freshly squeezed orange juice, but of course in the Cutter household any such transaction was out of the question —one did not mess around with fresh fruit and vegetables. And even now, before eight o'clock in the morning, Bone could see the basic reason for this in Mo's eyes, the soft glaze spreading in them and the lids growing heavier as she sipped her coffee, eating nothing, not wanting to weaken the effects of the methaqualone or whatever other downer she had ingested since taking care of the baby. Bone was not much of a drug man himself so he did not really understand the intricacies of her habit. Downers in the morning struck him as a totally illogical choice, like piling torpor on top of exhaustion, but according to Cutter that was all Mo ever took, morning, day, or night, only downers, and not too many of them either, just enough to soften the ragged cutting edges. And for all Bone knew, maybe the pills did accomplish this. But in the bargain they also aged her. Though she was no more than twenty-five, she looked a weary, beaten thirty. And another five years the way she was going — he would not care to see her then. The bone structure would still be there of course, and the finely crafted eyes. She would be beautiful still, maybe, but not very pretty.

"I don't think he'll be up before you leave," she was saying.

"That's all right. Let him sleep. I like it better with just us anyway."

"You do, huh?"

"Naturally."

"It's a shame I'm not more highly sexed."

"Isn't it."

"But he's your friend, Rich. Your host. You wouldn't betray a friend and host, would you?"

"Not normally."

"Abnormally then?"

"I don't think that's what I meant."

"You're a friend indeed."

Bone lit a cigarette. "Now you've finally got it. You're finally on track. I'm a friend *in need*."

"Sure you are. You need it about like Heinz needs ketchup."

"I didn't say anything about *it*."

83

"What then?" As she said this, she tried to maintain the same touch of easy raillery. But he did not answer, just sat there at the kitchen table watching her, and finally, looking flushed and somehow guilty, she lowered her eyes.

"You want me to call George for you?" she asked, starting to get up.

Bone had already taken her by the wrist, holding her there. "I'll call him," he said.

"I'm sorry I can't take you myself. But that shift in the Packard, you know what it's like. I just can't —"

"Mo." Bone was standing now too, and he had taken her by the shoulders. But she refused to look at him, had turned her face away.

"*Mo.*"

"Don't," she asked. "Please, Rich."

He let go of her then. He watched as she went over to the windows and stood there looking out, hugging her shoulders as if the bright morning sun somehow made her cold.

"At least, do me a favor," he said.

"What?"

"See a doctor. Have a checkup. And do what he tells you. Start taking care of yourself."

"Like eat right, get plenty of rest, and take Geritol every day?"

"Might be a good idea."

She turned now, smiling wearily. "You'd make someone a good Jewish mother."

"Maybe you could use one."

"I'll keep you in mind."

"And a gentile lover? How about one of those?"

"I've already got one."

"I keep forgetting."

After calling Swanson and asking if he could drive him to Montecito — which of course he could, George never being loath to get out from behind his desk — Bone packed his few belongings and, carrying them out to the front porch, sat down to wait and smoke a cigarette. Cutter was still in bed and Mo had gone back into the bathroom, to get away from him, Bone suspected. But when he finally heard Swanson's Jag snarling up the long hill, he went back into the house and tapped on the bathroom door, and Mo opened it immediately, as if she had been standing on the other side, waiting for him. Her eyes were red and her hand trembled at her throat, fussing with the open top of her kimono, which hung sacklike on her body except for the points of her breasts.

"George is here," he told her. "I'll be off."

She said nothing.

"I'll drop by later in the week."

All she did was nod. And Bone was about to turn away and leave her when he realized how unnatural that would have been, how much in violation of the moment. So he reached out and took her by the arms. And he kissed her, chastely at first, just on the cheek, but because there was no stiffening in her, none of the resistance he had expected, he moved to her mouth, kissing her deeply, gathering her body to his. And only then did it come, the pulling away, the convulsive turning of her face, as if he had slapped her hard.

"Get out of here," she said. "Please, Rich. Go."

He left then, almost stumbling over the baby, who was sitting on the floor happily playing with the empty vodka bottle from the night before.

According to Cutter, Swanson had missed out on the Vietnam War because he was busy trying to keep his pipe lit. And he would miss the impending Great California Earthquake for the same reason. Further, he was the only living American still seriously looking for the Lost Generation. Physically, he reminded Cutter variously of an Armenian rug merchant, the chief procurer for King Farouk, or John Wilkes Booth, wet-head. In short, there was seldom a time when Cutter did not consider it open season on Swanson. Yet if his friend minded, he never let it show. Still in his early thirties, Swanson could have passed for a decade older, having already achieved a comfortable middle-aged spread and an attitude of almost comatose aplomb, none of which kept him from playing a competent game of tennis or from forming troublesome alliances with attractive young married women about town. As Cutter's descriptions indicated, he had a distinctly Arabic look about him, slicked-down black hair and pencil-line mustache and saturnine hawk face, a classic villain physiognomy in fact, which made all the more surprising his easy unassuming good nature, the small still eye of sanity he maintained amid the storms that occasionally whirled about him, whether marital or Cutter-inspired.

Like Alex, he had once wanted to be a writer, in fact had spent a couple of years in Europe watching bullfights and fishing the old Hemingway streams and even renting rooms high in a Rhine castle tower, there to write cryptic little stories about disenchanted postwar youth. Now, tending to his realty company and gift shop, all that was behind him but definitely not over, not forgotten. There were few conversations he would not somewhere along the line try to bend to the subject of Hemingway and Fitzgerald and the other lost ones. Cutter in fact insisted that Swanson's first marriage had broken up because he could not keep from crying *Zelda!* during orgasm.

Bone did not care about any of that, however. He did not dislike the man so much as find him a touch unreal. He sometimes wondered if a day would not arrive when Swanson would take up an ax and give the nearest living thing the required forty whacks. But then Bone knew that was ungenerous of him. He was so used to his own unflagging nastiness, and now Cutter's, that he was afraid he had reached the point where he found its absence in another man suspect.

"So you've flown the coop," Swanson said, as they drove away.

"Two weeks is enough."

"Above and beyond the call of duty, huh?"

"I guess. But when I needed him, he was there. No questions."

"That's Alex, all right. He still in bed?"

Bone nodded. "Where I should be too."

"Rough night, huh?"

In his mind, Bone saw the tanklike Packard smashing into the Toyota, backing up, smashing it again. Grinning, he said, "Unusual anyway. Even for Cutter."

"Why? What happened?"

Bone told him, hitting just the high points. And Swanson laughed helplessly. "Oh God, I wish I'd been there," he said, eyes streaming. "He's an original, Alex is, no doubt about that."

"None," Bone agreed.

Frowning now, Swanson shook his head. "I don't know about him lately though, Rich. It's funny and all, but it's more than that — it's sick. I'm really worried about him. You know what he said to me last week? He said he'd *sell* me the next five years of his life — you believe that? Ten thousand a year, he said. And in return he'd promise not to 'harm my merchandise,' that's how he put it, can you beat that? *Harm the merchandise.* I told him he was crazy. Fifty thousand? Where could I get that kind of money? And for what? What would you call it? Reverse blackmail?"

"That's about it."

Again Swanson wagged his head. "God, what a character. Tell me, you ever seen a picture of him before Vietnam, the way he used to be?"

"No."

"Give you an idea what he lost. He wasn't, you know, what you'd call pretty-boy handsome. But he was good looking, all right, and he had this kind of magnetism — still does, for that matter. Anyway, I often think what he could've been if things had been different, you know? If his old man hadn't squandered their money, and if both parents hadn't died the way they did, and if there hadn't been any Vietnam —"

"A lot of ifs."

Swanson shrugged. "Yeah, I know. But they're what he must think about himself, you know? A guy'd have to. Jesus, I wish I could help him. And Mo too. She's really down lately."

Bone told him to turn at the next corner, and Swanson turned. He also changed the subject.

"Anything new on the killing? Police been in touch with you anymore?"

Bone said no, he hadn't heard anything. Which did not surprise Swanson at all — the goddamn police were too busy handing out speeding tickets to law-abiding taxpayers like himself to pay any attention to murderers, especially one who pitches cheerleaders into trashcans. Had Bone heard the one about the guy being an ecofreak, that he stashed the girl because he was against littering? No, Bone hadn't heard that one.

"Rock musicians," Swanson said, "they're the ones the police are coming down on, from what I hear. Probably one of them did it, that's what everybody says."

"The police ought to know."

"You think it was someone else?"

"I have no idea."

Swanson looked over at him quizzically, as if he hoped to be let in on a secret. "You really didn't see the guy then?"

"Not his face, no."

They were nearing Mrs. Little's house now.

"Next place on the right," Bone said.

"Nice," Swanson observed. "Uh, what kind of work you be doing here?"

"Handyman."

Swanson looked impressed. "Handyman — Jesus. Tell me, Rich, you ever going back? I mean, get a regular job again? Get married and sink into debt like the rest of us?"

"If I can."

"Well, why not? What's to stop you?"

"There's always something."

"Maybe I could find you a spot."

"I'd only blow it."

"Well, with that attitude, sure."

Bone shrugged. "That's what I mean. There's always something."

At Mrs. Little's the maid was the only one at home, and the reception she gave Bone was no warmer than it had been two days before.

"Mrs. Leetle in San Francisco with her husband," she explained. "She say you just move in and wait, do what you want. She be back two days. Food in the kitchen."

Bone tried to thank her but once again she gave him her back. Humbled, he picked up his few bags and moved into the garage apartment. The bed looked enormously inviting — the prospect of a long day and night of sleep temporarily more seductive to him than any woman could have been — but he knew that would only deepen the maid's hostility, and he wanted to make a good beginning here, he wanted things to go well, there were not all that many alternatives left to him. So he got out the lawn mower and cut the grass around the house, even though it did not really need it. Then he spaded the ground around the shrubbery inside the stone fence, hard steady work that made his body slick with sweat. Time and again he caught the maid peering out at him from behind one curtain or another, but he did not let on that he had seen her. Finally she came out of the house, somberly waddling across the lawn to him.

"You not eat today?" she said. "Why you not stop?"

He smiled. "Why not?"

In the kitchen she served him cold roast beef on rye bread, some highly spiced potato salad, and Chianti. Her name was

Teresa, she said. Teresa Chavez. And she did not understand why he worked so hard, since "thee woman" was away, why should he bother? He told her that he liked yard work, and that he figured she was in the house working, so why shouldn't he do the same, outside. She laughed at that.

"Work? What work is here? A house like this, one woman, no kids, and husband almost never home — I could keep it clean about two hours a week, all it take. Biggest job is find work, you know? Look busy. And I guess maybe that why she pay so bad. I could make more money at welfare."

"Couldn't we all?"

"What you say?"

"I could use a little welfare too."

She gave him an appraising look. "Other times she have boys here, for your job. College kids, you know? Bums. But you look like a man could make big money. Could be a boss. A big shot."

"I'm working my way up," he said.

For a moment she was not sure of his irony, then at his smile she shook her head.

"Oh, I think I know you now. You a macho, that what. Thee woman, she better watch out, huh?"

"I'll be gentle," he said.

And Teresa, his new friend, shook with laughter.

In the afternoon he slept for almost two hours and then wandered back to the house and joined Teresa, who was having a few drinks in preparation for her journey home to Santa Barbara's "mesa" and the small rented house where seven children and a beat postman were lying in wait for her. The prospect did not seem to cheer her and she compensated by having "one more for thee roads" — straight Red Label scotch — then finally drove off, in an early-1960s Cadillac that laid down a smoke screen heavier and darker than Bone's old MG had ever managed. Alone, Bone toured the house and found it even more luxurious than he had first thought. The furniture alone had to have a value of thirty or forty thousand, for only the six rooms. And he found the kitchen just as lavishly stocked. The refrigerator and freezer and pantry were loaded with so much fine food he had a hard time choosing, but finally settled for a thick porterhouse steak, mushrooms, and an enormous salad tossed together from every fresh vegetable he could find in the refrigerator. He washed it all down with champagne and then repaired to the game room, where he watched a Celtics–Bullets playoff game on television and read the latest issue of *Time*.

So when he went to bed at eleven o'clock, tired and comfortably high, he expected to fall asleep quickly and deeply. Instead he set out upon a flat dead sea of wakefulness, long hours in which his mind seemed to take on a life independent of his will, so that he found himself thinking about the one thing he did not want to think about. In the darkness of his room it took no effort to see the night street again, the big car braking and pulling into the apartment complex alley, the huddled figure moving against the headlight-illuminated background, going around the car and out of sight for a few moments and then back into it almost immediately and laying down rubber again, fishtailing the car through the complex and disappearing. A silhouette still, that was all the man was, there was no doubt about that. And yet the newspaper photograph, old country boy J. J. Wolfe grinning benignly over the burned-out shell of his rented LTD, there was no doubt about that either, no question that the picture had come up off the page at Bone like a fist, and no question that it lay in his mind still, a thing imperfectly seen and understood, a palimpsest, something he could not quite make out under all the other random scribbling and yet which he somehow recognized, had seen before. But in the apartment house alley? No, he could not be sure about that, not ever. And that was why Cutter's sudden enthusiasm, the "It's him" he apparently accepted as gospel, cut through Bone like salt spray in winter. For he knew better than he cared to the lineaments of Cutter's character, that his friend could no more leave the thing as it was than he could leave unopened a ticking box. But it was not avarice he feared in Alex so much as death, the recklessness unto death, the love of death that came off him like the reek of putrescent flesh.

Sleep brought release, however, and he dreamed of Mo and the baby in the park with him, along with the tourists and the Frisbee throwers and their dogs. The one different thing was in the rose garden, where someone had placed a pair of trash-cans with golf clubs sticking out of them. And far in the distance there was the sound of crying, a man crying. Cutter? he wondered.

When he woke the next morning, he heard Teresa already at work, scrubbing the walk between the house and the swimming pool. So he got out of bed and dressed, preparing to join her in another day of make-work at the Littles. Unexpectedly, he found her almost as cold and surly as she had been the day of his interview, but after he went into the kitchen and made his own breakfast she warmed noticeably, joining him for coffee and cigarettes. She had had a very bad night, she told him. Her husband had found marijuana in their oldest daughter's purse — he had been looking for money to go bowling with, she said — and naturally he had beaten the girl. He had locked her in her room but she had climbed through the window and had been gone all night. Meanwhile the husband had gotten drunk and accidentally gashed himself on a war surplus machete that he liked to threaten them with whenever he was "stinko." Someday she would kill him with "thee god-damn machete," she vowed. Bone would read about it in the newspaper — TERESA CHAVEZ CUTS HUSBAND INTO LITTLE PIECES. He suggested instead that she merely separate him from his *cojones,* because it was a less serious crime and yet would be almost as effective, and the idea so pleased her that she laughed until tears ran down her face.

After breakfast Bone resumed the job of spading up the ground inside the stone fence, and when he finished over two hours later he took a shower and put on his swimming trunks and lay out in the sun on a redwood chaise next to the swimming pool. For ten or fifteen minutes he lay there, trying not to think about anything except the feel of the sun on his body. And then a shadow fell across him, a shadow with Cutter's voice.

"Hey, fella, can I sit on your face?"

Bone squinted against the sunlight at the grinning specter above him. Then he saw the girl standing back a short distance, watching them, not smiling. Even in the brightness Bone could not miss the weary cool of her eyes, the tough and honest face. He looked back at Cutter.

"You had to do it, didn't you? You couldn't leave it alone."

"It wouldn't leave *us* alone."

"You bullshitter, Alex." As Bone got up from the chair, the girl came forward.

"I believe you two have met," Cutter said.

Valerie Durant smiled hesitantly. "I guess you could call it that."

"How are you?" For the moment Bone was unable to think of a less stupid greeting on this second day after she had buried her sister.

"Okay," she shrugged. "Alex is keeping me busy."

"He has a gift for that."

Cutter meanwhile was making a big thing out of his new surroundings, gaping at the Littles' sprawling house, the barbered grounds, the pool. "Land sakes, boy," he drawled. "You shore have a way of making out."

Bone slipped into his old terry robe. "Sure. Twenty minutes ago I was spading the front yard."

"Just think of that," Cutter marveled. "A common laborer just twenty minutes ago. And now here he is, lounging beside the pool. Which just proves a man can still make it if he's got pluck and grit."

"Let's sit down." Bone moved toward the umbrella table at the end of the pool.

"This old fox who hired you," Cutter asked, "just what you got on her anyway? You catch her being faithful to her old man, was that it?"

"Something like that."

"Way to go."

As he was about to sit down Bone realized that Valerie had not moved. Turning, he followed her gaze to the back of the house, where he saw Teresa standing just inside the screen door, staring out at the three of them.

"Is there some other place we could talk?" the girl asked. "Someplace private?"

Bone wanted to tell her there was no reason for privacy, that what little he had to say could be said right where they were. But her look, the steady open gaze, did not invite hostility.

"Sure," he said. "Come on."

They followed him into his room at the end of the garage, where he got out a bottle of scotch he had appropriated from the house. As he poured drinks for the three of them, Cutter again went into his cornpone wonderment act at Bone's rapid rise in the world.

"Red Label yet," he clucked. "Didn't I tell you, Val — we follow this cat and we shall wear diamonds."

"Diamonds I'm not interested in," she said. "That's not why I'm here."

Bone heard in that a clear suggestion they cut the small talk and get down to business. But Cutter apparently was not ready yet.

"So you think all this is better than our davenport," he said to Bone.

"All it lacks is Mo."

"Is the rent as reasonable, though?"

"About the same."

Alex grinned. "Sure. And God is love."

Bone looked over at Valerie, who had sat down in the room's only easy chair. Still very cool and controlled, she had taken out a cigarette, tapped it firm, lit it. And for some reason Bone found it irritating that there was not one thing about the girl, not her manner or her clear hard eyes or even her attire — the casual tan flare slacks and white cableknit sweater — nothing that hinted at loss or bereavement. She could have been a job applicant.

"I guess you know why I came here with Alex," she said now.

"I've got a fair idea."

"I was wondering if you'd changed your mind. I mean about what you saw that night."

Bone shook his head. "No. No change."

"Specifically I was wondering if you'd decided this man Wolfe was the one you saw."

"J. J. Wolfe, you mean? The tycoon?"

"Yes."

Smiling, Bone looked over at Cutter. "Now where could she have gotten an idea like that?"

Cutter shrugged innocently.

"I'm sorry, Mr. Bone," the girl kept on, "but none of this is a joke to me. It's very serious."

Bone did not feel like apologizing. "I never thought otherwise," he said.

"It's just his way," Cutter put in. "He can't help himself. He doesn't have normal human feelings like the rest of us."

"The truth is I can't see any reason for putting you through all this," Bone told her. "It's a dead end. And Alex knows it."

"He said you'd say that."

"Oh? And what else did he tell you?"

"How it happened. I mean what you said. And then how you changed what you said."

"You're talking about the picture now?"

"Yes."

95

Bone said that was not quite accurate. "Actually it was an offhand kind of thing," he explained. "When I saw the picture in the paper I guess I said something about it looking like the man — the silhouette — in the alley. But then, when I noticed my friend here about to have a coronary, I backed up and tried to tell him exactly what I meant. Which is what I told you in the police station, and what I'll tell you now — I don't know who killed your sister. I didn't see the man's face."

For a time Valerie sat there looking at him. And her expression made it very clear that none of this surprised her, just as none of it convinced her.

"So you didn't mean it," she said finally. "When you said *It's him* — it was only an offhand thing?"

"I don't think I even said *It's him*," Bone corrected. "What I said was *It could be him*, something like that."

Valerie looked over at Cutter, who was shaking his head.

"I take it you prefer his version," Bone said to the girl.

She did not answer.

"Well, you can believe what you want, of course."

"I'd like to believe *you*."

"I'd like that too."

Valerie crushed out her cigarette. "Let me ask you this, then — could you accept it that you might have been right without knowing it?"

Bone said he didn't follow her.

"I mean if what Alex and I have learned about this Wolfe makes it seem he actually *was* the man — then would you change your mind?"

"About what I *saw*?"

His emphasis on the verb must have been answer enough for her, for she shook her head now even before he did. And she turned to Cutter, her gaze inquiring, bleak.

"I told you, kiddo," he said to her. "You can't get blood out of a cadaver."

Bone raised his middle finger to him in silent reply.

Valerie meanwhile had decided on a different approach. "I'd still like you to hear what we've found out about Wolfe. That couldn't hurt anything, could it?"

"Do I have a choice?"

Evidently he did not, for she barely paused for breath.

"Well, in the first place, I guess you know Alex contacted me a couple of days ago, before the funeral, and I told him I was interested but of course we had to wait."

"Till after you got her in the ground." Bone immediately regretted saying it, even though what he saw in her eyes was not pain or anger so much as impatience.

"Till we buried my sister, yes. Anyway, yesterday at the library we got everything we could on Wolfe — the *Time* article and *Who's Who*, they were the main things. We Xeroxed them so you can go over them too."

"Fine. Thank you. I look forward to reading it."

"The *Time* article for instance tells how Wolfe likes to go into working-class bars alone and talk with what he calls 'the real people,' people different from the Harvard Business School types he hires to help run his conglomerate. And then — the important part for us — the article says he also makes it a habit to pick up hitchhikers, especially kids, because he likes their *inputs* — a favorite word of his."

"I see," Bone said. "Well, then of course he's guilty." He wanted to be straight with her, but raillery seemed his only defense.

She went on as before. "And Alex already told you about Wolfe being at the cocktail party across from the Stone Sponge, where my sister was earlier in the evening. If she left alone she would have hitchhiked."

"I see the connection."

"Later yesterday Alex and I checked gas stations between the apartments where he left my sister's body and the Biltmore. At a Union 76 just off the freeway one of the employees remembers selling a man two gallon gas cans and filling them with gas — around midnight, on the night it happened. Alex showed him Wolfe's picture from *Time* — just the picture, we didn't tell him Wolfe's name — but he wasn't sure. He said all he remembered about the man was that he had on a golf cap and sunglasses even though it was night."

Now Cutter joined in. "You dig the sequence, Richard? Let's say you are Wolfe. You've been to a cocktail party, you've got five or six drinks under your belt. And because it is your habit, you pick up this teenage hitchhiker. You kill her and dump her body for God knows what reason — an accident maybe — but no matter, whatever the reason, it's unimportant now. The important thing is you have this rented car, with blood in it. And you don't know if someone has seen you with the girl, either when she was alive or when you were getting rid of her body. So what do you do? Do you run into your motel room and get a wet rag and tidy up the car? Do you fold your hands and hope for the best? Not if you're slick enough to turn an Ozark chicken farm into an empire. No, you simply get a couple of cans of gas and soak the car with one of them, open the other and toss a match in the window. And then you cry militant. You claim some ecofreak like Erickson is out to get you, scare you. And of course the police and FBI and the media — everybody believes. Because you've got the bread. You've got the power and the glory, the God-given proof of your righteousness forever and ever amen."

Bone shook his head in wonderment. "You *have* been busy, Alex."

"You know it."

Bone got up and poured himself another drink, lit a cigarette. As he did so, he was not unaware of how Valerie was watching him, almost as if he were about to pass sentence on her. And it angered him, because this whole ridiculous affair was not his doing but Cutter's, and he felt Cutter should have been the one held responsible for any pain or disappointment that grew out of it. So for the moment Bone decided to play along, to let the thing die a natural death instead of killing it outright.

"Okay," he said, "so you have this new information, and this fine logical hypothesis. What next? What do you do with it? Where does it lead?"

Valerie looked questioningly at Cutter, as if for permission, and he shrugged assent.

"Blackmail," she said.

Bone laughed out loud.

"We *pretend* blackmail, that's all," Valerie corrected. "If Wolfe pays, then we have him. We can go to the police."

For a time Bone said nothing. He sat on the corner of his bed studying the two of them, Valerie all straightness and solemnity while Cutter predictably took the opposite ground, his canted smile suggesting the usual Chinese box of irony, appearance inside deception inside illusion.

Bone asked Valerie if she thought Cutter would be with her. "You think he's pushing this thing just to see a man brought to justice?" he added.

But Valerie had an answer for that too. "If it turns out Wolfe did do it, and if he does pay, Alex admitted he'd probably try to talk us into keeping the money and leaving everything just as it is, no police or anything. But he also said it would be up to me finally, she was my sister, it would be my decision. And frankly, Mr. Bone, I don't know which way I'd go. I'm not sure which would be truer justice — that the state get a conviction or my mother and I get some money. We had to borrow for the funeral. We're broke. And she's sick. So I admit I don't know what I'd do finally. All I know is, if there's any chance this is the man who did what was done to my sister — I want him to pay. He *has* to pay. And I don't much care who he pays — us or society."

Bone drained the last of his drink. He was still angry but in a different way now, not at Cutter so much as at himself, that the girl made him feel personally guilty, as if he were failing her somehow.

"If I were to join this thing, it'd be to help you," he said. "I'd like that. But I've got this problem. I can't see committing perjury so your new buddy here can goof off on Ibiza."

Cutter laughed at that, a flat mirthless laugh.

"You sanctimonious prick, Bone," he said. "Where do you get off thinking I got to justify myself to you? Who the hell are you anyway? The fastest dick on the beach? Big deal. That really qualifies you to go around moralizing, doesn't it. In a pig's ass."

The only difference between Cutter angry and Cutter joking were the words he used; his voice and expression remained the same. And Bone always figured this was because the man lived so consistently at the edge of rage that a hairline closer made no noticeable difference in him. But if Bone had seen and heard it all before, Valerie had not, and she stared at Cutter in open shock as he loped up and down the small room, grinning and murmuring in rage.

"But let me tell you, my friend. Just this once, just for the hell of it, for my own amusement, I think maybe I'll let you into the holy of holies for a moment or two and give you a taste of truth for a change, my truth, Richie, and it is simply this — I don't like this motherfucker Wolfe and all the motherfuckers like him, all the movers and shakers of this world, kiddo, because I saw them too many times, and I saw the people they moved and shook. I saw the soft white motherfuckers in their civvies and flak jackets come slicking in from Long Binh to look us over out in the boonies, see that everything was going sweet and smooth, the killing and the cutting and the sewing up, and then they'd grunt and fart and squeeze their way back into their choppers and slick on back to Washington or Wall Street or Peoria and say on with the show, America, a few more bombs will do it, a few more arms and legs. And I don't care if they were as smooth as the Bundys or as cornpone as Senator Eastland or this cat Wolfe, one fact was always the same, *is* always the same — it's never their ass they lay on the line, man, never theirs, but ours, *mine*."

He paused a few moments for breath, stood over Bone smiling still, trembling.

"So don't judge me, baby, okay? Don't put me down for a money-grubber altogether. Ninety percent maybe. But there's still the rest, this little tithe of rage I got, this ten cents of gut hate."

Bone did not apologize. With an actor as consummate as Cutter, one could not be sure of anything. There was also the little matter of last night's eery bedside confessional: it had presented a quite different rationale for blackmail.

"So you just pick out one of them," Bone said. "You pick him out and blackmail him."

"*You* picked him out!" Cutter shot back.

Lighting another cigarette, Bone got up and walked over to the open door. Across the yard, in the house, he saw Teresa again, this time busily cleaning one of the dining room windows, which afforded her an unobstructed view of his apartment. He almost waved to her, then thought better of it. Turning back to his guests, he decided it was time to put an end to their fantasy.

"It won't work," he said. "It *can't* work."

"Hell it can't," Cutter persisted.

"Let's say it turns out our Wolfe *is* innocent. Naturally he goes straight to the police. What happens then?"

"We tell them the truth," Valerie said. "The whole thing was just a way of flushing him, that's all. An attempt to find out if he was the one."

"It's still attempted blackmail, a felony."

"But the police would see why we did it, I mean, especially in my case. She was my sister. And we couldn't go to them with our suspicions, since you don't *know*, you aren't sure, you can't *testify* you saw him."

"And they just forgive and forget, huh? Drop the charges, wipe the slate clean?"

"So they wouldn't, so what?" Cutter said.

"But the other side's no better," Bone went on. "I mean if your hundred-to-one chance proves out, and Wolfe actually is the one. Well, he's no dummy. As you said, he built a two-by-four chicken farm up into a conglomerate, so it's safe to assume he knows his way around. Now, as the guilty party, one thing he'd know for sure is that I've already signed a statement I didn't see anything but a silhouette that night. No one's face. Not his, not anybody's. So how do I change my testimony, I mean change it and get anyone to believe it? No way. The dumbest thing Wolfe could do would be to pay up. It would be an admission of guilt — an admission he doesn't have to make."

For the first time Valerie looked doubtful, and she turned to Cutter, who of course had an answer.

"Sure, it would be dumb," he said. "Which makes it almost foolproof. Because that's just what scared people do — they do dumb things. I've seen kids pick up Cong hardware they *knew* was probably booby-trapped, yet they picked it up anyway, and got zapped for their trouble. So don't give us logic, man. If Wolfe is our boy, he's already proved how dumb he is, how sick. We come after him, he'll cave in. Believe me."

Bone said nothing more for a time. He sat back on the bed, practically sagged onto it, almost as if he were giving in, preparing to settle back and start making plans with his guests. Instead he slipped sideways and disappeared.

"Okay, then. You two are that sure, go ahead. You don't need me. Just tell him I saw him — that should do the trick. And that way you'll only have to split the money two ways."

Cutter snorted with contempt. "Come on, Val," he said, moving toward the door. "It's like trying to seduce a eunuch."

At the doorway, Valerie looked back at Bone. "Think about it though, won't you?" And then offhand, apparently as an afterthought, she said, "Did they show you her body?"

Bone shook his head. "There was no reason to."

"I was just wondering, that's all. Because if they had, I think maybe you'd be with us."

"Could be."

Mr. and Mrs. Little returned home that evening, pulling in just after seven o'clock in a Mark IV Continental. From his room at the end of the garage, where he had been lying in bed reading among other things the Xeroxes of the *Time* magazine article and the *Who's Who* entry on J. J. Wolfe, Bone was able to observe the couple as they alighted from the big maroon car, and separately, not speaking, crossed the driveway and entered their house, which was empty now, Teresa having once more abandoned these shores of Anglo tranquillity for the troubled seas of home. Mr. Little surprised Bone somewhat, looking more like a fiftyish male model than the fragile egghead types who in Bone's business experience normally turned up in computer services work. Little however was tall and lean, with a deep tan and close-cropped gray hair and that just-so look of hairy masculinity, authority, and success one found pushing expensive whiskeys and big cars in the pages of the national magazines.

Bone considered going over to the house and introducing himself to his new boss, and in the process letting Mrs. Little know that he was here and on the job. But he thought better of it. If Mrs. Little wanted to introduce him, all she had to do was come out and get him.

And minutes later that was exactly what she appeared to be doing. She came walking hurriedly across the yard, knocked once on his door, and entered.

"Good," she said. "You're still here."

"Still?"

"I talked with Teresa yesterday. Long distance."

"She didn't mention it." He had gotten out of bed now and was thinking of asking her to sit down, but her manner — breathless and excited — put him off.

"My husband's in the shower," she said, "so I rushed out here to tell you — I'd just as soon he didn't meet you yet. I told him I'd hired a new grounds *boy*."

Bone could not help smiling. "You don't want me to wander around outside, then."

"Not for a while, okay? An hour at the most. He'll be leaving by then — he's got a meeting in L.A. in the morning."

"No problem."

"After he's gone, though, you come on over. If you want, I mean. Naturally you're free to come and go as you please."

"I'm not going anywhere."

"Good. I'll tell you what — why don't we go out for dinner? I'm famished myself. How about you?"

"Most of the time."

"Well, fine then. And, uh — you do have a jacket? A sport coat?"

"Two. And shoes even."

She laughed at that, too eagerly. "Fine. I'll see you soon."

Alone again, and with nothing better to do, Bone once more went over the Xeroxed material on Wolfe. The *Who's Who* entry was spare to the point of brutality:

WOLFE, J. JAMES corp. exec.: b. Rockhill, Mo., Aug. 5, 1929; s. Oral and Sarah (Russell) W.; m. Olive Field Hawley, Dec. 15, 1949; children: J. James Jr., Oral C., Virginia F., and Harlan J. Founder & pres. Ozark Poultry Co-op. 1949–55; founder & pres. Ozark Markets, Inc. 1953–58; founder, pres., chrmn. Wolfe Enterprises, Inc. 1959–. Mem. Am. Soc. Sales Execs., American Angus Assoc., Kiwanis Club. Home: RFD Rockhill, Mo. Offices: Rockhill, Mo. 64840; 109 E. 42nd St., N.Y. 10017; 407 Unicorn Drive, Hollywood, Calif. 90028.

That terse, orderly listing bore about as much relation to the J. J. Wolfe in *Time* as a coach's blackboard diagram did to the blood and thunder of an actual football game. The story was not so much about Wolfe personally as about the general new breed of "conglomerateurs," as the magazine dubbed them. Wolfe was simply one of the group, and a smallish one at that, certainly no Perrot or Ling or Vesco. But he made for pretty good copy and thus earned himself star billing, the cover portrait and the full-page "box" inside, in which Wolfe the person — the husband and father, the cattleman and aviator, the cornpone maverick — was limned with *Time*'s customary slickness.

Essentially the story presented in the article and the "box" was a simple one, a cliché in fact. Wolfe had been born in southwestern Missouri, the fifth generation of dirt-poor hillbillies who believed in the trinity of hard liquor, a jealous God, and above all "kin," a concept whose corollary was instant mistrust and hatred of those who were not kin. The men were loggers and chicken farmers and hunters; the women were pregnant; the children, like Wolfe himself, seldom went past the eighth grade in school, dropping out to join their parents in chicken raising and pregnancy.

But from the beginning J. J. Wolfe had been different, almost different in *kind*, a veritable mutant. While his father and brothers and uncles hunted and drank and dreamed, he built the first automated pullet-raising and egg-laying houses in the country, then showed other poultrymen in the area how to do the same thing, and ultimately organized them into a marketing cooperative that rapidly extended down into Arkansas and west into Oklahoma. At twenty years of age, as president of the 400-member Ozark Poultry Cooperative, he borrowed money and started a feed company intended in theory to supply cheaper feed to the co-op's members, but which in fact ended up binding them to contracts that put Wolfe in virtual control of every member's operation, dictating not only the feed they were to buy and at what price but also where and when and at what profit they could market their eggs and fryers. Thus by his mid-twenties he had a large chunk of national poultry production in his pocket, and he quickly used it to gain control of a small supermarket chain, then a larger one, then moved on into discount stores and other fields entirely.

By the age of thirty he had holdings sufficiently diversified to warrant his setting up Wolfe Enterprises, Incorporated, the holding company that *Time* reported was now a significant factor in almost every segment of the national economy. Wolfe was the nation's single largest producer of poultry and poultry products; he was the second largest cattle feeder; his holdings in supermarket and discount chains accounted for almost four percent of *all* retail business; and as the article reported, he was also "into" banking and forest products and energy and communications. He was in short a conglomerate. And somehow, reading between the lines of the article, Bone got the feeling that it was a conglomerate held together by paper, a leaning tower of debt.

To Bone, the personal J. J. Wolfe did not sound much more interesting than the corporate one. *Time* tried to make him out as a dedicated family man, but the article also mentioned that he lived away from home much of the time, a good part of it in New York and Hollywood. The article made a big thing of his "folksiness," the fact that he went tieless most of the time and ate hamburgers for lunch and bought suits off the rack at his discount houses. And it mentioned his habit of going into working-class bars and picking up hitchhikers because he could "learn a damn sight more about people when they think you're just a dumb redneck — which I guess is what I am anyway." There were photographs of him with his family on his three-thousand-acre cattle ranch near his Missouri hometown, and there was another photo of him in a hardhat inspecting a new factory. But neither rang any bells for Bone. What he saw was just another tycoon enjoying his spoils. And oddly he did not seem to relate any more closely to the man in the Santa Barbara newspaper photograph than to the figure

Bone had seen in the alley. They all seemed like strangers, to each other as well as to him.

Like his slacks, both of Bone's sport coats were holdovers from his marketing v.p. days in Milwaukee, expensive double-knit jobs he had bought at MacNeil and Moore's in the Pfister Hotel building. Neither was altogether unpresentable, merely baggy, dirty, and worn at the elbows, a combination that more and more dictated he choose the darker one, the blue blazer, which in turn dictated the gray Farahs and his trusty peppermint-stripe shirt. So he was not feeling exactly spiffy as he waited in the Littles' game room working on a martini and watching *M*A*S*H* on the sarcophagus-sized television set, while Mrs. Little was somewhere else in the house putting the final touches on her disguise.

And minutes later, as she came down from upstairs, he saw what a successful disguise it was. From a distance she looked a smashing thirty-five, all lustrous black hair and long-lashed eyes and gleaming lips, the total effect an almost gooey Latin sexiness if anything heightened by her muted tan evening suit. In her smile, however, there was no hint of disguise. She looked happy and excited, and he could only wonder at her prodigious capacity for self-deception.

"You ready?" she sang.

"Sure."

"Anyplace special you'd like to go? Talk of the Town?"

"It's up to you."

"How about something out of the way?"

"Fine."

"There's one down the coast," she said, as they went out the back door. "Just past Carpenteria. It's new and small, and the food—well, let's just say the drinks are big."

"Sounds good."

At the garage, she tossed him the car keys. "You can drive, all right? Martinis, you know — I kind of got a jump on the evening."

"Sure."

The car, a late-model Buick Century, seemed to have every possible piece of optional equipment, including power seats, which Mrs. Little put to immediate use, stretching out almost supine as Bone backed around and drove off.

"I'm so happy," she said. "I'm so glad that motherfucking asshole is gone."

The "new small" place turned out to be only that, with drinks no larger or stronger than those served in other restaurants in the area. But Bone judged that what it did offer was safety from exposure, its resounding lack of cachet an almost certifiable guarantee that Mrs. Little would not run into anyone she did not want to run into. And Bone was fairly certain this did not include neighbors or friends so much as her husband's customers and business contacts, that vital group without whom she might not have been able to hire grounds *boys*. But if she was careful not to harm the man's business affairs, she had no such regard for his personal reputation, and right after drinks were served and the two of them had straightened out the name problem—he was to call her Beth, not Mrs. Little, and she in turn could call him Rich or Richard, not Dick, which he detested — she quickly picked up where she had left off in the car.

Jack Little was an insufferable bastard, pure and simple. Three days in San Francisco with the man, she said, and they had not even kissed, could Bone believe that? When Little took her out for dinner all the creep did was sit there and knead his earlobe and mentally strip and hump every girl in the room, while all she did was drink — too much, she admitted. Like tonight. Only this was fun drinking, drinking because she felt good, not bad, and that was all the difference.

"The man is totally business," she complained. "Nothing but business from the top of his woolly head to his pedicured feet. Even in sex he's business. Doesn't want any messy, time-consuming affairs, he says, so he confines himself to whores, would you believe that? It's true. He brags about it in fact — the very best call girls, he says, age twenty to twenty-five, professional, efficient, clean. Hundred to hundred-fifty a throw. Bang-bang, he's in and out and done — and back to business."

Like Mrs. Little, Bone was drinking steadily, and martinis at that. This night he figured he would need them.

"He talks to you about it, though? Straight out?"

"His sex life? Oh sure. He's proud of it."

"Well, that's something."

"Yeah — real togetherness."

"And there's nothing else? No children?"

She hit her martini again and looked away. He evidently had touched a nerve.

"Two," she said. "A boy and a girl."

"Where are they?"

"Boy's in college." And now in her glop-rimmed eyes the pain was raw, exposed. "The girl's married," she said. "And got two children of her own, which I believe makes me a grandmother, doesn't it?"

"Big deal."

"Well, isn't it?"

"Liz Taylor's a grandmother."

"That's hardly an answer."

"Put it this way, then — there are grandmothers, and there are grandmothers."

"This doesn't bother you then? You don't find it ridiculous?"

"What?"

"You, me — our age difference. And together like this."

"Does it bother you?"

"Not really."

"Then why should it me? If anyone doesn't like it, the hell with them."

She was smiling again. "My God, you're attractive, you know that? And nice."

"Of course."

109

"I'm awfully glad you dropped out or whatever you call it now. Maybe it hasn't been good for you, I don't know. But for me, tonight —" She shrugged in embarrassment. "I guess I'm a little smashed."

"That's what it's for."

The waitress came and served their food, a filet mignon for Bone, lobster for Mrs. Little. As soon as they were alone again, she suggested they eat hurriedly.

"I want to go home," she added. "I want *us* to go home."

Bone looked at her, the moist avid eyes, the anxiety quivering at the corners of her smile. "Sure," he said. "But everything in its season, you know. First, food."

"And then?"

He could not quite meet her eyes. "Home?"

"*Yes.*" She said it as if it were a nuptial vow.

Less than an hour later Bone found himself in the Littles' game room again, only now trying to get a fire going in the huge fieldstone fireplace. It was Mrs. Little's idea: "A cool night, and just the two of us, perfect for a fire." But she had not reckoned with his hands, which five martinis and a B&B had turned into catcher's mitts. The logs, however, were like those he had bought for Mo, pressed paper that burned in "a rainbow of colors." They also were easier to ignite, so he finally accomplished his mission and then made it back across the room to the bar, there to slosh some vodka and ice into a tumbler and carefully guide the libation to his lips. Laughing to himself, he reflected that this was one night he would not, as the schoolteacher put it, rise to the occasion. No, he would just have to be an old softie, and blame it on the booze. If the lady bitched and moaned — so be it. He wouldn't starve. He could always fall back on Cutter, couldn't he? Cutter and J. J. Wolfe. Again he laughed.

And it was then Mrs. Little made her second entrance of the evening, this time bumpily gliding down the stairs in bright red semi-see-through lounging pajamas that made Bone remember a Lenny Bruce record from his high school days, Lenny commenting on some old woman with "the kind of blouse you could see through — and you didn't want to."

Like Bone, Mrs. Little apparently needed one more sip of courage, for she swept to the bar and poured herself some brandy, all the while giving her new grounds boy a look of almost gloomy erotic anticipation. Taking a quick slug, she dropped the glass onto the bar and began her advance, weaving toward him across the broad shag carpet. Halfway there, however, her stride tightened into a little stutter step, like that of a Japanese serving girl. And then she was not moving at all, was just standing there in the middle of the room, her lacquered face suddenly the color of wood ash. Abruptly she turned and lunged back across the room and into the downstairs bath, where she began to vomit what sounded like a seven-course dinner. Bone knew he should have welcomed the clamor, that it amounted to a saving bell for him. But all he felt was aversion.

In a cool and deliberate expression of what he felt, he took three quick steps over to one of the lady's sculptures, an apparent bicycle chain welded rigid and sprouting a series of clockworks, and he kicked both it and its pedestal across the room, where it chipped a sizable corner off the television set.

Feeling better after that, he wandered over to the bathroom and looked in upon his unfortunate employer. She was standing back from the toilet, as if frightened by the great pool of filth she had spawned. And she was moaning.

Bone did not know what to say to her. "Not feeling too good, huh?" he tried.

But that only made her moan louder.

"It's a damn shame, all right," he allowed, waffling back from the door, preparing to leave. "Well, take care. I'll see you tomorrow."

"You can't go now!"

"Oh? Why not?"

"My nightie's wet!"

"So take it off."

"My robe. Get my robe upstairs."

"Sure thing."

In her room the only robe in view was a man's — heavy, opaque, one Bone would not be able to see through — so he looked no further. Coming back downstairs he found Mrs. Little hiding behind the bathroom door, with just her hand visible, reaching for the robe. Her Frederick's of Hollywood outfit lay in a heap in the tub.

"You'll be all right now," he said, hopefully turning away again.

But she disagreed. "No. You help me upstairs."

He saw no reason why she could not have made it on her own, but since he had no desire to be out on the street again tomorrow he muttered another "Sure thing" and helped the lady upstairs to her room, where she fell snuffling into bed, alternately begging him to forgive her and playing the *grande dame* totally aghast at her gaucherie: "I can't imagine what happened — it's never happened to me before. Never in my life." And then she made a clumsy grab for him, which he wearily eluded.

"You still smell of puke," he explained, in his best bedside manner.

"Then get the hell out of here," she whined. "Go play with yourself."

Bone started to leave, but she grabbed his coat sleeve and held on.

"No, you just shit here, Joe," she said, slurring her words. "Shit here and hold my hand."

Bone was sober enough to know he was not Joe, but he sat down on the edge of the bed anyway and took her hand. And suddenly he began to feel an enormous exhaustion. He wanted nothing in the world so much as to stretch out beside her and sleep, but he was not about to put himself in a position that could lead to a sexual showdown.

"Bet you think I'm ashamed," she said. "Bet you think I'm a mesh."

"Not at all."

"Not at all, your ash, Joe. Course I'm a mesh — I know that. But not always, lemme tell you. You know who you're lookin' at, Joe? You got any idea?"

"No idea."

"The Queen, thash who. Monmouth College Homecoming Queen, nineteen hunder and for —" She giggled at her ridiculous mistake. "And fifty-five. Thash old nuff, huh?"

"Congratulations," Bone said.

"Old hot lips, that was me, Joe."

"Hot lips, huh?"

"Body that wouldn't quit, let me tell you."

"And still hasn't."

"You bet your ash." And now she smiled reflectively. "Them Tekes, though — what a buncha hornies they were, huh? They had this auction, ya know. To raise money for some damn thing or other — I can't remember — and you know what they got me to do?"

"No."

"Shtrip, thash what! But just down to my unnerwear, course. We wasn't so fuckin' filthy back then."

"The good old days."

"You bet your ash."

"Again."

Bone said as little as possible from then on, and in time Mrs. Little's fond memories faded and her eyes began to flutter closed, probably unable to support any longer the weight of her half-inch false lashes. Finally Bone gave her a comradely pat on the arm and tiptoed out of the room. He was just starting down the stairs when her voice came after him again, like a harpoon.

113

"We try it again tomorrow night, okay? I won't drink sho much."

At that Bone raised his eyes to the ceiling in unthinking comic dismay, and immediately realized his mistake — a drunk's mistake — as his right foot missed the next step and he went tumbling the rest of the way down the carpeted stairs and rapped his head vigorously on the bottom baluster. For what seemed like minutes he lay there trying to decide whether to open his mouth and yell or run back upstairs and beat his new employer to death with one of her sculptures. Instead he got to his feet and went into the kitchen, where he picked up the wall phone and dialed.

For a change it was Cutter himself who answered, yawning and grumbling.

"This is Rich," Bone told him. "I've changed my mind."

"About what?"

"Wolfe."

"It's too late, man."

"Why?"

"I just slashed my wrists."

"Tape them," Bone said.

5

LATE THE NEXT MORNING BONE PARKED MRS. LITTLE'S PICKUP truck on Alvarez Street and walked to the point where he had first seen the man swerve his car into the alley next to the apartment complex. For a while he stood there alternately gazing across the street at the empty alley and then down at the picture in his hand, the newsphoto of J. J. Wolfe and his firebombed car.

He moved down the sidewalk a short distance and repeated the process. Then he did it again. Finally he turned and went back to the pickup. Driving south on Anacapa, he came to 101 and turned left. At the first Union 76 sign he saw, he exited the freeway and pulled into the service station. There were two men on duty, one about Bone's age and the other probably still in his teens. Both were working hard, trying to keep up with a steady stream of cars pulling in for service. So Bone had no choice except to hang back and wait for an occasional break in their gas-pumping to try some pumping of his own. He worked for the man in the picture, he told them. Maybe they remembered reading about it earlier in the week, the firebombing of J. J. Wolfe's car? Their reaction, bored and even hostile, gave him nothing. But he persisted. His boss was wondering if anyone had made any unusual sales of gasoline that night, Monday night it was, say a couple of gallons of gas, carry out? Maybe the purchaser had to buy gas cans too, he said, that was a possibility.

What Bone was hoping for of course was that Wolfe's picture might jar their memories — in it he looked different from the man in *Time*, which was the picture Cutter said he had shown them. And finally the teenager came around. Yeah, he remembered selling some cans and filling them for a cat last Monday night, but he hadn't got a good look at the guy.

"He was wearing shades and a golf cap," he said. "That's all I remember."

"What about his clothes? Was he wearing a suit?"

"I said I don't remember, man — we were hustling that night."

"Maybe he had on a sport coat," Bone tried. "Or a jacket."

The kid shrugged. "Yeah, a jacket, I guess. With a T-shirt underneath."

"That's all?"

"Yeah, just a T-shirt with this dumb pig on it."

"What kind of pig?"

"What am I, a farmer?"

"Was it a Porky Pig?"

"A *pig*, that's all I know. Just a fucking pig."

Again Bone showed him the picture of Wolfe. "Did the man look at all like my boss here?"

"I just told ya — I didn't get a good look at the cat." The kid shook his head in exasperation. "Jeez, everybody wants to know about him. Yesterday this freaky cripple, and now you."

"Things are tough all over," Bone said.

From the service station he drove on to Cabrillo Boulevard. He parked the truck again and headed out across the broad beach toward the water's edge, where the sand would be hard enough for easier walking. And he felt he had to walk. He had to think; he had to get some good clean oxygen into his blood to combat the poisons last night's drinking had dumped there. The thought of his own hangover led him inevitably to think of poor Mrs. Little back in her bed of pain in

116

Montecito. He had gone up to her room earlier to ask if he could use the truck for some personal errands, but she had had other things on her mind.

"My head! My stomach! My legs!" she bawled.

Bone had offered to get her something — scrambled eggs, he suggested — but that had only made her moan all the louder. In the interstices of her agony, however, she did manage to answer his petition — yes, he could take the goddamn truck if he wanted it. He could sell it, junk it, shove it, she didn't care.

As he moved along the beach he tried to get it straight in his mind, what he had done and for what reason. Even drunk last night, after making the call to Cutter, he had expected that when he woke this morning, he would quickly take it all back, call Cutter again and explain that it had just been a joke, an inebriate's midnight inspiration.

But he had not called, not changed his mind about seeing Cutter this morning. Hangover and all, he found that for the first time in ages the day ahead of him was not just something to be got through but a terrain that actually interested him, a field of unknown and intriguing possibility. And when he analyzed the phenomenon he could find no better reason for it than that he did not believe his own eyes. Because he still recalled seeing nothing that night except a dark shape. Yet he knew that if he had to bet on whom that shape belonged to, he would not have been reluctant to give odds that its possessor was J. J. Wolfe. So he could only assume that what his conscious mind had missed that night, his unconscious had not. There must have been something, a sight message, a visualization so swift and subtle he had not picked up on it except in his unconscious. What it came down to then was he *felt* he had seen Wolfe that night. That was all. But it was enough.

Beyond that he had no sure idea where he was headed or even where he wanted to go. Money was the essential thing of course, the carrot. Not for a second could he buy Valerie's hard-eyed protestations about bringing the guilty to justice. No, he was certain she was in the thing for the same reason Cutter was, and now maybe he would be, to ease the burden of living poor in this sunny sink of affluence. The stock market had been bumping along the bottom for some time now, unemployment was high, and every bar he went into, every straight and kinky party had its Jeremiahs predicting catastrophes ahead, depression and famine and political breakdown. And even if only a fraction of it proved true, Bone did not look forward to muddling through it as an aging beachboy in Salvation Army castoffs. No, like everyone else, he was going to need a shelter of his own, and it did not appear he was about to achieve it through any of the usual channels, like holding down a job. So maybe he would just have to turn to J. J. Wolfe for help. Like the survivors at Donner Pass, maybe he would have to stop thinking about himself in a certain way, and do what had to be done, survive however he could.

Bone of course realized that all this rested on two less-than-concrete assumptions — the first that Wolfe was guilty and the second that the man was sane, rational enough to give in to extortion rather than try to destroy its source or break before it, go to the police, and confess his crime. There was no way of knowing the first part of course; Wolfe himself would have to supply the answer there. But as for the second, the possibility that if he were guilty he might also be rational, Bone saw no reason why it could not be so, despite the brutality of the crime. For that matter, Bone saw no reason why the murder itself could not be interpreted as simply an accident instead of the purposeful act of a psychopath as everyone seemed to think it was. The semen in the girl's throat certainly was no basis for the psychopath theory. Over the years Bone himself had picked up numerous young female hitchhikers who turned out not to be traveling anywhere so much as reporting for work, ready to earn a fast ten or twenty dollars wherever he might have chosen to turn off and park. So the fact that

Valerie's sister had semen in her throat meant nothing really; in fact Bone would have bet that in the last year the girl had ingested more of it than she had ice cream.

No, it was the other that unsettled — the fractured skull, the crushed windpipe. And yet even these Bone could see as part of a normal scenario, things that grew out of the circumstances themselves rather than the compulsions of a psychopath. Wolfe — or whoever — picks up the girl, drives her around, talks, finally either makes out with her or buys her services. And as is so often the case, alcohol enters the picture, perhaps diminishing the man's capacity at the same time it exaggerates the girl's contempt for him, not only his performance but his very being, his age and appearance, his accent, his crewcut if nothing else. And, laughing, choking, she spits most of his meager production back at him, in his face or on his clothes — Bone could almost see the thing happening, the careless laughing girl, happy stoned, flying on her meth and beer while the man sits there in his middle-aged fat-sweat and stink, his outraged pride and shame congealing as the laughter washes over him, this child's scalding laughter. And he lashes out a hard beefy plowboy's hand straight into her face, into the laughter, again and again, and finally, when he is done, a gesture of contempt more than anything else, he shoves it away from him, this piece of poor spaced-out California child gash, he shoves it brutally away from him and the head strikes the windshield or cornerpost, something harder than bone anyway, harder than skull. And it is all over, canceled, twenty-five years of blood-sweat and thievery apparently undone in a matter of seconds.

But then it all must have come surging back to him, Bone figured, like adrenaline to an athlete, the old hillbilly obduracy and cunning. And he had dumped the girl's body. He had firebombed his own car. He had done his thing with the locals, whipping out the old aw-shucks routine as the visiting hayseed tycoon, a little surprised and puzzled at this weird bit of violence directed at him of all people, but at the same time not all that hot and bothered about it either, no sirree, not so put-out he couldn't hang in there grinning and pressing the flesh like any other good ole boy with a li'l dinky empire to husband. In other words, Wolfe had quickly reverted to character, the character of a man who would go belly up for the police at about the same time jackals turned herbivorous or the Ozarks voted communist.

All of which brought to Bone's mind an interesting corollary — would Wolfe then be likely to roll over for a trio of amateur extortionists? And about the only acceptable answer he could think of was *possibly* — if their demands were reasonable and if they covered themselves carefully enough. That was one of the reasons he was glad Cutter had brought Valerie into the thing — he considered three a neat, almost optimum conspiracy, too large for someone like Wolfe to handle easily and yet not so inclusive as to be unmanageable. Then too, as she had pointed out yesterday at Mrs. Little's, Valerie did in a sense legitimize the undertaking — if it ever began to come apart and Wolfe did go to the police, Valerie as the victim's sister would be able to cast doubt on their culpability. Who could prove the three of them were not simply trying to smoke Wolfe out? It would be a hard case to make, hard to prosecute.

So there were good reasons for including her, for giving her a share of Cutter's pie in the sky. Nevertheless Bone had his doubts that those reasons had been Cutter's — they were just too simple, too practical to have made it through the exotic plumbing of his friend's mind. Nor for a second could Bone believe that sympathy or generosity had been Cutter's motive. No, he imagined Alex had brought her in on impulse more than anything else, perhaps only because his prodigious ego required a larger and more appreciative audience than Bone alone. But that was not something to sweat over now, Bone reminded himself as he started back for the truck. That would have to wait, along with such other matters as to how to plan and set up the operation and how much money to ask for.

Above all, there was one simple question that needed answering. And there was only one person who could answer it.

It was almost noon when Bone entered Murdock's, expecting to sit at the bar and have a sandwich and maybe a free drink or two while he waited for Cutter. But surprisingly Alex was already there, sitting alone in a booth at the rear of the room. Besides him there were only two other patrons, a seedy pair of old men nursing draft beers at the bar, behind which Murdock was busy readying his supply of liquor, mixes, and glasses for the long day ahead. Still he took the time to give Bone a despairing look.

"Your buddy's here," he said.

Bone lit a cigarette. "So I see."

"You never learn, do you?"

"Probably not. But I did get out of his house, just like you instructed, father."

"Smart boy."

"You got any coffee?"

Murdock turned to the old men for commiseration. "You hear that? Coffee. Jesus, between the two of 'em I'm really gonna prosper today."

"That's what he's drinking?" Bone asked.

"Yeah — but lacing it with wood alcohol, I bet. Or bat blood."

"You do carry on." Bone waited at the bar for his coffee, then took it back to the booth and sat down. For a time Cutter did not acknowledge his arrival, just sat there lying back against the booth seat puffing on a cigar, blowing out an impressive chain of smoke rings.

"Something terrible's happened, right?" Bone said. "Something horrendous."

"Because I'm on time?"

"More — you're early."

"It's the new me, Rich. Why, I've turned over so many new

leaves this past week I'm practically through the whole damn book."

"Is that what that means — the leaves of a book?"

"What'd you think, a fig leaf?"

"I didn't think. I try not to."

Cutter said he could understand that, just as he himself tried not to run whenever possible. "Of course there's also the theory of compensation," he went on. "According to which you should be a world-renowned philosopher and I a wide receiver for the Rams."

"You'll make it first."

"You're probably right."

Bone sipped at his coffee and, finding it bitter, added sugar. All the while Cutter sat there studying him, the single bloodshot eye carefully working him over.

"Well, out with it," he said finally. "Last night you said there was still a problem, something bugging you."

"That's right. Before I sign on, I need this one answer."

"About what?"

"You."

Cutter grinned. "Now why didn't I think of that? *Me*. And here I thought it was Valerie. I figured you didn't want a girl in on it."

"No, there's no problem there."

"But there is with me, huh?" Cutter frowned deeply, burlesquing his puzzlement and concern. "Now what could it be? Let me think — you suspect my motives, right?"

Bone put out his cigarette. "Screw your motives. No, it's simply you, old buddy. Your sterling character. What I have to know is if you're serious about this thing, if you're on the level. Or if you're just playing the same old games, putting us peasants on just for the hell of it."

Cutter was aggrieved. "Have I ever put you on?"

"Many times."

"But not in something like this, Rich. Not when the stakes are this high. Not when it's important."

Bone thought of young Erickson and his holy war against polluters, and how Cutter had squashed him. And he thought of the first time he had ever seen Alex, at an election night party for a clean-cut local young professor who had just won his party's nomination for assemblyman, and how amid all the bubbly and pandemonium this one-eyed cripple in an apache dancer's outfit had scrambled up on a table and outshouted everyone. "A toast!" he had yelled. "A toast to the only politician I ever met with guts enough to face the truth about himself — to insist that a man's sex life is his own business, no matter how queer it may seem to someone else! So here's to him — your candidate and mine — Ralph Herman!" It had been typical Cutter — in fact Alex had not even gotten the man's first name right. Nevertheless a funereal silence had fallen briefly on the room, and the nervous laughter that trailed after it somehow failed to reestablish the original festive mood. And though undoubtedly for other reasons, "Ralph" Herman never made it to Sacramento.

So Bone could not attach much weight to Cutter's disclaimer. In fact it was his experience that the more "important" something was, the more likely Cutter was to deflate it.

"The whole idea," Bone said now. "It's pretty far out."

Cutter shrugged. "Life is far out."

"We could wind up in jail."

"I've been worse places."

"I haven't."

"Well, it's up to you, man. It's a question of priorities — how much you're willing to risk."

"What about the moral problem?"

"What moral problem?"

"Extortion is a crime."

"So's murder."

"Two wrongs don't make a right."

"May I quote you on that?"

"The thing bothers me. I can't help it."

"You're kidding."

"No, I'm not."

"In this world!" Cutter's grin did not believe. "This hellish planet. This jailhouse. This sinkhole of piss and misery. And you think it's immoral — prying a little bread loose from a murdering redneck creep like Wolfe? You actually think that?"

"For some reason, yeah," Bone admitted. "Maybe my Midwest puritan upbringing, I don't know."

Cutter nodded sagely. "I think I know what the problem is — our cause just doesn't sound noble enough. Which is all-important these days. Like if your thing is to liberate someone — Palestinians, gooks, leprechauns — then anything goes. You got carte blanche. You can slaughter the very people you're liberating, it doesn't matter. The important thing is not the end, but the means."

Bone had heard it all before. "Yeah, I know," he said.

"And it doesn't help?" Cutter affected a look of disappointment and perplexity. "Well, may be the problem is purely theoretical. Maybe what you need is a few minutes in Herr Doktor Cutter's Seminar in Rudimentary Philosophy Two-A."

"Don't bother."

"Do you believe in God?" Cutter went on, not waiting for an answer. "Of course you don't, you poor sinner. So let us examine this carefully. Since, according to you, there is no God, then it follows that our so-called moral law is man's invention rather than God's dispensation. It is an aspect of Rousseau's social contract, that's all, a convenient mechanism for greasing the gears of social intercourse, for doing business, for making trains run on time. Therefore it is relative. To shoot Yasir Arafat is one thing, to shoot Rodney Allen Rippey quite another."

Bone put up his hand. "Enough, Alex, all right? I was just about to say that despite this feeling I have, I can still go ahead with the thing — if you're serious."

For a time Cutter sat there meeting Bone's flat gaze. Then he looked down at the table, where his hand was absently trying to fit his now-dead cigar into an empty candleholder. "What can I say?" he tried finally. "What can I give you but my word? I am serious, Rich. I am totally serious. What is there beyond that? Do you want me to sign a contract? Do you want a blood oath?"

Bone heard the words but somehow they lacked the authority of the unconscious demonstration, the black cigar butt now standing obscenely in the candleholder. Bone tried to ignore the cigar's clear message.

"I don't want to go out on this particular limb with someone who's clowning," he said. "Or committing suicide — in his fashion. In other words, Alex, I don't want to get caught. I don't want to read about myself in the paper."

Cutter was shaking his head. "You really got a high opinion of me, you know that?"

"You're the one who told me about wanting to kill yourself."

"This is my reprieve, man. My stay of execution. Can't you see that? Can't you get it through that cover-boy head of yours? This is my last shot, Rich." And now for the first time Cutter's voice took on an edge. "So, yeah, I'm serious. Dead serious. Is that good enough for you? Can you buy that?"

Though these were the very words Bone had come here for, somehow they changed nothing, left him feeling as uneasy as when he first sat down in the booth. But that, he knew, was his problem, not Cutter's.

"Yeah," he said. "Why not?"

They had only one drink to celebrate Bone's decision. Cutter had to take Mo shopping, he said, and then later he and Valerie were going to get together and begin formulating plans, which he advised Bone to do too, so that when the three of them got together tomorrow — he would call Bone later and tell him where and when — they would have something to work with.

After Cutter left, Bone had a second drink at the bar and

followed it with a corned beef sandwich, which he told Murdock he would not pay the full price for since the bread was stale and the meat had a pale green cast at the edges. But then he absentmindedly ate all of it, which seriously damaged his case. Murdock was feeling generous, however, and compromised by giving him a third drink on the house and a few thousand words of advice regarding his poor choice of friends and general lack of ambition. Bone told him not to worry because he was about to turn to crime and would soon be buying drinks for the house every time he deigned to darken its chintzy door, a development upon which Murdock volunteered not to hold his breath.

Bone drove to the library and tried to find some other material on Wolfe besides the *Time* article and the *Who's Who* entry, but there was nothing more. He went into the periodical section then and settled down with recent issues of *Esquire* and *Harper's*, only to discover that he was reading just words, comprehending nothing. So he left. He walked around the downtown area for a while and ended up in a State Street theater that was rerunning the old James Bond films *Goldfinger* and *Thunderball*, which he figured might be just what he needed, four hours of campy violence and improbable girls, enough gore and tits to keep his eyes occupied while his mind was free to seek other entertainments, like considerations of crime and punishment. But as he settled into the rococo dimness with a box of overbuttered popcorn, he found his mind snagging on a single aspect of the subject, and that was the impending debut of Richard Bone, *felon*. The designation, the whole idea, struck him as preposterous, about as believeable as that the ravishing young girl sprawled across the screen — and about to sprawl into bed with Bond — was in reality a Russian superspy. The only difference was that his fantasy in time could prove out. All he had to do was keep moving in the direction he was going and Richard Bone, felon, might become all too real.

It was unsettling, this contemplation of one's own criminality. For until now Bone had always considered himself a law-abiding sort, despite the sinister-sounding "record" Lieutenant Ross had reeled off for the captain Tuesday morning. The truth of the matter was that all his record amounted to was a kind of precocity on his part, his having reached the typical organization man's psychological menopause about a decade earlier than was the custom. Suddenly at thirty years of age he had begun to think of himself as a kind of suited-up zoo animal pacing between the twin walls of home and job. Ruth for some reason had metamorphosed in those last few years into an utter and dowdy bore, a mother hen infernally clucking over her two precious chicks and anything and everything that touched their antiseptic little lives, a cosmology that embraced vitamins and orthodontics and the PTA and not much more. Sex between the two of them had become basically an act of masturbation, with her letting him use her body every second or third night as a kind of receptacle, not a great deal different, he imagined, from one of those inflatable life-size sex dolls sold in porno shops, in fact probably not as good, since Bone always had the feeling that Ruth was mentally fashioning shopping lists as he humped away on her, passionless and angry, like a laborer watching the clock, waiting for the niggardly release that lay ahead.

And his job offered no reprieve. Suddenly he saw the plush office and envied position as a stairway leading not to bigger and better things but merely to another stairway, and one he would not like any better than the one he was already on. So he found himself slipping into an almost deliberate program of career destruction, ranging from open ridicule of his superiors down through the usual dreary gamut of absenteeism and drinking and, in his case, sex — intense, constant, almost institutionalized extramarital sex — as a kind of therapy, compensation for the loss of what he had once thought of as a goal in life.

And this was about all his so-called record amounted to. The rape charge in Milwaukee, for instance. The truth of the matter was that he and the lady involved, Sharon Hartley — Mrs. John J. Hartley — should both have been convicted on charges of committing felonious low comedy. He had been balling the lady for a period of months, in fact had a standing reservation for the two of them at a downtown Milwaukee hotel. On the night of the "crime," however, they were comfortably quartered in her own house, John having been called away to Cleveland on business. But, feeling ill, he had returned home — to find the two of them committing sodomy in his very own king-size bed. Being a temperamental type, John rushed to his gun rack and proceeded to blow out two walls of the bedroom with a twelve-gauge shotgun, a demolition job he explained to the police as an attempt to apprehend the sex fiend who had just raped his wife. And a terrified Sharon had gone along with her husband. Yes, everything was just as John said. No, she didn't know this Bone character at all. He'd come to the door, a stranger whose car had stalled and who wanted to use her phone. So she had let him in — to her everlasting regret. So Bone was arrested, charged, and held — until he was able the next morning to get one of the detectives to show a photo of Mrs. Hartley to the desk clerk at the hotel he and Sharon had favored.

The charge of grand theft here in Santa Barbara was on the same order. The woman, Sylvia Columbo, was the ex-wife of one of the county's more successful contractors. In her late thirties, she was an attractive volatile woman given to alternating fits of impulsive generosity and neurotic possessiveness. Thus she thought no more of giving her new lover a Garand tape deck for Christmas than she did of having him arrested for stealing the goddamn machine the day after she was riding her Arabian gelding along Hope Ranch beach and came upon him and Mo lying alone on a large towel — Cutter was a few hundred feet away scuffing a gigantic HELP in the sand for the benefit of any air travelers passing overhead. So after a few days that charge too had been dropped. And as for the occasional nonsupport action by Ruth — well, Bone did not consider that very much in the way of criminality. Usually he was not even supporting himself at the time. So his record, if it could be called that, did not amount to much more than indiscretion, an embarrassing talent for getting caught with his pants down.

One thing was certain — there was nothing in it on the order of blackmail or extortion. But then neither was there murder. And for now that disparity, the difference between the *possible* murder and the *contemplated* extortion, would have to serve. Through all of history men had executed murderers. But here all the three of them would be doing was *charge* the murderer, let him pay for his crime in far lesser coin than his life. And if it turned out that the man was not guilty, and therefore not vulnerable, then he simply would not pay. Rather it would be *they* who paid. Looked at that way, the whole thing seemed an almost moral enterprise, like hunting lion with a spear. One could lose.

Bone was so lost in thought that he had barely noticed the three young girls who had taken the seats next to his, despite the fact that the theater was almost empty. But suddenly now he was aware of a pressure against his thigh, and looking down he saw its source, the long bare leg of a miniskirted girl in the seat next to him. Beyond her, two stout dark little teenagers — sisters, they appeared — were rocking and pounding their feet, about to explode with held-in laughter. It was only then Bone raised his eyes and looked into those of the girl next to him, she of the aggressive knee. She was long and blond, a tough tomboy type chewing a wad of gum and giving him the same look the superspies kept giving Bond, a sneer that said, "It's your move now, Buster." She was no older than the others, he estimated, fourteen or fifteen, but obviously their leader, their captain in crime. As her knee rubbed against his again now, the other two girls could no longer hold in their laughter and it came sputtering and hissing out of them like air from loosened balloons. At the same time the near girl's hand crawled onto Bone's arm.

"Hi," she said.

It could only be a dare, Bone decided, a kid's game. He wondered what the other two had bet her. A Donnie Osmond record? The latest Jackson Five? He hated to let her chase him out of the theater, to give her such an easy victory. But she was jail bait, he reminded himself. All of them were. And they were three to one, able to cry masher or child molester and if not make it stick at least give him the kind of trouble he did not need, now or ever.

So he got up and left. And all the way up the aisle their laughter clattered after him, like a tail of tin cans.

For hours afterward Bone was coldly furious with himself, not so much for letting the girls drive him from the theater as for having *invited* the attack in the first place, simply by being what he was, a loser and drifter, and looking the part from the top of his messy curly hair to the paper-thin soles of his battered Hush Puppies. He told himself that if there had been anything to him at all — if he'd had one crummy scintilla of property or position or responsibility — the bare-legged one would not have singled him out, not even if he had been in sports clothes and bagged in the bargain, because the reality still would have been there, the weight, the subtle ambience of *substance*. But instead all there had been was this seedy, over-thirty stud moldering in the cavernous theater and dreaming vodka-tonic dreams of blackmail and affluence.

Through the late afternoon he sat in the dark of the Bay Tree Bar drinking more vodka and worrying the problem, and in time he began to realize what a laugh it all was, what a sad, sorry, barely audible laugh, not just the scheme itself but even more his own participation in it, the exquisite little psych job he had performed on himself in order to make it all seem everything it was not — possible, reasonable, acceptable — because that was what he had wanted to believe, almost what a man *had* to believe when he was the kind who unintentionally invited teenage abuse in public. After his fourth drink, he decided that he had to do something drastic about his life, and do it right away, tonight, before he sank any deeper into the quicksands of Cutter's fantasies. He remembered that just the other day George Swanson had offered to help him find a straight job somewhere, and he saw no reason not to take him up on it now.

The matter seemed so urgent that he was soon out in Mrs. Little's truck again, driving the short distance to Swanson's place, a beautifully restored old house situated near the Mission, just a few blocks from Cutter's ancestral home. It was the area of the old rich, Californios whose families went back almost as far as those of their servants.

Bone knew it was not the best evening to drop in at Swanson's, since it was Saturday and George's wife was socially ambitious. She and George would either be going out to a party or suffering the minor ignominy of dining with friends at some newly discovered roach-ridden dive, the in-place of the month. It was still early, however, not quite seven-thirty, so Bone figured he just might catch George before he and his wife set out. But as he parked the truck, Bone saw that he was already too late — the street and driveway looked like the lot of a Mercedes-Benz dealership. And beyond the broad lawn the house was brightly lit, noisy with a party. Bone hesitated for a few moments, lighting a cigarette, and then he decided, what the hell, he would get a free drink or two, wolf down some canapés, and have his talk with George if and when the opportunity presented itself. So he got out and went up the walk, surprised to hear as he got closer that the music coming from inside was live. And he was even more surprised as he reached the house and found Tonto, the Swansons' gardener-chauffeur-handyman standing outside in a tuxedo. Tonto was Mexican, a short husky man with very black hair and very white teeth, which he bared now as Bone asked him if he was taking tickets.

"Mrs. Swanson's idea," the servant explained. "Black tie, she say. Ballet from San Francisco in town tonight. Big time, I guess. Everything real fancy."

Bone smiled. "Well, maybe it *was,* he said, indicating himself as he started to move past. But the little man stepped in front of him.

"Sorry, you can't go in," Tonto said. "Only invited guests, she say. Only black tie."

For a moment Bone could not believe the man was serious, moving in front of him this way, *blocking* him, as if Bone were some kind of untouchable. But his shock was short-lived, disappearing almost immediately under a sudden wave of anger, the kind of blind sweet surging rage he almost never felt, never even had to try to control, and which he did not control now as Tonto's chubby hand came up and touched him lightly on the chest, not a shove exactly, more an indication of the direction he wanted Bone to follow. But its effect was the reverse of that, and Bone shoved the little man sharply backward over a potted palm and into a French door that collapsed in a shower of glass. Immediately the music inside stopped — the schmaltzy four-piece rendition of *Aquarius* breaking in midbeat — and a number of men and women in evening dress and holding cocktails began pouring into the foyer. A few of them came out onto the front porch and then parted, making way for George's wife, who looked as if she were wearing all seven of Salomé's veils, and all brightly colored. Only her face was white.

"What is this?" she demanded. "What in the motherfucking hell is going on?"

Tonto was on his feet now, looking apologetic as he picked shards of glass out of his hair.

"He fell," Bone offered. "I pushed him and he fell. Send the bill to my attorneys." He was already walking away from them, heading down the sidewalk toward the street. Before he reached it there were footfalls behind him and then George was next to him, taking him by the arm, trying to get him to stop.

"Hey, what is it, Rich? What the hell happened anyway?"

Bone pulled his arm free and went on, not stopping until he reached the truck.

"Come on, Rich," George persisted. "I got to know what happened. I just can't figure it."

"Nothing," Bone told him now. "Nothing happened. Your doorman was just doing his job, that's all."

George shook his head mournfully. "Jesus, I'm sorry, man. It was just a mistake, that's all. You should have told him who you were."

Finally Bone had something to laugh at.

6

AS ALWAYS, BONE FOUND THE DRIVE UP TO SAN MARCOS PASS BOTH tortuous and beautiful, with the distant ocean every now and then slipping into view as the road climbed into the mountains still green from the winter rains, almost a Wisconsin summer green, so soft and lush it struck him as incongruous here, a parody, for in his mind the true Southern California was the one of summer and fall, with its yellow hills and dull brown mountains and desiccated flats, a withered land, a home for condors.

He still had no idea why Cutter wanted to get together at Cold Spring Tavern. Not only was it out of the way but it was a tourist haunt as well, a one-time stagecoach stop on the old coastal highway as it crossed the Santa Ynez Mountains, a way station carefully restored and preserved to offer at least a semblance of its original state. As such, on this Sunday afternoon it would be peopled with the usual representation of California tourists, a gamut running from hairy armpits to old lace. Nevertheless it was where Cutter said he and Valerie would be and where Bone was to meet them. "Around noon," he had instructed on the telephone. "If you can get away, that is. If the lady will let you dismount that long."

Actually there had been neither mounting or dismounting the night before. When Bone had finally arrived home he apologized to Mrs. Little for having tied her truck up all day

134

long, but he explained that a friend of his, an alcoholic, had fallen off the wagon and it had taken a good part of the day just to locate the poor stiff and get him home to his wife and kids. Mrs. Little said no explanations were necessary, that he could use the truck whenever he wanted because he worked for her, was after all her caretaker and handyman, and anyway she had her own car if she wanted to go anywhere. Then she insisted that he come in and have a bite to eat with her, cold barbecued chicken and imported Chablis. Afterwards they played straight pool in the game room, which smelled of Pine-Sol now instead of vomit. And they sat around drinking brandy and watching the fire in the fireplace, and in time Bone confessed his great problem to her, told her about the virulent case of gonorrhea he had contracted six months ago and how it had left him, how terrible it was to be impotent. Mrs. Little took the news like a real trooper, hardly batting her enormous eyelashes, and vowed that they would lick the problem together. She would get him the best psychiatric treatment in town. That was all it would take. Nothing could keep a good man down.

Knowing he had a source of food and shelter for the time being anyway, Bone felt a measure of confidence. But that confidence began to leave him the closer he got to his destination. And it was all but gone when he finally reached the tavern. Outside were a number of tourists' cars, a phalanx of Capris and Venturas and Malibus set in gaudy confrontation with the weathered old wood building, which seemed as much a part of the small valley as the surrounding rock walls and great spreading sycamores that shaded it. The cars in fact seemed like America visiting its past, a failed wanton home for a nervous weekend. If there was any link between the two it was Cutter's Packard, which sat off by itself in a spot predictably marked NO PARKING, always a sure invitation to him.

Inside, the confrontation began to break down. Though the main room had a fieldstone fireplace and plank floors and large wood beams overhead, it also had a garish bar clock that bubbled the time in colors matching those of the room's central feature, a leviathan jukebox that was blasting Billy Joel's "Piano Man" to the bemused clientele, most of them blue-haired widows, fugitives from Orange County, Bone imagined.

Going out through a screened porch at one end of the room, he saw the two of them sitting at a small table next to a log fence beyond which the valley brook trickled toward Lake Cachuma. Cutter was massaging her neck, sitting very close to her and saying something out of the side of his mouth, while Valerie, eyes closed and smiling, looked as if she were about to come.

As he saw Bone now, Cutter raised his good leg and pushed a chair out for him. "Well, by Jove, if it ain't his nibs right 'ere in the flesh," he said. "Yessir, Richard Bone Esquire, that's who — dildomaker to the queen, God's gift to little boys."

Valerie smiled easily, not at all embarrassed at how Bone had found them. "I'm glad you changed your mind," she said.

Sitting, Bone lit a cigarette. "A moment of weakness," he explained.

Cutter snorted. "A weakness well earned."

"Yeah, I've been working pretty hard."

"Serving his new mistress," Cutter explained to Valerie.

"Spading her garden as a matter of fact."

"And how did you find it, Richard? Just how *does* her garden grow?"

"Up your ass."

"Then it grows without cockleshells, I can assure you." Leaning back in his chair, Cutter began his single-handed cigarette lighting routine. "But seriously, Rich, how did you find the ground? Was it overworked?"

"Alex, I suggest you come out and have a look. You'll find the ground — and by what I mean the same dark crumbly stuff that lives under your fingernails — you'll find it spaded up around the whole goddamn house inside the fence. Spaded by hand."

"Oh really — by *hand?* Not her instrument of choice, I would imagine."

Valerie gave a pained laugh. "Oh come on. You two go on like this for hours?"

"Sometimes it seems more like days," Bone said.

A waitress came to the table and Bone ordered a round of Coors — the other two were already drinking beer. When the girl left, he turned back to Valerie. "I was just trying to explain my being here," he said. "My change of mind."

"Your moment of weakness?"

"Something like that."

"Sounds like maybe you haven't changed your mind," she said.

"If I hadn't, I wouldn't be here."

"For the money?" Valerie asked. "Or the other?"

Bone shrugged. "I'm like you. I'll cross that bridge when I come to it."

"Well, you'll come to it, old buddy," Cutter assured him. "Believe me."

"Why? You find out something new?"

"No need to. I just know, that's all. I have this gut certainty — based on my undying faith in the integrity and accuracy of your instinctive reactions."

Valerie smiled at that, or possibly at Bone's look, which he imagined was close to that of a man whose child was kicking him in public.

"As a matter of fact though, I ain't just been counting pubic hairs," Cutter added. "Like yesterday, Rich. I didn't tell you, but I was up early trying to find Wolfe's car, the LTD. See if there might be anything of interest in it, bloodstains or something that survived the fire. But they'd already scrapped the crate. It's probably a cube by now, headed for a blast furnace in one of Wolfe's own companies. He'd see to that, old J.J."

Bone put out his cigarette. For some reason he felt a need to play devil's advocate. "Did a little checking of my own this morning," he said. "The service stations off one-o-one, probably the same ones you two checked out. Know what I learned?"

Cutter blew out a stream of cigarette smoke. "They sell a lot of gas cans, right?"

"How'd you guess?"

"I'm psychic."

"Yeah, they say there isn't a day passes they don't sell someone a can and fill it up for him too, usually some guy stranded on the freeway. Happens a lot more lately, they said, with so many stations closed at night."

Cutter was unimpressed. "We know all that, man. And it's irrelevant. The only important fact for us is that on the night in question this one particular man, a cat in a very hasty disguise, did willfully purchase not one but two cans of gasoline at a station conveniently situated between the apartment complex and the Biltmore."

"You can make a firebomb out of *one* gallon," Bone observed. "Or a quart, or a pint."

"Granted. But a man like Wolfe, he doesn't believe in doing things by half, old buddy. He believes in overkill. He buys *two* cans."

"You're positive about that?"

"Of course."

"And what about the service station attendant? Wolfe has on sunglasses and a golf cap — big deal. I wear that, you wouldn't recognize me?"

"Unfortunately I know you better than the man knew Wolfe."

"Or whoever it was."

Cutter lifted his glass of beer and drank, put the glass down, all the while watching Bone. "You with us or not?" he said finally. "Because if you just came out here to gnaw on my ass —"

"I already said I was with you."

"Well, you'll pardon me if I say you don't much sound like it."

"You need what we used to call negative inputs, Alex. Good generals listen to the bad as well as the good."

Cutter shook his head. "One thing I ain't, kid, is a good general."

Valerie, reaching into her handbag, came up with two sheets of bond paper, neatly typewritten. "Shall we get on with it?" she said, placing them on the table.

"The girl's a flaming genius," Cutter told Bone. "Not only takes shorthand and types five thousand words a second, but dictates too. You better watch her — she gonna take over the world."

Valerie pushed the typewritten sheets across the table to Bone. "We both worked on it yesterday. Sort of a rough plan. An outline of our thinking so far."

"Outline, hell," Cutter scoffed. "It's a goddamn battle plan is what it is, just like in the boonies. Only here we're the ones who decide how we're gonna get zapped, not some ass-kissing motherfucker back at staff."

Valerie gave him a rueful look. "Do you have to talk like that?"

Cutter commiserated. "Sometimes I wonder."

Sitting back, Bone began to read through the two single-spaced pages. At first he considered it stupid and reckless, the whole idea of putting their plans down on paper. The sheets could be lost. There was no telling who might eventually read them and use them as evidence against the three of them, if it ever came to that. And while he did not completely abandon this criticism, he could see as he read further that there was value in putting it all down, spelling out the details of procedure, tactics, taboos.

The first rule of procedure was, rightly, that they deal only with Wolfe himself. They foresaw a problem in getting to him without first having to fight their way through protective layers of secretaries and vice-presidents and personal assistants, and being asked to reveal to them at least the nature if not the specifics of their business. But this of course was to be avoided at all costs. Absolute secrecy was implicit in any blackmail "contract"; without it, the victim would have no motive for being a victim. So they would have to be exceedingly careful in how they made contact with Wolfe. The best approach, they believed, would be for Bone to go in person to Wolfe's Hollywood office and tell the highest person he could reach there that he had to get in touch with Wolfe to give him a personal message relating to the night his car was firebombed in Santa Barbara. It was a message of vital importance to Wolfe, Bone was to tell them, and therefore he could give the message only to him. He was to assure them it was a message Wolfe would be grateful to receive — but only this way, personally, from Bone. Hearing it any other way, from the police for instance, would make Wolfe very unhappy indeed.

Bone was to give them the number where he could be reached. Once contact was made and Bone was invited back to Wolfe's office he was to pretend to go along, to meet Wolfe where and when the tycoon or one of his underlings specified. Face to face, however, Bone would improvise, move the "interview" to a place of his own choosing, like the sidewalk in front of the building or even the men's room, some place not likely to be bugged. For there was always the outside chance that Wolfe might not be the girl's murderer, and sensing some sort of blackmail attempt he might arrange to tape the meeting with Bone.

If and when the meeting did take place, Bone's first move would be to make clear that he was not alone in the undertaking, thus discouraging any violence Wolfe might contemplate. He was to show Wolfe a Polaroid shot of himself, Cutter, and Valerie holding up copies of that issue of the Santa Barbara newspaper which reported the news of Pamela's murder and the firebombing of Wolfe's car. Cutter's and Valerie's faces would be cut out of the photo. Thus Wolfe would know that the threat to him extended beyond Bone, but he would not know where, or to whom.

Bone would then proceed to make his nonnegotiable demand. He and his colleagues would remain silent about Wolfe's crime in return for payment of $150,000 yearly, which would be paid as a retainer to a dummy marketing consultant firm Bone would set up. Payment could thus be charged to Wolfe's corporation and not to him personally, since Bone and his colleagues had no desire to kill a goose that laid golden eggs. Payment would be made quarterly, beginning with $37,500 due one week from the day of their initial meeting.

Cutter and Valerie would go down to Los Angeles with Bone and stay in the same hotel with him in the event any emergencies arose, anything that might require discussion or action on their part as well as on his. Any differences of opinion would be settled by majority vote. And any of them that wanted out, at any time, would be free to go. But at the outset all had to agree to keep the matter strictly between the three of them — no present or future "lovers, spouses, or whatnot" were to be informed as to what the three of them had done, or what was the source of their income.

As he finished, Bone looked up at Cutter. "This last point here," he said. "That include Mo?"

Cutter shrugged indifferently. "It includes Mo."

Bone smiled. "Going to be a little hard, isn't it, to explain your sudden affluence?"

"Maybe I won't have to."

For five or six seconds Bone sat there looking at Cutter, waiting for him to explain this. But he offered nothing.

"What about the rest of the plan?" Valerie broke in. "Do you approve?"

Bone lit another cigarette. "I'm not sure. Kind of puts me out there all alone, doesn't it."

"On point," Cutter said. "Which is the place to be, Rich.

Purple Heartland, we used to call it. The ideal place to learn all about yourself."

"You're the logical choice," Valerie added. "Wolfe undoubtedly already knows that you were there and saw him, or at least his silhouette. You'll be believable in a way we couldn't be."

Bone did not argue the point. "How will we know when Wolfe's in L.A.?"

"We already knows, cap'n," Cutter said. "Duh big white bossman, he be flyin' in tomorrow afternoon. And dat's when we gwine be dere too."

"How'd you find out?"

"Another one of his impressions," Valerie said, smiling. "Ozark hillbilly."

Cutter corrected her. "Not hillbilly really. Just a good ole boy, southern fried. I called his Hollywood office yesterday on the off chance someone might be on the switchboard, and lo and behold, this sweet young thing answers. Wolfe Enterprises Incorporated, she say. Well, I jist told her my name was Tommy Joe Didwell and that me and J.J. used to fish together when we was kids and I jist moved here to Los Angeles from Muskogee and jist wanted to give old J.J. a call when he was in town and shoot the shit with him a little, you know how it is, and that if old J.J. was anything like he used to be, he'd be madder'n a wet hornet with a cob up his ass sideways if he ever heard old Tommy Joe tried to get in touch with him and couldn't — jist cuz some intelligent, sweet-soundin' little filly like yourself wanted to be contrary." Cutter finished off his glass of beer. "Well, to make a short story shorter, she allowed as how my old friend J.J. was flying in Monday morning for three days of conferences before returning home to Missouri."

Cutter poured the last of his bottle of beer into his glass and then appropriated Valerie's bottle for the same purpose, and Bone found himself wondering how much beer Alex had had so far. It was still early afternoon and Bone did not look forward to spending the rest of the day with him in a thirsty mood, which usually meant a hassle of one kind or other.

Bone got his answer only minutes later, when a pair of motorcycle freaks came swaggering out of the tavern and took a table near theirs, took it as if they were raping and stomping the thing, slamming their beer bottles down onto it, kicking chairs out of the way, collapsing into others, banging their booted feet onto the top of the table. One of them was sloppy fat, with a short ratty beard and a fringe of long, equally ratty hair falling from a prematurely bald pate. The other was thin as a ferret and commensurately ugly, with a sullen chinless face the color of dirty flour and a greased-down mane of blackish hair gathered into a ponytail at the back. Their costumes were alike only in their general raunchiness and in the black leather vests each of them was wearing and which bore a tiny emblem identifying them as OUTSIDERS, a totally superfluous designation as far as Bone was concerned. The other patrons meanwhile were working hard at pretending nothing had changed — all except Cutter. From the beginning he sat staring at the pair, particularly at the ferret-faced one, who for a time seemed unable or at least unwilling to believe such a sacrilege could take place, here, out in public, in the land of the straights. He would look away from Cutter for a few moments, pretending interest in something else, scratch the tattoos on his belly, spit, contemplate his cigarillo, his stubby fingers and hagiographic rings, then inevitably he would look back at Cutter — and the Eye would still be on him, *laughing* at him.

Bone and Valerie meanwhile were trying to keep to the subject, discussing such problems as operating funds — to come from her, she said, money she was in the process of borrowing on her car, a three-year-old Pinto which she had just recently finished paying for. But almost immediately the ferret and his friend got to their feet, just as they had seen it done a thousand times before in *Gunsmokes* and John Wayne westerns and the bike flicks of their own adolescence, both of

143

them rising slowly, almost wearily, with the proper touch of macho resignation, knocking over a chair in the process, and then ponderously setting out across the no-man's land between them and the *enemy,* this freaky-looking one-eyed fag who for some incredible reason actually thought he could stare at them and get away with it.

As they reached the table Bone reflexively got up himself — he had no intention of having his head opened with a beer bottle — and he was relieved somewhat to see that he was bigger than either of them, though not as heavy as the fat one.

"Who the fuck you staring at?" the ferret demanded of Cutter.

Alex thought about it. "Let me guess. Ann-Margret?"

That seemed to cost the ferret his voice. For a few moments he just stood there gulping air and staring at Cutter. Then he turned to Bone.

"Look, what is it with this character, huh? He wanta get hurt, is that it? He wanta lose his other eye?"

Bone tried to appear calm, a shrink at a group therapy session of psychopaths. "Just take it easy," he said. "Don't waste your time on him. Come on, let's go over there. Maybe I can explain." He gestured toward the far end of the patio.

But Cutter would not quit. "Liberace? Roy Rogers?"

Valerie pleaded with him to shut up.

"That good advice, mama," the fat biker said.

Bone had started across the patio. "Come on, hear me out anyway," he said. "What can you lose? He ain't going anywhere."

The fat one, shrugging, started after Bone. And then the other followed, through tables that were largely empty now, most of the patrons having scurried inside at the first sign of trouble.

"Tiny Tim?" Cutter called over.

The ferret started to turn back, but his friend pulled him on.

144

"What can I tell you?" Bone told them. "He's just what he seems. He's bananas. And he's been that way ever since Vietnam. In one hospital or another all this time. He's out on a kind of leave right now, for just a week. I got to watch him like a hawk. He's always trying to kill himself."

"Well, he better be careful," the fat biker said. "Someone else do it for him."

"He wouldn't mind, believe me." Bone looked back at the table, where Cutter sat smiling pleasantly at them. "You notice the cane," he went on. "His legs are gone too. And he's got no control over his bowels or bladder. A one-eyed paraplegic who wants to kill himself — that's my brother, fellas. Or what's left of him anyway. What they gave back to us."

The ferret suddenly brought his fist crashing down on a table. "That fucking war!" he cried. "That dirty fucking war!"

The fat biker gave Bone a comradely slap on the arm. "No hassle, man," he said. "No sweat. We go inside."

"Thanks," Bone told him. "I appreciate it."

"Don't mention it."

After they had taken their drinks inside, Bone went back to the table and sat down.

"That was real cute," he said to Cutter. "In fact it was so cute, my friend, you just lost your point."

Through the rest of the afternoon Bone held to his decision to pull out of the Wolfe affair. He told Cutter that the thing was dangerous enough in itself without having to undertake it with a suicidal prankster as a partner. Cutter of course argued the matter with him, alternating between amused scorn and old-buddy cajolery, insisting that Bone was comparing apples with oranges, that the situations were entirely different. Just because Cutter might want to put on a couple of half-assed bike freaks here, now, in Santa Barbara, *before* the project began — well, that certainly didn't mean he would pull a similar stunt later, in L.A., when it counted, when the whistle had sounded and the game was on. Certainly Bone could see that, couldn't he?

As a matter of fact, he could not. In fact Bone had no trouble at all believing that someone who would pull the kind of stunt Cutter just had, on the weekend *before* going to L.A., with all their plans neatly spread out on a table before them — that kind of character, Bone said, would do just about anything, anytime, anywhere, just so long as it tickled his funnybone.

Valerie stayed out of it for the most part, probably because she found herself stranded somewhere between the two of them. She undoubtedly wanted to go ahead with the project, yet at the same time Bone felt she must have shared some of his doubts about Cutter's fitness for it. When Bone returned to the table, she almost had been in tears. And when the three of them left the tavern she was very quiet, reluctantly going with Cutter in the Packard, probably anticipating what a harrowing ride down the mountains it would be, a tossup between Cutter's heavy foot and the car's unreliable brakes, steering, and just about everything else. Bone, following in the pickup, three times watched them go off the twisting mountain road and then swerve back on so sharply that they went over the center line, and he could feel in his own body some of the tension Valerie had to be experiencing.

They finally made it, however, and Bone followed Cutter through town to the beach, where the three of them walked out to the end of the breakwater and skipped stones across the water toward the hundreds of small boats and yachts in the harbor. Then they went to Murdock's for a few more drinks, these at Bone's expense since Cutter claimed to have reached bottom again, already having gone through Swanson's "loan." The question of Bone's participation in the project came up only now and then, as Cutter would happen upon some new line of argument, and then when it would fail they would turn to other subjects, or even better, just sit back and listen to records, the pop stuff Cutter had ridiculed with Erickson and the black girl less than a week before. In essence then it was just another Alexander Cutter afternoon, a whitewater float with occasional stretches of calm. And along the way Bone learned a good deal more about Valerie.

Her father had "pulled a Boner," as Alex put it, running out on her mother when Valerie was still in grade school. For a time the mother had coped, working as a waitress at the Biltmore and doing what she could to find another husband, but as she pushed over forty and her looks began to go, she had turned more and more to liquor, and by sixteen Valerie found herself pretty much in charge of things, caring for her mother and keeping house and cooking and trying to raise her little sister, all while she was still going to high school. When she graduated, at seventeen, she was made pregnant by a handsome young Levi pants salesman, who graciously introduced her to the same abortionist who would later serve her sister. Soon after, her mother had her first nervous breakdown, requiring hospitalization and extensive psychotherapy, which in turn was followed by the loss of their home.

Meanwhile Valerie had begun her career with Coastal Insurance, working her way up to her present position as a customer service representative earning the princely sum of four hundred dollars a month, which did not begin to cover her family's living and medical expenses. And since her mother refused to apply for welfare — the "nigger-spic dole," as she called it — Valerie had to find added funds elsewhere. For a time she stole small amounts from the office-party kitty. But that of course was a doomed operation as well as petty. So one desperate Saturday night she put on her sexiest dress and drove down the coast to Oxnard, to a beach hotel–marina complex, where she sought out the poshest bar she could find and there settled in over martinis, alone. She made her first score within a half hour, an all-night trick that netted her as much as she earned all week at the insurance company. That was the first of many weekend trips, some to Los Angeles and even to San Francisco, but most of them to the same Oxnard bar. And always when she came home she would wind up asking herself the same question: "Why not full time? Why not make it while you can?"

The answer, she told them, was always the same:

"I couldn't bear to be a whore."

She laughed at that, a small dry laugh more like a cough than any show of merriment.

"Did your sister know?" Bone asked.

"I don't think so. She was gone so much herself. I think she probably figured I had a boyfriend."

"Which you did," Cutter put in. "Boy*friends*."

"And such *good* friends they were too. Real salt of the earth."

Bone finished his beer. "It explains a lot," he said.

"What does?"

"This. Your avocation. I wondered how Alex reached you."

"He didn't know."

"But he reached you nevertheless. And I wondered how. I mean, well, the girl *was* your sister. Most people in your position would've gone straight to the police with what he told you."

"I thought about it," she admitted. "But Alex said you'd never tell the police it was Wolfe. And if you did, they wouldn't do anything against a man like that."

"And then there was the money," Bone said.

"Yes. Then there was the money."

"It mattered."

"Sure. Just like it did for you."

Bone said nothing for a few moments. He already knew he was back in, probably had not even left in the first place, except as a ruse, a lesson for Cutter. "*Does*," he said. "It still does — depending on Alex."

148

Cutter gave him a questioning look. "On what?"

"On whether you do me a favor."

A half hour later, after picking up a couple of pizzas on the way, the three of them arrived at Cutter's house, where Alex was to meet Bone's price for staying on the project.

"It's not much," Bone had told him. "I just want you to let Mo in on the thing, tell her what we're doing and why."

Cutter's reaction had been a shrug. "Why not? I can tell you now, though, she won't want any part of it. If bread mattered to her, all she's gotta do is lift the phone and dial Mama down in Beverly Hills. But then she won't interfere either, 'cause she is mah woman. What Alex wants, Alex gets."

Bone did not expect her to join them either. In fact he would pull out if she did. But he did want her to *know*. He wanted to give her that anyway.

George Swanson's Jaguar was parked out in front, so they expected to find him inside, though not in the kitchen wearing an apron and washing dishes while Mo sat watching him from the table, her feet propped on top of it while she nursed a jelly jar half filled with what appeared to be cold duck. Under the table the baby was contentedly banging a ladle against a saucepan.

With his usual grace, Cutter introduced Valerie. "This here's Val. We just picked her up on the highway." Then, opening the pizzas, he told George to sit down and have a bite with them but that he'd have to leave after that because they were going to have an orgy and that, as he well knew, five was a crowd. If the baby interested him, well then he might be able to stay, it was up to him, but Cutter couldn't guarantee anything, as George could see, because the little fellow was already happily occupied with a six-inch spoon and might not want to fool around with anything half that size. Swanson came up with the required laugh and then begged off, saying that pizza and beer did not fit in with his diet and that he had to be leaving anyway, his wife expected him home for dinner, and that he had already gotten "everything I ever dared hope for." With this last, he winked at Mo, who sat watching all of them with her usual torpid gaze and the light trace of smile, the imperfectly dissembled contempt. Swanson also said a few words about the night before, how sorry he was at what had happened and that his house was always open to Bone, and Bone slipped past it with a nod and smile, not wanting to blow the matter up large enough for Alex to take an interest in it.

Valerie meanwhile sat delicately eating her pizza, unsure of herself in this new milieu, with its damp firework display going on all about her. Even after Swanson had left and the four of them settled in to finish the pizza, the girl did not unbend. She was better dressed than Mo, wearing a white blouse and beads and checkered slacks in contrast to Mo's chinos and sweatshirt. Yet she seemed tacky in comparison, and Bone wondered if this was simply in his own eye, the eye of a biased beholder, or whether it came from the girl herself, that she *felt* tacky confronted with Mo's thoughtless ease, that Beverly Hills and eastern school background that somehow authorized her to sit where she was behind the table all this time, not bothering to move or welcome Valerie or even talk to her until now, and in a voice that only added to the effect, its clean heedless timbre in some way yet another badge of old privilege.

"I'm sorry about your sister," she said. "It was a terrible thing to happen."

Considering Cutter's flip introduction of Valerie, Bone was surprised that Mo knew who the girl was. And apparently she also knew that Cutter had been spending most of his time with her, for there was a marked coolness in the way she sat looking at the girl, at all of them for that matter. So it was an awkward meal. While the three of them cleaned up the pizza, Mo just sat there sipping her cold duck and going through Pall Malls as if they were beads on a rosary. Finally Cutter started to tell her something but she cut him off, getting up from the table and saying it was time to feed the baby.

Cutter made a pot of his incredible coffee then — instant grind dumped unmeasured into warm tap water — and the three of them went into the living room and sat down around the boat hatch. There did not seem to be anything to say. Valerie picked up an old copy of *Penthouse* and sat looking at the nudes while Cutter and Bone waited for Mo.

When she came in finally, carrying a new glass of wine and a freshly lit cigarette, she asked what was going on. "Are we having a wake?"

Then, looking at Valerie, she caught herself. "I'm sorry. I wasn't thinking. Just putting my foot in my mouth as usual."

"It's all right," Valerie said. "I didn't even connect it."

Cutter was giving them his pontifical gesture. "Peace, my children," he said. "I have a duty to perform."

"Not in here," Mo suggested.

"Funny girl. No, sweetheart, this is for here. For you."

Mo faked a shiver. "I'm so excited."

"You remember our little talk the other night? With Rich about this Wolfe character and what I'd found out?"

"Vaguely. I do remember something about your parking the car that night, some difficulties you were having. And some conjugal complaints later."

Cutter, going along with her, smiled pleasantly. "That's the very night, my dear. Well, since then, you might say things have crystallized. Val and Rich are with me now. I mean we all figure it was Wolfe who killed Val's sister. And we're going to get in touch with him. We're going to try to blackmail him. If he pays, then we've got him by the testes. We can go to the fuzz."

Mo said nothing, just sat there looking at him as if his nose were turning into a carrot.

"Telling you was Rich's idea," Cutter went on. "I figured it'd be better to wait, tell you all about it afterward. Simplify things."

"Oh, of course. Of course." Mo smiled at Bone now. "But I do thank you for your consideration, Richard. You're a gentleman and something else, I'm sure."

"You're welcome, Mo."

And now she let it out, the laughter, about even parts amusement and scorn. "Now let me get this straight," she said. "You're all going to try to blackmail this J. J. Wolfe for killing her sister." And she nodded at Valerie here, smiled, as if they were all discussing Tupperware. "And if the man pays, then you're going to turn him over to the law — along with the money."

"That's our plan, yes," Valerie said.

"I see." Smiling still, Mo turned to Cutter. "This is insulting, Alex. I mean, do you really expect me to buy such horseshit? You're scraping bottom lately, you know that? You're becoming a jerk. A pitiful jerk."

Cutter shrugged. "If you say so."

"I say so."

Valerie broke in again. "It could work out just as he said. I know that's what I want anyway — I mean, to turn the money in and convict Wolfe."

Mo gave her a rueful look. "Oh, go take a flying leap, will you?"

Cutter clucked his tongue. "Now don't get abusive, love."

"*Abusive!*" Mo laughed again. "How in hell could anyone abuse the three of you — a kinky little band of would-be extortionists."

Cutter shook his head in mock sadness, as if he were being put upon by some ill-mannered child. But Bone could see the anger rising in him.

"I think maybe you're forgetting a few things," Cutter said to Mo. "Valerie here just did happen to lose a sister, you recall that little fact? And if Wolfe is the one who killed her — which we got good reason to believe — then I say whatever we or anybody else does to him comes under the heading of justice, that's all, pure and simple justice."

But Mo would not back off. "Oh sure, Alex. You tell 'em, kid. Talk about newspeak — you're becoming a real past master, you know that? Nixon could've used you in the White House. You and Ron Ziegler. By now all the old words would be *inoperative*. Not only justice but truth too. And pride. Honor. You remember any of those?"

Cutter frowned. "I try, Mother. I really do."

"And how about guts?"

"You know a lot about guts, do you?"

"You bet I do. Guts is sitting around this pigsty month after month waiting for you to find the nerve to start living again. And instead, here you are, planning some stupid crime." She laughed bitterly. "God, I am some princess. I kiss a toad long enough, he turns into a snake."

Cutter was pale with anger. He started to say something, but Valerie broke in.

"Well, I don't see much purpose in any of this." She got to her feet. "I think I'll be leaving."

"You're one very cool customer, aren't you?" Mo said to her. "Your sister is, what, two days in the ground? And here you are already trying to cash in."

"We said we're not going to *keep* the money," Valerie told her. "We're —"

"Oh, come off it. Give me that much credit anyway."

Moving toward the door, Valerie shot Bone an urgent look. "It's getting late," she said.

"All this was Big Dick's idea anyway," Cutter was saying, turning to Bone now. "You're the one wanted to tell mama all about it, right? So speak up, man. Defend the faith."

Bone shook his head. "I've got nothing to say."

Again Mo laughed, this time almost with enjoyment. "Of course not. And why should he? All this is pretty much in

153

character for him. And I can buy that. At least he doesn't go mooning around, crying over the great might-have-been. And neither does he mock and vilify every poor bastard who crosses his path."

Cutter had already put his drink down. And very carefully now he limped over to Mo and slapped her hard in the face. Immediately Bone was on his feet and across the room, seizing Alex's wrist before he could hit her again.

"I wouldn't," he told him.

Cutter was trembling. "Gets to you, does it?"

Bone ignored him. "You all right?" he asked Mo.

Her eyes were dry, furious. "Oh, beat it, will you? You think this is the first time?"

He turned to Cutter. "Make it the last, Alex."

Cutter tried to pull his arm free. Failing, he smiled thinly. "Why not?" he said. "Why the fucking hell not?"

On the way back to Montecito, Bone dropped Valerie off at her home, a small rented bungalow near the freeway. Beyond giving him directions, she did not utter a word all the way there. But as he pulled up to the curb and she opened the truck door, preparing to get out, she turned back to him.

"It'll work out," she said. "I know it will."

"Why?"

"Because it has to."

"I'll try to remember that."

"I'm not joking — it *will* work out."

"Because it has to."

"Yes."

Bone said he hoped she was right and she smiled then, a small bereft smile. He watched as she got out and hurried toward the tiny frame house.

Later, after he had quietly parked the pickup truck in Mrs. Little's garage and then even more quietly walked to his room and entered, he found a new pair of men's bikini swim trunks

154

on his bed, with a gift card bearing a message written in lavender ink:

How about a midnight swim?

And Bone found himself almost convinced that Valerie was right. It would all work out. It had to.

7

IF BONE LEARNED ANYTHING AT ALL IN HIGH SCHOOL IT WAS THE importance of initial decisions, those casual first steps that could effortlessly lead to a second step and then a third and before one knew it had locked him into some miserable marathon without end. It was a lesson he learned best of all in freshman track, a sport he was really not all that interested in and probably would not even have gone out for if it had not been for the urging of his father, who had earned his only varsity letter as a member of the mile relay team back in the good old Jim Crow days when white boys only had to run against other white boys. So Bone had gone along, had suited up and run with the rest of the hopefuls, not very fast actually, just trying to stay with the crowd, that was all. But for some reason the coach had liked his stride and had singled him out: "You, Bone — think you could run the mile?" And Bone, indifferent, had shrugged: "Sure. Why not?"

Over the next four years he was to learn why not, as he endured the pain of the daily five-mile grind just to stay in shape and then the heightened suffering of the clocked runs and finally the races themselves, the true crucibles of agony, as he pared his time from five minutes down to four-thirty and finally a four-nineteen that made him feel as if his heart had beaten him to death.

But Bone learned his lesson. One did not volunteer. One did

not shrug and go along. One bit one's tongue and watched carefully and made the big moves, the initial moves, as if one's life depended on it. Because it so often did. So he did not go out for college track. Nor did he meekly submit to his Selective Service draft notice, any more than he would have volunteered for the marines. Instead he spent the Vietnam years going to college and being married and having children and rising in a competitive business. And similarly his renunciation of all that these last years was in its way yet another cautionary move — one could lose his life selling paper in Milwaukee just as surely as he could shooting gooks in Vietnam.

So Bone was not feeling very happy late Monday morning as Valerie drove him and Cutter in her small Pinto back and forth on the streets above Hollywood Boulevard near La Brea. Time and again they turned onto Unicorn and drove past the elegant old five-story one-time apartment building that now served as the West Coast office of Wolfe Enterprises, Inc., and each time they did so Bone had the uncomfortable feeling that he was a kid again, a stupid cocky kid who had just been asked if he could run the mile and had answered *Sure, why not?* — to Coach Cutter sitting in the back seat, leaning forward between him and Valerie and darkening the air with the reek of his breakfast pancakes, ham, and scrambled eggs, already going sour in his stomach in the heady excitement of the morning.

"The whole top floor's Wolfe's apartment," he was saying. "*Time* says he spent a couple hundred thou having it redone to suit him. He's a maniac for gadgetry, sort of an Ozark Hugh Hefner. Push a button and there's a waterfall. Or a belly dancer. Or pickled pig's feet."

Bone muttered his misgivings. "Goddamn place looks like it'd be easier to see Howard Hughes."

"If you'd seen Hughes do what this cat did, you'd be able to get an interview with him, believe me."

"You're so positive these days, Alex."

"What's the matter, you got the shakes?"

"Let's just say I wish it was over."

Valerie gave Bone a reassuring smile. "It will be, before you know it."

"Yeah, I know. Just waltz in and make my spiel. Uh, miss, I'm here to blackmail your boss — who do I see?"

But Cutter was in no mood for comedy now. "Bullshit, Richard — you've got it cold. Nothing could be simpler. You just do it the way we practiced, that's all. In ten minutes you'll be home free."

Sure, Bone thought. Just do it the way we practiced. The place of practice had been their ninth-floor room at the Sheraton-Universal, a hotel Cutter had chosen because an old college chum of his was now a Sheraton vice-president and according to him might come in handy if and when any problems developed regarding Valerie's Master Charge card, which the three of them were using to finance what they could of this initial part of the operation. The most likely problem of course was that someone at the hotel would run a credit check on her and set a low limit on her card, which would force the three of them to fall back on the six hundred dollars she had borrowed on her car. The room rate alone was thirty-eight dollars a day; four rounds of drinks last night at the poolside bar had come to twenty-three dollars; and thanks largely to Cutter's increasingly go-for-broke attitude, even breakfast at the coffee shop this morning had totaled ten-fifty. At that rate, and if it took more than a few days to make contact with Wolfe, Bone figured Valerie would stand a fair chance of ending up in bankruptcy court, a prospect that apparently had occurred to her as well, for she had not shared Cutter's almost festive attitude last night in the hotel room.

After changing into pajamas in the bathroom, she had come out and pulled back the covers on one of the double beds. But before she could settle in, Cutter said he wanted a practice session, "a war game," as he put it. Pulling the room's small desk out from the wall, he told Valerie to sit behind it.

"And remember," he told her, "you're not some measly small-town insurance clerk. You're a Hollywood receptionist — which means you've got at least two years of high school behind you, you don't snap your gum between nine and five, and you know all about handy purse-size douches. Above all, you've learned how to talk high class, with that kind of cool sexy hauteur, you know? Like this — 'Anymore, there just ain't nothing left between he and I.' You got that, Val? You think you could manage that?"

She was giving Bone a pained look, recognition of what they both were in for.

"You think you could?" Cutter persisted.

"I can try."

"Okay then. Now you're going to have to use your imagination here, as I come through the front door," he told her. "I walk tall and straight, you see, with an air of easy authority. And my eyes are Paul Newman blue, my smile dazzles. I have this very special look that combines a sort of knowledgeable self-confidence with a certain physicality, you know? Like, say, a billy goat in rut."

Bone lit a cigarette. "Get on with it, for Christ sake."

Cutter nodded grimly. "You're right, Rich — this ain't no laughing matter. It's business. So let us proceed. You enter the building, the reception room, and the girl of course takes you in. You look okay personally, physically, but not exactly *successful*, you know? I mean, well, your clothes aren't exactly today, are they? More like yesterday, or even the day before. So the girl's probably gonna be a touch cool. You cross over to her —" Here, Cutter gestured to Valerie, who shrugged.

"Good morning?" she tried.

Cutter shook his head. "Jesus, you are really with it."

"Well, how do I know what you want me to say?"

"All right, then. I'll play both parts."

Valerie got up from the desk. "That I can live with."

Cutter ignored her. "Okay, Rich — you go up to the girl and

the two of you say good morning or up yours or whatever. She then asks what she can do for you, and you tell her the truth, straight out. 'My name is Bone. Richard Bone. And I know this may sound a little unusual, but I came here to see Mr. Wolfe. I *have* to see Mr. Wolfe.' She asks if you've got an appointment and of course you got to say no, at which point she starts the brush-off routine. And that's when you've got to move in close. You draw up a chair, say, and give her the old eyeball whammy. 'It's a very personal matter,' you tell her. 'A very crucial matter. And all I can say is it concerns the night Mr. Wolfe's car was firebombed in Santa Barbara — and that he'll be very grateful to hear what I have to tell him. But it has to come from me personally. No intermediaries. Now I can tell other people — his assistants and so forth — I can tell them this same story, just what I'm telling you. But that's *all*. The information I have for Mr. Wolfe, I have to lay it on him alone. Just the two of us. No other way.' "

Cutter evidently felt he was doing a pretty good job, for he smiled grudgingly, as if in approval of someone else's performance.

"By now, you got the girl by the short hairs," he went on. "But she'll try a cop-out, give you the no-authority bit, tell you all she can do is call her boss, old Miss Iron Crotch, and let her handle it. Then you just slide this one in on her — you say, 'Well, you do what you have to, miss, but I can guarantee you the Great Man ain't gonna be happy if very many people are let in on this. My advice to you is to go as high as you can with it, over as many heads as possible.' You put the fear of God into her, and she'll come up with someone above Iron Crotch — probably young Mr. Whozit. And you say, 'Fine, call him.' "

And so it went. Without bothering to come down, Cutter then winged it through the interview Bone would have with Whozit, and then Whozit's boss, that person or point where Bone would realize he had gone as far as he could go verbally and now would have to give them the typewritten note addressed to Wolfe and marked *personal*, but which Cutter expected to be opened and read by an intermediary, though of course without the fullness of comprehension Wolfe alone would bring to it. The note read:

> Dear Mr. Wolfe:
> You may recall reading in the newspaper that on the night your car was firebombed in Santa Barbara, a man was witness to another crime in another part of the city. I am that man.
>
> I have vital information for you — and you alone. At three o'clock this afternoon (Monday, April 7) I will phone your office to arrange a personal meeting between us. Be advised that time is of the essence.
>
> RICHARD K. BONE, *witness*

In time Cutter closed his one-man show. And Bone, taking a pillow and cover down onto the floor, told him not to be offended but he didn't sleep with fellas. Cutter in turn said that it was just as well because his hemorrhoids had been acting up lately. Valerie gave them both a despairing look and again went into the bathroom — she had been drinking Tom Collinses down at the bar. But when she opened the door to come out, Cutter crowded her back in and locked the door behind them, and Bone expected to hear nothing then except heavy breathing. Instead he heard an argument, Valerie quietly shouting for Alex to take his goddamn hands off her while Cutter's voice, bored and exasperated, kept up a steady "Aw, c'mon, c'mon." And finally there was a light crash against the wall and the sound of a plastic cup striking the floor and bouncing. Valerie came out and got into her bed. Cutter emerged a few moments later. Dropping into the other bed, he explained things to Bone.

"She's got a sick headache." Then he added, "Goodnight, all."

For almost an hour Bone lay awake on the floor. And when he finally did drop off, all he found was a few hours of shallow sleep that ended around four in the morning. He got up and went out onto the narrow balcony to smoke a cigarette and watch the traffic on the freeway, the endless headlights streaming endlessly past, even at this unlikely hour of the night.

He had been there only a few minutes when the drapes behind him parted and Valerie came out, with a sheet wrapped around her.

"Can't sleep?" she asked.

"I guess not."

"Worried?"

"Shouldn't I be?"

"I don't know. It all seems safe enough to me."

"Maybe I'm the worrying kind."

"No. You're the one who'll be going in — 'the point,' as Alex says."

"He ought to know."

"I'm sorry about that earlier."

"About what?"

"In the bathroom. Alex doesn't like no for an answer."

"Who does?"

For a while she just stood there looking at him and shivering on their little promontory above the city.

"I wish you liked me better," she said finally.

"I like you fine."

"No, you think I'm hard and hungry — which I guess I am."

"And I'm such a paragon? Someone to sit in judgment?"

"No, I know you don't. Still, you must wonder. I mean, Pam *was* my sister, my flesh and blood. And she hasn't even been dead a week, yet here I am, like Mo said, trying to cash in."

"You've got your reasons."

"I know. But still, it's kind of odd. I mean when I try to look at it straight and honest, I have to admit I don't feel much of anything. About Pam, I mean. Her death. It's almost as if it'd happened to some other kid, someone in the newspaper, and all I feel is the usual vague outrage and anger because of all the creeps in the world. But that's all. Nothing important. Nothing like grief. No real pain."

"Maybe you weren't close."

"That's what I mean. We weren't. No more than my mother and I are. And I have this terrible feeling sometimes that we're not all that exceptional, that almost everyone I know, and others I watch in public, the families, I mean, that they're just people who live together, you know? And don't give a damn about each other."

Bone thought of Milwaukee and his own budding band of strangers. "You could be right," was all he said.

"Why is it like that, Rich? Are we all sick or something?"

Bone did not particularly like the subject, especially at four in the morning, and on this day. "What do you take me for?" he asked. "A wise man?"

"Sometimes."

"Sure. And I come bearing frankincense and myrrh."

"Don't put yourself down."

"Was I?"

"I get that feeling. And I think I know why. Because you're ashamed. You really don't want any part of this, do you?"

"I'm here."

"In body anyway."

"In spirit too. If we score, and you and Alex decide to keep the money, I'll be right there with my hand out."

"But you don't like the idea."

"I like it fine."

"And will we score?"

"You tell me."

"Are you thinking it wasn't him now?"

Bone shook his head. "No, that hasn't changed. I still have

this *feeling* it was him. But nothing more. I still couldn't swear to it, not in court."

"We have a chance then."

"And a chance to put our asses in a wringer."

"You want out?"

Bone did not answer. He took one last drag on his cigarette and ground it out against the steel railing of the balcony.

"You're pretty tight," she said.

"You noticed."

"Can I do anything for you?"

He turned to look at her, to see if he had read her right, but in the darkness her eyes gave him nothing save the light of the cars down below, bright blips darting across her gaze.

"Like what?" he said.

"Can I relax you?"

"You sure Alex would like that?"

"He's asleep."

"Never for long."

She shrugged. "I'm not his girl. I'm a hooker, remember? Li'l old weekend hooker, me."

Bone could already feel the excitement beginning in him, but for some reason he felt compelled to resist it. He shook his head. "Maybe you're not his girl. But then, maybe he thinks you are."

"So what? What does that matter?"

"I guess it matters to me." Bone did not expect her to accept the rejection gracefully, nevertheless he was surprised at how her mouth twisted in anger now, even hatred.

"Whatever you say," she snapped.

Then she went back inside. And only moments later Bone heard Cutter's voice, a grunt of irritation at being awakened, followed by soft laughter and whispering and then the slowly building other sounds of sex.

But all that was in the past now, irrelevant to the deepening sense of dread Bone felt as Cutter directed Valerie to pull over to the curb. Wolfe's office building was across the street, in the next block.

Cutter clapped him on the back. "Well it's about that time, Rich. What our sergeant used to call the wet-ass hour."

"You're a big help." Bone opened the door.

"It'll go fine," Valerie said. "You'll do fine."

Bone did not respond. Getting out, he went around the car and across the street, heading along the sidewalk toward the white stone building in the next block. And it seemed that every step he took only intensified his feeling of dread, as if he were setting out on a cinder track without end.

Opening the heavy glass and stainless steel front door, he entered the glacial air of the reception room. And nothing was as he had expected. The man who bought ready-made suits off the rack at his own discount houses showed no similar lack of taste here. The decor was contemporary, but so beautifully and expensively done that the room had an almost antique ambience, dark and quiet and restful despite the huge nonobjective paintings and art objects and the indirect lighting and sleek modern furniture, most of it made of leather and brushed wood. And it was an ambience the receptionist only reinforced, no teeny-bopper pretending at hauteur but a gray-haired woman of fifty or so, well groomed and intelligent-looking, with a soft voice and a trace of English accent. At the moment she was with a young man who would have looked more at home at Hollywood and Vine, with his long hair and suede jacket and cord slacks and Dingo boots. But he did have a briefcase, and also some sort of problem, which gave Bone time to wander over to a wall display across the room. It was very handsomely done, wood-framed and discreet, obviously the interior decorator's solution to one of his client's more gauche demands. For it was quite simply a celebration of J. J. Wolfe, the man and his empire. There was an arrangement of photographs, all in sepia tone, some of them real Kodak box-camera antiques showing Wolfe as a kid on his Ozark farm and as the teenage businessman carrying a crate of eggs. And there was the first supermarket; the first discount house; Wolfe pushing the button to start the feed rolling in an automated cattle feedyard; Wolfe piloting a jet; Wolfe and his family grouped around a champion Angus bull at a Denver show. Next to the photographs was a three-dimensional graph, a kind of inverted family tree showing how the Wolfe empire was structured, flowing from the single entity at the top, the man himself, down into the stout tree trunk of Wolfe Enterprises, Incorporated, which in turn put out a series of heavy branches, corporations that owned corporations that owned corporations, and oddly it was only at the far reaches of the tree, the small single leaves, that the words meant anything, were in fact true household names in American business, flabby venerable giants that had been gobbled by the upstart Wolfe.

"May I help you, sir?"

The receptionist, alone now, was speaking to him from across the room.

"Yes," Bone said. "I was to meet a friend here. He said he had some business upstairs, and when he was finished he would wait here for me."

She smiled warmly. "I see. And his name?"

"Alexander Five."

"Five?"

"Yes — same as the number."

"That's one you'd think I'd remember." She was scanning an appointments list. "But I don't. And — no, he isn't here. I'm afraid I don't have any record of him. Are you sure this is the right address?"

"The Wolfe building, he said. Yes."

"I see. Well, perhaps if you gave me your name."

"George Swanson."

Once more she scanned her appointments list.

"I don't think you'll find me there either," he said.

"No, I don't suppose." She smiled again. "I guess about all

166

we can do then is wait. If you want to wait here, it's perfectly all right."

"Thank you. Maybe five minutes or so."

"Of course. There are some magazines over there."

She indicated a davenport and coffee table near the front door, the *glass* front door beyond which Valerie and Cutter would be driving past every few minutes.

"Forgot my glasses," he said. "I'll just wait over here."

"Fine."

At some distance from the door, Bone angled his long body into a soft short-backed chair. Under his clothes — the new checked shirt and the navy blazer and gray slacks — his body was slick with sweat. But he felt fine, he felt free, as if someone had just rolled a gravestone off his chest. Until the moment he opened his mouth and actually spoke to the woman, he had not known what he was going to say or do, whether he would run from the thing or stand his ground with Cutter like some poor terrified rabbit freezing on a highway. He felt no shame at all, nothing except relief and a hearty dose of self-disgust, anger at what an ass he had been, what a fool. Hadn't he known Cutter well enough to recognize all this for what it was, simply one more of his self-destructive gambits? What did it matter if some sixth or seventh sense told Bone that Wolfe *probably* was the man he had seen that night? In fact what did it matter even if the man slaughtered and dumped a teenage girl in every city he ever visited? It was all beside the point — which, very simply, now and forevermore, was *power*. And power was the inverted tree across the room. It was the building enclosing Bone and the network of similar buildings spread across the whole amber-waved continent. It was money, finally, big money. And the fact that Bone had temporarily ignored this cardinal fact of life, for a time had dreamed with Cutter his bizarre little dream of affluence and independence — well, better late than never.

So Bone felt no guilt for what he had done, or more accurately, not done. He had backed out at this late moment not just to save his skin but theirs too, Cutter's and Valerie's. And he was sure Valerie at least would see the truth of this if she could have been with him now, here at the "point," Cutter's vaunted Purple Heartland. Yes, Valerie might understand and go along. But Cutter? Not likely. No, Bone would have to let him down slowly, like a canister of nitroglycerine.

Because Cutter had expected someone to follow Bone, he had instructed Valerie to park the car just off Unicorn, two blocks from the building. Thus a few seconds after Bone rounded the corner — and was temporarily lost sight of by his hypothetical pursuers — he could slip into the car and be gone, the three of them in the Pinto quickly disappearing in the La Brea traffic. And except for any pursuers, that was just how it happened. For fifteen or twenty seconds neither Cutter nor Valerie said a word to him. Cutter was busy staring out the rear window for any sign of a "tail" while Valerie frantically worked the car down the narrow off-street and onto La Brea.

Finally Cutter wheeled from his post: "Well?"

Bone shrugged. "Who knows?"

"What the hell does that mean? Come on, what happened, man?"

"Your Mr. Whozit turned out to be an administrative assistant name of Price. Very swishy. And very bored. Acted like what I was really after was a job."

"Couldn't you go over him?"

Bone lit a cigarette, taking his time, making clear his feelings of anger and disappointment. "Mr. Price reports to Mr. Brown, who reports to Mr. Hudson." This last name Bone stole from a street sign as they were moving along Hollywood Boulevard now.

"You mean the thing has to go through two more people!" Cutter bawled. "Before it gets to Wolfe!"

Bone nodded. "That's the way it's done, old buddy. If you'd

ever worked a day in your life you'd know that. The old organization chart. You go over your boss's head, and he'll have yours. On a platter."

Cutter sagged into the back seat. Valerie, weaving through the traffic, took the time to glance over at Bone, and her look was not worried so much as searching, trying to read him. Quickly Bone threw out a bit of lifeline:

"We did get one break, though — Brown and Hudson weren't there this morning. So I really put it to the fairy. I told him the message was just what it said on the envelope — personal — that it had to do with something Wolfe was *personally* involved in up in Santa Barbara, and I could guarantee him Wolfe wouldn't like it if the matter went through two other men."

Cutter was sitting up again. "Good boy."

"I even laid the old office jargon on him — I said it was his big chance to make Brownie points with the old man."

"What'd he say to that?"

"He asked how he could be sure the thing wasn't a letter bomb — that's one we didn't anticipate, huh? I suggested he get one of his own envelopes and I'd take the note out of ours and put it in his."

"Did he?"

"No, he took my word for it. I told him letter bombs wer ﹥ fat, which I think they are. Anyway he's our man. If we get through to Wolfe today, or if we don't — it's up to him."

Cutter was definitely in the ascent now. "Well, Christ, Rich, that's all we expected, wasn't it? A foot in the door. The note'll do the rest."

Bone shook his head. "I don't know. I didn't like how the guy came on, so goddamn condescending."

"Well, he doesn't sound like a loner anyway," Valerie put in. "Like he'd take it on himself to censor the boss's mail."

"Or run upstairs with it," Bone countered. "It cuts both ways."

In answer Cutter belched luxuriously, giving them the ghost of his breakfast again. And he began to pound Bone on the back.

"Come on, come on!" he laughed. "Get with it, will you, man? You did it! We're in like Flynn, for Christ sake! Face it! You did it!"

"You think so, huh?"

"I know so."

"No, you don't. We won't know till I call back at three."

"So we'll know then."

"And I told him it'd have to be Wolfe, I wouldn't talk to anyone else."

Cutter took a bow. "Just like we rehearsed."

But Valerie, as she drove on, had a puzzled look. "I still don't see why we have to get through to him today. Why not tomorrow or the next day? It's the same message. The same situation."

Clucking his tongue, Cutter took hold of Valerie's cheek and playfully began to shake her head back and forth. "Bad little Valerie," he said. "Stupid little Valerie. She should try to remember each day that passeth means that many more people get into the act — secretaries, vice-presidents, janitors. And that don't leave Mr. Conglomerate much choice except to stonewall it, like his ex–commander in chief. Only in this case stonewalling would mean calling in the fuzz. The man. You dig?"

Valerie, looking angry, pulled her cheek free. "Yes! All right — I dig!"

Cutter checked his watch. "Eleven-ten," he announced. "Four hours to kill."

Following Cutter's lead, they killed the hours in style. They had some drinks at a dark comfortable steakhouse bar near their hotel, then ordered a round of New York–cut steak "sandwiches" at seven dollars each, altogether diminishing

Valerie's estate by another thirty dollars. Then, back at the hotel, Cutter decided that they should take advantage of the weather, which was clear and warm, and go down to the pool for a swim.

"And maybe I'll just go in too," he said. "Can you picture it? I come gimping out there, maybe coughing a little to add to the general effect. And then I carefully take off my robe and test the water — with my stump!" At this he flapped his left arm, what was left of it. "And zap! Everybody's up and running, like it's starting to rain turds."

"Very funny," Valerie said. "Very sick."

"Okay then. Just you two go. I'll watch."

She told him they had not brought swimsuits.

But Cutter was undaunted. "Just leave that to me."

More to humor him than anything else, Bone and Valerie went along, following him downstairs and into a clothing shop located at one end of the lobby. Like the gift and sundries stores on each side of it, the shop was small, understocked, and overpriced. In the elevator Cutter had told the two of them what the object was, to get a pair of swimsuits without surrendering any cash. They were to pick out the swimsuits and he was to do the talking. And talk he did, hitting Bone with a dry toneless monologue that started the moment they entered the shop and continued uninterrupted as Bone and Valerie examined the swimsuits offered, held them up against their bodies and quietly discussed their merits and prices with each other and the sales clerk, a lady who seemed to think she was Greer Garson.

Cutter had had a bellyful of the cattle operation, that was all there was to it. The goddamn thing simply had to go, he said. He had put up with it long enough, each year expecting the thing would take hold and show a little profit, but no dice, the operation was a loser pure and simple and the sooner they realized it the better. And he didn't give a good goddamn what the price of red meat was, he was simply going to unload the herd no matter what. Hell, the Ojai avocado ranch had half as many acres, didn't it, and you sure as hell couldn't call the profit it produced small change now, could you? And as far as that went, just one well in the Marshall field — just one, mind you, not twenty or fifty — just one of their lousy little wells there produced more long green in one year than that whole cattle operation had managed in ten. And, oh sure, he knew it was a good tax loss and all, but what the hell — *ten years* as a tax loss? That was carrying things a bit far. No, the whole lousy setup had to go, he had made up his mind and there was no talking him out of it. The ranch hands, well he was sorry about them but what the hell did Bone think he was, a welfare state? Let them eat food stamps.

And so it went. Bone and Valerie chose their swimsuits, and Greer Garson happily bagged them and wrote up the sales ticket, which Cutter grandly snatched away from Bone. "Here, let me get this — you got lunch." And then he began to pat his pockets, searching for his wallet — which, alas, was not there but probably still up in his room — he would forget his leg if it weren't attached to his body, a joke the lady seemed to miss. Would she let him charge the bill to his hotel account? Of course, she would. So he whipped out his nineteen-cent Bic pen and signed the check, carelessly scrawled his name across it, from the bottom to the top: *Valerie Durant*. Miss Garson, probably a touch impressed, graciously thanked him, and the three of them left.

The pool was situated in a large courtyard bordered on one side by the high-rise part of the hotel and on the other sides by a two-story structure housing cabana rooms and the pool bar. Throughout the courtyard there were real palm trees and other flora not likely to be found in Peoria, which Bone believed to be the main criterion for any successful Southern California tourist enterprise. But now, in April, the pool was deserted except for a few sunbathers like Bone and Valerie, who had stretched out on a pair of chaise longues next to the umbrella table where Cutter sat sipping a scotch-and-water. And he evidently was feeling the pressure as keenly as Bone, for there was no more talking now, no more hijinks and yeasty self-confidence, no more counting of Wolfe's dollars before they were extorted. But where Cutter undoubtedly had run up against a real anxiety, the anxiety of not knowing what lay immediately ahead, Bone's only problem was technical, *how* to bring about that very situation which his colleague dreaded.

The more he thought about it, however, he could not see any real problem beyond that of the telephone call, making sure Cutter could not overhear what was said at the other end of the line. So Bone would have to resist any last-minute reck-lessness on Cutter's part, any suggestion that they call from their room instead of from a pay phone and thus enable him and possibly Valerie too to crowd in close and try to hear what was being said at the other end. Bone would have to insist that they stick to their plan and call from a pay phone, ostensibly to keep anyone from tracing the call to them. The phone booths in the hotel lobby would be a logical choice. Bone could not see even Cutter wanting to crowd into one of those with him, not with scores of people looking on. And if he tried — well, Bone would simply push him out. The call was his to make. He after all was the "contact," the man out there alone on point.

As for what he would say to Wolfe's switchboard operator, that was no problem. He would not even listen to her, just go on with his side of the conversation, give Cutter at least that much to overhear. He considered dialing the time or the weather but decided it would not be worth the risk. If Alex caught on, everything would hit the fan.

As he lay there thinking, Bone could feel the sun slipping through the trees. Once Cutter got up and went into the bar for a refill and Valerie immediately turned her head toward Bone, as if she were going to say something. But he did not look at her and after a few seconds she settled back again.

Cutter returned and worked on his new drink for a time. Then he pushed back his chair and got up.

"Fourteen-thirty hours, kiddies," he said. "Two-toity to youse. Zero hour draws nigh."

Squinting, Bone stood up. "So it does."

A half hour later they were dressed and in the lobby. Valerie, looking ill with anxiety, sank rigidly onto a davenport and sat watching Bone and Cutter as they crossed over to the row of telephone booths, only one of which was occupied. Entering the last booth in the row, Bone got out a dime, inserted it, and dialed the number of Wolfe Enterprises, Incorporated — while Cutter stood not two feet away, leaning against the open folding door, his lesioned face drawn with tension.

Bone was relieved to hear the voice that answered the phone now, a woman's voice, but not that of the receptionist he had spoken with earlier.

"My name is Richard Bone," he said. "Mr. Wolfe is expecting a call from me."

The voice said "One moment please," and he was switched to another line, another female voice, this one announcing, "Mr. Wolfe's office."

And for the second time that day Bone felt sweat slicking down his spine. He repeated his message. The woman said she had no record of the expected call. Mr. Wolfe was in conference.

"I spoke with a Mr. Price this morning," Bone told her. "I gave him an urgent message for Mr. Wolfe. And he said —"

The woman interrupted: she did not know of any Mr. Price. But Bone pushed on, as if he had not heard her.

"Yes — Mr. Price. He assured me the message would be given to Mr. Wolfe and that —"

Again the woman interrupted, her voice clipped now, cold. There was no Mr. Price, no one in the building by that name.

"All right, I'll wait," Bone put in. "Yeah, check with him. Do that." He covered the mouthpiece of the phone.

"Wolfe's secretary," he said, shaking his head. "Doesn't know anything about me calling. Wolfe didn't tell her a goddamn thing. She's checking with Price now."

Cutter had begun to pound his fist helplessly against the door frame. "I knew it!" he moaned. "I knew it! I knew it!"

Hearing the phone go dead, Bone took his hand off the mouthpiece and he began to nod grimly, as if he were listening to someone.

"He did, huh?" he said finally. "He did give Mr. Wolfe my message, then? All right, I see. Yes. Thank you."

He hung up then, angrily. "No dice," he said. "The man got the message. Price gave it to him personally. And that's all there is. No response. Nothing."

Cutter looked ill. "The bastard," he muttered. "The murdering bastard."

Bone put his hand on Cutter's shoulder, but Alex shook it off.

"You believe him?" Cutter snapped. "You believe this fairy Price actually delivered the note?"

Bone shrugged. "He struck me as too scared not to."

By now they had crossed to where Valerie sat waiting for them.

"No sale," Bone told her. "He didn't bite."

"So I gathered." She got up.

Cutter stared at both of them as if he expected them to do something, anything — start screaming or join him in tearing apart the hotel lobby — and when they did nothing but stand there and look back at him he turned on his heels and, loping over to the bank of elevators, charged into one that had just opened and which guests were still trying to get out of. One of those he jostled, a frail old woman, gave him a reproachful look and he in turn gave her the finger. Then the doors closed and he was gone.

175

"We better stay with him," Bone said. "He's pretty shook."

Valerie coolly regarded Bone. "Unlike you."

"Yeah — unlike me."

In the elevator, alone together, she kept at him. "Admit it — this is kind of what you wanted, isn't it?"

"Failure? Sure, it's my bag."

"I'm serious."

Bone met her snowy gaze for three or four floors. "Could be," he said finally. "Anyway, this way we stay out of jail."

"Did you really deliver it?"

"What?"

"The message, of course. The note."

"No, I ate it."

"The truth," she demanded. "Please, Rich."

"It tasted kind of dry," he told her.

When they reached their room Cutter went into the bathroom and locked the door. After a few minutes of ominous silence he came out again and told Valerie to give him some more money.

"Twenty anyway," he said. And when she hesitated a moment he shouted at her. "Come on, goddamn it! It's *our* bread, remember! *Our* gig, sweetheart. So *give!*"

Valerie gave. And Cutter, stuffing the bills into his pocket, left the room.

"Where's he going?" Valerie asked.

"The bar."

"You said we should stick with him."

"Up here, yeah. But he can't jump out of the bar. Ground floor, remember?"

"I still think we should be with him."

"Whatever you say."

That was not enough for her. "You know how he is."

"I know how he is."

Her look now was not unlike that of the Dakota schoolteacher, resentful and aggrieved. Saying she had to freshen up first, she went into the bathroom.

Bone lit a cigarette and walked out onto the balcony to watch the Los Angelenos on the freeway below, hundreds of them pouring past every minute, a cataract of steel and plastic and humanoid hate-sweat roaring down the poisoned air. And he found it singularly appropriate that just last night Valerie — this day's new enemy — had offered him a kind of love or at least what had come to pass for love, here, just a few feet above it all, this modern Inferno, this better hell built by man. As always, just the sight of it somehow fortified Bone's cynicism, gave second wind to his enduring despair. He knew it all really was not worth thinking about anymore, had become a kind of catechism at best. Life was brutal and ugly and one endured it alone and any love or beauty he found along the way was purely accidental and usually short-lived. Nothing in and of itself had value. There was no gold standard in life. The currency was paper, a constantly devaluing paper. Of course. And what else was new?

Valerie finally emerged from the bathroom, looking no different as far as Bone could see. In silence the two of them took the elevator down to the lower lobby and the cocktail lounge situated at the end of the pool. It was large and sunlit, hardly the sort of place Bone would have preferred for an afternoon of drinking, especially with Cutter in the mood he was in. But then the choice as usual was not his to make. Alex had taken a table almost in the center of the room and he was leaning back in his chair against a pillar while his right leg, the steel-and-plastic one, was propped on a corner of the table, close to a double martini. And he was smoking a cigar, a panatella with a silver band still on it. Seeing Bone and Valerie, he waved them in like a Mafia don granting an audience.

After they had ordered drinks, Cutter pounded the table. "Now isn't this just goodsie fudgie," he said. "The three of us here together again, old palsies having a few drinkies, saying a few words over the body."

"Oh, come on," Valerie protested. "I don't see why we're so down. We can still keep trying to reach the man. What difference will a couple of days make?"

Bone explained. "The note said it all. And if that didn't bring him around, what will? We keep trying to reach him, he'll call in the police. It's that simple."

"Maybe he didn't get the note," Valerie said.

Bone looked at her. "He got it."

"Then I say write another. Keep trying."

Cutter buried her in cigar smoke. "Aw, come off it," he told her.

"Off what?"

"Face it, lady. We bombed."

"I can't see why it's so final. We can't just give up so easy. We've got to keep trying."

"Pollyanna want a cracker?" Cutter offered her one of the pretzel sticks the waitress had just served, along with a round of drinks.

Valerie ignored the offering.

And Cutter snorted derisively. "Jesus, I am some winner, huh? Ain't this some beautiful streak I got going? You know what I am, kiddos — a modern Midas. A reverse Midas. Everything I touch turns to shit."

Bone drank to that. "Bravo, Alex — that's the attitude. No sense just accepting it, that Wolfe isn't our man. Let's wallow in self-pity instead. Let's cover ourselves with crap."

Cutter nodded in solemn mockery. "I'm with you, Rich. As always. My captain."

Valerie asked them what would happen next, what would they do, and Cutter told her they were already doing it.

"You mean all night?" she asked. "The three of us, in this town, and on my money?"

"Why not?"

"I'll go home broke."

Cutter shrugged. "So what? You've always got your avocation to fall back on, if you'll pardon the pun. As Swanson

178

would say — as Hemingway said, you will have found your profession. All you have to do is give in to it. Relax. Why shee-itt, I could even be your man, baby. A player, as they say. All I'd have to do is get me some satin threads and one of those wide-brim floppy hats and a chartreuse Caddie with a water-melon radiator cap, and we be in bidness, me and my woman, my own private ho. How's that sound, huh? Just you and me, babe — against the world."

"I don't think I'm gonna like tonight," Valerie said.

And Bone found he did not much like it either. They had a second round of drinks and then a third and fourth, and the bar gradually began to fill, not with tourists so much as sales-men and a few show business types including some unusually beautiful girls, probably starlets from the nearby Universal Studios. And as the crowd grew larger, so did Cutter grow louder and more verbal.

One of his great strengths, he said, was his ability to objec-tify his own experience, to see it clear and dispassionate, a trick he'd used in Vietnam in order to keep his sanity. "You just sort of rise up out of yourself, you know, like a chopper, lifting right up out of there, so you can look down all cool and un-afraid and say, 'My, my, look at that poor grunt about to get his ass zapped, yes it sure is a crying shame about him, isn't it, the little creep down there locked in time and place, an *object* really, nothing more.' But not me, kiddos, I mean this other me — up there above it all, above all this shit, this sea to grimy sea. I just float free."

"So you feel no pain?" Bone said. "No disappointment?"

Cutter made a face, judicious, contemplative. "Well, I must admit that right now maybe I do feel something. Let's say I mourn to a degree for that gimpy fellow down there at that table being indulged, nay mocked, by his bonny unmarked friend."

Bone told him no one was mocking him.

"Does it matter? No, I was just saying I objectify that poor fellow's pain. I feel it not. I do wish him well, however. In fact it has always been my ferventest prayer and dearest wish that he might one day strike it rich — and by that I don't mean some squalid financial score like the one that has just fizzled for him — and of course for his attractive friends too. No, I mean a real score — some spiritual or philosophic or maybe even political coup, like say that neat little job Saul of Tarsus brought off on the road to Damascus. Something like that, you know? A blinding light, and yea, maybe even a time of darkness too, preparation. But for what, huh? Epiphany? Apotheosis?"

Bone looked over at Valerie and it was obvious she had not heard Cutter carry on like this before, had not known just how high he could fly when the mood struck him, and she looked almost awed. But Bone had been here before, had gone this route many times, so he just sat back and drank and ate pretzels and listened.

"You see what I mean, don't you, Val? A gift from above, you know? Sort of like Erickson's or Wolfe's. You wake up one day and lo and behold, there it is — the Way, the Truth and the Life. Now it doesn't matter if it's setting fire to rich folk's property or marketing cheaper eggs or for that matter being a together dude pimp — the important thing is the way of it, the truth and the life of it, it's got to reach you down in here —" And at this point he touched his stomach, and frowning, feigning consternation, moved on to his chest and shoulder. "— or here, or well, the right place, you know?"

A waitress happened to be passing their table just then and Cutter seized her by the arm and poured out the rest of his story.

"But it's never happened, would you believe that? The gods have denied me. Indeed, they have pissed upon me, they have shat upon me. They have used me as a toilet bowl. Now I ask you, is that fair? Is that any way for gods to carry on?"

The girl, looking both bewildered and frightened, pulled her arm free and began to back away, all the while staring at Cutter as if he had crawled out of a grave. But he was smiling benignly. He raised his hand and gave her one of his papal blessings.

"Peace, my child," he intoned. *"La plume de ma tante est dans votre derrière."*

As the afternoon crawled toward night, Cutter gained strength and Valerie grew increasingly quiet. One after another she smoked her Virginia Slims and drank her Tom Collinses, but she said almost nothing and in fact barely moved except when Cutter would ask her for more money, which she would then obediently dig out of her purse and hand over, as if that were her only purpose in being there. When they left the hotel, it was Bone who drove the Pinto while she sat meekly between the men, submitting to Cutter's hand under her sweater and up her skirt, and even accepting his kisses too, this despite the fact that he had thrown up in the hotel men's room not even an hour before and his breath would not let them forget it.

Bone had had five or six drinks himself and he was not keen on driving anywhere, especially not on the Hollywood Freeway to Sunset and then making his way through the heavy night traffic to the strip, but Cutter had insisted that was where they must go, that no other place except Sunset Strip could possibly do justice to the misery of the occasion, and if Bone did not want to take the wheel, well Cutter would be happy to do the honors himself and in the bargain would save them a good deal of time. So Bone drove. But he had to fight the alcohol every mile and every block of the way, forcing himself to concentrate hard on the traffic signals and the cross streets and the cars hurtling at him on Sunset. Once he had parked, however, it was like giving in to sleep — the alcohol seemed to pour through him, deadening and dulling all but his ego, making his mind a kind of fisheye lens blurring and shrinking the strip and all its florid fauna while at the same time it magnified him and Cutter and Valerie at the center. And that was how the night progressed, this small bagged epicenter of the universe moving erratically down the street, from one bar to another, from topless to straight to bottomless to gay. And even high as he was, Bone found the topless-bottomless mills as depressing as ever, sexless and castrating, soul-killing cells of gloom in which red- and blue-lighted girls listlessly swung and stroked and bumped their sleek spayed bodies before the uplifted and oddly bovine gaze of the crowd, dead men all. Even Cutter could not endure it for longer than a drink, nor find a blasphemy to equal it.

A gay bar up the street, however, proved no such obstacle as he loudly asked where all the girls were. And as one, the cool cosmeticized faces swiveled on him, like a firing squad of B-B guns. But Cutter laughed it off:

"Just kidding, girls. Actually I'm a latent from Fresno. I'm thinking of coming out."

Bone knew there were few surer ways of getting stomped than by abusing homosexuals on their own turf, so he hustled the three of them out of the bar, while Cutter loudly explained to Valerie that the place was a good example of what he'd meant by epiphany: "These bastards really got something to believe in — the priapic principle, the cock as God."

But somehow they made it to the street, with Cutter laughing happily and banging his cane against anything that would make a racket. Because this was the strip though, he barely drew a glance, fitted in as unremarkably as a coyote in a zoo. The street in fact reminded Bone of those old movies about Hollywood, with the inevitable studio scene showing the hero and heroine as they made their way across the lot crowded with "extras" hurrying here and there — cowboys and Indians, slave girls and Roman senators, pirates and Foreign Legionnaires — all managing somehow to look quite normal, workers costumed for a job. Such was not the case, however, with their modern counterparts on the strip. For some reason the costume had become the reality. Indeed these actors did not even appear to know that they *were* costumed. And so they paraded the street — Cochise and Billy the Kid, Apollo and Venus and the Count de Sade.

A block from the gay bar, Cutter, Valerie, and Bone came upon a young black man dressed almost exactly as Cutter had said he would get himself up to serve as Valerie's pimp, and of course Alex could not resist approaching him. Whispering and limping, Cutter asked him if he could fix up his "kinky friend here" with a Great Dane — his tastes were "positively bestial." Fortunately the pimp enjoyed the put-on, going into a kind of limp dance of amusement and even giving Cutter's wry, outstretched hand the sharp slap of brotherhood. But the comedy and amusement were all on his side — Bone did not miss the look of desperation in Cutter's eye. And yet he had no idea what he could do about it, how to arrest the steep angle of their descent. So he trudged along with Valerie as Alex led them into a joint that advertised "Rassle a Naked Lady." The price was ten dollars, which naturally did not give Cutter a moment's pause — he simply snapped his finger at Valerie and she resignedly gave him the money, which he then handed to the proprietor, a chalk-skinned little rodent of a man who looked as if he retired each morning into a coffin. He said that Cutter could strip down to his pants if he wanted to, but he had to keep them on. There would be "no hanky-panky here."

"Just rassle," he said. "Just what you pay for."

Cutter took the man at his word, probably to a degree unprecedented in the history of the establishment. The girl was a tall Chicano built along the lines of a Lachaise sculpture, with great swelling breasts and thighs. And her gaze was lithic, unmoved, as Cutter took off his sweater and T-shirt, revealing the stump of his arm and the terrible quilt of shrapnel scars dimpling his torso. She knew what he wanted of course, what they all wanted, to squeeze her great bazooms and touch her big black pussy, and she would suffer it, she was paid for it, it was a job. Instead Cutter walked up to her and, grasping her by the arm, threw her face-down on the mat. Then, forcing her arm up behind her back, he told her to say uncle or he would break her ulna and possibly her Volga too. For some reason the girl preferred to lie there and scream for the proprietor, who came running out of a back room with a small baseball bat in his hand. But Cutter would not let go.

"Tell her to say uncle," he persisted.

"Say it! Say it!" the man yelled at her. "Jesus Christ, tell him uncle!"

And finally the girl caught on. "Uncle! Uncle!" she cried.

Cutter got off her then, mugging triumph, holding his good arm and the stump together above his head. The proprietor was yelling at him and threatening to call the police, but Cutter barely glanced at him. The bat the man held could have been a breadstick for all the attention Alex gave it.

"You said rassle," he told the man. "So I rassled."

Down in the street again, he gave Bone and Valerie a different reason: "The poor kid, having a job like that. I decided to give her something to remember. For a day or two, at least."

Between eleven and midnight Cutter led them into the Bergerac, a small posh restaurant with a domed ceiling and a large fireplace and soft globe lights burning over a very voluble clientele, most of them young, mod, and successful-looking. One look at Cutter and the maître d' hustled the three of them into the bar, an even smaller room with birdbath tables crowded along a row of leaded stained-glass windows. Bone, hoping to avoid the drunk tank, asked the waiter for a menu and was told in exceedingly fine diction that the kitchen was closed. But the long night of drinking had not been totally lost on him either, and he crooked his finger at the undoubtedly once-and-future actor and told him pleasantly to reconsider his answer or Bone would personally shove the table

184

lantern up his ass sideways. The waiter reconsidered, brought them menus and drinks, and took their orders, petit filets mignons all around. But almost immediately Cutter wondered out loud why he had bothered to order any food, since he couldn't possibly eat anything.

Valerie asked him what was wrong. Was he feeling sick again?

"Of course," he told her. "Always."

"Throwing up sick, I mean," she clarified.

"Of course. Always."

Valerie turned to Bone, her look almost accusative. "Say something. Do something."

"There's nothing to do," Alex said. "Nothing he can say. I'm just not hungry, that's all. Thirsty, yes. In fact, I think I'll probably be thirsty the rest of my life."

"Why not?" Bone put in.

"Listen to him, will you? The old Bone credo — why not?"

"Why not?" Bone said again.

And Cutter laughed. "*Because*, that's why. Simply *because*. Didn't anyone ever teach you anything?"

"Because, huh?"

"Hell yes!" Cutter started to laugh then, hard, doubling over his drink. And a number of people in the small room turned to look at him, which only caused him to shout at them. "What's the matter with you cats anyway? Can't a man laugh? Can't a man be happy?"

Bone suggested that he quiet down, and Cutter asked why he should.

"It's like you just said — because."

"I said no such thing."

"My mistake."

But Cutter would not be mollified. "Will you please get the goddamn hell off my back, both of you. And let me try to deal with this thing in my own way. Try to remember, kiddies — this morning we were just a few hours away from payday,

185

hotels on Park Place and Boardwalk. And what've we got now? — not even an outhouse on Baltic Avenue. So let me laugh, okay? Let me weep."

"Whatever turns you on," Bone said.

"Killing him, that would turn me on," he said, so loud a number of people in the bar turned to look at him again, though not with alarm so much as condescension and amusement.

"What's more logical?" he went on. "What's more human than to kill the killer, huh? Execute the executioner? Is there any better gauge of a society's moral fiber than its willingness to take an eye for an eye and a crushed trachea for a crushed trachea? So why not aim high, huh? Why not kill the motherfucker?"

Bone casually lit a cigarette, trying to communicate a sense of calm. But his words went the other way. "Alex, for Christ sake, can't you just talk? Do you have to shout?"

"Who's shouting? You just don't like the idea, that's all. Because you're chicken. A tit for a tat, that's your style. Or possibly two tits. So how about this — why don't we auction it off? Why don't we sell it right here? These creeps look like they ain't hurting for bread, right? So why not sell it to them?"

"Sell what?" Bone asked.

"Our knowledge, man. That special bit of info we got about J. J. Wolfe. Why, hell, there's bound to be a buyer here."

"Come on, Alex. Please. Knock it off."

"Why, huh? Why not sell it? What else we got, huh? Silver ingots? Thousand shares of IBM? Like hell we have. All we got is J. J. Wolfe — but by the balls, my friend! By the old lemon drops!"

Even the patrons across the room had turned to look at Cutter now, and Bone was getting desperate. Slowly, patiently, as if he were talking to a raging child, he again asked him to quiet down, to knock it off. And suddenly in Alex's eye Bone saw the whole thing shrinking to the distance between them, becoming personal, charged. Cutter's mouth curled with malice.

"Sure, man!" he said. "Of course — the second you tell me why I should, the second you give me one good reason to." Then he pushed back his chair, evidently preparing to get up and begin the "auction."

Bone felt the muscles in his own legs leap tight, he was that close to walking out, leaving the two of them to whatever fate Cutter's demons might bring down on them. Instead Bone found himself reaching inside his coat and pulling out the envelope, the *personal* note he was supposed to have delivered to J. J. Wolfe. Now he delivered it to Cutter.

And for long seconds Cutter did not understand. He stared down at it in confusion and then looked up at Bone and finally over at Valerie, where he must have found the answer, read it loud and clear in the contempt her weary eyes had focused on Bone.

"Why?" Cutter asked him. "Why, Rich? In God's name, *why?*"

Bone shrugged. "You just said it, Alex. I'm chicken."

8

SOMEHOW BONE MANAGED TO GET THEM BACK TO THE HOTEL, probably by driving twenty miles an hour all the way though he could not have sworn to it, since he remembered almost nothing of the journey except a vague feeling of personal heroism, as if he were a half-dead Saint Bernard dog dragging his poor lost charges to safety. In the hotel parking lot Cutter showed his gratitude by throwing a punch at him, but he missed and hit a parked Cadillac instead. Yelling in pain, Alex then dented the car's hood with his cane and finished it off by urinating on two of its whitewalls. In time, however, the three of them managed to reach the right floor of the hotel and even their very own room. Once inside, Bone submitted meekly to the booze and with two exceptions did not stir from his oblivion until almost eleven the next morning. The first exception was when he rolled over once at a hammering sound counterpointed by heavy panting and he had the distinct impression he saw Cutter performing calisthenics out on the balcony. Another time he seemed to recall seeing Cutter, naked and shower-drenched, opening the door for room service, a stooped old man who pushed a breakfast cart into the room as if he had no real expectation of ever getting out alive. But Bone could not have cared less. Sleep was what he needed, sore hangover's bath, and he drifted contentedly in it until a chambermaid came clattering into the room at eleven and, not seeing him

188

zonked out on the floor between the beds, began to tidy up the bathroom, all the while singing a soft Spanish dirge. Bone thought of rolling under a bed and letting her complete her work in peace, but there was not enough room, so he did the next best thing — he slipped up onto one of the beds and began to yawn loudly. The maid came out of the bathroom in a crouch, her eyes round with terror.

"I no see!" she cried.

Bone shrugged. "*De nada*. You come back, *si?*"

"I no see!"

"Right. I understand. You come back, okay?"

"Hokay!" She backed out of the room carefully, knowing a *brujo* when she saw one.

Alone, Bone wondered what time Cutter and Valerie had left. Remembering the calisthenics and room service during the night, the coffee and the showers, he assumed Cutter had tried to work his hangover off instead of sleeping it off, that he had been that anxious to pick up where Bone had left off yesterday. And Bone did not have to look far for confirmation. On the dresser mirror across the room was a lipstick-scrawled message:

YANKEE GO HOME!

Below it, an arrow pointed to the top of the dresser, where Cutter had continued his message on a sheet of hotel stationery:

> Dear Chickenshit,
> During the night it comes to me like a hot flash — I need you like I need more glass eyes. Who's to say *I* wasn't on Alvarez Street that night? Who's to say *I* didn't see old J.J. dump the bod same as you did? Not J.J. hisself — that I guarantee.
>
> So what it comes down to, dear heart, is this — me and

189

V. hereby include you out. In a word, you are fired —
free to return to the sands of S.B. and contemplate the
utter perfection of your ding-dong.

Meanwhile, J.J. is ours. *Mine.* Today we don't send a
boy out on a man's job. Today I go. And tomorrow —
well, someday y'all come visit us on Ibiza, hear?

But for the nonce — get lost.

Yrs. in Jesus,
ALEXANDER IV

All in all, Bone considered it pretty good advice, if not actually to get lost at least to put as much distance as he could
between himself and them, and the sooner the better. Even
handled expertly — that is, the way Bone himself would have
tried to handle it — the operation would have been a long shot
at best. It required a negotiator who knew something of the
corporate labyrinth, because unless one reached Wolfe with
the product intact — not picked over by underlings, ripped
open, light-exposed — then one really had nothing to sell.
Wolfe would have no alternative except to call in the gendarmes and bluff it out, play his power game to the full, which
would probably mean jail — and not for Wolfe. Considering
all that, Bone simply could not imagine Cutter bringing the
thing off. Somewhere along the line, probably within minutes
after he entered Wolfe's domain, he would run up against one
variety or other of bureaucratic lunacy and his response would
naturally be both swift and outrageous, the kind of act that
would bring everything crashing down upon him. A mad lame
bull in a plastic shop, that would about describe him. And it
was a description Bone could not see leading to anything but
failure. So he was glad to be out of it, anxious to be on his
way.

There was still his hangover to deal with, however, his need
for oxygen and food and movement. Getting out of bed, he

decided that if room service was good enough for Cutter and Valerie it was also good enough for him, and he phoned down an order for French toast, scrambled eggs, bacon, coffee, and a pint of freshly squeezed orange juice, this last a specification that threw the order-taker into such a panic Bone wondered if he had been connected with the Sheraton-Iceland kitchen by mistake. He then smoked a cigarette, defecated splendidly, and spent the next fifteen minutes in the shower, grateful that the world's reputedly impending water crisis was still a few years distant.

The breakfast proved to be almost as cold as it was expensive, though this last he solved à la Cutter, scrawling his version of Valerie's signature across the room service check. By twelve-thirty he was ready to go, fed and dressed, with the few things he had brought with him, extra shirt, socks, toilet articles, all stuffed into his venerable attaché case. Downstairs he strode across the hotel lobby and out through the bustling entrance like any other successful young executive. Only where they all seemed to be hailing taxis, he walked casually across the parking lot, shortcutted through some bushes, and headed down the hill to Lankersham. Another block and he was on the freeway entrance ramp, thumbing with his usual touch of calculated restraint and even embarrassment, hoping to make clear to that Great American Majority thundering past that his customary place was right there with them *on* the road, not next to it as now, for it was his experience that people were more likely to pick up their own kind. And normally it was the women who came through for him, usually young ones, two or three of them riding together and thus able to combine a sense of adventure with some measure of security. But this day it was a man who did the honors, a heavy middle-aged sales type with a bright red face and a whiskey voice. He drove one-handed and very fast, chain-smoking Camels as he cruised along the freeway, tailgating, changing lanes, slipping through openings that would have given a Hell's Angel pause. But as

Bone quickly learned, the man was not really being cavalier with anyone's life except his own, for the simple reason that he did not seem to realize that there were any others out there. Bone in fact believed that if he had been an armed Black Panther or a Hari Krishna monk or a bull dyke fondling a bicycle chain, it would have been the same — the man would not have noticed. All he wanted, all he had stopped for, was a pair of ears, a hitchhiker confessor, a surrogate shrink.

In the less than ninety minutes it took to reach Santa Barbara, Bone learned in crushing detail the history of the man's three rottenfuckin' marriages. He learned all about the ingratitude and stupidity of the man's rottenfuckin' daughters and pansy-ass sons and in the bargain got a straight-from-the-shoulder analysis of the housewares business, starting with the manufacturers and moving down through the jobbers and salesmen (the best of the goddamn lot, the backbone of the whole economy) to the rottenfuckin' retailers themselves, who never discounted anything unless it was simple old-fashioned honesty, an honest product for an honest buck. Like most businesses, housewares was simply no place for an honest man, a good man, and especially not an honest good man who was also a crackerjack salesman. Him they just didn't know what to do with. They cheated him and lied to him and stabbed him in the back. They shaved his commissions and pirated his accounts and failed to recognize his considerable achievements. All of which convinced Bone that he had more than earned his way back to Santa Barbara, and in fact had a little something extra due him. So as they reached the downtown area and the man started to pull off the freeway to let him out, Bone told him to go on to the next corner and hang a right.

"There's something you've got to see," he explained. "It's just a couple of blocks."

Murdock's Bar actually was six blocks from the freeway, but the housewares tycoon did not complain. As Bone got out, though, the man asked for an explanation.

"Well, what is it I got to see?"

Bone frowned, smiled. It should have been obvious. "My destination," he said.

Unfortunately Murdock's turned out not to be much in the way of a destination, for Murdock himself was gone, which meant Bone would not be able to drink on his tab or borrow the man's car for a run uptown to see Mo and the baby. Nevertheless Bone did settle in long enough to have one vodka tonic, to sit there in the pleasant darkness working on the drink and picking at his decision to come here, all the way downtown, instead of getting out on 101 as it passed through Montecito, not even a half mile from Mrs. Little's, which after all was his new home, his place of bed and board for now. But as he thought about it, he had to admit no decision was involved, that he simply had come straight here like a homing pigeon following the radar beam of its nature. The fact that Cutter would not be there did not really enter in. Bone had been alone with her before, dozens of times, and nothing had happened. So why should he expect anything to happen this time? Oh, he could hope, all right. And he could even try, make the old half-hearted try. There couldn't be any harm in that, he told himself. There was never any harm in that.

On the way out he ran into Sergeant Verdugo, one of the detectives who had rousted him the night of the murder. Verdugo said he was still assigned to the case, but was getting nowhere fast. He asked Bone if his memory had improved any and Bone said he was on his way uptown, that maybe the sergeant would give him a lift and they could talk about it. Verdugo had the look of a man who knew he was being suckered, but he went along anyway, driving Bone the few miles to Cutter's place. And all he did was nod wearily when Bone said he had nothing to add to his original statement. For his part, the sergeant did not have much more to offer. Every lead so far in the case had reached a dead end. The department was nowhere. Lieutenant Ross was back on warm milk and baby food. And to top it all, the victim's sister seemed to have disappeared. Her mother didn't know where she was, and neither did her employer.

"Ross thinks we'll find her dead too," Verdugo finished.

Bone said nothing.

They were at Cutter's now. "Still staying here, huh?" the sergeant observed. "On the floor?"

Getting out, Bone smiled. "Home is where the heart is."

There was no answer to his knock, so he went on into the house, expecting that he would find her asleep in bed with the baby. Instead he found her out on the deck dozing topless in the sun on one of the webbed folding chairs Swanson had given Cutter. Alex Five was at her feet, asleep in a pile of blankets on the deck floor. For a short time Bone just stood there in the doorway saying nothing, not moving, as if he feared the slightest sound would bring it all crashing down, this tableau that looked almost contrived by a French impressionist — the half-nude madonna and child asleep in the gold pool of the sun, with the mountains and the sea and the red-roofed city beyond. He thought of bending down and touching his lips to her breasts, but he knew that would probably gain him nothing except a punched nose, so he lightly rapped on the doorjamb instead. And Mo reacted about as he had expected she would, with her eyes mostly, a look of bland surprise. Not bothering to cover her breasts, she raised her finger to her mouth to silence him — she did not want him waking the baby. Getting up, she followed him back into the house and closed the French deck doors behind her.

"What the hell are you now, a cat burglar?" she asked, slipping into a sweatshirt.

"I knocked."

"Not very loud."

Bone smiled. "Just loud enough. For my purposes."

Flopping back on the davenport, she lit a cigarette. "Well, I hope you enjoyed yourself."

"Immensely."

"Yeah, they're pretty great," she admitted. "All thirty-four inches."

"I'm not a tits man."

"What then? Elbows? Ankles?"

"Eyes, Mo. I have this thing about certain kinds of eyes."

"Bloodshot, no doubt."

"Usually, yes."

She said nothing for a few moments, evidently having temporarily run out of sarcasm. "You're alone?" she asked finally.

"I came back alone, yes."

"He's still there, then?"

"Still there. Still on the job."

She sat looking at him, smiling slightly. "Are you going to tell me why?"

"Sure. I chickened out. Once I hit Wolfe's place, I found I couldn't go through with the thing. But I pretended to anyway. Went through the motions. You know."

"Why?"

"Why couldn't I go through with it?"

"Yes. Why the sudden bout of sanity?"

"That about says it."

"Why pretend you went through with it though?"

"I figured when nothing happened — when Wolfe never got in touch — the whole thing would just peter out. Alex would lose interest, give it up."

"I take it he didn't."

"No. Today he's carrying the ball."

"And will he drop it too?"

"Not if he can help it."

"Is there any chance he could bring it off?"

"Let's hope so. For your sake anyway."

195

"You figure I might benefit somehow?"

Bone shrugged.

"Sort of a share-the-wealth thing?"

"I can't see why not."

"Can't you now?"

"No, I can't."

Mo's smile seemed to appreciate the effort he made, but she still was not buying. "And the girl? I take it she didn't chicken out either."

"No. She's still hanging in there."

"Plucky little thing."

"Yeah, she's a plucky little thing."

"And with you gone, that sort of throws them together, doesn't it?"

"In a business sort of way."

"Kind of like colleagues, you might say."

Bone did not pick it up.

"Or partners," she went on.

"Whatever."

"Bedmates?"

"Not while I was there."

"Of course not. Not with old blue-eyes on the scene. I mean one couldn't very well expect Alex to beat that kind of competition, could one?"

Bone went along. "Now that you mention it."

"Except with me, of course."

"Of course."

"But now if he *were* screwing her — you'd tell me, wouldn't you?"

"Would it matter?"

"Which. Their screwing, or your telling me?"

"Take your pick."

The smile came again. "You're right, Rich. I guess it doesn't really matter, does it."

"No."

The baby was awake now. Through the French doors Bone could hear him jabbering, see him on his hands and knees at the deck railing, trying to squeeze his head through.

"It's all right — you can go get him," Mo said. "You can do your little domestic thing."

Bone gave her a despairing look. But he went out onto the deck and got the baby anyway.

"You want to change him?" she asked.

"No."

"Feed him?"

"I'll watch."

While Mo took the baby into the bedroom, Bone went back onto the deck and stretched out in the sun, whose brilliance and warmth did nothing to diminish his feeling of rising spirits. Just yesterday he had had one foot in the abyss, yet here he was today back on solid ground, safe and sane if not solvent. And as for any uneasiness he might have felt about coming here alone, Mo herself had quickly dispelled that, Mo in the flesh, the ever astringent flesh. He stood about as good a chance of abusing her as he did a bulldozer. More likely, she would end up rolling right over him. But even that prospect held no terror for him. He was content in the knowledge that he just might find out something this day, maybe get her out of his system for good — or help her set the hook even deeper. Either way, it would be a kind of release, one less point for anxiety.

While he was on the deck the phone rang in the living room, in fact rang seven or eight times before Mo finally answered it. And even then she did not say much except for an occasional "Yes, I heard you," or "Yes, I'm still here." Finally she said, "Why don't you tell him yourself? He's here."

At that, Bone got up and went back inside, where he found Mo holding the phone out to him as if it were a wet diaper.

"It's the great blackmailer," she said. "With wondrous tales to tell."

Bone said hello, and Cutter's voice boomed out of the receiver:

"Keeping the old home fires burning, uh, Rich?"

"Trying, anyway."

"That's the ticket. You hang in there, kiddo."

"Sure thing."

Cutter came on even stronger now, the juices of his ego fairly oozing from his voice. Was Bone at all interested in how the day's activities had gone? Yes, of course he was. Well, Cutter was sure happy to hear that, because he hated to think his old buddy might be pissed off at him, and for no good reason either, like that half-assed note Cutter had left in the hotel room for him, which had just been a put-on of course, certainly old Rich was able to see that. Anyway, the wheels of time had done their thing and so had he. Yes, this fool had rushed in where Bone had rightly feared to tread, and would Bone believe that the thing was done, the fait already accompli? Would he believe old Alex had made high-echelon contact and was now waiting to hear from them?

"A young executive type named Pruitt," Cutter went on. "How about that? Not Whozit but Pruitt — now is that a favorable sign or is that a favorable sign? And in the young man's own words — he'll be in touch with us *today*. He'll send us a message."

For some reason Bone could only repeat the phrase: "He'll send you a message?"

"That's right."

"Which means he knows where you are? Where you're staying?"

"Yeah, I had to improvise a little. With you gone, certain little changes had to be made in the game plan."

"Suppose he sends you a message via the L.A.P.D.? Or a cannon?"

Cutter laughed. "No chance — believe me. I scared them shitless."

Bone believed it. "Well, congratulations," he said. "And good luck. I think you're going to need it."

"You too. Tell Mo I said she should be extra nice, because your ego has been so badly bruised of late. Tell her I said you can use the Packard if you need it. You can even sit in my chair."

"Gee thanks."

"It's nothing. Goomba for now."

Bone hung up. Mo was standing in the deck doorway, staring out at the sea.

"He tell you what happened?" Bone asked.

"More than I care to know. I don't give a damn. Let him get his ass killed or jailed, I don't care."

For a time neither of them said anything more. Bone stood there looking at her sun-limned in the doorway, her face and hair a furze of honeyed fire.

"It's only three o'clock," he said finally. "Anything you want to do?"

She gave him a thoughtful look and then nodded, very positively. "Yes. First, I'll feed the baby. And then I have a gallon of pretty good Chianti and some ridiculously expensive Romano cheese compliments of George. Also some Triscuits and half a loaf of dago bread. So we'll drink and we'll eat and we'll drink some more and maybe play a few records and possibly even dance. How does that sound? Does it sound like something a pair of quasi human beings could manage?"

Bone was not sure. "We could try," he said.

And try, they did. Through the late afternoon they sat around drinking the wine and listening to records by Carole King and Elton John and Seals and Crofts, albums by Streisand and the Beatles and Sarah Vaughan and Stevie Wonder. They watched the baby and played with him and they danced together, Bone occasionally kissing her forehead or cheek, chaste kisses she did not seem to mind or even notice. Then during Wonder's *Golden Lady* Bone slid his right hand inside her chinos and onto her buttocks at the same time he kissed her on the mouth. And when she did not resist he brought his left hand into the act too, reaching up under her sweatshirt and lightly taking hold of her breast. But at that she pulled away, very casually, however, more as if she had simply tired of dancing. Dropping onto the sofa, she told him not to bother.

"You'd only be disappointed," she explained. "You wouldn't be gaining a lover, you'd be losing a friend."

Bone said he was willing to risk it, but she shook her head.

"No, I don't think I'm in your league, Rich. I remember the night you had the black girl here, the night of the killing. I thought you two would never quit — God, was I jealous! I hated her."

Bone tried not to look too pleased. "That was athletics, Mo. Right now I have something else in mind."

"Like what?"

"Why don't we find out?"

She smiled with wry affection, almost as if he were another Alexander Five, who at the moment was sitting on the floor happily ripping up a copy of the *Village Voice*.

"You poor sap," she said. "You really are a slave to it, aren't you?"

"I don't want any *it*," he told her.

"What then?"

"You. *Us*."

"Love?" She said it without total mockery, almost as if she were testing the word, testing him.

"Why not?"

And she laughed. "A thousand reasons."

Bone was sitting next to her now, leaning back, about ready to give up, for he had learned a long time ago that one rarely talked a woman into the act. One made his move and either succeeded then or not at all. But suddenly he realized she had changed her position on the davenport. Tucking one leg up under her and turning toward him, she began to search his eyes with her own, a long cool unreadable look that he had to force himself to meet. And then suddenly she kissed him, on the mouth, barely touching his lips. At the same time her hand came to rest on his lap, on the mound of his erection.

"I guess it'd be worth a try," she said. "What could we lose?"

Bone tried to take her there on the davenport, but she put him off, saying she first had to take care of the baby and then herself.

"You wouldn't want to make love to a slob, now would you?" she asked.

She changed the baby's diapers and then gave him to Bone while she took a bath. So Bone found himself lying in bed bouncing the baby up and down on his stomach, lifting him above his face, shaking him and rubbing noses, making the little fellow gurgle with laughter. And it made the whole thing seem very routine, very orderly and domestic. That was how she came back into the room too, like a wife, very matter-of-fact, casually pulling shades, turning on the one dim dresser light, picking up the baby and placing him in the makeshift playpen next to the bed formed by two walls and the back of a chest of drawers and the bed itself, so that he had the option of standing next to them and observing their lovemaking if he wished. But he was more interested in an old coffeepot and an alphabet block, which he carried to the center of the pen and, sitting down, began to bang together.

It was in this simple domestic setting then that Bone and Mo came together in the bed. But from the moment he touched her, took hold of her shoulders and gently pulled her down onto him, there was no single routine second between them. It was Bone's experience that lovemaking was almost never that so much as a mutual act of masturbation in which the partners used each other's bodies in place of their own hands or other devices. And he found nothing wrong in this, in fact believed that it led to sex at its fullest and best, as with the black girl last week, those hour-long sessions in which the participants practically fed on each other, carefully searched out those special little morsels of sensation and then picked them clean, blood and sinew and bone, tearing and crunching and sucking, devouring all in a long sweet feast of the flesh, a kind of gluttony perhaps, but still very satisfying and very human, hurting no one. At the same time, neither did it reach Bone's spirit or touch his heart. That kind of lovemaking he had known only rarely in his life, first as an eighteen-year-old boy with a church summer camp director's wife and then in the first months of his marriage to Ruth and in only two affairs since then, just four times in all his life when he had made love to a *person*, someone who had lived in his mind as surely and vividly as he himself. And ironically the sex then rarely had been the best, had almost always been complicated and weakened by the human feelings sweeping back and forth between him and the loved one. Yet even then, during these less than perfect performances, what he had felt as he held his woman and entered her had no counterpart in the other "lovemaking," the masturbatory variety. For what he had felt was a kind of death of self, an immolation, as if he had briefly penetrated to the cool still fire at the heart of things.

And he felt something like this now as he made love to Mo, his lips brushing her hair and eyes and cheeks before twining with her mouth finally in a kiss that lasted until he could feel her begin to come and then he burrowed his face in her neck as he rushed to follow, crushing her body to his, killing it, killing his own. And immediately she was weeping in his arms, her face a lovely saltlick to his mouth. It was then he heard himself uttering the heavy, forbidden words:

"I love you, Mo. I love you. I love you."

In response she held his body tightly, locking him in the bracelet of her legs, and began to return his kisses, ardently, her mouth suddenly the sweetest spring in all the desert of his life. So it was only natural that within a short time they were making love again, but more slowly now, more deliciously, like a pair of moths playing at the very edge of fire. And possibly they played too near, for when they reached climax this second time it was as if they had consummated a kind of death instead. Suddenly the whole thing was gone, murdered. In her touch alone Bone could feel the thing's death, feel it draining out of her as surely as the blood from his penis. Wordlessly he got off her and lay back on the pillow beside her, but apparently even that was not separation enough, for she abruptly rolled away from him and reached out to the baby, who was still sitting on the floor, engrossed in trying to get the alphabet block out of the coffeepot. But he gave it up for his mother's finger, squeezing it, lifting it to his mouth.

And for a while that was how things remained — Mo lying at the edge of the bed, broodingly playing with the baby, while Bone lay alone, waiting. Finally she spoke:

"So you love me, do you?"

He was slow to answer. "If not you, then no one."

"Maybe no one, then?"

"No — you, Mo."

"How much?"

Bone could almost feel the ground opening under him, the abyss forming, again. "I'm no good at math," he said.

"You love me enough to be my man? Enough to go to some lousy job every day and make the bread so I can take care of this one, feed him, clothe him?" The baby was standing at the side of the bed now, playing with his mother's hair. She waited a few moments before making the hole wider. "And in the middle of night, Rich, when I wake up and can almost hear my terror scratching along the walls — will you be here then? Will you be here to hold me, Rich? Will you love me then?"

He thought of asking her whatever had happened to that hard-nosed women's-libber who expected nothing of men, who would not even accord them the role of fatherhood let alone economic dominance. Apparently that Mo had only been a front, a pose. But he did not bother to ask. Silence was so much safer. And of course it answered all her questions anyway, better than any words could have. Sitting up, she gave him a slight enigmatic smile, a look carrying something beyond its usual burden of irony, something new and subtly alien, as if the light gray-green of her eyes had turned a muddy brown.

"Well, I guess you can relax now, Rich. No more holdouts. The Richard Bone fan club is complete." She started to get out of bed.

"Mo —" Bone took hold of her arm, staying her for the moment.

She was smiling brightly now, falsely. "Yes? Was there something more?"

He waited, but her smile did not change. He let go of her.

"Good. I must be about my son's business." After slipping into her kimono she picked up the baby and took him into the kitchen.

Bone got up and dressed slowly, feeling almost ill with disappointment, the way it all had ended. But it was not his fault, he told himself. Nor hers either. It was just life, that was all it was, always just life, the inability of people to do what they wanted, have what they wanted. Always something else would enter the picture, some need or condition or commitment, some complicating factor that democratically robbed the rich and poor alike, robbed them of fulfillment. Mo understood his position, there could be no question of that. In fact, more than anyone else she and Cutter were always giving him the needle about it, what he was and how he lived, old Golden Boy, the Duke of Unemployment, the Prince of Welfare. So even as she was saying all that a few minutes ago, putting him on the spot that way, she already knew what his answer would be, what it had to be. This winner among winners who could barely feed and clothe himself — how in God's name was he suddenly to become the All-American Provider again? There was no way. And Mo knew it, had known it all along. So it was not his fault, not his worry. There was no need for him to sweat the thing. She would be all right. It had been the wine talking, that was all. The wine and the sex. She had probably already forgotten the whole thing. Why shouldn't he do the same?

In the next hour Mo dragged back and forth between the kitchen and the bedroom and the bathroom, taking care of the baby, changing and feeding him and getting him ready for bed. Every so often she would take a drink of the wine, which was over half gone now. And once Bone saw her in the bathroom shaking a few pills into her hand and popping them into her mouth like peanuts. He tried to stay out of her way. He sat in the living room perusing the ravaged *Village Voice* and he drank a little more of the wine and finished off the last of the bread and cheese.

After she had put the baby to bed, Bone suggested they put on something warm and go out on the deck and watch California doing her thing, the lights of her cars moving along the coast. Shrugging, Mo brought along the bottle of wine but rejected the idea of putting on a coat — keeping her warm would be his responsibility, she said. And after he had sat down in the one sturdy deck chair, she settled snugly onto his lap, pulling his coat — Cutter's actually — around her and tucking her head in under his chin. The night was beautifully clear, with a late Santa Ana coming down out of the canyons and pushing the normally heavy night air out to the islands, so Bone was able to see up the coast to Goleta and beyond, a kind of miniature electric Milky Way through which the traffic on 101 moved steadily, like a river of meteors. Mo did not bother to look. The air was cold and she lay against Bone shivering, her eyes closed. He kissed her on the forehead and in her hair a few times but she did not react at all, and when he tried to tell her about the events of last night, Cutter doing

Sunset Strip, she said she was not interested. In fact about all she did seem interested in was the wine she had brought out with her and which she sipped at every now and then.

After a while Bone suggested they go back inside, and she went along as indifferently as she had gone out in the first place. She was still shivering, however, so he got a blanket out of the bedroom and spread it over her on the davenport. And then he lay down next to her, behind her, holding one arm around her, over her breasts. And the position must have made her feel better and more secure, for she laughed suddenly, a soft wry laugh muffled against the stuffing of the old davenport.

"I kind of had you going back there, didn't I," she said.

"Where?"

"The bedroom."

"You still have."

"Not the sex part, dummy. What I said, I mean — all that gunk about love and security, getting me a shield and protector."

"I knew you didn't mean it," Bone said, and wondered whether he would have tried it looking her in the eye. "I know you better than that," he added.

"Of course you do. And in the biblical sense now too, isn't that sweet? I am known by Richard Bone — why it's a regular lyric." She laughed and then repeated the phrase, almost sang it. "I am known by Richard Bone."

Bone squeezed her breasts. "And it's been nice knowing you."

"I bet you say that to all the girls."

Bone told her to shut up and go to sleep and for a while she did not say anything more, just lay there against his body breathing shallowly. And then, as the rhythm of her breathing changed, he realized she was weeping.

"You'd better leave now, Rich," she said finally.

"Soon."

"No, now. I don't want to fall asleep . . . this way. And then wake . . . alone."

"I'll stay."

"No, you won't. When I'm asleep, you'll get up and leave. You'll sneak off carrying your shoes. I know you."

"I told you to go to sleep," he said. "Now do it. Relax. Give up the fight a few minutes, okay?"

And in time she seemed to drop off occasionally, going down into sleep like a tiring swimmer into the sea. But then she would come up out of it again and laboriously push on.

"I didn't expect anything from you, Rich," she said finally.

"There was no reason to."

"Of course not. I mean it's not as if you were the first in line." She had begun slurring her words now, and she spoke so softly Bone could barely hear her. "Course the line, it goes way back — back to Daddy, I guess. Old numero uno. And then a teacher was next, a woman, so brilliant and pretty, my idol, my secret love. And then a whole marching band of boys, one at a time, and one just like another. And then the drugs, and Jesus. And now Alex — Alex and you and the baby."

Bone snored softly, pretending sleep. But it made no difference.

"When you're gone," she went on, "I'll wake up alone. In the middle of the night I'll wake up and I'll probably run in there to see if he's still there. I'll look at him sleeping, my little monster, my jailer. I'll look at him and I'll tell myself, oh you love him now, now when you're the Big Enchilada and he needs you every hour of the day. But later? Later, when he won't need me either? 'Cause, really, who needs old ladies, huh, Rich? Who wants them?"

"Right," Bone said. "He'll reject you too, just like everyone else. No one likes you, Mo. No one ever has. No one ever will."

If she heard him, she gave no sign of it. "Oh, I could go home, I guess. I could sit around the pool with my mother and drink margaritas. I could swim and get a good tan again and we could talk about face lifts and clothes and new places to eat. But I won't do it."

"You won't do it."

She turned in his arm, unthinkingly thrusting her buttocks tighter against his erection. "You know how I always see myself?" she said. "How I always picture myself? And I can't stop. I mean, I try. I really do. But I even dream it. It's like a kind of precognition. I'm, oh I don't know, forty or fifty, and even skinnier than now and pale as death and my face is just a kind of blank, you know? I'm sitting alone on this bench outside somewhere, on the grounds of some kind of institution or hospital, it seems. And I never smile. I never cry. I just sit there. And I wait."

Again Bone told her to sleep, told her that he would stay.

She tried to laugh then, at least made a kind of derisive sound, an expulsion of air. But she ended up crying again, with her body if nothing else. Holding her tightly, Bone waited, and after a while she stopped trembling and seemed to slip under the surface of her consciousness again, but only to rise out of it moments later.

"Will you stay, Rich?" she asked. "When I wake, will you be here?"

He said nothing for a time, hoping she would fall asleep again. But she persisted.

"Will you be here, Rich?"

He squeezed her body reassuringly. "Sure," he said. "So go to sleep now, Mo. Rest."

And he could almost feel her descending into it for good now, filling her lungs with air and arching her body and letting go, plunging steeply into the stillness.

Bone did not get up until he was sure she was sound asleep, then he moved quickly, getting the keys to the Packard off the mantel, where Cutter invariably threw them, though occasionally missing and depositing them in the fireplace instead, and a few times even in the fire. Bone quietly went out the front door then and locked it behind him. He slipped into the Packard, choked it lavishly, and got it started on the first try.

Ten minutes later he parked the car a half block from the Littles'. He took off his shoes and walked gingerly around the sprawling structure toward his room, all the way fearing that the lady of the house would somehow sense his arrival and come running at him with her hair up in rollers and her eyes taped back and her face mudpacked and chin-strapped for the night. He made it in safely, however, locking the door behind him and quickly undressing and slipping into bed.

He almost felt guilty admitting it to himself, but he was feeling pretty good about how things had turned out. He was not very proud of having to run out on Mo like that, but then she had not left him much choice, coming on the way she had, like some poor knocked-up teenager, all tears and need and self-pity. That simply was not the Mo he knew. It was an impostor, some weird mime doing a one-night stand. Tomorrow she would be herself again, he was sure of that, and she would understand. Certainly she knew that in this world you saved yourself. Either you did it, or no one did.

But beyond that, his disappointment in her, he felt a kind of relief too, because he no longer felt vulnerable where she was concerned. It was as if he had got all his markers back. He was his own man again, all his emotions once more in fairly good shape, a trifle hard maybe, overtrained, but durable, good for the longer distances. So there was really nothing much to think about, nothing to keep him awake.

And nothing did. He slept until a banging sound woke him at dawn. Getting up, he saw George Swanson standing outside his door in the soft mauve light. George was wearing a raincoat over denim pants and what appeared to be a pajama top, and for once his hair was not combed, his face was not shaved.

Bone opened the door.

"You know where Alex is?" Swanson asked.

"In L.A. — why?"

Swanson's eyes filmed over. "Mo and the baby — I guess you haven't heard."

"Heard what?" Bone felt oddly foolish saying it, like a man already struck by lightning but waiting around for the report, the thunder that would announce his own demise. "*Heard what?*" he repeated.

"There was a fire," Swanson said. "They're both dead."

9

BONE AND SWANSON, WHO HAD ALREADY GIVEN THEIR STATEMENTS to the police, were waiting on the front steps of the station house when Cutter finally emerged, at almost ten in the morning. Bone gave him a cigarette, lit it, waited. And Swanson too said nothing, apparently expecting the same explosion. But it never came.

"Not much to it," Cutter said finally.

"Not much," Bone agreed.

"Here today, gone tomorrow." Cutter grinned crookedly through the cigarette smoke.

Swanson's eyes suddenly filled. "Let's go to my house now, Alex. You're staying with us, okay?"

Cutter ignored him. "Win a few, lose a few."

"Long as you want," Swanson said.

"The Lord giveth, the Lord taketh away."

Bone dragged on his cigarette, looked down at the steps.

"Blessed be the name of the Lord."

Cutter had started moving now, limping slowly down the sidewalk. Bone and Swanson followed.

"Wasn't anything to it," Cutter said. "The police were just beautiful. Hardly any red tape at all. Just sign here, please. No sweat, no hassle."

Swanson explained. "Well, you weren't here, Alex, when it happened. And since you and Mo weren't married, her parents are still next of kin. So I guess they're the ones to handle everything, identify the bodies and all."

Cutter shook his head. "Mr. and Mrs. Harris Johnston. Two of my staunchest fans."

"Well, they can't blame you," Swanson said. "You weren't even here."

Bone expected Cutter to turn on him then, with the same bent smile. 'No, *I* wasn't here.' But he said nothing.

And they had reached Swanson's car now, the small two-seat Jaguar, one of the reasons Bone had brought Mrs. Little's pickup downtown.

"Valerie coming back for you?" he asked Cutter.

Cutter shook his head. "Not likely."

A half hour earlier, after letting him out, she had driven off like a panicked drag racer, burning rubber right in front of the police station.

"You can come with me, then," Swanson said. "Rich can follow in his truck. We got plenty of room at the house. And you can stay as long as you like."

Cutter did not move. "My benefactor."

"You can use one," Bone told him.

"Bowman Brothers," Cutter said. "I hear that's where the bodies are."

Swanson nodded.

"We're gonna stop there on the way. I want to see them."

Swanson asked him if he was sure. "It was a terrible fire," he said. "Terrible."

But Cutter was already moving toward the pickup parked down the street.

"We'll see you there, George," he said.

In the truck, Bone could not think of anything to say, and Cutter evidently did not feel the need of words, for he sat slumped in the corner of the cab, squinting against the smoke that curled up from the stump of his cigarette. Bone was sure that Cutter knew the whole story — there was no reason for the police not to have told him everything — and yet if he did know, it beggared belief that he could sit beside Bone now, saying nothing, asking nothing.

The fire, which had started with a gas explosion, had burned the house to the ground, consuming everything except the plumbing and sinks and a few major appliances including the kitchen range — which was discovered to have one of its gas jets turned on. The investigators also turned up a melted medicine vial next to the bodies of Mo and the baby, which were found lying together in what was left of Mo's bed. The evidence thus pointed to the likelihood of murder-suicide, that Mo had turned on the gas jet herself, had ingested a quantity of downers, and then had taken the baby to bed with her — there to await the painless death of carbon monoxide poisoning. The explosion and fire had been an accident, it was theorized, an oversight of Mo's drugged mind. Unfortunately — from the standpoint of the police — none of this was provable. The bodies were too far destroyed for any accurate postmortem testing. The medical examiner therefore would probably have to rule that the deaths were accidental.

So as far as Bone was concerned there was still much to talk about, much between him and Cutter that needed airing.

"I was with her yesterday, Alex," he tried now. "You remember that."

"So?"

"So I'd think you'd want to know how she was."

"Okay, how was she?"

Bone found himself almost stammering. "Well, she was down, all right. But not unusually so, I didn't think. Not —"

"Suicidal?" Cutter almost sneered as he said it.

"Of course not. I wouldn't have left her if I'd thought she was."

"You don't have to tell me that."

"Well, the police — they must have told you about the gas jet being on. And the empty pill bottle."

"Yeah. I heard their theory."

"You don't believe it?"

Cutter laughed softly, scornfully. "*Mo*? Mo kill that kid? *Never.*"

And Bone felt a swift rush of relief and gratitude. "That's what I think," he got out. "It was an accident, Alex. It had to be. I figure she was stoned on quads and turned the jet on to heat coffee or something. And the baby must have cried and she went to get him and forgot all about the gas being on. The pilot must have been off, and she didn't notice. She just went straight to the baby and took him to be with her. And—"

But Bone could not go on. His voice was strangling and his eyes had filled. Next to him, Cutter was nodding. But his sardonic look did not agree.

"Yeah, that *could* have been," he said. "It's as good a theory as the other."

"What else is there?"

"Maybe someone sent me a message."

Bone, just then pulling into the parking lot behind the mortuary, was not able to look at Cutter until he had parked the truck. And when he did, he could not believe what he saw. The man's face was void of irony.

"Who?" Bone asked, though he already knew.

"I told you on the phone."

Bone tried to smile. "You can't be serious."

"I can't?"

"It doesn't make sense, Alex."

Cutter got out of the truck. "We'll see," he said.

After Swanson arrived, the three of them went around to the front of the building, cutting across the barbered lawn. When they entered the reception room they found Bone's old inquisitor, tiny Lieutenant Ross, talking softly with an elderly well-dressed couple and another man whose gray pinstripe suit and unctuously deferential manner suggested he was the proprietor of the establishment. It was the couple, however, who commanded Bone's attention, for on seeing Cutter they reacted as if some monstrous serpent had come gliding into the room.

"Him!" the woman cried. "Why couldn't it have been him — that animal — instead of our baby, our Maureen?"

Her husband took her by the shoulder and turned her away. "Don't bother about him," he said. "He doesn't matter anymore. He's nothing now."

Cutter stood there looking at them. "I love you too," he said.

Lieutenant Ross told him to shut up and move out.

"*Move out?* What's happened? We back in the marines?"

The woman was crying heavily now and her husband was trying his best to comfort her, hugging her to him with one hand while he used the other to daub her face with a handkerchief.

"You killed my baby!" she screamed at Cutter. "You killed her! You filth! You pig!"

Ross told her to take it easy. "He's leaving, Mrs. Johnston. He's leaving now." He turned to Cutter. "Aren't you, pal?"

Cutter shook his head. "I'm gonna see the bodies first — pal."

The lieutenant grinned. "No, you're not."

Swanson, heading for the door, tried to pull Cutter with him. "Come on, Alex. Let's leave for now. Maybe we can come back."

But Cutter shook him off. "I'm going to see the bodies."

Bone could see that Ross had already spent his small fund of patience, so he moved quickly, asking the proprietor where the phone was.

"I want to call the paper and our lawyer," he explained. "The lieutenant must have forgotten — common-law marriage has certain rights these days. There's no way you can legally keep Mr. Cutter from seeing the bodies of his wife and son. He'll be able to sue your ass — I guess you realize that?"

Evidently the mortician did, for his color was rapidly beginning to resemble that of his clients. He turned imploringly to Ross, who had quickly shifted his hostility to Bone, Bone the uncooperative, the myopic, the deadbeat who had helped him back onto baby food.

"You get around, don't you?" the lieutenant said.

Bone did not respond, and Ross turned to the Johnstons.

"This is Richard Bone," he told them. "He was the last one to see your daughter alive."

Bone was not sure how Ross knew this — he had given his statement to a Sergeant Waldheim down at the station — and in fact he had no idea what Ross was doing here with the Johnstons in the first place; a simple body identification would not have seemed big enough to warrant the services of a lieutenant. But then that did not matter now, Bone decided, not with Mo's parents staring at him.

"That's right," he told them. "I dropped by yesterday evening. She gave me some supper. And I think you ought to know she didn't seem unhappy or depressed. She loved her baby. What happened was an accident. I'm sure of that."

This set Mrs. Johnston crying again, but her husband gave Bone a nod of understanding and perhaps even gratitude, and Bone was glad for what he had said. He only wished he could have believed it himself, beyond all doubt.

The lieutenant meanwhile had changed his mind. He nodded to the mortician, who then asked Cutter to follow him. Bone and Swanson went along, through a wide door and down a corridor to a small room. In it were two high wheeled tables covered with white sheets gently mounded in the middle. Casually, without a touch of ceremony, the mortician pulled back the sheets, revealing a pair of clear plastic sacks each containing what looked like blackened mummies, eyeless, hairless, skinless, one almost life-size and the other very tiny, a doll, a plaything for beasts.

Swanson gagged and turned away, doubling over as if he

had been kicked in the stomach. Bone withstood it a moment longer, waiting to see if Cutter would need him, then he too turned and followed Swanson out of the room, feeling as if his body were splitting from the inside, like an egg about to bear some hideous crawling thing. Inside, the mortician was enjoying himself with Cutter:

"When they're this bad they don't even post 'em. Just bring 'em straight here."

Cutter made no comment. When he came out a few moments later he looked calm, almost serene.

"Let's go have a drink," he said.

The Bay Tree Bar was around the corner from the mortuary, so they went there on foot. They went in silence and settled into the midmorning gloom of the place like bears into a winter cave. They were the only patrons, which only added to their reticence, made them like strangers with each other. For a time Swanson tried to talk about the tragedy, and he tried to get Bone to tell them about yesterday afternoon, how Mo had seemed, what she had said. But Cutter interrupted, saying he didn't want to hear any of that, it was unimportant now, it was beside the point. There he stopped, however, not going on to explain just what "the point" was, not uttering one word about J. J. Wolfe or any "messages" the man supposedly had sent him. Instead he sat there drinking scotch and chain-smoking cigarettes, a new habit for him, apparently willed him by Mo.

And Bone waited. Feeling like a ticking bomb, he leaned back and waited for the minutes to drop away one by one and free him in the end. He was in no hurry. He tried not to let on how he felt or what lay ahead of him, just sat there calmly drinking with the other two, a little faster than he normally did perhaps. But they did not notice. Swanson was busy giving Cutter counsel. He knew how hard it would be for Alex to stand by and watch Mo's parents take over, take the bodies back to Beverly Hills and arrange the funeral and everything, probably even exclude him from the proceedings altogether. But Swanson advised him not to do anything about it, to accept it.

And Cutter nodded indulgently. "Don't worry about it, George," he said. "Funerals ain't my forte. If it was left up to me, the bodies probably wouldn't even get buried."

The coarseness of the remark seemed to upset Swanson. Taking a deeper drink than was his custom, he wound up choking and coughing, and Cutter reached over and patted him on the back.

"Don't sweat it, old buddy," he told him. "They're dead now. Gone. Hell, those things over there ain't even bodies — they're *remains.*" His voice scorned the word. "So let old Mom and Pop have 'em. Let them have all the goddamn ceremonies they want. I got other business."

Swanson did not ask him what it was. He was sure about one thing, he said — Alex was coming to stay at his place. And it wasn't going to be some little overnight thing either, not if he could help it. No, Alex was going to have his own room and money too, and above all, *time.* Time to get his head on straight again. And Swanson didn't care if it took him a month, a year, or five years — he'd still be welcome.

"You remember that spring vacation your folks took me with you, to Sun Valley?" he asked.

Cutter's eye was distant, bleak. "Vaguely," he said.

"Well, that was the biggest thing that ever happened to me as a kid, the first skiing I'd ever done. And the first real living. I haven't forgotten it — even if you have. So you're staying with us, Alex. Open end."

Cutter looked over at Bone and grinned. "Well, I've finally got it made," he said, lifting his glass. "Let's drink to George's place. My new home. *Requiescat in pace.*"

It was close to noon when Bone left them, claiming that he had to get the pickup truck back to Mrs. Little. Instead he bought a pint of scotch at a nearby liquor store and drove up to Franceschi Park at the top of the Riviera. It was a small park, not much more than a few acres of grass fringed with eucalyptus trees and three or four picnic tables. And though it offered a stirring view of the coast, that was not the reason he had chosen it. More important to him was its remoteness, its distance from the beaten tourist path. He figured that with any luck at all a man would be able to drink there in peace for hours. And that was just what he planned to do.

The only other persons he could see in the park were two lovers sitting on a table at the far end, the girl leaning back between the man's legs as they both stared out at the sea, its great sweep somehow diminished by the oil-drilling platforms strewn along the channel, like an armada of monstrous crabs. Bootlegging the bottle of scotch, Bone made his way down through the trees until he found a place to his liking, a flat grassy niche in the rocks, with a slight overhang above. Sitting down, he opened the bottle and took a deep pull on it, so much he almost gagged as it went down. And he thought about what he was doing, why he had to get drunk this day. He did not think it was because of his feelings of guilt and remorse, that they were insupportable. They should have been, he knew. But they were not. And he did not believe the reason was simple grief, the knowledge that she was gone now, gone forever, and the baby with her — the terrible and final knowing that he would not see her again, not talk with her, not hold her, not ever. This knowledge, this grief, had become for him an unrelieved and oddly localized pain, as if an artery in his chest had burst and was now spilling his life there. Even this he could have endured, however, could have faced it sober. He did not need the liquor for that, nor as a kind of ritual thing, part of some private memorial service, a lone man's wake. No, he imagined that the reason for the bottle was simply that he did not care to live through the rest of this day as his customary self, his sober self, Old Faithless in the mirror. Today he needed to take his eye off the ball. He needed an unsteady hand and an unsure foot. He needed a vacation from the grubby little scavenger that was Richard Kendall Bone.

So he drank. Like some poor skid row wino he huddled back in his little hole and nipped steadily at the bottle, carefully building his oblivion. And it came as slowly and surely as twilight, the brilliant spring sun dulling to a kind of diurnal moon that muted all color and softened the biting edges of the world stretched out below him, and in time the pain in his chest began to ease and he found entire minutes passing without his hearing her voice asking him to stay, asking him if he would be there when she woke, and then his own voice answering: Sure, go to sleep now, Mo, rest.

He finished the bottle and left the park, drunk, but not so drunk he was unaware of it. Nevertheless he made no allowance for his condition and drove recklessly, jockeying the truck like a stoned teenager through the afternoon traffic. And instead of choosing a safe bar like Murdock's he stopped in the barrio and entered a Chicano joint where he knew Anglos were not welcome. He did not bother to specify scotch and so found himself drinking bourbon, standing there at the bar in the seedy storefront tavern putting down shot after shot as if he were trying to slake an honest water-thirst, all the while vaguely aware that the bartender and the other patrons were watching him, in fact had put him at the center of their attention like a cock in a pit. He remembered later sitting at a table for a while, and perhaps even dozing for a time. And he had a vague recollection of some kind of trouble in the men's room, some pushing and shoving and a tall thin young Mexican groaning on the floor in front of the urinal, and there was blood, Bone's own blood running down his chin and soaking his shirt. And then, abruptly, it seemed he was outside, wandering up and down the street looking for the truck, and finding it eventually with the keys still in the ignition — a discovery that for some reason amused him greatly and had him laughing out loud as he drove off, not knowing where he was headed. Evidently the traffic flow was easier to the south, for that was the direction he took, crossing the freeway and winding up on Cabrillo Boulevard, which he followed past the yacht harbor to the Leadbetter Beach parking lot, where he left the truck.

The moment his feet touched sand he knew he had come to the right place, that this had been his true destination all day long, only for some reason he had overlooked it, had forgotten that on this day above all others he had to run, and run, run like that poor long-striding adolescent mark in freshman track, run as if the old life depended on it, yes, run Richard Bone right down into the sand, run him until he was stump-legged and windless, broken, his heart a pump of piss and bile. And so he started out, heading into a real twilight now, a dim fogged shore strewn with kelp and lost dogs and lovers and lonely old men.

Bone ran past them all, sometimes veering into the surf and stumbling back out and plunging on. And within minutes, it seemed, he had come to the end of the beach, the point under the cliffs where the tide each day gave and then withdrew strips of narrow rocky sand, isolate and wind. This day the tide was taking, rising to turn the gray ribbon of beach into separate headlands cleaving the waves as they thundered in. So part of the time Bone was running knee-deep in water, fighting through it to another strip of beach and then on into the water again.

And suddenly it occurred to him that there would never be a better time to go for a swim, to try for that hundred yards too far. Immediately he began to stagger and hop about the small stretch of beach, trying to get out of his sea-wet clothes. And when he made it finally he stood there naked for a few moments, breathing deeply, preparing himself for the initial assault against the breakers, which he knew would be the most difficult part of the swim, the part like climbing a mountain in the midst of an avalanche.

Then abruptly he was in the water and swimming for his

life, coming up for air in the trough between the waves and diving again, stroking frantically as the great freezing tides thundered over him, tugging him toward shore. But with each wave he gained a few feet, and in time — how much time, he had no idea — he found himself out beyond the breakers, where the swimming should have been easier. But somehow each stroke was like lifting a log out of the water and dropping it, trying to force it down through a substance with the consistency of freshly poured cement. His breath ripped out of his lungs, his heart sprinted, ached. And still he kept on. He swam in the failing light. He swam in darkness. He swam until he could swim no more. And then he gave it all, this ridiculous swim, this ridiculous life, his easy benediction:

Go to sleep now. Rest. I'll be here, yes.

And that was what he remembered, the logs coming to rest in the water and his head settling back just as hers had done, his body arching the same way, and then plunging, going deep into his own forever sea.

But all he found was sand, another small prow of beach where a driftwood fire burned and voices fell over him like salt spray, cool stinging voices laughing at what the sea had coughed up. And then there were blankets dropped over his shaking shoulders and a bottle at his mouth, wine as sickly sweet as Kool-Aid followed by the dryness of smoke, grass smoke instead of wood, balm for his savaged lungs. There was flesh with him in the blankets then, warm slick woman flesh, and this smiling stone-eyed face that disappeared every so often, huddling down over his body as if she were building a fire there, trying to blow it into life. And apparently she succeeded, for his only recollection of the beach from then on was the sex, the stone-eyed girl and then another one astride him and under him and locked with him mouth to groin, sometimes just one of them alone and other times both, and yet there never seemed to be any release for him, only the tumescence, the fire the stone-eyed one had built in him and which the alcohol kept from going out, and so there was cheering too, he remembered that, voices urging him on, like a performing animal, a circus freak. Supersalt, they called him.

He remembered the floor of a darkened minibus, wrapped up in blankets and shivering as the stone-eyed girl huddled near him, bracing herself against the bumping of the vehicle. And then there was only silence, a great long tunnel of nothing, a sleep that could have been death for all he knew of it.

He woke in daylight alone in a cluttered room, a small efficiency apartment plastered with peeling posters of youth-cult and rebellion: the inevitable Che and W. C. Fields along with Henry Kissinger as a nude Cosmopolitan Man and other non-pictorial ones proclaiming such profundities as *Shit* and *Bitch, Bitch, Bitch* in artsy typography. Empty clotheslines crisscrossed the room above a floor strewn with sleeping bags and broken chairs and scattered books and sheet music and cans and ashtrays, along with a torn bass drum and a guitar without strings. The kitchenette, buried in beer cans and dirty dishes, was such a mess that Bone almost expected to see Mo come shuffling out of it — which was the wrong thought for him to have, for abruptly he was conscious then, aware of who he was and what had happened, and with that realization he also discovered his hangover, the cold dishwater that was his belly, the stake being driven into his head. Slowly he sat up, not surprised to discover that he had been sleeping on a davenport instead of a bed. Of three doors in the place, one opened into a closet and the other was obviously the front door, so he was about to set himself in the direction of the third, hoping there to find relief for his seared throat and aching bladder. But just as he was about to try to stand, the door opened and someone came out, a small dark creature with a boy's haircut and build and clothes — rope sandals and Levi's and a leather jacket over a UCSB T-shirt, whose slight pointed rise at the U and B suggested the creature might be female.

"You're awake," she said.

"Could be," he admitted.

"Well, put something on, for God's sake. Don't just sit there showing off."

Bone pulled a ratty blanket over his lap. "I'm sorry," he told her. "I thought you were a boy."

"Thanks."

"Don't mention it." Standing, he pulled the blanket around him. "Uh, can I go in there now?" he said. "I've got problems."

"You sure have." She moved out of the doorway.

Bone did not ask for clarification. The problems he knew about were sufficient for now. Closing the door behind him, he did what he could to end them. After urinating for what seemed like twenty minutes, he drank a glass of cold water and promptly threw it up. Trying warm water then, he stood for a while staring at the derelict in the mirror, trying to psych him into keeping the water down. He was only mildly surprised to see that he had a bruise under his left eye and a cut running from his hairline down to his earlobe. It was already dried, a fine handsome scab.

Wrapping the blanket around him again, he went back into the apartment. The girl was standing at the front windows, which looked out on a straight ugly street bordered by California's answer to the brownstone, four- and eight-unit stucco apartment houses, pastel boxes built to last a decade.

"Isla Vista?" he said.

She nodded sourly. "Yeah — the ghetto."

"The kids on the beach — I take it they brought me here."

"My roomies, yeah — Carla and Josie, the clap twins."

"I hope you're wrong."

"You remember, then?"

"What?"

"The beach. Coming in out of the waves 'like a fucking Greek god' — I believe that's how Carla described it."

224

Bone shook his head wonderingly, in pain. "Beautiful," he said.

"Isn't it? She didn't specify which god though."

"Bacchus."

The girl looked dubious. "Aphrodite came out of the sea."

"Okay — her, then."

"No, Carla wouldn't agree. She said you were spectacular, whatever that means."

"Whatever."

"But then of course I wasn't there."

"Why of course?"

"Because I'm the Virgin of Isla Vista — didn't you know?"

"No, I'm afraid not. But congratulations anyway."

"Well, that's what everyone calls me."

Bone said nothing as a fresh wave of nausea swept over him. He carefully sagged back onto the davenport.

"That or Monk," she said.

"Fine," he got out. "Keep up the good work."

"It isn't hard, believe me."

"Good."

"Josie's at work, and Carla's got an art class. She told me to take good care of you. She's looking forward to meeting you sober."

"You sound like an answering service."

"That's about it," the girl admitted.

Bone asked her what time it was.

"A little after one."

"I got any clothes here? Did they find —"

She was shaking her head. "Nope — they brought you just as they found you. In all your glory."

He could not help groaning. "Beautiful. Oh Jesus, that is just beautiful." He remembered having seventy dollars left after buying the bottle of scotch yesterday, fifty of which — two twenties and a ten — he had secreted in his wallet between his driver's license and a three-year-old American Express card.

The wallet of course had been in his pants. And his pants were now in the sea.

"Where'd you leave your clothes?" the girl asked.

"On the beach."

"Maybe they're still there."

Bone shook his head. "Tide was still rising."

"How neat. When the tide brings it all in again, they'll think you're dead. You'll be a free man. You can start a brand-new life."

"Yeah — how neat."

"It isn't, huh?"

"I'm too successful with this one."

"Feel kind of lousy, huh?"

He did not bother to answer.

"How much did you have?" she kept on.

"I wasn't counting."

"Obviously."

She seemed to have nothing else in the world to do except stand there and stare at him, something like a lonely tomboy sister with a big brother back from the wars. Even sick as he was, the intensity of her interest embarrassed him and he wanted to tell her to get lost. Instead he asked if there was any coffee.

"Yeah, instant. You want some?"

"I could try."

She nodded approvingly. "Bravo. That's the spirit."

While she busied herself in the cluttered kitchenette, Bone got up and rummaged through an equally cluttered closet until he came up with something he could wear, a white terry beach robe with a large Budweiser beer label printed on the back. Putting the robe on, he pulled the sash tighter than he should have and found himself struggling not to retch. His legs suddenly were fileted and his stomach felt as if it had been wadded by a large hand. With his head booming, he teetered back to the davenport.

From the kitchenette, the girl asked him who Mo was.

"Why?" he said. "What do you mean?"

"You talk in your sleep."

"He's just a guy I know."

"And you're in love with him?"

"Yeah, I'm mad about him."

For a time the girl just stood there watching the kettle heating on the burner. Finally she said, "I know three things — Mo is a woman, she has a baby, and you are sorry. You are very sorry."

Bone looked away from her, convinced that he had never felt worse in all his life. He could not remember a time when his body and spirit were so all-of-a-piece, so consonant in their pain and disrepair. It made him wonder why men held life precious. Just the possibility of there being days like this somehow devalued all the others, at least for him.

Idly, he looked out the window at a vacant lot across the street, where some students or street people had a fire going, a bonfire of paintings, evidently some twenty-year-old artist finally throwing in the towel, succumbing to the forces of darkness. The paintings appeared to be portraits or figure studies, one of a nude woman whose golden skin turned a brief brown and then black and then disappeared altogether as the flames consumed her. And Bone could not help thinking of the blackened mummy in the clear plastic sack. His stomach crumpled again, pumped something bilious into his throat, where he choked it off, trembling, tear-blinded. He put his head down for a time. Then, drying his eyes, he looked up at the girl.

"Let's forget the coffee, okay?"

"Sure."

"Maybe some hair of the dog," he suggested. "You got anything?"

"Beer," she said. "And an old bottle of brandy."

"That'll do. Even old."

Standing on a chair, she got the bottle out of a cabinet over the refrigerator. "You want a glass?" she asked.

"No. Just the bottle."

She brought it over and gave it to him, grudgingly. Taking his first pull on the bottle, he closed his eyes and waited, straining to keep it down. And then he felt it, the special gift of brandy, the sudden stain of warmth spreading through his stomach.

"You gonna get drunk again?" she asked.

He shook his head. "It's the hangover, that's all. A little of this and I'll feel better."

"How about a little food?"

"Later."

She looked at him dolefully. "Don't stay here, okay?"

Bone tried to smile. "Not too keen on me, huh?"

"On *them*. The clap twins. They won't be good for you."

"I can believe it." He took another drink.

"I'm getting out too."

"Can't blame you. The place is a pigsty."

"I know. I just gave up after a while."

"One does."

She watched him as he took another pull on the bottle. "What's your name?" she asked.

"Richard Bone."

"You drink pretty fast, Richard Bone."

"Not fast enough."

"I thought you weren't going to get drunk."

He was feeling better now, as the warmth continued to spread in him. "I'm not. I meant something else."

"What?"

He met her gaze for a few moments, the unblinking eyes above the pugnacious tomboy mouth and chin. "I forget," he said.

She seemed to give up on him then. Turning away, she went back into the kitchenette. "Is there anybody you want me to call?" she asked. "Someone to come and get you?"

Bone thought about it. "Yeah," he said finally. "I don't know the number — George Swanson in Santa Barbara. Ask for Cutter. Mister Alexander Cutter."

She got the phonebook and began to leaf through it, looking for the number. "You don't want me to call Mo?" she asked.

Bone could not remember alcohol hitting him so hard before. The bottle of brandy had been only half full when he started and though there was still at least a third of it left he felt totally and painlessly high. And he imagined the reason was that he had started out already halfway home, with a respectable level of alcohol still sloshing about in his blood. But whatever the cause, he was not about to complain, for his hangover had gone the way of his sobriety, and he missed neither of them.

As he drank, he sat on the davenport looking out the window at the few raunchy kids still left around the fire, poking and worrying its smoking ashes like scavengers at a city dump. He also watched the Virgin of Isla Vista banging around in the kitchenette, putting things away and straightening up and starting to wash the dishes. And then he stretched out and slept again, for how long he had no idea. There was no question, however, as to what it was that woke him finally — a cane sticking him in the ribs. And then Cutter's voice:

"Wake up, my son. Thy father hath need of thee."

Bone remembered trying to push the cane away, but it kept prodding him in new places. And he remembered getting up finally, teetering there in the middle of the room like an infant while the two of them struggled to dress him. As they were working him into his jockey shorts, he recalled warning them to look the other way because he was actually the Virgin of Chicago Plains and it was rumored that anyone who dared look upon his private parts would be blinded by their purity and perfection. And Cutter went along, saying something to the effect that, yes, he and the girl were aware what a signal honor fate had visited upon them. But then he ruined the moment by observing to the girl that probably never before in human history had so little given so many so little, and Bone remembered the girl laughing, smiling happily, and how unexpectedly beautiful that smile had seemed, lighting not only her drab little face but even for a few moments the alcoholic wastes of his own spirit.

Dressed finally, and clutching his precious hangover antidote, the fifth of Christian Brothers, he let Cutter and the girl lead him downstairs and outside to a late-model Ford station wagon, which Bone recalled seeing in Swanson's driveway and garage, the family utility vehicle, something for George and his wife to fall back on in such dire emergencies as having to carry a third person or an extra sack of groceries. At the car Bone noticed that the girl had brought her own suitcase with her, an expensive overnight bag which she stuffed into the back of the wagon, next to Bone's own luggage from his room at Mrs. Little's. It crossed Bone's mind that none of this made any sense — the girl going along, and his own things being there, packed and loaded — but it just did not seem important to him, not where he was, gliding up above it all like a beatified seagull. And even when he got into the back seat of the wagon and had to make a place for himself amid all the junk — the rifles and shotguns and cameras and tape recorders — he still did not bother to ask any questions.

After driving back to Santa Barbara, Cutter pulled into the parking lot of Swanson's real estate office and got out. He said he would not be long and he was true to his word, coming out of the building within a few minutes and grinning as he fanned himself with a piece of paper — a check which he promptly cashed at a drive-in bank near the freeway. For some reason Bone remembered his instructions to the teller:

"Make it twenties, my good woman. *Fifty* of them."

And Bone thought: good old George, trusting Cutter to pick up a thousand dollars for him.

But instead of going back to George's house, as Bone expected him to do, Cutter swung south on 101, which caused Bone to look up from the bottle of brandy long enough to inquire where they were headed — Hollywood? Tijuana? Chile? — he thought it might be a good idea if he knew. But Cutter said he was not to worry; they were just out for a drive, that was all, a quick spin down the coast in order to give Bone time to sober up, because, as he well knew, George's wife wasn't keen on lushes or one-eyed cripples, and while they couldn't do anything about the latter, the former was a different matter. So he advised Bone to drink up, finish what he had started, and then once he was safely back on the wagon, they could all repair to Santa Barbara, there to live happily ever after. Bone said he would drink to that, and he did.

They were not much past Carpenteria, however, when Cutter announced that he was starved, and turned off the freeway. Pulling up to a Sambo's restaurant, he gave the girl twenty dollars and sent her off with instructions to load up on hamburgers and fries and Cokes and anything else that tickled her fancy. When she was gone, he reached back for the brandy and took a few pulls himself. Then he sat there looking at Bone and shaking his head.

"Did it help?" he asked.

"What?"

He gestured with the bottle. "This."

"Help what?"

"Richard Bone, the secret bleeder."

"That's me."

"Old blood and tears."

"Now you know."

"Well don't sweat it, kid. We gonna get ours. We gonna make 'em pay."

Bone took the bottle back. "Right on. Let's stick it to 'em."

Cutter was not taken in. "Who?" he asked.

Bone grinned. "You name 'em, pal. I'll do the sticking."

"You don't know who, do you?"

"*Them.*"

And Cutter laughed. "Of course, *them*. Who else?"

Cutter let the girl drive from then on. Bone ate some of the fries and about half of a hamburger — his first food in almost two days — but most of the time he stayed with the brandy, and by the time they reached Los Angeles he had finished the bottle and had stretched out on the seat with a rolled-up coat under his head. He was vaguely aware of their stopping once, in some crowded urban alley, where Cutter scooped up most of the junk on the floor and disappeared for a while, for what purpose Bone did not know or care. Again sleep seemed so much more important.

When he woke again, he woke in pain and thirst and cold, the latter roaring out of the car's air conditioner. Slowly sitting up, he looked about him and all he could see were the rolling wastes of the Mojave Desert, gray in the twilight, a lunar terrain scored by the twin bands of the blacktop freeway stretching ahead of them. The girl was still driving. Cutter, next to her, raised his head to look back at Bone.

"It lives," he announced. "It has risen."

Bone was in no mood for comedy. "Where the hell are we?"

"Just past Barstow."

"Barstow!"

"Yep, Barstow."

"Why?"

"Because it's on the way."

"On the way where?"

"That we don't know."

"*Where*, Alex?"

"Monk and me," he said, "we got to thinking about it back in L.A. And we decided why the hell not just keep right on going. See America first and all that."

Again Bone asked him where they were headed, what was going on.

Sighing, Cutter sank back into the car seat. "I told you he wouldn't dig it," he said to the girl. "The man is other-directed."

She looked back from the wheel, flashing Bone an anxious, almost frightened look. "You were asleep," she said. "And when Alex brought it up — well, it seemed like such a super idea, you know? Just to keep right on going, the three of us."

"Yeah, super," Bone muttered.

"We got the bread," Cutter assured him. "And it's like I was saying to Monk just a few miles back — school keeps. It'll all still be there."

"When we get back," the girl put in.

By now Bone was feeling sick, puking sick. But he fought it down. He was angrier than he was sick. "Not me, Alex," he said. "Not on your goddamn life."

"Well, it's up to you, old buddy. We sure want you to come along. But if you feel you got to go back — well, we can let you out anytime, anyplace. Just say the word."

Bone wanted to tell him to pull over right then, but the words would not come. He knew what shape he was in. And he knew the desert. He knew it that well anyway.

"Needles will do," he said. "You can let me out there."

"You sure?"

"I'm sure."

Cutter was still slouched down in the seat, staring out at the darkening desert. "We'll miss you, Rich," he said. "It just won't be the same."

10

WHEN THEY REACHED NEEDLES, CUTTER ANNOUNCED THAT HE AND the girl were going to stay the night and get an early start in the morning, and he suggested that Bone do the same, since he looked like a dead man and smelled worse and his only hope for a lift back across the desert would be a Hell's Angel with advanced rhinitis. Bone had not intended to start back yet anyway, not feeling the way he did, but he knew that his staying the night in a motel, or for that matter even eating, depended on Cutter's generosity, which, as he soon found out, was not excessive. He asked him for a loan, or more accurately, compensation.

"A hundred," he suggested. "I figure that's about what you owe me. Sort of a kidnapping fee. The cost of getting me back where I was."

And Cutter shrugged a grudging agreement. "Of course, my son. But not now. Not tonight. You'd only spend it on spirits, poor souse that you are. I'll give it to you in the morning. Meanwhile, you can stay with us."

Bone did not object. If he had really wanted the money now, he knew he could have insisted, he could even have strong-armed Cutter for it. But the next morning would do fine, he decided. For one thing, it meant he would not have to pay for his food and lodging for the night. And for another, he wanted to find out if Cutter was serious about this aimless little

234

tour through the motherland or whether it was all a put-on, a smokescreen he was laying down for the girl as well as for him.

They rented a twin-bed room in a dreary rundown little motel with a sign out in front that succinctly recorded the nation's recent economic history — an original *$6 per nite* with a crudely painted number *1* inserted to make *$16*, which in turn was crossed out with a large and angry X. All bets were off, all contracts canceled. It was a lodging for today, tonight. No one was making any promises about tomorrow.

Once inside, Bone waited for Cutter and the girl to finish with the bathroom and then he preempted it for almost an hour, most of which he spent in the shower, first trying to steam the alcohol out of his system and then resorting to the shock treatment of a full cold spray the final ten or fifteen minutes. After dressing, he continued the pursuit of his lost health by talking Cutter into dining at a nearby steakhouse instead of the usual hamburger joints he favored whenever haute cuisine was either unavailable or unaffordable. There Bone tried to restore some of his vitamin loss with a fourteen-ounce New York–cut steak and french fries and a tossed salad washed down with tomato juice and milk and coffee, all in quantities that had the waitress watching him with wary hostility, as if she were afraid he might be putting her on. She was middle-aged and hard-faced, with a beehive of champagne-colored hair that she kept patting and touching to reassure herself it was still there in all its glory. But she was not a bit out of place in the steakhouse, with its linoleum-covered floor and tube-steel furniture and blaring, country-rock jukebox. Bone did not care about any of that, however, for the food was good. And he noticed that the Virgin of Isla Vista seemed to be taking almost as much pleasure in his eating as he was, probably because she had considered him a doomed alcoholic until now. She even insisted on giving him part of her own steak, had cut off a sizable portion and forked it onto his plate almost ceremoniously, like an offering, a bribe to keep him sober. Then she settled back, arms folded, eyes shining, looking every inch a twelve-year-old First Class Boy Scout who had just done his good deed for the day.

"You know, I still don't know your name," he told her now.

"Monk."

"That's not a name."

"It's an insult, yeah," she laughed. "The clap twins hung it on me."

"Well, the hell with them," Bone said. "What's your real name?"

"Monk's fine," she insisted. "I'm used to it now. I like it."

Cutter was lighting a cigar. "We've already been this route, Rich," he said. "The alternative is Dorothy or Dot."

Bone gave in. "Okay — Monk it is."

"Monk from San Jose," Cutter continued. "Surname Emerson, nineteen years old, English Lit major, only child of divorced parents. Daddy's a dentist, Mom's a social worker, and Monk herself is a nigger-loving, com-symp, atheistic socialist with allergies. And a bad case of virginity. It just won't go away."

The girl gave Cutter a rueful look. "Don't talk about that, okay? I'm sorry I told you."

"You should be," Cutter scolded. "Shame on you. With all your advantages. And in this day and age."

Bone tried to rescue the girl. "You've been busy, Alex. No grass growing under the old foot, huh?"

"You forget, Rich, you been bombed out for some time now."

Bone could only agree. "Yeah, a day and a half, as I recall. And it seems like a month and a half. Last time I touched ground was the funeral home. And now here I am, sober in Needles."

"Stuck in Needles," Alex amended.

Bone did not pick it up. Mention of the funeral home had

236

suddenly brought it all back. He would never understand why the sea had rejected him.

"The funeral," he said, "is it tomorrow?"

Cutter looked away and shrugged, almost as if he had been asked the time. And Bone did not understand. He sat there waiting, shaken. Finally he turned back to the girl.

"I forgot to thank you for helping me," he said. "I guess it isn't your fault I wound up here in the desert."

"I'm afraid it's my doing as much as Alex's," she said. "I thought you'd be all for it. And I still think it's a super idea — the three of us just taking off, going nowhere in particular."

"You sure there's such a place?" Bone asked.

"Might as well give it up," Cutter advised her. "The man would just be a drag anyway, looking for hidden meanings and grand significances all across this great land of ours. I can just see him poring over every greasy spoon menu — 'What does it really mean, *over easy?*' And that we don't need, Monk. We can get by."

Bone tried to set the matter straight. "Hidden meanings I'm not after, Alex. Just a few answers, that's all I want."

"Like what?"

"Like what went wrong at George's? Why this sudden flight into the desert?"

Cutter flicked ash off his cigar. "Nothing big," he said. "George's wife just wasn't enamored of my bathroom deportment. She's very keen on closed doors and individual towels, toothbrushes, toilet paper — you name it. I think the lady has a Ph.D. in personal hygiene."

Bone was grinning, but he did not believe. "What about the car?" he asked.

"What about it?"

"George give it to you, loan it to you, what?"

"A *kind* of loan."

"The kind he didn't know about?"

"I left him a note."

237

"That was considerate."

"Thank you."

"And the check?"

"Simple generosity, that's all. I told him it was a matter of life and death, which it is — and that I will repay him, which I might."

"George the generous."

"He can afford it."

"And the stuff in the car — the guns and cameras and all that — his too?"

"It was."

Bone smiled now, in open wonderment. "Now let's see — you loot his house, you load the stuff in his car, you drive to his office and hit him for a thousand-dollar 'loan,' and then you take off — in his car."

"In *one* of his cars, yeah. And then I fence the purloined items. You forgot that."

"When I was sleeping."

"In L.A., right. A guy I know, name of Slats. Terrific fence, old Slats."

If Cutter had expected a laugh, he did not get it. Bone looked over at the girl and found her staring at Alex as if sight were a new experience for her, a frightening experience. Seeing this himself, Cutter reached over and covered her hand with his own, patted it.

"Don't sweat it, kid," he said. "It's nothing. Which is why I didn't bother to fill you in before. The car is just borrowed, like I said. And the rest, hell, the man has probably already written it off — a debt to an old friend. A guilt payment. Because he's loaded. Because he was 4F. Because he's what he is. So take my word for it — not to worry."

She looked at Bone, and he nodded. "He's probably right. George would give him both kidneys if he asked."

"And I probably will," Cutter said.

After that, they finished the meal largely in silence. Toward

238

the end, Bone mentioned that he had trouble figuring out the sequence of it all, just how it had happened. He remembered Monk making the phone call from Isla Vista and he remembered their dressing him, he said, but he could not figure out how they got from there to here.

"I mean, just what happens when Alex shows up?" he asked. "He says hello, I'm taking this lush on a trip, and do you want to join us? And you say sure, give me a minute to pack? Is that how it goes?"

The girl was staring down at her plate. "It wasn't like that," she said.

"Then how was it?"

"Does it matter?"

Bone said it mattered.

"It was *you*, jackass," Cutter broke in. "You and that old black magic you weave so well."

The girl did not raise her eyes. "I asked to go," she admitted. "I don't know much about alcohol and I was worried, the way you were going at it, and the way you kept saying *Mo* over and over, like you wanted to die."

Bone could feel Cutter's eye on him, but he did not look up.

Back at the motel Bone waited until the girl was asleep and then he pried Cutter loose from the room's vintage black and white television set, on which Johnny Carson and Ed McMahon were doing their vacuous little thing for a grateful nation. Bone pushed Cutter's jacket at him and practically dragged him out of the small room into the cold desert night.

"What the hell is this?" Cutter groused. "What's with you anyway?"

"We have to talk."

"So why not back inside? The kid's asleep."

Bone shook his head. "Out here. I want you alert. I want answers."

239

"Don't we all."

The motel courtyard was asphalt, a parking lot with a small empty swimming pool in the center, a concrete hole guarded by a chain-link fence with a NO SWIMMING sign attached. Cutter, unzipping his fly, observed that there weren't any NO PISSING signs in evidence and proceeded to water a dead potted palm just over the fence. Bone lit a cigarette and waited.

Beyond the highway and the buildings lining it — the drive-ins, motels, and gas stations — he could see patches of the Colorado River running black in the night light, a vein of lifeblood trickling through the vast corpse of the desert. For some reason he thought it would be better to talk over there, under the scrawny trees scattered along the riverbank, and he headed in that direction. Cutter limped alongside, suddenly a wondering Celt.

"Aye now, Richard me boy, is it not a sight to behold up there? Stars so big and bright a body could almost reach out and touch them, he could, if a body'd a mind to, mind you."

Bone did not respond. When they reached the bank, Cutter found a large rock at the base of a tree and sat down. Sighing, leaning back, he lit a cigarette.

"Okay," Bone said.

"Okay, what?"

"Okay, give."

"Give what?"

"The truth, Alex. Once again — what is going on?"

Cutter laughed and shook his head. "I got this weird sense of *déjà vu*, you know? Like I've already lived through this moment, like about a half hour ago."

"Just tell me your destination. That would help."

"We already told you, man. Nowhere. We're just tripping, that's all. Car tripping."

"No particular destination, then?"

"None."

"And direction? How about that?"

Cutter picked up a pebble and tossed it, waited until it plunked into the water. "Well, there is this one cat I know from Nam, he's got some kind of lake resort near Tulsa. I figured we just might move in that general direction. See what develops."

"And after that?"

"You tell me."

Bone's attention momentarily had strayed to the river, where an inflated raft was sliding past, unmanned, empty. And though he knew this was a phenomenon that merited comment, and even concern, he gave it nothing. He already had enough problems.

"Tulsa," he said. "Pretty close to Missouri, isn't it?"

"Pretty close."

"And in Missouri, down near Arkansas, there is this little town of Rockhill."

Cutter dragged on the last of his cigarette and dropped it on the ground, interred it with his foot. "Yeah, Rockhill," he said finally. "Home of J. J. Wolfe, as I recall."

"As you recall."

"As I recall, yes sir."

"But you wouldn't be heading there?"

"Now why would I want to do that?"

"It was just yesterday morning, Alex — you forgotten already? You telling me that Wolfe had 'sent you a message'?"

"I said that, huh?"

"You said that. And you believe it, too. It's the only explanation for all this."

"All what?"

"Leaving town. Taking George's car and the money. And even more, your attitude. Yesterday morning you were a man in shock, and now — well, it's like nothing had happened. You're back at the same old stand, without a hair out of place. And Mo and the baby — it's like they never were."

"And somehow this all relates to Wolfe, huh?"

"In your head it does, yeah."

"Then lay it on me. Explain."

"You know the old phrase about beating swords into plowshares — well I think you've beaten your grief into a sword."

Cutter pretended to lose his balance on the rock. Grinning, he struggled to right himself. "Such eloquence, Rich — I just wasn't prepared."

"Screw you."

"All in good time."

For a while neither of them said anything more. Cutter got up and limped a few steps closer to the river, a move that seemed without purpose, except that it put his face beyond the reach of Bone's eyes. For a span of minutes he stood there staring out at the night and the river and then finally he turned and came back, and though he was grinning again, slightly, crookedly, all Bone really saw was his eye and the tears that filled it, made it seem incandescent in the starlight.

"Vengeance?" he said. "You think that's what I'd have in mind, Rich, just because of what happened to Mo and the kid? Hell, you know how I treated them — like so much dirt, wasn't it? Just because she wasn't ugly and had this thing about loyalty and didn't get all choked up about stumps and scar tissue, you think I'd lay the ticker on the line? Or just because she pulled out all the stops and gave me old Brown Pants, myself all over again, only all in one piece, with the four limbs and the two eyes working so fine a man couldn't even bear to look at the little bastard for fear some goddamn toy might go boom or the highchair topple over and crush a little footsie or maybe even the baby formula come up poison — who could know? Not his old man certainly. No, all he could do was run and hide, right? Drink too much and stay out of the house, try not to be there when it happened."

The smile came again, rueful and crimped, a scar running

under the open wound of his eye. "And I *wasn't* there, was I?" he got out. "So why should I want revenge against Wolfe, huh? What did the man ever do to me except free me from anxiety, kill the old fear and trembling?" He held out his hand now, held it shaking in Bone's face. "See, old buddy? So who needs revenge, huh? Who needs to get his own back?"

Bone said nothing for a while, unwilling to trust his voice. It was the first time he had seen Cutter cry, the first glimpse he had ever had beyond the man's carapace of raillery and black humor. And it crossed his mind as vaguely as a feeling of guilt that he probably loved him, that if anyone's pain was automatically his as well, it was Cutter's. So he dealt from weakness.

"You *are* going to Missouri, then," he said.

"I guess so."

"To kill him."

"I don't know that yet. Maybe just the blackmail bit still, I won't know till I get there. Till I see him, face to face."

"Then you do believe it," Bone said. "You actually believe the man had something to do with Mo and the baby."

"Not possible, huh?"

"Not possible, Alex."

"Oh, yeah it is." It was a statement, a matter of fact.

"You're out of your tree," Bone told him.

"Maybe so. But I was there, man. I know what happened. I know how they reacted to what I laid on them. And I know they knew who I was, where I lived. Name, hotel, phone number — I gave it all to them, because I was feeling that reckless, Rich, that confident. I couldn't see any reason not to tell the bastards." He shook his head. "Now I know better."

"But it doesn't make sense," Bone said. "Forgetting whether or not the man *would* do it, there's still the problem of *how*, the time element. I don't see how —"

"You don't have to."

"The hell I don't!"

"Face it, Rich. What are the alternatives? Suicide or accident, right? And you know as well as I do how Mo loved that kid, how she took care of him. Oh, she was a pillhead, yeah. And maybe the world's worst housekeeper too. But tell me — you ever see a time when she wasn't able to take care of him? When she wasn't there?"

Bone thought of the afternoon he had found the baby alone at home and had taken him to Mission Park, which in turn led him to the sound of Mo's voice — *How touching, How too, too sweet* — and her face above him, the smiling mockery he had no idea he would ever miss, but did miss now. He said nothing, however. And Cutter pushed on:

"You ever see him when he wasn't fed and clean and healthy? Like hell you did. And as for suicide — well, you said it yourself, she wasn't depressed. And you were the last one to see her."

Bone heard the words like a judge's sentence, words he had known he would eventually have to listen to and deal with.

"That wasn't exactly true," he said.

"What wasn't?"

"What I said before. She *was* depressed."

Cutter had sat down on the rock again. His eye was dry now. "How depressed?" he said.

"I don't know. Very, I guess. She had cried while I was there. She was asleep when I left her. And I'd promised to stay, to be there when she woke up. She'd made me promise."

"But you cut out anyway?"

"That's right." Bone was not breathing now, was just standing there, waiting, his body tensed. For he did not plan to move, not if Cutter hit him, not even if he caned him. But, unbelievably, all Alex did was smile slightly.

"It figures," he said. "With that leviathan ego of yours, you'd naturally assume a girl would run straight for the gas burner the second you walked out on her. I mean, after all, what other choice would she have, right?"

"She was *depressed*, Alex." Somehow he thought the statement would be definitive, that it would put an end to the matter.

But Cutter only scoffed. "Who ain't?"

Bone stared at him. "You take it real good, don't you?"

"Which part? The dying? Or the screwing?"

"Take your pick."

Cutter shrugged and reached down for another pebble. "I try, man," he said. "I try to feel something. But it just isn't there. The two of them, they could've been a couple of dogs for all I care. For all I feel."

"I don't believe you."

"I don't want to either."

Bone's fists shook at his sides. "You're lying," he said. "You're posing. You're a fucking poseur."

"I don't feel much of anything, no loss or grief or any of those nice normal feelings. Maybe I just scooped up too many guys and dumped them in body bags, I don't know. Maybe there were just too many pieces."

"And what about all that a minute ago?" Bone asked. "About Mo and the baby, and you not even wanting to look at him for fear — ?"

Cutter held up his hand for silence. "Like you said, a pose. I thought I'd try it on. A noble, if phony, reason for going to Missouri."

"Then what's the real reason?"

"Must be greed, huh? Our little blackmail bit? Especially now, with you and Valerie pulling out, and no one to share the proceeds with. Why shee-it, man, I be able to re-tire on Ibiza."

"And vengeance — 'getting your own back' — that doesn't figure in?"

Cutter tried to grin, he tried to meet Bone's gaze, but neither worked. Finally he just looked down and shook his head in bewilderment. "I don't know," he said. "But I'm going. For some reason I've got to. I've got no choice."

Bone nodded slowly, understanding nothing, except that he would be going along, that this time at least he would not be walking out on someone who needed him, even if that someone suddenly made his flesh crawl.

When they went back to the motel, Bone told Cutter that he was not ready to go to bed yet, that he wanted to walk for a while by himself and do some thinking. And Cutter said he thought it was a capital idea, he often recommended thinking to those who were jaded and wanted to do something unusual, but he advised Bone not to overdo, and of course not to accept any candy from strangers.

Bone had to walk almost to the other end of the small town before he found an outdoor booth with a workable telephone. There, first, he placed a collect call to Mrs. Little, who was understandably waspish at the outset. She hadn't liked it one bit, the way his gimpy friend had stormed in and cleaned out Bone's apartment. She herself had not been there at the time, but Teresa had, and when the poor soul tried to find out what was going on, "your friend told her he was FBI and that you'd been arrested for impersonating an officer and indecent exposure and God knows what all, and that if Teresa didn't get her ass out of his way he was going to deport her to Mexico. That's what he told her. Why, the poor thing was scared half to death."

Bone commiserated with her, said yes he knew all about that offensive character and he too wanted nothing more to do with him. It was another friend of his he was concerned with now, a nice guy who had just kicked his teenage son out of the house for stashing drugs there and now the father was worried sick, was looking all over for the kid, and Bone was helping. It was too complicated to explain it all now, but one of the things he'd had to do was abandon her truck, had left it in the Leadbetter beach parking lot — a fact Mrs. Little was very happy to hear, she said, because tomorrow she'd planned on reporting the thing stolen and she would have regretted getting him into trouble with the police. Bone thanked her, said he appreciated all she had done for him, and that he thought she was one hell of a lady. In return, she told him that the job and apartment would always be open to him. "We've got some unfinished business," she said. Bone slipped hurriedly around that, thanking her again, then saying goodbye.

Next he called George Swanson, and once again he found the man more than a little tainted by sainthood. Yes, George had read the note Alex had left for him, so of course he knew about the car and the other "items" that had been taken. But he had no intention of calling in the police and reporting anything stolen, Bone could put his mind at rest on that. Bone thanked him and explained about his binge and his not having known what was going on, in fact that he still was not sure what their destination was. But he said that if he was able to stay with Cutter now he thought he'd be able to see him through "this problem of his, this obsession," and with luck he'd even be able to get the car and the other items back to George within a week or so, hopefully with Cutter still in one piece and out of jail. George asked if Bone could tell him any more about Cutter's "problem" and Bone said it had to do with the deaths of Mo and the baby, maybe someone Cutter held responsible and wanted to get even with, or possibly he was simply running from the tragedy — Bone was not sure, was still pretty much in the dark about everything, except that the man was close to the edge, that he needed time. And of course George gave him all that and more. He told Bone that if he needed anything else, any help or money, just to call him and he would send it. And for a few moments Bone found himself speechless in the face of the man's effortless generosity and loyalty. Finally though he managed a few words of thanks. He told him that it would work out and they would all be back in the sun in no time. And George said he hoped so. "Take care of my boy," he added. "I wouldn't want to lose him too."

Only then did Bone realize the man was crying.

Cutter's "early start in the morning" did not take place until eleven o'clock and Bone was glad of the delay, for the long night's sleep and the leisurely breakfast of pancakes and bacon and eggs had left him feeling almost normal again. But if the start was unhurried, the going turned out to be something else entirely, in fact was close to a steady eighty miles an hour under Cutter's heavy prosthetic foot. And even though he had to drive one-handed, he still managed to smoke and drum the wheel and fiddle with the radio, all the while serving up an almost unbroken commentary on a wide variety of subjects, which Bone would not have minded if only the man had not also found it necessary to keep looking away from the road to read his audience, bright little Monk sitting next to him in the front seat thirstily imbibing his every word.

Bone however contented himself with the scenery, the numbing grandeur and variety of the Great Southwest. Leaving the green vein of the Colorado River Valley, the freeway climbed steadily into Arizona, up out of the mesquite and desert into the high country around Flagstaff, all snow and rock and ponderosa pine, a cold clear Valhalla that abruptly ended ten or twenty miles to the east, changing into mesquite country again, barren rolling land with small mountainous formations whose dark red hue explained the color of the freeway at that point, before it moved on into the flats of eastern Arizona and then the deserts of New Mexico, Little Joe country, a vast dun wasteland strewn with buttes and mesas of unlikely configuration. Except for Bone, it was wasted scenery, superfluous splendor, nonexistent for the two in the front seat, both of whom were caught up in the apparently more fascinating scenery of Cutter's mind.

As usual, Alex was roaming his fields of death and gore, and though Bone wanted to tune him out, to fix his mind on the geological phenomena out the car window, he found that he could not, that he was almost as caught up as Monk in some of Cutter's stories, for instance the one about the honky in his platoon.

"A mean little crew-cut redneck Okie named Oral Roberts Russell," Cutter described him. "One of God's really gifted haters, a boy who had learned well at Mama's knee. Niggers, spics, papists, Jews, commies — he knew us all for what we were, *the enemy,* more enemy than old Charlie out in the bush could ever be. So Oral was on guard, in fact he was snapped to attention twenty-nine hours a day, those tight little pale gray eyes of his swiveling back and forth like a brace of twenty-millimeter cannon, taking it all in, you know, taking the role for up yonder, get-even time, for him and that mean, jealous God of his. He even called me the devil, old Oral did — yeah, Lieutenant Satan I was, even though the kid saw me resting, knew I rested most of the time. Anyway he watched. And he hated. And then it happened — his undoing — a replacement kid name of Dewey White. Only Dewey wasn't white, he was black as coal and beautiful as sin, cool and smart and with just too goddamn much of that one unforgivable thing the blacks got, that thing we all secretly hate them the most for — their laughter, their "soul.""

And here Cutter digressed to give Monk a theory he had about soul, that Caucasians and Orientals had it once too, long ago, but that the "old debil" natural selection had worked its remorseless mechanics here as well, with survival of the fittest proving true in civilization just as in a state of nature. Only in civilization the "fittest" were the shrewd, the calculating, the unemotional. In a civilized society they were the ones to survive and thrive. So naturally, over the millennia, the "soul" had died out of the race. And proof of this, he said, existed for anyone to see just by observing the emergent black middle class, already as restrained and soulless as their white counterparts ever were. Monk by now had the look of a fervent acolyte, and she leaped upon the idea — of course it was true, it was there for anyone to see, but not just anyone had. No, it took someone with special insight to have seen it.

"It took *you*, Alex," she said.

But Cutter was already back with his honky in Vietnam.

"Anyway, little Oral, he couldn't deal with Dewey, just couldn't handle the phenomenon of him. Because the kid wasn't just cool and beautiful, you see, he was also *friendly*. He actually seemed to like us whites. And he liked slants, dogs, newsmen, anybody, everybody. I guess what he was, was a fucking saint, old Dewey." And here Cutter paused to light a cigarette, one-handed, as the station wagon roared down the freeway, uncontrolled. When he went on, his voice was flat, matter-of-fact. "And, well, he bought it, Dewey did. Tripped a mine and came down in little pieces. Which wasn't exactly unusual, in fact was happening to somebody all the time. But Oral Roberts Russell, he just wouldn't accept it, wouldn't let it go. For days he kept going on about that 'stupid nigger, that stupid sonofabitching nigger.' Over and over he kept saying it, and he was crying all the time and he didn't know it. Then just as suddenly he quit. And from then on, his bag was silence. Silence and killing. Overnight he became the best grunt we had, a real killer, a mechanic. Girls on bicycles, little kids, old people, even a tiger once, a goddamn big beautiful Bengal tiger — if the thing moved and wasn't us, he shot it. And he always wanted point, he insisted on it. But it never did him any good. He never got a scratch. He just went on living and killing, untouched, a charmed life."

As he finished, Monk regarded him with shining eyes. "That Dewey," she said, "he wasn't the only one beautiful."

But Cutter pretended not to catch her meaning. He busied himself lighting another cigarette.

That night Cutter said he refused to spend the rest of his life in "worst western" motels — "Vinyl furniture is one thing, vinyl food another" — and he suggested that the three of them take turns at the wheel while the other two rested or slept. Monk of course was eager to do anything he asked, so Bone decided to go along too. They drove all through the night and into the next day, stopping only for gas and food. And Bone gradually began to lose that normal feeling of physical well-being he thought he had recovered at Needles. The car seats apparently had been designed for five-and-a-half-footers and his six-one simply could not find comfort or rest. He slept poorly, worrying about what lay ahead of them and what he could do about it. And sometimes he just lay there listening to Cutter or the girl, who occasionally and grudgingly surrendered a fact or two about herself, as if she were confessing to small crimes. She could not remember ever having a conversation with her father, she said, always just a polite word or two, an attempt at intimacy and then failure, embarrassment, silence. He had not kissed her since grade school, nor could she recall seeing him embrace or kiss her mother except for perfunctory pecks of hello and goodbye. What little time he wasn't poking and drilling in other people's mouths he spent in the dark of skin-flick theaters, she claimed, gorging popcorn with hand while he held himself with the other — a detail Bone could only assume was Monk's invention, since he could not imagine her spying on the man that closely.

Nor was the girl any fonder of her mother, a short-haired, earthshod liberal Democrat who was forever marching the highways of the Salinas Valley with César Chavez and his grapepickers. In her caseload as a social worker, the Mexicans and blacks all had first names and were victims of the "goddamn system," while the whites came with last names only and invariably were freeloaders, leeches, creeps.

Even before her parents' divorce, the three of them had been like strangers living together. Words were spent like dollars and Monk had always thought she was the cause of it all, that if she'd been prettier and brighter everything would have been different. So what life she had, she found in television.

For years Lucy and the Beaver and Rob Petrie were the realest people in her existence. She had tried the Catholic church and the Girl Scouts and the YWCA and occasionally a friend, but none of it had turned out, none of it worked as well as television. Summing up, she said she was a loser, an outsider, a nebbish, and finally the notorious Virgin of Isla Vista. So these last two days were just about the best thing that had ever happened to her. She felt free and happy for the first time in her life.

To all of this Cutter predictably gave her the backhand of understanding, saying that it was all her own fault, that there were all kinds of drugs to take and the sex fiends and religious freaks there for the asking, and if she would only try, she could be just as jolly and successful as everyone else. She laughed at that and then in a much softer voice told him about the night her roommates had brought Bone home with them, and how the thought that he'd made love to them just about drove her crazy, how she'd hated them for it.

"He's so — well, you know."

"No, I don't," Cutter said.

"Well, *attractive,* I guess the word is. Even drunk the way he was. But then the more I was alone with him, I began to see he wasn't what he seemed — I mean all cool and together, you know? Can I tell you something?"

"Anything."

"He was in love with Mo. *Your* Mo."

"In his way, maybe. But she wasn't *my* Mo."

"Well, you loved her, didn't you?"

"No."

"But you said she had your child."

"So?"

"Well, what are we making this trip for then? I mean, what you said about not being able to stay on the coast anymore, not with her there, in the ground."

"I *liked* her," he said.

The girl's voice was suddenly cowed, frightened. "I don't understand you."

"It's a beginning," Cutter said.

By the second afternoon Cutter's loquacity began to seem clearly compulsive to Bone. For one thing, he spoke faster and more stridently than Bone had ever heard him before, as if he were in a desperate race to get it all out. But even stranger was *what* he talked about. If there was any subject he had always avoided, it was his childhood in Santa Barbara, and yet now, almost all the way through Oklahoma, this was what he recounted for Monk. "Our little plutocracy's Indian summer," he called it. "The last doomed days of innocent wealth, before the GI Bill generation took over." And then he went on to describe how they came in wave after wave, acquisitors and climbers and pirates all buttoned-down and gray-flanneled and other-directed, but not a bad lot actually, not when compared with their offspring, today's sorry lot of socially aware managers and communicators with their razor haircuts and gunfighter mustaches and mod clothes and liberal politics and, above all, their *eyes,* Cutter said, their frightened eyes, the eyes of a herbivore at the waterhole. "They watch and they wait. When will it come? they wonder. When will they finally hit, our poor abused black and brown brethren?"

But mostly he gave Monk the past, a nostalgia he tried to minimize and ridicule, but the warm sepia tones of it still managed to slip through intact: long uncrowded days in the beautiful seaside city, the fine old house under the wine palms and sycamores, with its gardeners and servants, its stables and tennis court and swimming pool and white wicker lawn furniture and guests in organdy and Palm Beach suits, some who came even then on horseback. And there were the polo matches viewed from the roofs of heavy Packards and Cadillacs, white-walled and waxed, gleaming in the coastal sun. There was the constant sailing on the succession of yachts his father kept buying and selling as if he were looking for the platonic *idea* boat, but on all of them the experience for Alex had been beautifully the same: the smell of wood and canvas and sea air, the salt spray free then of any trace of petroleum.

There were the Sunday dinners at the country club and, just as invariable, supper at the Biltmore Hotel, that still lushly beautiful Sarazen palace spread along the Pacific shore, where Bone once had spent three days in a cabana with a Seattle divorcée whose name he could not even remember now. Cutter, however, had no problem remembering those Sunday suppers, for they had seemed like the high church service of his parents' set: the large dining room with its great wood beams overhead, the waiters who were almost like old friends, *obsequious* old friends, and then the music, the doors thrown open to the patio where couples danced decorously to the live music of an eight-piece band, Mexicans mostly, and all so happy, Cutter said, all of them smiling just as happily as the waiters and the busboys and the maître d'.

"They were fine days," Cutter went on. "Good days. Good for us anyway. The world was our oyster for a time, with that sweet strip of seacoast all ours. And I never even thought about it. I guess I figured it was for good, that it would never end. But it did. Just like for the Canalinos, the Indians who lived there when the Spanish were still home in Castile burning each other at the stake. Things change."

"Parmenides," the girl offered.

"Bless you too," Cutter said.

Through the afternoon and evening Bone did the driving, and though he occasionally found himself listening to Cutter and the girl, most of the time it was his own thoughts that occupied him, flowing like stale water into the lowest spots in his mind: the continued feeling of loss and guilt, the sense of dread at what lay ahead of them and what he could do about it.

They would be in Missouri soon, which meant they would

probably reach Wolfe's hometown by midnight. And the prospect scared him. He felt that if only he had a more exact reading of Cutter's state of mind, he might have some idea how to deal with the situation. But as usual all he had got from him was chimera and confusion. He doubted that even Alex himself knew which was real — Cutter the avenger, the anguished survivor of a wife and son he had loved almost too much to endure; the war casualty who might have lost a pair of dogs for all the grief he felt; or the coolly persistent blackmailer merely trying to get to Ibiza.

This last one Bone felt he could eliminate. And as for the other two, all his instincts told him that both entered in, that Cutter's true state of mind probably lay somewhere between them. In the thirty-odd hours of driving since they left Needles, Bone had used what opportunities he had — whenever the girl was asleep or gone for a few minutes to stretch her legs or use a restroom — to find out more from Cutter about what had happened in Los Angeles and afterward. And though he did manage to fill in a number of empty spaces this way, nothing he learned altered the essential picture. The "they" Cutter had talked about in Needles turned out to have been only one man, Pruitt, some kind of special assistant to Wolfe. To this man Cutter had peddled himself as an eyewitness to another crime — "a *very* serious crime" committed in Santa Barbara the same night J. J. Wolfe's car was firebombed. Cutter told Pruitt that the information he had "involved Mr. Wolfe, and would be very valuable to him," but that Wolfe would have to hear it from Cutter himself. Pruitt had been very quiet, very impressed, and when Cutter gave him his phone number and the name of the hotel where he was staying, and finally, recklessly, his name, Pruitt had very carefully written it all down. And then he had said it: they would be in touch with Cutter, they would *send him a message*. The hour was about eleven in the morning — approximately the same time that Bone was hitching a ride back to Santa Barbara. Theoretically, then, there had been enough time for

Wolfe and his minions to learn Cutter's home address and strike him there, through his family rather than directly at him, and thus not risk one of those situations in which an eliminated witness leaves behind a letter addressed to his lawyer or a district attorney. So the elements of possibility did exist. If a man wanted to, he could concoct a scenario involving arson and double homicide and intimidation of a witness. And a further proof of this scenario for Cutter was Valerie's reaction to the news of the fire and the deaths of Mo and the baby. After Bone's phone call from Santa Barbara, Valerie had practically collapsed. Cutter had had to pack for them and check them out of the hotel and it was he who drove them back to Santa Barbara in the Pinto. And almost all the way the girl had sat beside him crying and trembling and saying over and over that Cutter should not have given them his name, and that she was out of it now, she wanted no more part of J. J. Wolfe.

Bone had been surprised to learn this, that Valerie too apparently had inferred a connection between the deaths and the blackmail attempt on Wolfe. But he was just as surprised at how Cutter told him about it — about all of it — with a kind of irony and obliqueness that seemed to dare Bone not to believe it. And Bone did dare. He still considered the whole story nothing but a theoretical possibility at best. But then of course he had the advantage of having been with Mo that last afternoon and evening. Only he knew exactly how far down she had been, and how much further down he had kicked her. So he did not need some bizarre scenario. The simple reality was more than enough.

Nevertheless he could not control his feeling of dread as they drove on into the night and the road began to wind through the Ozark hills. The one thing he feared most was in himself, in his own mind — the belief that J. J. Wolfe might actually have been the man he had seen in the alley that night. Yet here he was, driving toward the man's home, heading for a confrontation which might corroborate that belief, make it a fact. He wondered what would he do then.

11

THE LONGVIEW MOTEL, RESTAURANT & BAR WAS SITUATED, LOGI-
cally, on the crest of a high hill, and except for the two-lane
highway running past it and a few scattered farmyard lights
burning on the surrounding hills and in the valleys, it offered
the only visible trace of civilization in the rain-swept Ozark
night. Even then, it was a faint trace. The neon had been left
burning only in the MOTEL part of the sign, and the manage-
ment similarly was not wasting wattage on parking lot lights or
VACANCY signs. Nevertheless Bone, Cutter, and Monk did manage to get a pair of adjoining rooms, and by eleven-thirty the
girl was sound asleep in hers while the men abandoned theirs
for a short visit to the bar to have a few drinks before turning
in.

Bone did not like the idea. Somehow the motel and bar only
added to his feeling of unease. Though the building itself was
not new — its cement-block construction and interior fake
wood paneling showed clear signs of age — the motel still
managed to seem oddly unused, as though the people who had
been running it and working there and the guests who had
been tracking through it all these years had left no mark at all,
no real sign of their passing. For one thing, the place was
almost totally undecorated. There was not a photo or a paint-
ing or a gewgaw on its virginal walls, no fishnets or mounted
mooseheads or sports trophies or even an out-of-date calendar,
nothing other than the elements of construction themselves:

the brick, the pressed wood, the plastic and aluminum. And the staff somehow only added to this aura of sterility. In the dining room a younger model of Billy Graham sat at a Wurlitzer organ spinning out a funereal version of "Tea for Two" for three tables of late diners, all of whom had a look of bovine contentment as they sat watching him, apparently grateful that his leaden hand spared them the chore of talking with each other. The women were heavy and overdressed, with elaborate Sun King coiffeurs strikingly at odds with the short-cropped hair of their men, who were leaner and sun-darkened and gaudily resplendent in discount-store sportcoat-and-slacks coordinates. The woman who was waiting on them also served as the barmaid, and the bartender turned out to be the man who had checked Bone and Cutter into the motel a half hour before.

Seeing them together, Cutter said to Bone, "American Gothic sans pitchfork." And Bone could only agree. They were middle-aged and bored, and equally gave off the same air of dour and aggrieved authority. Bone assumed that they were the owners, husband and wife, dead souls responsible for the soulless character of their establishment.

At the bar Bone followed Cutter's lead and ordered scotch, a double, because he did not intend to drink very long. Even though it was Saturday night, the place was almost empty, with just two old men at the bar and three young cowboys sitting around a table drinking beer straight from the bottle. Two of them could have been movie extras, burlesque bad-guy types with booted feet propped up on chairs and their heads thrown back so they could see out from under low-slung cowboy hats with eyes properly squinted against the smoke rising from nonfilter cigarettes raffishly dangled at their lips. But it was the other one, the third cowboy, who prompted Bone to forgo the stool between Cutter and one of the old men and instead take the stool at the corner of the bar, on the other side of Cutter. That way, as Alex did his usual barroom number, Bone would not have to sit with his back to the cowboys and wonder how they were taking it, and especially this third one, who for some reason struck Bone as a man who bore watching, possibly because he was not hoking it up like the others but just sat there hatless, cool, almost mannerly — except for his gaze, which was that of a bull rider assessing his next mount.

When the bartender served their drinks, Cutter gave him a big hick grin. "Uptown Saturday night, uh?" he said.

The man nodded primly. "Yep, it's Saturday, all right."

"Yep, so it is." Cutter turned to Bone. "You hear that? I was right — it's Saturday here."

The bartender was looking wary now, his eyes skittering between Cutter's eyepatch and the empty sleeve, the knot.

"What's your name, pal?" Cutter asked him.

"Mister Morgan."

Cutter smiled as if he had just received some very good news. "Well, I'll be damned — *Mister* Morgan, uh? You probably remember us from the front desk. I'm *Mister* Cutter and my friend here is *Mister* Bone. We're here to do bidness."

Morgan's response to this was to turn away and busy himself washing beer glasses. But Cutter sailed on, undaunted.

"What county is this, Mister Morgan?"

"Rock."

"County seat is Rockhill?"

"Yep. A mile back, half mile off the highway."

"Ah, that's why we missed it, then."

Actually they had driven through it in the rain, around the small square with its old brick stores and covered sidewalks facing a modest, rundown courthouse. Everything had been festooned with bunting and signs welcoming visitors to Bank Day. On a street leading from the square a traveling carnival had sat shuttered in the rain.

"We didn't see any other bars driving through," Cutter said to Morgan. "You got a monopoly?"

"Nope. There's two beer taverns and another motel this side the state line. They got a bar too."

"Not a very wet county, then."

"It ain't dry."

"But the people do most of their lushing at home, uh?"

Morgan muttered that he wouldn't know what that was, so Cutter showed him, tipping up his hand as though he were taking a drink. But the bartender had had enough. He turned away, still holding his rag, and began to polish the cash register. At the same time the old man nearest Cutter leaned toward him.

"Folks around here mostly goes to church," he said. "Wednesday nighters, we call 'em."

"I take it you're not one of them," Cutter said.

"*Me?* Oh, hell no. And not old Charley here neither," the old man said, indicating Morgan behind the bar. "Not anymore. Not since he added on this here ginmill of his."

"They cast him out of their midst, did they?"

"Yep, they told old Satan here to get his ass behind 'em!" The old man whooped with laughter, and Morgan strode out of the barroom, probably heading for the front desk to restore his sense of dignity.

While he was gone, Bone told Cutter that it would be a good idea if he shut his mouth and drank up. Instead Alex patted him on the hand.

"Now, don't you fret, moms," he said. "One more belt and we'll turn in. We'll flip a coin to see who gets to rape little Monk tonight."

Looking past him, Bone saw that all three of the cowboys were watching them, but with a difference. While the movie extras were busy giving each other elbow digs and looks of droll stupefaction, the third one sat as before, his expression unchanged. And Bone took another drink, lit a cigarette, wished he believed in prayer.

A few minutes later Morgan made a dignified reentry and

resumed his post behind the bar. Cutter promptly shoved his empty glass at him.

"One more, my good man," he said.

As Morgan took his glass, Cutter asked him if he knew a J. J. Wolfe, and the bartender nodded grudgingly.

"Big man, huh?" Cutter pressed.

"You could say that."

"He spend much time around here? Or does he just fly in and out."

"Wouldn't know."

"Well, I would," the old man at the bar put in. "What'd you want to see him for, young fella?"

"Oh, we just want to buy some cattle," Cutter said. "Thought maybe we'd drop by his place tomorrow and look over some of them fancy critters of his."

The old man laughed. "Tomorrow's Sunday, boy! And Bank Day on top of that."

"Big time, huh?"

"Our annual wingding, that's what. A parade, picnics, and a carnival the next two nights. Should've been last night and tonight, but we got rained out. Churches don't like it, I hear — carnival on the sabbath — but I guess they holdin' still for it. Probably gettin' a piece of the action, if the truth was knowed."

Cutter asked him what a bank day was, and the old man laughed again. He was obviously feeling good. "Well, ourn was a robbery," he said. "Back in ninety-seven, it was, even before my time. These three gunslingers got caught inside the bank, with the townsfolk surroundin' 'em on all sides. And everybody armed and ornery. Well, sir, by the time it was over, they was five dead — two of us, three of them. Almost as bad as up in Coffeyville with the Daltons. Yessir, biggest thing ever happen in Rockhill."

"Hell, I thought J. J. Wolfe was," Cutter observed.

"Naw, he's only second. No parades in his honor, far as I know. Though he does lead 'em, come to think of it."

Cutter asked if Wolfe would be leading the parade tomorrow.

"Like as not, if he's home."

"Well, we'd better try to see him early then. Before the parade."

Bone had noticed that every time Cutter mentioned Wolfe, Morgan's eyes had swiveled uneasily to the cowboy table, to the third man, the bull rider.

"Shit, you don't have to see Wolfe hisself just to buy some of his cattle," the old man was saying. "Why, he's got so many hands workin' that spread of his, they steppin' on each other half the time. Fack, we got three of 'em here right now, includin' his foreman. Jist ast him."

But Cutter apparently was not listening to the old man, and instead asked now how to get to the ranch from the motel. At that point the bull rider finally moved, uncrossing his legs and edging a cigarette into his mouth.

"Jist who is it wants to know?" he drawled, lighting the cigarette.

Cutter scanned the ceiling, as if he had heard a celestial voice. "Hark," he said to Bone. "Did you hear something?"

The cowboy patiently repeated his question. "Jist who is it wants to know?"

And Cutter, grinning, found him now. "Jist who is it," he said, "wants to know jist who is it wants to know?"

One of the other cowboys was already on his feet, pushing back his chair, getting ready for combat. But the third one called him off with a look. "Cool it, Sam," he said. "Man's jist trying to be funny, that's all. His way of being friendly, I guess. So maybe we ought to be friendly back." He smiled at Cutter and Bone. "My name's Billy," he said. "What's yours?"

"Humperdinck," Cutter told him. "Engelbert Humperdinck."

The one named Sam faked a laugh. "Why, he's a card, Billy."

"He shore is," Billy concurred. "A cattle-buying card is what he is. Tell me, Humperdinck — which of Mister Wolfe's exotics you interested in?"

"Exotic what?" Cutter asked.

"Exotic what!" Grinning now, Billy turned to his friends. "By gawd, fellas, that do sound like Mister Humperdinck don't know cattle from Shinola."

Cutter looked at Bone and shrugged. "I think I have erred."

"Big surprise," Bone said.

Billy was explaining: "What I mean is, do you want to buy Limousin or Simmental or Charolais, or jist one of the traditional English beef breeds?"

To counter all the high-toned words, Billy had hoked up their pronunciation, playing the rube. But Bone was not taken in, could see simply in the man's clear intelligent gaze that he was not a rube and never had been, that Cutter did not bewilder him or scare him or fill him with rage.

"I was thinking more along the lines of weimaraner," Cutter said. "Wolfe got any of those?"

"Nope. Too small a breed. Their weaning ratio is poor, real poor."

"What about auto-da-fés?" Cutter asked. "Your boss in that line at all?"

"Nope. Though we do have barbecues. Afraid you came to the wrong place, friend."

Cutter turned to Bone. "Folks around here shore is friendly, ain't they?"

Bone told him to shut up, and Cutter pretended to pout.

"Never trust a friend," he said.

Billy was on his feet now, getting his cowboy hat off a rack near the door. Morgan asked him if he didn't want another round and Billy shook his head.

"No, reckon we've had enough, Charley," he said.

And Cutter jumped on that. "Reckon it's about time to mosey on back to the spread, uh, Billy Boy?"

The one named Sam told Cutter not to push his luck. But Billy, paying at the bar, gestured for Sam to let it go.

Cutter would not let them, however. "Yep, time to get back to the old corral and bed down with old Bessie. Each cowboy gets a hole. Billy gets the biggest."

Billy shook his head sadly. Picking up his change, he came down the bar. He stopped at the vacant stool next to Cutter and stood there for a few moments, giving the stool a spin.

"Humperdinck," he said finally, "could I give you a few words of advice?"

"Why shore, Billy Boy."

And Billy went on, unexcited. "Well, the main thing is you look like you've caught enough shit in your time — I wouldn't go around looking for more. Especially I wouldn't go into bars around here and make fun of the locals."

"Never crossed my mind."

"Good. 'Cause, let me tell you — most of the guys around here are good old boys, which means they feel kinda naked without a bunch of guns in their pickups. And most of 'em don't drink any better'n you do. So you could get in trouble, Humperdinck. Real trouble."

Bone was feeling not only relief but downright pleasure. He could see Cutter's frustration. Honest friendly advice was not what he had been looking for, not what he could handle.

Nevertheless he tried now, turning to Bone and lisping, "My, isn't he the nicest person."

But Billy was unflappable. "Far as that goes, Humperdinck, maybe you ought to ask yourself why make fun in the first place? What's the purpose? I mean it's not like it could change anything, make you all one piece again. Ain't nothin' gonna do that, ever."

And finally Cutter had no comeback. He just sat there staring, not drinking, while Billy made a gesture of goodbye, first to him and then to Morgan and the two old men at the bar. Then he left, with the other cowboys trailing respectfully behind.

For a time the bar was like a wax museum. The two old men sat staring at their drinks, while Morgan contentedly contemplated a row of beer glasses he had just washed and dried. Cutter was equally silent. And Bone could not think of one thing to say, no glib lie with which to counter the cowboy's brutal truth. Finally Cutter finished his drink. He dropped a twenty-dollar bill on the bar and told Morgan that he wanted a bottle of Red Label "to go."

"Something to see me through the sabbath," he mumbled.

Morgan gave him the bottle, took the bill and brought back his change, all without once looking at him. And Cutter left, not waiting for Bone.

By the time he returned to his room, Bone's feelings of anxiety and dread had withered into resignation. Cutter obviously could not control his recklessness. He was going to get the two of them killed or maimed or thrown in jail, and there was not one thing Bone could do about it except run out on the man, and that he knew he wouldn't do. He was caught. Trapped. He felt about as he imagined a soldier felt the night before storming some lousy bloody beach somewhere, almost that kind of impotence and outrage.

So he was not feeling very sociable or communicative as he got ready for bed. Cutter kept offering him a nip from the bottle of scotch he had bought, and Bone kept refusing. All he wanted was sleep, he said, and maybe a little silence, if Cutter thought he could manage such a tall order. Frowning, Alex said he would work on it, he always enjoyed a challenge.

But he did not work very hard. As Bone turned out the lights and got into bed, Cutter promptly drew open the drapes on the window wall at the front of the room. Then, dropping into a plastic chair there, he began to hum Brahms' Lullaby.

And Bone wished he had had some small modicum of light-heartedness left in order to appreciate the comic absurdity of the moment, but all he felt was weariness, a weariness that very soon awarded him with sleep.

He had no idea how long that first sleep lasted — probably no more than an hour — for it seemed that almost immediately he began to hear this strange sound, this soft inhuman keening, like the cry of an animal caught somewhere, wounded, dying. As sleep-drugged as he was, it took a while for him to determine the source of the sound: Cutter, still dressed, standing at the window, his face pressed against the glass while outside the rain was still coming down, drumming on the cars parked beyond the sidewalk. Only as Bone struggled to a sitting position in his bed did he notice the drawing on the window, where Cutter's breath had clouded the glass: a tick-tack-toe form filled with zeros.

Swinging his legs out of the bed, Bone groped for his cigarettes. "What's up, old-timer?" he said. "You got a bellyache?"

Cutter moved unsteadily from the window, sagged into the chair again. "I'm drunk, I guess," he admitted.

"I guess."

"But you right, Rich — I ache. Yeah, I do ache."

"Why not go to bed?"

"If it would help, I do it."

"But it won't, huh?"

Cutter shook his head and looked over at the bottle next to him on the table. It was one-third empty now. He started to reach for it and then gave up, let his hand fall. And again he shook his head back and forth, like an animal contemplating the bars of its cage.

"You ever feel divided?" he asked finally. "I mean, like you was split, like some goddamn worm cut in two, and the two parts of you keep crawling around looking for the other, for the whole of you?"

Bone said nothing. He wanted to respond, but the right words would not come, and he was afraid of the wrong ones.

"I'm scared, Rich," Cutter went on. "I'm way out here, and I don't think I can get back this time."

"Back from where?"

"I don't know. I guess that's the problem. I'm out here, and I'm alone. And I don't think I can get back."

Bone seized the opportunity. "We could leave tonight, Alex. Right now. Try some bigger town, with the right kind of doctors. The right kind of hospital."

"Why not aspirin? Or a Band-Aid?"

"All right — no doctors or hospitals. But what then? What else is there?"

Cutter tried to grin. "There could be God."

"Could be."

"Then again, there could not be."

Bone dragged on his cigarette, exhaled. He was trying not to look at Cutter, not to stare, for he had the feeling that in some subtle and irreversible way the man had changed in this last long unknown hour while Bone had slept, and gone over some ultimate edge into an area that was somehow totally *other*, beyond Bone's ken and reach, and both of them knew it.

"Tell me what to do," Bone said. "Anything. I'll do it."

Cutter had reached out for the bottle and now he took a drink. Finished, he set it between his legs. "There's nothing," he said. "Ain't nothing you can do, old buddy."

"I could take the bottle away."

Alex shook his head. "Wouldn't do any good. I'd still be here. And you'd still be there."

"We could get some sleep."

Cutter tried the grin again. "Why, you got problems you don't even know about, you poor sap."

"Like what?"

"Like you trusted me. You believed me."

"Believed what?"

"I don't know, maybe it's better you don't know."

"Know what?"

"You don't want to know, Rich. Believe me."

"Why not let me be the judge of that?"

"You're better off."

"It's up to you."

"But then, I guess I should tell you. I mean, it's the right thing to do, the moral thing. And if I don't do it now, whilst I am smashed — then I probably shan't, ever."

Bone was almost out of patience. "So do it," he said.

"Right. Well, what it comes down to is — I ain't sure what we're doing here."

"You care to explain that?"

"You heard about the cat who lies so much he winds up believing his lies?"

"I have."

"I think I'm that cat."

"What lie, Alex?"

"Wolfe."

For a time Bone said nothing. Just hearing that single brutal syllable, he felt he already knew what Cutter was getting at. But it was almost too much, too absolute an outrage for him to want to hear it all now, spelled out, done and done. Yet he had no choice.

"You mean you changed your mind?" he said. "About Wolfe having Mo and the baby killed?"

Cutter shook his head. "Naw, I mean the whole thing. I mean I don't seem to know what's real anymore. Like, I think I know what really happened in L.A. after you left. And then I know what I told Valerie and you afterward — two different things. But it seems it got all mixed up since then, like I can't tell the difference anymore. Otherwise, why would we be here, huh? Does it make any sense?"

Bone crushed out his cigarette and lit another. He was trying hard to keep his cool, to keep it all the way to the truth. A muscle in his jaw began to leap and he stilled it with his hand, casually, as if he were rubbing his face.

"L.A.," he said now. "What did happen there, Alex?"

268

Cutter smiled again. "That's my problem — I'm not sure anymore."

"Of course you are."

"I am?"

"You were there, man. Just tell it. Like it happened."

"In space and time."

"Right. Just the boring dimensions."

Cutter shrugged a minor resignation. "Yeah, I guess maybe I could keep it all separate, give it the old college try. Let me think — version one. The old time and space routine. Well, let's see — there was this cat named Pruitt, that was fact. Or so I remember anyway. But Pruitt wasn't no assistant to the president — no, he was some kind of office boy, that's all. A kid. A nobody. I tried to tell him what I was doing there, what we were after, but it was like talking to a water cooler. All he did was nod his dumb head and look at me like I was from outer space or skid row. And then when I was finished he gives me a sharp pencil and an employment application and tells me to fill it out and leave it with the girl at the front desk."

Here Cutter had to break off, he was laughing so hard, doubling forward over the bottle of scotch in his lap. On the bed, Bone sat smoking and waiting.

"So you lied," Bone said finally. "Like me."

Cutter shrugged. "Maybe so. I'm not sure. It didn't seem important at the time. It gave Val a kind of high. And then when you called the next morning about Mo and the kid, I think Val right away connected the two. It was Wolfe, she said. He'd had it done — because I'd been careless and stupid, she said, giving them my name and number and all. And for some reason I latched onto the idea. I think that's what happened. But I'm not sure anymore, Rich — honest to Christ. Maybe I just remember it that way now because I have to. Because the truth scares me. Like that cowboy tonight. Because I know I can't break these people — they'll break me."

"Bullshit."

"What is?"

"That you don't remember. Tell me this — do you have any recollection at all of meeting this Pruitt you said was an assistant to Wolfe? The one who said he'd *send you a message?* You remember that ever happening? In time and space?"

Cutter thought about it for a while, frowning and grinning. Finally he shook his head. "I guess not," he said. "I guess I made it up."

"Yeah, I guess you did."

Bone got up and took the bottle from him. He took a long pull on it and then set it back on the table. Going over to the window, he stood looking out through the tick-tack-toe design at the sodden Ozark night. And it crossed his mind that he was here, almost two thousand miles from the coast, on a *whim,* a vagary of Cutter's playful psyche. Surely that was reason enough for rage. On the other hand, suddenly he no longer had to worry about storming some lousy bloody beach in the morning. Wolfe and his kin and their rock hills were out of the picture now, and that should have been cause for rejoicing or at least relief. But Bone felt neither rage nor relief. What he felt instead was numbness, a numbness cousin to death. He no longer cared. Had Cutter finally and inevitably gone bananas? Maybe so. And so what? What else was new? Was any of it as important as the sleep Bone was missing right now or a good breakfast in the morning or the prospect of sun and sand within a few days, with perhaps an occasional lay thrown in to keep the plumbing open, the nerves all fat and sleek? Not hardly. Because nothing he did here and now would matter. It never had and never would. One could spend all his life climbing onto crosses to save people from themselves, and nothing would change. For human beings finally were each as alone as dead stars and no amount of toil or love or litany could alter by a centimeter the terrible precision of their journeys.

So there was nothing to do. There were a few questions to

ask, that was all, some bewilderment and outrage to express. And Bone went through the motions now.

"All this way, Alex!"

Cutter did not answer.

"Why not in Needles?" Bone asked. "Why couldn't you have owned up then? Were we still too close to home? Wouldn't the damage have been great enough? And why all that static in the bar tonight? Why go through all that for nothing? For no reason at all?"

Still Cutter said nothing.

"No answers, huh?"

Cutter shook his head. "None. Because I don't know myself, Rich. I don't know anymore . . . why I do . . . what I do."

Bone looked at him. For the second time since he met him, the man was crying. His eye shone in the night light, slick with desolation.

"It's like I said before," he went on. "I'm way out here, and I can't get back."

Bone tried for a bedside manner. "Sure you can, Alex. Give it time."

Cutter sagged back into the chair and his head lolled forward, as if he were falling asleep. But his eye remained open, fixed not on the floor so much as the space it filled. Bone sat there watching him, saying nothing, and finally he made one more try.

"If there's anything, man — anything you want me to do — you just ask. I'll do what I can."

But Cutter did not respond, did not even look up. And after a while Bone settled back into his bed, to lie there smoking and staring at the ceiling, helpless and silent. Then, again, he slept.

He was not sure what woke him this time — the first light of dawn building like a thunderhead outside the glass wall or the sounds coming from Monk's room, the rattling bed and desperate breathing, the soft little-girl cry coming over and over. One look at Cutter's empty bed and the abandoned chair and Bone did not have to wonder what the commotion was. What he did not know was whether it was a consenting act or otherwise, in which case he would have felt compelled to interfere, even at the risk of driving Cutter further from him. So he slipped out of bed and went over to the door that connected the two rooms and which now was slightly ajar. The drapes in Monk's room were still closed, so it took him a few moments to determine that despite the girl's cries she was not being violated. Her legs and arms were right where they should have been, holding Cutter's body fast to hers.

Bone quietly shut the door. He drew the drapes in his room closed and got back into bed, hopefully to sleep through the rest of the morning. And he was surprised at how good he felt all of a sudden, surprised because he normally did not derive much pleasure from being a spectator to sex instead of a participant. But this bit of voyeurism had been different, had been like seeing a deathly sick friend suddenly up and around again, alive again. Bone could hardly believe that the Cutter of a few hours before could now be making love. And the only explanation seemed to be that while Bone had slept, Alex had negotiated the same ultimate edge, had come back over it to rejoin the living.

For Bone it was a pleasant thought, as narcotic as alcohol. He stretched and yawned and felt the slow sweet slide beginning again, for the third time since he went to bed. Only this time he carried nothing extra with him, no baggage of useless worry and fear. Wolfe was out of the picture and apparently Cutter was himself again, or at least sufficiently so for the three of them to leave this scenic backwater and return to the coast, in time for the earthquake. Again he slept.

12

LATE IN THE MORNING BONE LEFT HIS ROOM AND WENT TO THE
motel restaurant to have coffee and read a newspaper while
he waited for Cutter and the girl to join him for breakfast. In
daylight the room pleasantly surprised him. For one thing,
Billy Graham the Younger was not on duty behind the organ,
and for another the view outside the huge windows at the rear
of the room turned out to be spectacular, overlooking a chasm
with a steep limestone cliff on the other side, fringed with
cedar along the top and plunging a good two hundred feet to
a narrow strip of white water that widened a short distance
beyond, turning calm and limpid as it slipped on through
lesser green hills spattered with rosebud and dogwood. And
the rain had ended. The sun was out.

So Bone was feeling almost contented as he sat at a table by
the windows sipping black coffee and catching up on the
calamities of the world, which not unexpectedly had kept pace
with his own. Maybe the sunshine and the scenery were an
omen, he told himself. Just maybe Alex would be out of the
woods now, free of both the Wolfe fantasy and his last night's
deep depression, and the three of them could be packed and
on their way back to the coast by evening — after the parade.
For Bone accepted it that he would have to go that far at least.
He would have to see J. J. Wolfe in the flesh and once and for

all settle the matter in his mind, whether Wolfe had indeed been the man in the alley, the Santa Barbara police captain's own true Prince of Darkness. Bone did not think he would be, not now, after Cutter's confession last night. Somehow all the lies about Wolfe and Los Angeles had only made Bone more unsure of who and what he had seen in the alley.

He had been sitting there about twenty minutes when Monk came in, alone, looking like a typical California runaway in her old jeans and Adidas sweatshirt. Her eyes were red from crying or loss of sleep, and when Bone said good morning, she asked him what was good about it.

He gestured at the window. "Well, God seems to be out there trying."

"You believe in God, do you?"

"Sometimes."

She put her face in her hands and shook her head disconsolately. "I guess you know what happened."

"I guess."

"He's out walking now. He's been gone for over an hour."

Bone said nothing. The thought of Cutter, in the condition he was in, wandering the cliffs behind the motel alarmed him more than he let on.

"It was so terrible," the girl went on, her eyes filling.

"I'm sorry. I guess I should have —"

"No, I don't mean that. Not the sex part," she explained. "I'm glad about that. It's like getting rid of acne or something."

Bone grinned, and for a moment the girl brightened too. Then she remembered. "No, it was the other, Rich. The things he said. He kept calling me Mo. And there were other weird things too, like private jokes between the two of them and when I couldn't pick up on them, he got all upset."

"He'd had a lot to drink," Bone said.

She shook her head in denial. "No, it wasn't like that, I mean just a guy being smashed, you know? Mixed up. It was more like — well, like he was sick. Like he couldn't get it all straight in his head, who I was, and where we were."

Bone took his time getting out his cigarettes, giving one to the girl and taking one himself, lighting them. He wanted to calm her. He wanted to calm himself. "Booze can do that," he said finally.

But the girl was adamant. "It wasn't booze."

"Maybe not."

"No maybe about it."

Bone would not concede the point. "You don't know that, Monk. It could be, but that's all. *Could* be. The fact that he spent a long time with the shrinks in VA hospitals doesn't mean anything — his wounds made that inevitable, for anyone."

"I know that."

"All right, then. Let's just wait and see, okay?"

Monk's face was puckered now, the face of a lost child. "I was so happy at first. So shocked and yet so happy when he came in. He shooshed me. And then he pulled back the covers, and —"

Bone put his hand on hers. "Take it easy, all right? Forget it for now. Let it go."

At this late morning hour only two other tables in the room were taken, but the patrons at each of them had fallen silent and were watching him and Monk with growing interest. Monk, however, was oblivious of them.

"And now this!" she said. "What do you think it is? Will it be permanent? Do you think he's —"

"Why hell no," Bone cut her off. "What are you talking about? He's just rundown, that's all. Strung out. He'll be okay."

"You think so?"

"Sure. We'll cut out of here this afternoon. And we'll take our time going home. We'll eat in restaurants and stay in motels. Swim and take it easy. He'll be all right. I promise."

Monk, looking past Bone at the entrance to the room, suddenly started to dry her eyes with a napkin.

"Oh boy, here he comes now," she said.

Bone did not understand her *oh boy* until Cutter came into view and sat down. He had not shaved or combed his hair. And instead of his customary black turtleneck he was wearing only a filthy T-shirt out of which the stump of his left arm protruded like a large white carrot.

"Nice country," he said. "Nice morning."

"Alexander Cutter the Fourth out taking a morning constitutional," Bone observed. "Hard to believe."

"Constitutional, my ass. I just stood on a rock."

"A rock?"

Cutter motioned at the window. "Yeah, out there. A big flat baby sticking out over the edge, with about five miles straight down. You just stand there. You close your eyes and get your toes out over the edge and play chicken with yourself."

"Sounds like great fun," Bone said.

"Oh, it is. It's a real high. Better than dope."

Bone said he'd try to remember that, but meanwhile he was more interested in food. "Either of you guys hungry?" he asked.

Cutter winked lasciviously at the girl. "Well, I don't know," he said. "I already did quite a bit of eating this morning."

Monk, turning scarlet, closed her eyes.

But Cutter was enjoying himself. "Kid must be part Chinese, though, because I am kind of hungry again."

"Nice to have you back," Bone said.

"Oh, great to be here. Just great."

"But you'd better be on your good behavior now," Bone advised. "Because I think we're about to be visited by your old friend, American Gothic."

She had just come out of the kitchen, and it appeared that morning had not altered the lady's spirit. Unsmiling, she came to their table, whipped out her order pad, licked the point of her pencil and held it ready, as if she were about to stab one of them with it.

"What'll you have?" she demanded.

"Coffee," Cutter said. "Just a pot of coffee for me, dearie."

The woman glanced at him and looked away, in studied revulsion. She practically sniffed. "We don't serve coffee in pots," she said. "You get it by the cup or not at all."

Cutter grinned. "You got to be kidding."

"No. That's the rule, I'm afraid."

Cutter looked hopefully at Bone. "Tell the lady she's kidding."

Bone was becoming uneasy now. He knew the look in Cutter's eye, had seen it too many times in the past, just before all hell broke loose. So he tried to throw himself into the breach, hurriedly ordering breakfast.

"Well let's see, I'll have a stack of wheatcakes, two scrambled eggs, a rasher of bacon — and coffee by the cup."

But Cutter was not to be put off. "Lady, you got a coffeepot in that kitchen?"

The woman ignored him. "And what will you have, miss?" she asked Monk.

At that, Cutter reached across the table and picked up the glass sugar dispenser, held it straight out from him and let it drop onto the tile floor, where it shattered loudly, spreading sugar out in a broad, almost geometric pattern.

"We'll also need some sugar," he said.

But by then the woman was gone, scurrying for the door.

Bone moaned quietly. "Yeah, it's sure great to have you back."

"A pot of coffee," Cutter said. "Is that so much to ask?"

"Evidently."

Across the room, American Gothic was already making a triumphant return, trailed by Mister Morgan from the front desk. As the man reached the table Cutter slapped his thigh and grinned.

"Well, Jesus H. Christ, if it ain't Mister Morgan hisself! You may remember us from the bar last night."

Morgan, standing tall, cleared his throat. "What's the problem here?"

"Coffee and sugar," Cutter said. "I want some."

"I'm going to have to ask you to leave," Morgan said.

"And I'm going to have to ask you to piss up a rope, sweetheart. While you're at it, give Miss Congeniality here a shot at it too. Might settle some of her crotch dust."

Morgan and the woman fled as if they had been scorched by a flamethrower. And Cutter tried to call them back, saying that they could get the goddamn rope later, *after* he had his coffee and sugar. Monk meanwhile was laughing and crying at the same time, and Bone felt like joining her, for he knew Morgan and the woman were hurrying off not to find a rope but to call the police. So he got up and followed them, reaching the front desk just in time to ask Morgan to put the phone down and hear his explanation. Then he went through a routine almost identical to the one he had laid on the motorcycle freaks at Santa Barbara's Cold Spring Tavern. Cutter was his cousin, he said, a poor maimed Vietnam veteran, a deranged paraplegic out on a week's leave from the Colorado Veterans' Hospital in Bone's care. Bone sincerely regretted his cousin's outlandish behavior. He apologized for him and promised to pay for any damages and to have the poor guy out of the motel before checkout time. But Morgan was not an easy sell. He was awfully put out, he said. He just didn't think war wounds was any excuse to talk to a lady the way Cutter had, especially a real Christian lady like his wife. And Bone of course agreed. He also offered to pay ten dollars for the sugar container, and that finally seemed to touch the man's forgiving spirit.

"Well, okay — one more chance. But that's all he gets. And you have him out of here by three, understand?"

Yes, Bone understood. He thanked Morgan and returned to the table.

Smiling thinly, he told Cutter and the girl that for the moment things were calm again and that if anyone did anything

278

to disturb that calm he personally was going to break off that person's plastic leg and beat him to death with it.

"Well, what are friends for?" Cutter asked.

Another waitress came to their table, took their orders for breakfast, and poured them each a cup of coffee. After she left, neither Bone nor Cutter said anything for a time, and the silence apparently got to Monk, for she began to babble like the stream out the window: God, wasn't it gorgeous here! And who'd ever have thought it — the Ozarks! Why she'd always thought of Missouri as flat and full of corn, would they believe that? And instead look how it was, how really beautiful. Why, even Santa Barbara wasn't this beautiful — oh, maybe if there weren't so many people there and if it had been the way it originally was, maybe then it might have been like this, so clean-looking, so fresh and green, with all that rock and those evergreens too — what kind were they, fir trees? Cedar, Bone told her. But she did not seem to hear, was already going on about the air, how clear and fresh it was. Hadn't he slept well? Wasn't it just about the greatest sleep of his life?

"Not really," Bone said. "No, I've slept better."

"Well, you'd been drinking again. Maybe that's why."

"Could be."

"Anyway, I think it's just super here. I'm glad we came." And here she gave Cutter a new and special look, almost a lover's look. Only there was something else in it too, something like terror. And it made Bone want to reach over and pull the kid onto his lap and try to console her or help her in some way, as she had helped him. But he knew there was really nothing he could do or say. The thing had happened to her, had actually and finally happened. The Virgin of Isla Vista was dead and buried and she was happy for the loss, she was joyous, she was probably in love. Yet here was her lover and liberator, grim as an executioner.

Lighting a cigarette, Bone asked them what they wanted to

do that day. "Want to head back or should we take in the local parade first?"

Monk looked surprised. "You mean, that's all? That's all we came here for?"

Bone shrugged. "Might be a great parade. Who knows?"

"But what about this character Wolfe or whatever his name is? I thought the reason we came here was to see him."

"He'll be in the parade," Bone said.

"I don't mean that kind of *see*. I thought there was some kind of heavy business you two had with him. Something about Mo and the baby."

"Not anymore," Cutter said.

"Why not?"

When Alex did not respond, Bone stepped in. "A change of plans," he said. "We decided to leave well enough alone."

The girl said she still did not understand.

"Never mind," Cutter told her. "Let it go."

Bone was surprised that the girl knew even this much, that Cutter had told her anything at all about Wolfe.

"Oh well, who cares?" she said. "It was worth the trip anyway."

Then, catching herself, she put one hand to her mouth while the other found Cutter's arm. And for a few moments he let it lie there, did nothing except gaze down at it as if it were excrement. Then he looked up at the girl with the same expression.

"Will you get your goddamn hand off me," he said.

Monk withdrew it.

"That's better," Cutter told her. "Jesus, Mo, just because we fornicated doesn't mean we're friends, you know."

The girl looked genuinely frightened now, close to tears.

"Quite a comedian, your new boyfriend," Bone said.

Cutter sneered. "Boyfriend, my ass. Between her and the goddamn kid, I've about had it."

Bone sat there watching him, waiting for the tip-off, the

beginning of a smile, a touch of light in his eye. But there was nothing.

By the time they returned to their room Bone was convinced that Cutter's condition — and starting back home with him immediately — were more important than the idle curiosity of seeing J. J. Wolfe in the flesh. And he tried to convince Cutter of this:

"The hell with Wolfe and the parade. Who needs it? Let's start for home now."

"No, you got to eyeball him," Cutter insisted. "That's why we're here."

"But I don't give a damn, Alex. I don't care one way or the other."

Cutter shrugged. "Well, I do. And anyway, I feel like a parade."

Outside, without saying a word, Cutter gave Bone the car keys and slipped into the back seat, as though out of long habit. And he positioned himself sideways, giving Monk no choice except to get into the front next to Bone. She too was very quiet now, had said almost nothing since the hand incident in the restaurant. So they were not a very festive group as they headed toward the festivities of Bank Day.

At a service station on the highway Bone asked about the parade and was informed that it would not start for an hour yet. It occurred to him then that he might still be able to see Wolfe at home, at his ranch, and thus avoid the risk of taking in the parade with Cutter in the condition he was in. He asked for directions to Wolfe's ranch and the attendant, husbanding a huge wad of chewing tobacco, allowed that it was harder not to find the place than it was to find it.

"Six whole sections last time anybody bothered to count," he said. "And with buildings you wouldn't believe. I tell you, them cattle of his'n live a darn sight better'n most people hereabouts, me included."

Bone tried to look properly impressed. Again he asked how to get there.

"Three miles up, turn right on County K. Another mile, you be there. Place got a gate cost more'n my house trailer, and that's a fack."

Bone thanked him and drove on, expecting some reaction from Cutter. But Alex said nothing, just sat in the back seat staring out the window, his eye — in the rearview mirror — registering nothing as the car swept on through woodlands and rocky dells and steep green hills stippled with grazing cattle.

Within a few minutes they came upon the ranch, which looked like a small town spread out along the rim of a hill about a quarter mile back from the road. The buildings, fences, corrals — all were white, dazzling in the sun. And as the service station attendant had said, the entrance was an impressive piece of architecture, with huge native stone pillars and stout white board fences bordering the drive, running all the way back to the ranch. In each of the pillars was a marble square engraved with the words Wolfe Farms, as if the place were some hallowed old institution. To the Santa Barbara horse set it would have been a hilarious gaucherie, but Bone imagined that here it got the job done effectively enough. J. J. Wolfe did his boasting in marble.

For a moment, after he had turned into the drive, Bone considered going on ahead to the house and trying to see the man now, get it over with. But the moment passed and he braked the car, reversed onto County K, and started back for Rockhill. He would be able to see Wolfe in the parade, he told himself. That would be sufficient, one quick look just to make sure whether or not he was his man. And either way, it would not make any difference. Either way, the three of them would simply pick up and leave.

As he turned around he expected Cutter to comment on the move, on the sudden flagging of his will, but Alex said nothing. And Monk seemed more interested in the ranch itself.

Wouldn't it be great to have such a place, she said. Wouldn't Bone dig owning it?

"It depends," he told her.

"On what?"

"On whether I'd have to live there."

"You wouldn't like that?"

"No."

"Why not?"

Bone tried to think of a reason. "People," he said. "You could go a whole lifetime and never run into the clap twins."

"Big loss!" the girl scoffed.

Bone laughed and looked in the rearview mirror, hoping to see Cutter smiling at least. But he was not. He had not heard them.

Bone drove back past the motel and made the turnoff into Rockhill, where he discovered a very different scene from that of the night before. Cars were parked everywhere, on the streets and lawns and sidewalks. And after he had parked the station wagon and the three of them had followed the crowd to the square, he found it filled with people, most of them from out of town, judging by their number. And he was surprised at how homogeneous they all seemed, with none of the melting-pot, multiracial character found in California and the northern cities. The vast majority looked Anglo-Saxon and Celt, not unlike a single huge extended family — a divided family however. For the sexes were like two races apart: the men lean and sunburnt and improbably pleased with themselves, laughing, spitting, japing with each other as they swaggered about in stovepipe Levi's and pointed boots and wing-brimmed cowboy hats, while their women were somehow like chaperones, old and fat and peevish, struggling along in armor-plated girdles under frilly Sunday dresses and constantly fussing with yesterday's permanents, endless tight little waves of blue-rinsed hair, black-dyed hair, bleached hair. Their facial expressions pretty well told the story of their lives: while the men had cattle and corn liquor and each other, they had to make do with Jesus and the Bible. And they weren't happy about it. They didn't think it was fair. Walking among them, Bone was convinced that nine in ten would have dismissed the female orgasm as a vicious rumor. The thing he disliked most about them, however, was their reaction to Cutter, the way they turned and stared at him with the same sour disapproval as the woman at the motel.

But it was a disapproval Cutter himself did not even seem to notice as he limped along next to Bone and Monk, as silent as he had been in the car. And here at least, Bone was relieved, for he doubted that the natives would have understood or put up with Cutter flying at anything like his normal altitude. As the cowboy Billy had warned them last night, almost every pickup had a rack of rifles and shotguns inside the back window, and Bone had no difficulty believing that most of them were loaded, judging by the macho air of the men, that look and attitude which proclaimed them goddamn ready and eager for any commie revolution the pinko nigger-loving government might be cooking up. And since the pickup seemed to be the prevailing mode of transport — the good old boys' answer to Santa Barbara's *de rigueur* Mercedes and Porsches — the crowd constituted a fairly well armed army.

This day, however, the men and the children at least did not seem concerned about much of anything except having a good time. There was a considerable amount of beer flowing, and occasionally a pint or half-pint of whiskey would make a furtive appearance, all of it smuggled in of course, certainly not being sold openly in Rockhill on this fine Southern Baptist sabbath. Yet, despite this puritan note, the general mood was decidedly festive, which as far as Bone was concerned meant discomfort more than anything else: noise and sweat and unwanted body contact. And he would not have endured a moment of it if it had not been for the parade and the chance to see J. J. Wolfe — perhaps for the second time.

But this possibility seemed of no interest to Cutter, no more than did the Bank Day celebrants: the huddles of chawing men and their spouses already settled into aluminum folding chairs, patiently fanning themselves and gossiping, waiting for the great event, while herds of hyped-up kids stampeded the streets and sidewalks, kids every bit as long-haired and raunchy as their coastal counterparts but somehow wilder by far, perhaps because their natural brutish vigor had not been leached out by dope and money and the soporific rays of the Pacific sun. Every few steps one or more of them would come crashing into Bone, playing tag or generational war, and he would shove them out of the way. Even Monk began to yell at them, trying to protect herself and Cutter, who just limped along, serene and apathetic, his eye fixed on something ahead of him, something that moved wherever he moved. Nor did he show any interest in the square itself and its picturesque old buildings, some with cast-iron façades and covered walks in front, and others made of cut stone and ancient clapboard, but all equally adorned with decals celebrating God and country: *America — Love it or leave it. My God is alive — sorry about yours. What a friend we have in Jesus.*

At the same time, Bone had never seen so many bullet-riddled street signs before, not even in a ghetto. But then he reflected that there was nothing anomalous in this: if piety and patriotism ever had a bedfellow, it was violence.

Contrary to what the old man in the bar had said, J. J. Wolfe did not lead the parade. That honor belonged to the Bank Day queen and her court riding in an open Cadillac convertible, five teenage girls whose soapy bright-eyed pretti-ness reminded Bone how uncharacteristically celibate he had been of late and that he should be careful not to carry the situation to extremes. After the girls, came the usual school bands and pompon girls, the Boy Scout troops and fire com-panies and the inevitable American Legionnaires, three venerable men who shuffled up the street with a fragile dignity.

Compared to Santa Barbara's famed annual Fiesta parade, this one was slight and unimaginative, yet somehow much more "American" to Bone's midwestern eyes. Where the Santa Barbarenos spent small fortunes getting themselves up as Spanish grandees and nubile senoritas, costumed to the nines and often borne by a coach-and-four, here there was an almost religious shunning of costumery and pretense. For the most part the parade was simply horse owners riding their horses, a few in full cowboy regalia but the rest making do with jeans and cowboy hats no different from those worn by half the watching crowd.

When the parade began, Bone and Cutter and Monk had insinuated their way to the curb in front of a boarded-up general store, and among the people they shared this stretch of sidewalk with was a small family that looked as if they had been lifted off an 1890 tintype: two severely plain old women in long gray dresses and bonnets sitting on wooden folding chairs in front of two men, one who appeared to be in his sixties and the other probably in his forties, though there was almost no difference in their appearance, both small and wiry and wearing overalls and blue work shirts buttoned to the neck and old-fashioned straw hats that covered all but a fringe of close-shaved hair. Like the women, their look of severity was shaded by fear, an intense wariness, as if they were in the camp of the enemy. And Bone judged that in their minds that was exactly where they were, probably true hillfolk, members of some small fanatic sect to whom even Bible Belt Southern Baptists were busy doing the devil's work.

Strangely Cutter did not seem to sense this difference in them at all, and as he began to come out of his silence now he talked to them almost as if they were fellow Californians doing the Sunset Strip together. Some goddamn parade, wasn't it? he said. A cat wouldn't know which were the horses and which were the pom-pom girls if it wasn't for the horses shitting every few feet. Or was that the pom-pom girls? Hard to tell, but one thing was for sure, there would be grass growing in the streets of this fucking burg this summer. And speaking of grass, they didn't happen to have a joint on them, did they?

By now Bone was trying desperately to shut him up, for the hillfolk already looked as if they were in shock, mesmerized by this satanic presence that had materialized right in front of them. And for a few moments Cutter pretended to cooperate, nodding to Bone that, yes, he understood, would knock it off. But all he did was take another breath and start in again.

"Just one more thing," he said to the hillfolk. "You cats know J. J. Wolfe? Why, hell yes, you do — all God's chillun knows de Big Chicken, don't dey? Well, you point him out to us when he comes by, will you do that? 'Cause we don't want to miss the sonofabitch."

Bone tried to drag him away, but Cutter pulled free.

"My friend here saw him kill a girl," he went on. "He made the chick blow him first and then he crushed her skull and dumped her body in a garbage can."

By now everyone around them was staring at Cutter in stunned disbelief. And still he kept on:

"And then the bastard burned my old lady and our kid to a crisp and tried to make it look like a fucking murder-suicide, would you believe that? And there was Vietnam too, we can't forget that, can we? A mighty hawk, old J.J. — a few more arms and legs, well hell yes, he was willing to pay the price. Plenty more where those came from. So you point him out, okay? Point out the cocksucker and leave the rest to us."

But there was no need for anyone to point him out, for Bone saw Wolfe now coming around the nearest corner of the square. Bone knew it was Wolfe simply by looking at the man, at the same heavy smiling avuncular face he had seen in the photographs in the Santa Barbara newspaper and in his Hollywood office. And for Bone the moment was somehow like being caught in the middle of a highway between cars speeding at him from opposite directions: he had to see Wolfe close up, and yet he knew he had to get Cutter out of there before the crowd got its wits together and began beating him to a pulp.

Wolfe rode as part of a family unit, himself and a middle-aged woman and two young girls all dressed like Roy Rogers and mounted on matching palominos. As the four horses clattered past, Cutter moved close to Bone.

"Well, lay it on me," he said. "Is it him? Is he our boy?"

Bone did not answer for a few moments, mostly out of fear that he would giggle if he opened his mouth, betray to the whole wide world just how absolutely hopeless he was, how totally and irredeemably a loser.

For he *still* did not know if Wolfe was the man. Even looking right at him, he still could not tell if Wolfe had been the man in the alley. His head was large and his body thick, just as the killer's was. But that gross and swollen animus which somehow had thrived even in silhouette — it was not there. Instead there was just this costumed fat man sitting a horse, grinning, waving, the tycoon as clown. And the disappointment Bone felt, the letdown, for some reason only added to the comedy of the moment. Of course it would be thus. How could it have been otherwise? Why should Bone's life suddenly have developed a sense of symmetry and purpose? Would he have traveled across half a continent *except* in a fruitless cause?

As he was about to answer Cutter, he found himself staring flatly into the eyes of the cowboy at the motel last night, Wolfe's foreman Billy, standing alone across the street, oblivious of the parade passing between them. Bone nodded slightly, a greeting of sorts, but the cowboy did not respond. Cutter meanwhile was still watching Wolfe.

"Come on, come on!" he urged Bone. "Is it him? Is Wolfe our boy?"

Bone shook his head. "No, he's not the man," he said.

And Alex laughed. "Of course, he ain't. So let's go, jackass. Let's eat."

A few minutes later Bone found himself following Cutter and the girl down the street that held the small carnival, which close up had the look of the sorriest show on earth, the kind of outfit that pulled into a town loaded into three or four battered trucks driven by geeks and bearded ladies and other colorful carnie types. There were only two rides: a Ferris wheel and a "Spinaroo," a huge wheeling mechanical octopus with individually whirling cabs at the end of its tentacles, each of them filled with kids screaming in ear-stunning terror. There was also a funhouse and three or four game booths offering such prizes as Day-glo plastic dogs and satin pillows beribboned with slogans in gold thread: *Sex — try it, you'll like it . . . Too much sex is hard to swallow . . .* and the ever-popular *The family that plays together, stays together.*

As the three of them pushed their way past the garish booths Bone asked Cutter if he was sure he didn't want to turn and run for their lives and Alex said no, everything was okay. But he did not look at Bone as he said it. So Bone pressed.

"You sure you're all right?"

"What's all right?"

"Normal."

"I'm okay."

"You could've got us strung up back there."

"Naturally. This is the place. Or didn't you notice?"

"What place?"

Cutter gave him a searching look, ironic, unbelieving. "Don't put me on," he said.

"About what?"

"Here. We're here and you know it."

"Where?"

"Where *they* are. Didn't you see him back there — old Billy Boy? They've come for me. They've finally come for me."

Bone said nothing, did not know what to say.

And Cutter grinned, the wound again. "I said I was hungry."

"So you did." Bone turned to Monk. "What about you?"

"Sure. Hot dog and a Coke. Everything on the hot dog."

"Brave girl. And you, Alex? The same?"

Cutter was shielding his eye, gazing up at the Ferris wheel. Thinking he nodded, Bone went over and joined the crowd in front of the food stand. Most of them were children and teenagers, not a few with lumps of tobacco working inside their lower lips. Occasionally a bit of it would run over, like brown blood, and the kid would turn and spit, already a good old boy. Bone stayed alert and unspattered, and finally he made it back with the Cokes and hot dogs.

Monk was alone.

"Where's Alex?"

She nodded in the direction of the Ferris wheel.

"He went up in *that?*"

Again the girl nodded. "I asked him if he wanted me to go with, but he didn't answer. He just walked away."

Bone squinted up at the harsh afternoon sky, at the great wheel turning slowly against it. He tried to make Cutter out as the seats came around one at a time, and finally he saw him, sitting back alone, his eye fixed ahead of him, on space, on nothing.

"What's wrong with him?" Monk asked. "Was it last night? Was it me? Shouldn't I have let him?"

"No, it wasn't you," Bone said. "He was like this earlier last night. Troubled, I mean. Not himself."

"But was he scary like now? I mean so wild one moment and so quiet the next?"

"No. This is something new."

"Well, what is it?"

"Depression, I guess. Sorrow, grief — you name it."

And suddenly Monk was crying. "Oh God, I'm so scared," she said. "I'm so scared."

By now, five or six young boys had stopped to stare at the two of them as if they were part of the carnival, another side-show. Finally one of the boys puckered up and began to cry himself. "Ma, I lost my puddy tat!" he bawled. "I lost it! I did, I did, I did!" And his friends began to laugh and hoot until Bone ran them off.

He took Monk by the arm and led her over to a spot next to a boarded-up blacksmith shop. They were in the shade here, which made it easier to watch the Ferris wheel as the contraption continued to turn against the sky, its ponderous grace so at odds with the demonic tempo of the calliope music that pervaded the street. Monk had dried her eyes and blown her nose, and now she began to eat her hot dog, while Bone watched the wheel. Twice the huge thing stopped and new riders took the place of veterans — except for Cutter. He stayed on the machine, and Bone watched his seat come around time after time, and always it was the same: the slender figure sitting back, stiff, unmoving, the single eye never straying.

The next time the ride came to an end and it was Cutter's turn to get off, the operator began to shout at him and even tried to pull him off. But Alex would not budge. Bone immediately started through the crowd toward him, but before he got there the wheel was moving again, with Cutter still in his seat. And the operator, a young long-haired hippie, was yelling over to another employee to go for the police.

"And tell 'em to haul ass!" he said. "The bastard won't get off!"

Vaulting a fence, Bone went over to the operator and told him he was a friend of the man who wouldn't get off the Ferris wheel. He said that he would pay for all his rides so far and that the next time around he personally would drag his friend off the thing if it was necessary.

"But call off the police," Bone asked him. "Please. The man is sick."

The hippie did not answer. He was still busy moving the wheel around, letting riders off and putting new ones on. Bone tried again.

"Please — as a favor. I'll give you ten bucks. Just call off the police. Let me handle it."

The hippie finally looked at him, and at the bill Bone had taken out.

"No chance, fella," he said. "Save your money. That asshole up there's crazy and we got to get him off this thing, it's that simple. So back off, okay? Cool it."

Bone stood there trying to think of something else he could say or do. But there was nothing. It was out of his hands, and he knew it. So he went back to the fence, where Monk was standing now, holding onto it with a death grip. Her eyes were streaming and she kept saying something over and over, but Bone was not sure what it was. He could not take his mind or eyes off Cutter as the wheel started around again, at full speed now. Some of the riders screamed and others laughed and a few took it calmly, sitting back and watching the world below. None, however, sat as Cutter did.

By now a small crowd was gathering as word spread that there was some sort of trouble on the Ferris wheel. Most of them were kids. But on their outer edges Bone was surprised to see the cowboy Billy, standing as before, by himself, patiently watching Cutter.

Bone had no time to wonder about him, however, for the second employee had just arrived, followed by a policeman, a beefy middle-aged sheriff's deputy sweating through his suntans. The hippie said a few words to him and the deputy nodded. Then he stepped back and looked up as the wheel came around again and stopped — at Cutter's seat. Bone felt his own hands begin to shake as the hippie unfastened the bar in front of the seat and swung it clear. The deputy moved forward and said something to Cutter, something Alex apparently did not hear, for he did not move or change his expression, just sat there as before, staring ahead, his hand gripping the side rail of his seat. Both men began to tug at him then, easily at first, evidently not expecting much resistance. But when they failed to move him, when both of them together were unable to break his grip, the hippie angrily went around to the side of the seat and began to kick at Cutter's hand, as if he were stamping the life out of a snake.

Bone remembered very little after that. He remembered hearing Monk scream and he remembered plunging ahead and driving his fist into the hippie's face and seeing the youth fall on his back, his nose and mouth spurting blood. And he remembered hearing behind him a kind of grunt, just before the back of his head exploded. Just before there was nothing.

13

BONE'S STAY IN THE COUNTY JAIL LASTED ONLY FOUR HOURS, MOST of which he spent in the drunk tank holding his ears and head against the vocal assault of a beer-filled teenager who kept squalling at the top of his voice a refrain of Janis Joplin:

Oh Lord wontcha buy me a Mercedes-Benzzzz
My friends all have Por-scheees I must make aay-mends.

So Bone was considerably relieved when the sheriff finally came for him. He was a big easygoing man in his fifties, and he told Bone that for over thirty years he had been carrying six pieces of fine Krupp steel around in his right leg and therefore could understand a guy coming to the aid of a buddy who had lost an arm and a leg and an eye fighting for his country. The sheriff even apologized for Bone's headache but said it couldn't be helped, "Junior" just didn't know his own strength and was forever bringing people in half-dead, people who "shoulda knowed better than tangle with a officer with twelve-inch wrists."

Bone agreed with the sheriff. He thanked him for releasing him and asked how to get to the veterans' hospital in Fayetteville, where Cutter had been taken, along with Monk, who apparently had told the police that she was Cutter's wife. The sheriff reflected that he didn't envy anyone who had to go there, in fact anyone who even had to leave Rock County for that matter, but he gave Bone the directions anyway. And he returned his keys and wallet. He even shook hands goodbye.

In the patrol car, driving Bone to his station wagon, Junior observed that "a body shouldn't believe all that patriotic bullshit the sheriff dishes out." The only metal in the old man's leg was buckshot from a hunting accident, the deputy said. And the only reason Bone was getting off so easy was the sheriff didn't think it was a crime to hit a hippie, as a matter of fact took a poke at 'em hisself whenever he could. So naturally he'd talked the carnival kid out of pressing charges. Which meant Bone was one lucky sumbitch, and Junior hoped he knowed it. If it had been up to him, Bone would still be in the slam, because assault was assault, by God, and there just wasn't no two ways about it.

Bone naturally neglected to comment on any of this. When they reached his car, he thanked the deputy for the lift and told him not to brood about busting his head the way he had, that with any luck it would probably mend in time. But Junior was not listening.

"I'm gonna follow you to the motel," he said. "The owner wants to make sure you check out pronto, without causin' any more fuss."

Bone thought of the pair of them, Cutter's American Gothic, and he was not surprised. "Whatever you say, pal," he told the deputy.

Junior had more for him. "And after you've checked out, you follow me in your car. Someone wants to have a talk with you."

"Who?"

"Never mind who."

"And suppose I don't go. Suppose I just take off."

The idea did not impress Junior very much. "No pollution crap on this baby," he said, patting the squadcar's steering wheel. "I'll ketch you right off and run you in for resistin' arrest."

"Arrest for what?"

"Speedin'."

A half hour later Bone found himself trailing Junior over a route he already knew: three miles south on the highway, then west on County K. But this day, as he turned in at the stone portals of Wolfe Farms, he did not stop and back out. He continued up the curving crushed-rock drive to the top of the hill, following the deputy past the lane that led to the house, a modernistic sprawl of wood and glass and native stone with an empty swimming pool in the front.

When they came to the outbuildings, Junior parked and got out. Bone pulled in next to him but remained in his car. In the nearest corral two cowboys were working with a group of small black calves, crowding them down a narrow chute toward a headgate where a third man was inoculating the animals, shooting them with a hypodermic that looked like a silver pistol. Bone remembered one of the cowboys from the motel bar, the one "Billy Boy" had called Sam. And now Sam caught sight of Junior. Giving a calf one last brutal whack with the cane he was carrying, he came out through the corral gate. Junior said something to him and the cowboy looked over at Bone and grinned, all the while slapping his open palm with the cane, which was long and unpainted, as stout as an ax handle. Nodding to the deputy now, he sauntered over to the nearest building and went inside.

Bone by now had his hand on the ignition key, held it sweating there while he tried to decide whether or not to make a run for it. His throat was dry. Television and movie images raced through his head: federal backhoes digging in red clay soil while deputies just like Junior stood around joshing and elbowing each other, having a fine old time. Even as Bone was thinking this, the deputy sidled over and cut him off, sat back against the fender of Bone's car and began to pick his teeth with one hand while the other fondled his holstered thirty-eight.

Within a few seconds Sam came back out of the building, followed by his boss — the third time Bone had seen the man that day. Only this time it was with a feeling of relief, for somehow Bone could not imagine him — Billy Boy, the cool peacemaker of the night before — as part of some bloody, honky cabal.

"Okay, you — get out here," Junior bawled.

And Bone obeyed, moving on legs that felt like stilts.

Billy's grin was relaxed, easy. "Well, if it ain't old Humperdinck's buddy," he said.

"Big surprise, huh?"

"In a way, yeah. We weren't sure we could catch you before you left."

"You caught me."

"*Catch* as in contact," Billy explained.

"Sure."

Next to Billy, Junior had the look of a hunter who had shot his limit. But Billy had bad news for him. "We can handle it from here, old buddy," he said, clapping the deputy on the back. "You best get back to fighting crime."

Junior's face fell. Yet he managed a laugh. "You know it, Billy! You sure as hell know it!"

As the deputy drove away, Billy tried to explain things to Bone. "I guess all this seems sort of like a command performance. And we're sorry about that. But we just wanted to talk over a few things before you cut out."

"Who's *we?*"

"Mister Wolfe mainly."

"I don't know the man. I've got nothing to talk with him about."

"Well, he seems to think so. Why not give him a few minutes, huh? What can it hurt?" Billy started to turn away. "He's out in the bull barn, messin' with this new Angus we got."

But Bone did not follow. He did not like the idea of leaving the open ground of the farmyard for the dark recesses of some distant barn. "Why not here?" he asked. "Why can't he come here?"

Billy shrugged. "I don't know, I guess he could. But what's the difference? I mean, all the man wants is to ask you a few questions, that's all. Five minutes from now you can be on your way."

Billy's look of veiled amusement did not give Bone much choice. "All right," he said.

They went down a kind of main drag between the low white buildings, some of which were filled with bales of hay while others stood empty except for a few tractors and other implements.

"Too bad about your friend," Billy said, as they walked. "I was there, you know. I saw the poor guy freak out. I wonder what it was — fear of heights, you think that was it?"

"Could be," Bone said.

Near the end of the road he followed Billy into a barn with rows of stalls on either side of a central alley cluttered with stacks of baled straw. The building was dimly lit, most of the light in fact coming through the door behind Bone — a door that went closed now. And turning, Bone saw the reason, the cowboy Sam. He had not known Sam was following them.

"Well, it appears old J.J. ain't here," Billy observed.

"Then let's go where he is."

Billy shrugged. "Oh, I guess maybe I could handle it alone."

Bone knew by now that he had walked into it, that he was trapped. But he tried to tough it out. He tried to act as if nothing essential had changed. "You said Wolfe would be here," he said.

"And Wolfe is. I'm a Wolfe, same as J.J. His nephew as a matter of fact."

Bone started to turn away, but Billy reached out and held him, lightly. "Okay, the truth, then," he said. "I'm the one with the questions, not J.J."

For a few moments Bone said nothing, just stood there looking down at Billy's hand on his arm until it fell away. Then, leaning back against a stall gate, Billy fished a cigarette out of his jacket pocket — evidently a prearranged signal between him and Sam, for at that moment the cowboy drove his cane into Bone's back and Bone dropped to his knees in the straw, silent, silently screaming at himself not to scream, not to black out. And then the cane struck again, in the same place, and Bone's face rapped against the straw and concrete of the floor.

Still he did not pass out. He was aware of the door behind him opening and closing again and then long seconds passing, time droning in a stillness broken only by the sounds of the bulls in their stalls. And he was thinking, trying desperately to get some sort of fix on his predicament, some idea how to get out of it. A few thoughts stuck: that Wolfe and Billy probably knew nothing about him, that he was there because of Cutter's rantings at the parade, that his one chance was to separate himself from Cutter as much as possible.

Slowly he pushed himself up, aware of Billy standing above him, still leaning back against the stall, and casually lighting his cigarette now with a kitchen match that he carefully blew out and returned to the pocket of his battered denim jacket. Bone worked his way across the alley from him, scooted up against the stall there, to protect his kidneys and spine, which had melded into a single clot of pain.

"Too bad about that," Billy said finally. "Too bad we had to do that."

"Why me?" Bone got out.

Billy ignored the question. "Mister Wolfe don't know you're here," he said. "Fact, he don't know anything about you. I want to keep it that way."

Bone, trying to keep the pain and fear out of his voice, again asked what was going on, why they had singled him out.

"You can thank Humperdinck. All that shit he was broadcasting this afternoon."

"You saw him crack up. You just said so outside. So what's it matter, what a psycho says?"

"Oh, it matters," Billy assured him. "People just don't say stuff like that around here — especially not about J. J. Wolfe."

"Well, I don't know your J. J. Wolfe," Bone said. "And I barely know Humperdinck."

"Barely know him?"

"That's right."

"Just traveling companions, huh?"

"An employee is more like it. His driver. Maybe you noticed — he's missing a few limbs."

"I noticed."

"About four days ago, on the coast, I was at this party. And he came over and said he heard I was loose and would I drive him out here. He offered meals and expenses."

"That's all?"

"That's all."

"Not part of the take, huh?"

"What take?"

"Extortion."

"I don't know anything about any extortion."

"You don't, huh?"

"That's right, I don't."

Billy exhaled a smoke ring, then sailed a smaller one through it. "You lie pretty good," he said.

"Not when I'm scared."

"You scared now?"

"Yeah."

"Why?"

"For good reason."

"Me?"

Bone shrugged. "On my own turf, with just the two of us, maybe not. But here, yeah. You people scare me."

"That's smart. Too bad Humperdinck ain't smart."

"He's sick, that's all."

300

Billy looked down at Bone and shook his head, in contempt and wonderment. "J. J. Wolfe killing some teenage girl and dumping her body in a garbage can — now, why would anyone say a thing like that, huh?"

"I don't know. Ask the man who said it."

"I'm asking you."

"And I can't help you. I drove the man's car here, that's all. I don't know what he's up to. I don't know what your beef is. But it ain't with me."

For a while Billy said nothing. He was standing in front of the stall now, almost facing it. "You get a look at that critter in there?" he said finally. "Bad Dream, we call him."

Bone had crawled up onto a bale of straw, hoping to ease the pain in his back. Through the stall's two-by-ten slats he could see the animal inside, a great horned black beast as long and tall as a thoroughbred racehorse but twice as wide, twice as deep, with a head the size of a barrel, nostrils he could have stuck his fist in.

"Yeah, I see him," he said.

"But can you believe him? Angus-Chianina cross, he is, over a ton of black nigger rage. Can you imagine what he'd do to some poor sonofabitch happen to get caught in there with him? Somebody, say, tied up? Can you picture it?"

Bone could, and in cold terror. But all he gave Billy was a flat "Yeah."

"Yeah, I bet you can. It's like I was telling Humperdinck last night about the good old boys around here. Them and their pickups loaded down with guns. This just ain't a healthy place to come in and slander somebody, especially somebody like J. J. Wolfe."

"I can see that," Bone said. "I'm sorry it happened. But I didn't have anything to do with it."

"You didn't, huh?"

"No."

Billy took a drag on his cigarette and slowly exhaled, all the while studying Bone with his icewater gaze. "Why'd you come here?" he said finally.

"I just told you."

"Why'd he come here?"

"I don't know."

"Blackmail? Did he come here to blackmail J.J.?"

"Blackmail Wolfe? For what? What'd he do?"

"Who said he had to do anything? A man like J.J., he's a sitting duck. With all his responsibilities, all his holdings — it just takes a rumor, my friend. That's all. A little dirt. And then some creep thinks he's in business."

Bone said nothing. And Billy went on, his voice suddenly hard and urgent, as if he were revealing a terrible secret. "J. J. Wolfe is the straightest man you'll ever meet. He's the best there is. The hardest working. The straightest."

"I don't doubt it," Bone tried.

"And anyone say any different, anyone think he can waltz in here and call him a murderer and sex maniac — and figure we'll just roll over and pay, pay 'em not to lie about us — well, let me promise you they ain't gonna be able to hide nowhere. You understand that? *Nowhere.*"

It was growing warm in the closed barn now, and Billy absently unclasped his jacket. As it fell open Bone was able to see his T-shirt underneath, and the emblem on it: a red Arkansas razorback hog, name and symbol of the state university's sports teams. And for some reason that emblem began to scratch at Bone's attention, like a face he could not quite place. He wanted time to think about it, but Billy's voice kept at him.

"You got that, friend?"

Bone nodded. "I don't know anything about the man. I didn't come here to harm him."

"And your buddy — that go for him too?"

Bone did not answer immediately, for it had come to him now, what it was about the razorback. *Just a fucking pig,*

302

the service station attendant had described it, the picture on the T-shirt of the man who bought the cans of gasoline in Santa Barbara. And Bone wondered if he was not looking at the man now, the firebomber, not Wolfe after all but his nephew, even at this moment idly scratching at the small red rampaging boar on his chest. Bone could almost see the thing taking place, J.J. drunk and blood-spattered, coming back to the motel in shock and panic, probably not even sure what had happened, probably even wanting to call the police — and Billy stepping in, the iceman, the man with the quick hard answers.

It was an intriguing theory, but only that, Bone knew. The razorback was not proof enough. Nothing was ever proof enough.

"What about it?" Billy repeated. "That go for your buddy too?"

"He's not my buddy."

"No, of course not. And that scene this afternoon at the Ferris wheel, you smashing the hippie — what was that?"

"The man's a cripple," Bone said. "The hippie was kicking him."

"So he's not your buddy, huh?"

"No."

"Then you can't say what he'll do, can you?"

"I can tell you what he won't do. He won't remember any of this. They'll give him shock treatments. Electrotherapy."

"How do you know that?"

"Mutual friends. They say he's been in and out of hospitals ever since Vietnam."

This information seemed to impress Billy. "Then he is a psycho."

"Wouldn't you be?"

Taking another drag on his cigarette, Billy shook his head thoughtfully. "I want to be done with this whole goddamn thing, right here and now. But I gotta be sure. J.J., he's not just my uncle and boss — I owe him. My old man was no good, a lush, but J.J. made sure we never did without. Whatever we needed, he gave. He even sent me to college."

"Arkansas," Bone said.

"Yeah. Biz Ed and wrestling. And now I run his farms for him. And I travel with him some. He likes to talk cattle."

"You were in Santa Barbara." It had slipped out, a mistake. And Billy did not miss it. Something new came into his eyes, something Bone could not read.

"What do you mean by that?" the cowboy asked.

"Nothing," Bone said, trying to cover. "I just figured whatever the hassle was, I mean between Wolfe and Humperdinck — well, maybe you were in on it. Maybe you were there."

"Yeah, maybe I was. And then maybe there wasn't any hassle at all, just two totally separate events. J.J.'s car gets bombed and this local girl gets herself wasted and dumped in a garbage can. And you two clowns pick up on it. Easy money, you figure. You add one and one and come up with what — ten thousand? Is that about it? That what you figure he'd pay not to be bothered, not to have the publicity?"

Bone was shaking his head, denying it all. "I told you — I don't know anything about it. I drove the man's car here, that's all."

"Sure, you did."

"That's right."

"And that's why you said I was in Santa Barbara — because you don't know anything, right?"

"That's right."

Billy smiled grimly. "Of course that's right."

Bone was on his feet now, taller than Billy, bigger. And he found that he could manage his pain, could fight if it came to that. "It doesn't matter," he said. "It's not important."

"Oh? What is then?"

"That you've got my word — I don't know anything about Wolfe. I don't know what any of this is about."

"That's all?"

"And I'm walking out of here. Now."

"Just like that?"

"Just like that."

Billy thought about it. With his boot he cleaned a place in the straw on the floor, then dropped his cigarette and carefully ground it out. "You and your 'employer' are some odd couple," he said finally.

Bone made no response.

"Yeah, old Humperdinck, he don't just pay the price, he ups the ante. He can't *wait* to pay. But now you, you figure you can get in scot free, right? You figure you can put on that pleasant harmless face and everything's okay, everything's sweet and easy."

"And that's wrong, huh?"

"That's wrong."

"So be it. I'm still leaving."

"Well, of course you are. You jist gonna waltz on out of here, free as the wind, right?"

Bone said nothing.

And Billy was not smiling now. "You best get started then," he said.

As Bone left, he did not give the cowboy his back, not until he reached the barn door. Then he turned and went out into the failing light. He forced himself to walk unhurriedly all the way to his car and he drove slowly down the hill and out through the stone gate. Only then did he slam the accelerator to the floor.

It was almost midnight when he arrived at the hospital. He found Monk in the waiting room, sitting by herself in the dimness. When she saw him, she gave a cry and practically knocked him down diving into his arms. Then she let it out of her, the fear and tension of the last eight hours, crying like a child. In time she told him what she could, what little she knew. Alex was sedated somewhere, asleep. She did not even know his room number. She had not seen him. She had given the doctors all the information she could, but they had not told her anything, in fact were not even shrinks. A psychiatrist would not be on duty until morning, they said, and even then it would be a while before he got to Cutter or would have anything to tell her.

Bone talked the girl into leaving the hospital then, and they checked into a nearby motel. She asked about the way he kept holding his back and he told her he had been in a fight at the jail and had fallen against a table. She ran a tub of water for him then and even helped him into it. He was not sure what would be better for his back — hot water or ice packs — but he knew that the heat felt good and he settled for it, for almost an hour. And all that time Monk held forth on the profound new depth her relationship with Cutter had reached. Her coming to Missouri with them had been preordained, she said. The gods or stars or whatever had known Alex would be needing her eventually and so had forced her to come along, against her will really. For she hadn't wanted to come, had never done anything like this before, yet here she was, right when he needed her most. Alone she was nothing, a zero, always had been and always would be. But not as part of Alex, his lover or gopher or doormat, she didn't care what her role was, as long as it was what Alex wanted. Because he was a very special human being — Bone could see that, couldn't he? Had he ever known anyone like Alex before, anyone who could talk the way he could, anyone who behaved the way he did, anyone with *that look* of his, that special look that said he knew it all and had seen it all, felt it all? And he would be well again, be himself again, Monk knew that, did not question it any more than that the sun would rise in the morning. Simply because he was Alex, because he was he.

Bone kept nodding and yawning. And finally, ready for bed, he kissed her on the forehead and said goodnight. But he did not sleep. For a long time he lay there in the dark thinking about all that had happened that day, and he found it incredible that he still was not sure that Wolfe was guilty. He had seen the man in the flesh and no bells had rung, no lights had dawned. And yet, if the man was innocent, then he certainly had overreacted to Cutter's charges, having a deputy bring Bone out to the farm and letting his hired hands beat him and grill him the way they had. If Wolfe's only worry had been a nuisance blackmail attempt, why would he have gone to such lengths to stop it, outside the law?

On the other hand, if he *was* guilty, then why had he let Bone go? Billy had not been acting on his own — Bone did not believe that for a moment. Wolfe undoubtedly had heard what Cutter said at the parade. And he had learned that Bone was with Cutter, had traveled all the way from Santa Barbara with him, and therefore was probably his partner in crime. Yet they had let him go.

So Bone could only conclude that Wolfe was either innocent or the next best thing, a noncriminal at heart, a muddler like most people, like Bone himself, and in letting him go had opted for inaction and uncertainty rather than undertake a cold-blooded execution. Either way, Bone considered the matter over and done. He was safe. He was out of it. And Cutter too — but out of it in a way Bone did not want to think about now, not tonight. Tomorrow would be soon enough for that.

In the morning, stiff and sore, he returned with Monk to the hospital. And they had to wait till almost noon before a doctor finally saw them, a doctor who turned out to be the long-awaited psychiatrist, though in the flesh he could have passed more easily for a Los Angeles used car salesman, snapping his gum and glad-handing them, giving them a big Sears grin to match his computer-coordinated red and white print shirt with red tie and slacks, white belt and white shoes. Doc Wheelright, he called himself. And if they were expecting a lot of psycho-analytic jargon, then they'd come to the wrong store.

It was kinda hard to tell about their friend. He was still in a depressed state, that was for sure, but it was too early yet to say whether what he had was a genuine psychotic depressive reaction or just some sorta blue funk. Their friend had this weird kinda light in his eye — a kind the Doc had seen before, plenty of times — and it usually meant the patient was playing games of one kind or another. Which didn't mean the boy wasn't sick — oh, he was that, all right, no doubt about it. The doc had called L.A. for Cutter's VA record and judging by it and what the girl here had told Doctor Ramsey last night, well it was obvious the boy needed to spend some time off the streets, safe from society. And quite often that's all these things were, breakdowns like this — a kid knows he's had it, knows he's sick, and so kinda lets it all go, kinda commits himself to the hospital by his own hand. Sort of a *soldier, heal thyself* situation, if they knew what he meant.

The doctor paused at that point to grin and reflect on the phenomenon of his verbal felicity, then he got down to the business side of the case. This VA hospital did not have a psycho ward — he himself worked for the university, was here only in a consultancy capacity — so Cutter would have to be transferred soon, either to Little Rock or back to the coast, depending on family, finances, and so forth. Bone told the doctor that there was no family left but that a Santa Barbara businessman, a Mr. George Swanson, came closest to filling the bill. Bone himself was not in the most secure or affluent time of his life and — here he tried, and failed, to think of Monk's real name — *she* was still in college. So the nearest source of moral and financial support, outside the VA, would be back in California. Wheelright, writing all this down, said that he imagined that was where they would probably transfer Cutter then, send him back with an orderly.

"And me," Monk put in. "I go with him, wherever he goes."

308

Wheelright nodded agreeably. "That's fine — if you pay your way, of course. And if I don't find out in the meantime you're part of the patient's problem."

"She's not," Bone said.

Bone had a hard time convincing the doctor to let him see Cutter that same day, before he started for the coast. And even then Wheelright said that he would have to accompany him.

"I don't want that sick boy gettin' any sicker," he said.

On the way, as they went past all the rooms, all the men on crutches and in wheelchairs and lying lost and broken in their beds, Bone began to feel more keenly than before the enormity of Cutter's breakdown. He had lied to Billy about the electrotherapy — Cutter had never been that sick before — but now, following the doctor down these long waxed corridors of pain and despair, he had to wonder if it would not come to that, if in the end they would not wire Cutter up and burn away his mind and spirit, quench his antic flame with their cold fire. The more he thought about it, the more unendurable it became. And by the time he reached Cutter's room he was not even sure he could speak. He felt as if he were strangling. His eyes burned with a terrible dryness.

The room had three beds and an orderly in attendance, a short husky black youth who told Wheelright that the new patient was conscious now and fairly relaxed, not fighting the sheet at all. The doctor nodded and Bone followed him to the corner bed, situated behind a white plastic curtain. In it Cutter lay on his back, motionless and slight. And only as Bone drew close did he understand why Alex might have fought his sheet, that it was in fact a restraining blanket, a heavy canvas cover strapped down. His expression was indeed relaxed, even serene. But his eye looked dead to Bone, that eye where the doctor had detected a "weird kinda light." Dull and drugglazed, it flicked briefly at Bone and then resumed its blank gaze at the ceiling.

"Only a few seconds now," the doctor cautioned.

Bone nodded, still staring down at Cutter, hoping he would look back at him again.

"Hey, old-timer," Bone said. "What's the big idea?" And he tried to smile as he said this, knowing it was ridiculous, as ridiculous as his words. But he did not know how else to do it, how to talk to this unknown being lying before him. He remembered the last strange words Cutter had uttered, at the carnival, that *they* had come for him, finally come for him, and Bone wondered if he might reach him there, help him to understand that *they* did not exist, were only men, that was all, little men caught in little webs.

"I went to see Wolfe," he said. "I talked with him. He wasn't the one, Alex. He didn't have anything to do with the girl, or the fire." He wanted to add that Wolfe had not set the claymores in Vietnam either, or raised the sea at Point Conception. But Cutter would not have heard him, any more than he had heard the first part.

"Okay, I think that's enough," the doctor said. "You can see how he is."

And now Bone could not keep it out of his eyes any longer. As they filled he reached down and touched Cutter, squeezed his shoulder.

"You find your way back," he got out. "You hear me, kid? You come back to us. We need you."

But the doctor was already gently pulling Bone away. He led him back across the room and out into the corridor.

"Now, don't you give up," he said. "That's why I didn't want you to see him yet. The first day like this, you just can't tell. But a couple days from now, why he could just snap right back. You never know."

Bone nodded, grateful. It was something.

That afternoon, he found a room for Monk. He helped her move her things in, gave her two hundred of the four hundred fifty dollars he had left, then he kissed her goodbye. She cried a little and said she loved him, loved him almost as much as she did Cutter. And Bone grinned.

"I'll settle for that," he said. "Any day."

After he left her, he drove into a service station and called George Swanson collect in Santa Barbara, reaching him at his real estate office. He briefly told him about Cutter's breakdown and that the VA would probably be sending him back to the coast soon. Bone gave him the telephone numbers of the hospital and of Monk's roominghouse, and he told him how devoted she was to Cutter and that it would be a good idea to stay in touch with her, that she would be able to keep him informed on Cutter's condition and when he would be returned to the coast. As for himself, Bone said he was going to leave that afternoon and would have George's car back to him within a week. He tried to tell him about the money then, how much was left and who had it, but George said he didn't care about it, that the important thing was that Cutter was still among the living and would be getting the help he needed, thanks to Bone.

Bone wanted to hang up then but George asked if he could tell him now what the trip had been about, why Cutter had wanted to go to the Ozarks.

"A wild goose chase," Bone said.

"What goose?"

Bone told him, explaining about the picture of Wolfe in the newspaper.

And George whistled. "*The* J. J. Wolfe?"

"The same."

"Well, how'd it turn out — was he the man you saw?"

"I don't know."

"What do you mean, you don't know?"

"Well, put it this way," Bone said. "If you never see Alex or me again — if we wind up in a ditch somewhere — then yeah, I guess Wolfe was the man."

For a few moments there was no sound at the other end of the line. When George spoke again his voice was thin, frightened. "Are you serious?"

Bone tried a laugh. "I hope not," he said.

After he hung up, he pulled the car around to the gas pumps and had it filled. He had the oil and water and tires checked. At a store down the street he bought a blanket, some packages of dried fruit and nuts, and a canteen he filled with water at a roadside fountain. Then he drove out of town, heading west. And he liked the feeling, putting the Ozarks behind him, this country of Billy and Junior and J. J. Wolfe, with their easy smiles and easier brutalities. And somehow, now, in daylight, leaving, the whole Wolfe affair suddenly seemed unimportant. Deep down Bone believed the man was guilty, yes, but of an accident more than murder, some unfortunate stew of lust and alcohol, youth and age, mindless swinging California and the dark rages of the hill country. Bone believed it. But he did not really care. He was glad to be putting it all behind him. He only wished he could have done the same with Cutter.

He would take the long way home, he decided, the northern route up into Colorado and Wyoming and down through Utah and Nevada to San Francisco, then down the coast to Santa Barbara. He would drive alone. He would sleep in the car at night and during the day he would eat only the food he had brought with him and he would talk to no one. And maybe then he would begin to deal with it, the pain, the sense of loss, the knowledge that they were all gone, Mo and the baby, and now Cutter too, gone in his own way.

Back in Santa Barbara he would clean up his affairs. He would settle with Swanson how much he owed him and how he would pay it back, and then he would hitchhike down the coast to San Diego or Oceanside or one of the smaller beach towns and get some half-assed job to keep him in food and cigarettes. In time he would have a few friends. He would find a congenial bar somewhere, a place to talk and drink.

312

And he would run on the beach. He would have an occasional girl and give his body sweet peace for a night or two. But that would be all. The friends and the girls, he would not let them into his life, not as he had Mo and Cutter. He would not love them.

Within an hour he had crossed the state line into Oklahoma and was heading north on a country blacktop when he noticed the pickup truck in his rearview mirror. It was a late model, black, and seemed to be holding at about three hundred feet in back of him. To test it, he increased his speed to seventy but the pickup did not fall behind. And he began to feel a first faint breath of alarm. He accelerated even more for a few seconds and then thought better of it, slowing the car instead, easing it down to forty-five to see if the truck would do the same. But it did not. It rapidly came up behind him and pulled out to pass.

Relieved, Bone pushed in the car lighter and started to get a cigarette out of his pocket. At the same time he glanced out the window at the pickup as it was moving past and he saw two men in it, the driver mostly in silhouette, a squat, large-headed figure staring straight ahead, while the man next to him, his cool bull-rider eyes hidden behind sunglasses, swung a shotgun out the window and held it there for just a moment before firing, just long enough for Bone to know.